KT-431-429

The Women of Lilac Street

ANNIE MURRAY was born in Berkshire and read English at St John's College, Oxford. Her first 'Birmingham' novel, *Birmingham Rose*, hit *The Times* bestseller list when it was published in 1995. She has subsequently written sixteen other successful novels. Annie Murray has four children and lives in Reading.

PRAISE FOR ANNIE MURRAY

Soldier Girl

'This heart-warming story is a gripping read, full of drama, love and compassion' *Take a Break*

Chocolate Girls

'This epic saga will have you gripped
from start to finish'
Birmingham Evening Mail

Birmingham Rose

'An exceptional first novel' *Chronicle*

Birmingham Friends

'A meaty family saga with just the right mix
of mystery and nostalgia' *Parents' Magazine*

Birmingham Blitz

'A tale of passion and empathy which will
keep you hooked' *Woman's Own*

ANNIE MURRAY

The Women of
Lilac Street

PAN BOOKS

First published in Great Britain 2013 by Macmillan

This edition published 2013 by Pan Books
an imprint of Pan Macmillan, a division of Macmillan Publishers Limited
Pan Macmillan, 20 New Wharf Road, London N1 9RR
Basingstoke and Oxford
Associated companies throughout the world
www.panmacmillan.com

ISBN 978-0-330-53521-2

Copyright © Annie Murray 2013

The right of Annie Murray to be identified as the
author of this work has been asserted by her in accordance
with the Copyright, Designs and Patents Act 1988.

The lines on p. 23 are from 'There's a Wideness in God's Mercy'
by Frederick W. Faber, Oratory Hymns, 1854.
Every effort has been made to acknowledge the sources of material
reproduced in this book. If any have been inadvertently overlooked, the
publishers will be pleased to make restitution at the earliest opportunity.

1 3 5 7 9 8 6 4 2

A CIP catalogue record for this book is available from
the British Library.

Typeset by SetSystems Ltd, Saffron Walden, Essex
Printed and bound by CPI Group (UK) Ltd, Croydon, CR0 4YY

Visit **www.panmacmillan.com** to read more about all our books and
to buy them. You will also find features, author interviews and
news of any author events, and you can sign up for e-newsletters
so that you're always first to hear about our new releases.

February 1925

One

'Aggie? Come 'ere and peg these out for me!'

Though her mother's shrill call could not have failed to reach her ears, Aggie didn't move from the front window where she stood peering out at the street, her little sister May balanced on her right hip, clinging to her like a monkey.

Aggie was a slender but sturdy twelve-year-old, her solemn face sprinkled with freckles and flyaway red hair cut severely at jaw length. May, who was three, looked quite different, her hair dark and curly, eyes a gravy brown.

Upstairs, Dad was coughing.

Though barefoot, Aggie was too caught up in her own thoughts to notice the cold or anything else, like her grandmother's tutting from behind her. Aggie moved even closer to the window, the ragged net curtain bunched in her left hand. There was a long singe mark at the bottom edge where Dad had fallen asleep with his Woodbine too close to it. Nanna said they'd been lucky the whole house hadn't gone up.

'Aggie Green,' she whispered, 'took a stand by the window, where her enemies could not see her. They had no idea that Aggie was on their trail...' That's how spies talked, she thought, though she didn't really know.

Outside, passers-by were like blurred ghosts in the

murk. A feeble winter sun was just beginning to strain through a fog that was so thick you could hardly see the houses on the other side. The terraces faced each other like a resigned old married couple across Lilac Street, in an ordinary Birmingham neighbourhood.

'Aggie!' It was a furious shriek now.

'Coming, Mom!'

But still she didn't obey.

'Better shift yerself, wench.' Nanna's voice broke into her thoughts. 'Or there'll be trouble.'

Nanna was perched on the edge of the sagging horse-hair sofa, 'keeping out of the road' – which meant out from under the feet of her daughter Jen, Aggie's mother, who was not in the most reasonable of moods.

Aggie's grandmother, Freda Adams, was dressed, as usual, in black from head to foot. She sat ramrod straight, her right arm holding up her walking stick, the other massaging her sore hip, wincing now and again. The cold in the room didn't help. Some people had nice front parlours, kept for best. Theirs was an overspill room with only the old sofa in it. The fireplace held no comfort, just a pile of cold ash. But Nanna seemed to be able to sit endlessly waiting, as if her whole life had been made of patience.

It was Saturday. Aggie's two brothers and her other sister had all been sent out to play, out of the way, but May, the youngest, had a cold and Mom had kept Aggie, the eldest, in to help.

As well as spying, Aggie was waiting for Mrs Southgate to come out of her house two doors down, to go to the shops, and she never went anywhere without Lily. Lily was four, a year older than May, and sometimes at the weekend, Mrs Southgate would let Aggie bring May into her house, or for a special treat they'd go out for a little walk to Small Heath Park where the girls could play and listen to the band.

But instead of Rose Southgate, something else caught her eye. Two little lads, about seven and eight, were sneaking down the road with some string and a look of mischief on their faces.

'Look at them two,' Aggie said to May. She hoicked May further up on her hip, then rested one of her feet on the other, trying to warm them. 'Ooh, they'd better not be going to Mrs Taylor's – bet they are!'

Aggie could see what the boys were up to. They were going to tie string to someone's knocker and probably the one next door as well and sneak round into the entry to pull the string.

'What's going on out there?' Nanna asked.

Pointing for May, Aggie said, 'Look, see – the knocker'll go bang and there won't be no one there.' May watched with wide eyes. 'They're going to Mrs Taylor's,' she told her grandmother.

'Ooh,' Nanna said, sucking air in through her remaining teeth with a look of mischief. 'There'll be fireworks.' She looked at Aggie, po-faced, then winked.

Aggie wished they lived over the other side, so that she could see Mrs Taylor come cursing to her door. Even though Phyllis Taylor was an upright, religious woman who sailed around with an air of being above everyone else, when provoked enough she would drop her lah-di-dah voice and swear like a trooper and that was all part of the fun.

A moment later though, before there was any hope of the knock-knock trick, Aggie saw Mrs Taylor herself come storming along the street in one of her hats.

'Aggie!' Jen Green erupted into the room, sleeves rolled, apron on. 'Why d'you 'ave to make me call you a dozen times? As if I haven't got enough on my plate with *him*,' she jerked her head towards the floor above, 'in bed again.' She shot her mother a look which implied without much doubt that she was part of what was on her plate as well.

'What's got into you, wench? What're you gawping at?'

She came over, about to administer a slap, but seeing Aggie's intent gaze, she was drawn to the window.

'Ooh, my – look at that! What's up with Her Majesty?'

Jen Green was a short, plump woman with the vivid red hair which her mother, Freda Adams, had once had and which had been inherited by some of her children. She wore it scraped back into a half-made bun from which bits were escaping. Today her face had an especially sallow, sickly look. Though she was in her mid-thirties she looked older, worn out by hard work and poverty. But her permanent air of being put upon was counteracted by the girlish, upturned angle of her nose, which made her appear more cheerful than she felt a lot of the time, with a sick husband, a mother and five children to look after.

Aggie could smell her mother's sweat mixed with rough washing soap as she leaned over her. Jen absent-mindedly reached round and stroked May's head and Aggie watched with jealous hunger. When was Mom ever nice to her like that? All she got was being ordered around.

'What's going on then?' Nanna asked again, never one to be left out.

'Ooh – that one looks as if she's lost a pound and found threepence!' Jen's breath steamed the glass. 'And oh, my –' She giggled. 'Look at that hat!'

Mrs Taylor was striding away along the street. She was a huge, swarthy-faced, handsome woman, built altogether on a grand scale and today seeming to hold herself even more loomingly than usual. She was given to extravagant dress. She had on her usual bottle-green coat and a wide-brimmed hat, its brim positively bristling with fruit and feathers all round. And there was a bursting, storm-cloud look to her.

Jen leaned closer to the window as Mrs Taylor receded along the street.

'Don't pull that curtain out too far, Aggie – she'll see us. Blimey, she looks like one of them tanks. No one'd better get in *her* way – she'll flatten 'em!'

Craning their necks, they watched until Phyllis Taylor's fearsome figure had disappeared past the Mission Hall at the end and out of sight.

'I wonder what's eating *her*?' Jen said, moving back from the window. 'Anyway, miss – the washing . . .'

'P'r'aps it's 'cause Dolly's come home,' Aggie interrupted.

Jen turned, frowning. 'What – Dolly Taylor? How d'you know?'

'I saw her, this morning, in the road with her hat on and a bundle. She never saw me – she was all sort of bent over.'

'I s'pect it was the next one up you saw – Rachel,' Nanna said. 'You'd be hard pushed to tell 'em apart.'

'No,' Aggie insisted. 'It were Dolly, I know it was.'

'Well, there you are,' Jen said, digesting this gossip with relish. 'She's supposedly in service with some Mrs Lah-di-Dah or other – out Sutton way I think it was. I wonder what *that* one's doing back so soon.'

'She might be paying a visit, mightn't she?' Aggie suggested, lowering May to the floor, despite her squeaks of protest. 'No, get down, May – you're doing my back in.'

'She might,' her mother said with the tart air of someone who knows better. 'And she might not. Now come and get these bits of clothes out for me before it flaming well rains.'

The Terraces were the better end of the street. They were cramped two-up two-down little houses, but most of them had attics and since a couple of years back, they also had a tap inside. After the back-to-back houses Jen had grown up in, with only one room on the ground floor and a shared tap out in the yard, they seemed like luxury. Many of them housed business workshops as well as domestic life: a silver-mirror maker, a brush manufacturer, a barber and a coal merchant just to name a few, as well as Price's fried fish shop next to the Mission Hall, sending its mouth-watering fishy, vinegary smells along the street. Opposite Price's was the all-purpose huckster's shop run by Dorrie Davis, the queen of gossip. At the other end, towards Larches Street, the buildings came out in a rash of back-to-back houses arranged around courts, like the Mansions at the very bottom, where Aggie's friend Babs Skinner lived.

Lilac Street was a crowded, sooty-faced, workaday place, the houses full and the streets teeming with children. One thing it was, without a doubt, was full of life.

Two

Phyllis Taylor had to get out of the house.

Had to, or she'd have knocked Dolly's block off. Knocked her from here into next week.

The girl had turned up before they'd even finished breakfast, the four of them round the table, her older three children, all of them neatly dressed and heading off to their jobs: Charles at a successful printer's works, which among other things printed Christian tracts, Susanna to the draper's in town and Rachel to Mrs Dunne for whom she worked as an assistant milliner. In struts Dolly, no hint of a warning, carrying a bundle and with that look on her. So damn pretty, her Dolly, with her sultry eyes – and that figure. Of all her girls she reminded Phyllis most of herself at the same age – reminded her far too much, in fact. But today Dolly's face was pale and sweaty as a summer cheese. As soon as she'd staggered through to the back room she fell on to a chair and pushed her head down between her knees.

'What in heaven's name're *you* doing here?' Susanna demanded. She'd been about to get up and ready herself for work.

Charles had had his Bible open at the table and he closed it with a thud, as if to protect it from infection. Rachel, eighteen and the next up in age from Dolly, just stared, horrified.

'Oh, Mom!' Dolly burst out. 'Oh – I don't feel well!' And she fled out to the privy.

They all gaped at the empty chair.

'Go on, all of you – out,' Phyllis commanded the others ominously. 'I'll get to the bottom of this.'

And the others, as they normally did – even Rachel – obeyed without question.

Dolly came back in, wincing at the sour taste in her mouth. She poured herself a cup of tea and sat cradling it in front of her, her hands mauve with cold. She had dried her tears now but she kept her eyes cast down.

A dangerous silence stretched across the table. Rage flickered in Phyllis like a pilot light about to erupt into flames. There were her three good-looking, respectable children and here was Dolly, the little bint. After all the chances she'd had of a decent start, she had flown in the face of all her mother's wishes and advice and gone into service. *Service* of all things! Jobs were terribly hard to come by, it was true. The men who'd come back from the war wanted their jobs back and there weren't enough to go round. Some of them were reduced to begging on the street. The trick, she had advised the girls, was to take on women's work – hats and clothes – the sort of thing a man wouldn't want.

But when had her youngest ever listened to her advice? Thought she knew everything, that one. 'What I want is to get away from *you*,' Dolly had raged. But she'd stopped raging now, the stupid, wicked girl – oh, yes! Phyllis knew what was coming. Just at that moment she wanted to reach over and slap Dolly's pert little face.

At last, in a strangled voice she said, 'Well, madam – what've you got to say for yourself?'

Dolly raised her dark eyes. 'She told on me – that mean, spiteful little bitch!' she burst out, more tears running down her cheeks. 'I hate her!'

Phyllis was thrown by this. 'What d'you mean?'

Dolly gave a sharp, angry sigh, dashing away the tears with the back of her hand. 'That Lizzie, the tweeny who slept in the same room as me. She was spying on me! She heard me being—'

'You're expecting, aren't you? You've got a bun in the oven, a bastard baby, you filthy little hussy!'

The words roared out of Phyllis's mouth before Dolly could even finish.

The two of them stared at each other then, their eyes stretched wide by the terrible truth that had been spoken. For a few seconds Dolly met her mother's gaze defiantly, then she crumpled, head in her hands.

'What'm I going to do? She's given me my notice and no references. Oh, Lord, I'm sorry, Mom – it wasn't my fault . . . What's going to become of me?'

It was then, looking at her daughter's thin, heaving shoulders, that Phyllis knew she had to leave the house. She seized her coat and hat and yanked the door open, storming along the road, before she had even managed to master her expression or the enraged pounding of her feet on the pavement. She tried to slow down. *Stop making an exhibition of yourself.* All the nosey parkers round here would be prying, asking questions, out to drag her down . . .

But it was almost impossible to contain her bursting fury. Here they were, getting somewhere in the world, with Susanna promised to that nice David boy and

11

Charles training to be a lay preacher. And here was Dolly, about to disgrace them all. She had to do anything, *anything* at this moment except be in the same room as that reckless, wayward, *stupid* girl of hers. Otherwise she'd most likely take the poker to her and give her the hiding of her life.

Jen Green, Aggie's mother, dragged herself up the stairs, pulling on the rail Tommy had fixed to the wall. She stopped halfway up, feeling sick and faint. Reaching the top at last, she could already hear her husband's coughing from behind their bedroom door.

When she went in, he was curled up on his side, as if trying to get warm. She felt her innards clutch at the sight of him. All she could see was a tuft of his dark hair which was getting quite long, and this tiny, almost childlike figure under the blanket. She kept trying to tell herself he had a dose of his bronchitis, that he was not getting thinner by the day, that this was nothing unusual. He'd always been sickly, boy and man, but he'd always bounced back. She kept telling him they ought to get the doctor, but he was adamant – no doctors.

Hearing her, he turned his head, then painfully rolled over. He gathered his face into a grin. In a rasping whisper he said, 'Hello, kid.'

'D'you want a cuppa tea?' she asked, sounding irritable when she meant to be tender but somehow it came out wrong. She felt so anyhow herself today and she knew, with terrible foreboding, just why she was feeling sick.

'Ar – that'd be nice,' he said.

'You'd better eat summat.' For a moment she perched wearily on the side of the bed.

12

Tommy moved his hand dismissively. He had no appetite.

'Just a piece of bread – just summat,' she argued. 'You've got to get yourself stronger.'

Tommy sighed. 'All right, wench. If you say so.'

'I do,' she said, more softly now. She wanted to crawl into bed with him, to hold him tight, to sleep. But there was far too much to be done.

'Feeling any better?' she asked.

Tommy swallowed. 'Course – course I am. I was just thinking about old Bob Stevens. Dunno why.'

Jen smiled. Bob had been a childhood friend of theirs. His family lived next to Tommy's in one of the back-to-back courts in Balsall Heath. Jen had grown up in an almost identical house further along the street. Both of them were full of pride that they had managed to move up into a proper terrace. They worked hard to pay the rent, but it was worth it for not just a front door but a back as well and more rooms to call their own.

'He was a mad sod,' Jen said. 'What made you think of him?'

Tommy began to smile, but he caught his breath and started coughing, jerked to a sitting position by his need to breathe. His lungs seemed to foam and rattle and he coughed up a load of stuff into his piece of rag. Jen went to sit by him, horrified by the sound. As the fit passed she ran her hand down his back. His ribs were like piano keys. *Oh, God*, she thought, horrified again. Her mind swam away from the implications of this, of just how ill he was and how stubborn.

'I'll go and get you your tea,' she said.

He lay back, too exhausted to answer.

Jen went downstairs with a cold, frightened feeling wrapping itself round her heart.

Three

Rose Southgate had woken early that morning.

It was dark, save for a faint blur of light seeping round the curtains.

She knew she had woken because of Lily, though at that moment she could hear nothing except Harry's breathing beside her, his quiet, almost surreptitious breaths. She called this his 'sleep of the dead' when he went quiet like that and she could barely tell he was there beside her. At other times, in the small hours he would let out yells, sometimes jerk up to sit panting, in what seemed terrible anguish. This had gone on all through the six years of their marriage, but if she offered comfort – he seemed so frightened and distraught – or asked him about it once daylight had returned, he pushed her away furiously, refusing to talk about it. So she had given up asking.

Lily was out there, she knew. Despite the silence, Rose could sense her through the door. She could picture her, in her little white nightshirt, her long, ghostly hair in a plait down her back – without the plait there were such tangles and tears in the morning – sitting waiting on the top step in the cold. She imagined the chill of her soft little feet.

Rose lifted up her head to listen. Yes, there it was – a tiny creak of the floorboard at the top of the stairs. Lily was waiting. She knew never to knock or come into

14

their bedroom. Harry wouldn't have it. He was so touchy about everything.

Hardly breathing, Rose shifted the bedclothes off her and in a smooth, almost melting motion, removed herself from the bed. Snatching up her long cardigan she crept to the door, which was unlatched in readiness. It opened with a squeak and she looked back at Harry, but he slept on. She crept out, drawing the door closed again and in the gloom, smiled down at the person most beloved to her in all the world.

'Hello, sweetheart,' she whispered. Even being away from Harry's sleeping presence made her feel light-hearted. Lily was looking up at her. 'Shall we go and light the fire? Find our shoes?'

The two of them linked hands and slid silently downstairs, each with their long fair hair in a braid. They looked as if they could have been sisters just as well as mother and daughter, a twenty-one-year gap between them.

The clock in the back room said six-fifteen. Lily curled up in a chair and Rose put a blanket over her while she, mousey quiet out of habit, dealt with the coal bucket and lit the range to warm the house and boil water. While they waited for the water, Rose did a few little jobs tidying up and folding some dry washing. She made tea, and warm milk for Lily.

'Can I have a story, Mom?'

Rose pushed the chair as close to the range as possible and sat Lily on her lap, both of them under the blanket, and they cuddled up and read Lily's favourite story. It was called *Ameliaranne and the Green Umbrella*. A kind lady at the church called Mrs Muriel Wood had given it to her, along with some other little tales which had belonged to her daughter. Poor Mrs Wood had lost her husband and daughter Elizabeth to the Spanish influenza and was left with just her little boy, Oliver, who did not like girls' books. Lily loved the stories and could not hear the adventures of Ameliaranne Stiggins enough times.

Her daughter's head on her shoulder, her warm, sweet weight in her lap, Rose read softly and sipped her tea. With the story finished she put the book down and wrapped her arms around Lily, looking out over her head.

' 'Nother one, Mom?' Lily said hopefully.

'In a minute, dear.'

Rose let out a long sigh. If only it could always be like this: just her and Lily, snug and warm together. The fact that the books had belonged to poor Muriel Wood's little girl made Lily's sweet, warm existence even more precious.

'Make sure you always read, won't you?' she said suddenly. Lily looked round at her. 'Once you get to school – you read and learn all you can and make the best of things, won't you?'

Lily, barely understanding her but aware that this seemed important, nodded solemnly.

'Good girl,' Rose said.

Silently, she thought, *So you don't have to end up like me.*

She had a pot of porridge ready for when Harry came down. He went silently out to the privy to relieve himself, then stood shaving in the scullery in his shirt-sleeves. Rose watched him, standing at an angle to him where she knew he could not see her in the little rectangular mirror.

Harry was just a year older than her. He was a strong, stocky man with bristly black hair, swarthy skin and very dark brown eyes. By trade he was a painter and decorator, a job in which the summer was the best time, so in the winter he tried to make up his earnings by doing odd jobs. Yesterday he had been out fixing someone's back door. He was strong and competent. He had once also been lively and humorous, in those early days, and now and again his old self popped out. Increasingly, he was a mystery to Rose and a hostile one at that. She knew it was partly her fault – but not all, surely? The war had made strangers of some men.

Patting the damp from his newly shaved cheeks, Harry sat at the table and when she served his porridge, he gave a low grunt which she knew was a thank-you of a kind. She poured tea. Lily sat watching him, warily. Rose also sat down, trying to gauge his mood.

'What will you do today?' she asked finally. His Saturday afternoons were either football or fishing.

Harry finished his mouthful and looked up, peering out of the window. The sight of the brightness outside seemed to cheer him.

'We're gonna finish that little job from yesterday.' He chewed, swallowed. 'Then I'll take my rod out.' There was a time they'd have laughed at him saying that, but not now.

So he'd be out all afternoon. Harry was a keen fisherman, even just in the cut – but he liked to go further afield to do it, often cycling right out of town with the rod strapped to his bike.

'That's nice,' she said. 'Looks a good day for it.' A weight lifted from her at the thought of him being out all that time. She'd be able to sew. That set of place linen was almost finished.

'Ar – it does.' Harry looked up then and gave her almost a smile. Rose smiled back and Lily beamed in delight.

'You going fishing, Dad?'

'Shame you're not a lad – you could come with me.'

It rankled with him all the time that he had no son. That she was so unwilling to give him more children.

'You could teach her,' Rose said pleasantly, knowing he never would.

He seemed in a good mood. She'd try asking now, she thought.

'The thing is, Harry – love – I was thinking . . . It's time we had someone in to tune the piano.'

'What? That old thing? Nah –' He scraped his bowl out and flung the spoon down. 'What d'yer think you're going to use for money then, eh? Middle of the winter? Forget it – the damn thing's no use anyway.'

'But I want Lily to have a few lessons soon.' Rose tried to speak sweetly, persuasively. She could see Harry's chin jutting already in opposition. She quelled her own anger. Why was he so mean and stubborn about everything? 'She's nearly old enough and I only know a little bit, hardly anything. Mrs Wood'd teach her for next to nothing, I'm sure. She's said so. And playing my mother's piano – it'd be nice to hear her . . .'

'Piano lessons!' He pushed his chair back scornfully. 'What bloody use is any of that? You can forget that idea – all your airs and graces and frills. I'm not wasting good money on your fancy ideas. If I had my way I'd sell the rotten thing, taking up half the room . . .'

He went out to the back again and Rose knew he had gone to sort out his fishing tackle.

'But you're not going to get your way,' she whispered to herself. She had been stowing away the money for it. Harry didn't know she still sewed, how good she was at embroidery or about Mrs Lacey over in Moseley, who was eager to buy the things she made . . . One day, when it was safe, she would get the piano tuned.

'Is Daddy cross?' Lily asked. She was an anxious child. His moods moved across them like clouds in the wind.

'Oh, no!' Rose said brightly. 'Your dad's all right. He's going out fishing. Tell you what, if it stays sunny, shall we see if Aggie and May want to come to the park with us?'

Lily brightened up immediately.

'Ooh, yes – can I take my hoop?'

'Of course you can,' Rose said. She caught sight of her husband through the back window, doing something intricate to his line, his eyes narrowed, intent. She thought how odd it was that she lived with this man and tried to find in herself a grain of tenderness for him, but it slid away from her grasp.

Four

'Can we come in and see yer?'

Rose opened the door that Saturday afternoon to find the two little girls hand in hand, shivering, gazing up at her pleadingly. The brief burst of sunshine was over and a bitter wind was blowing the smoke from all the chimneys horizontally along the rooftops. Aggie's teeth were chattering and May's face was stained with a crusty mixture of tears and snot.

'Only,' Aggie told her, 'our mom says I'm to take May out from under her feet, but it's cold out here and it's making May bad.'

'Didn't you think to put a coat on?' Rose scolded gently, before realizing she had been tactless.

'I ain't got a coat,' Aggie said, in a voice which implied that the thought of having such a thing had never occurred to her. She was wearing a brown skirt cut down to fit, after a fashion, the hem rucked up in a thick ridge round her shins. Her shoes were clumpy charity boots like so many of the children wore. May at least had an extra jumper on which came down almost to her knees, but the child seemed to be full of cold.

Poor little mites, Rose thought. She smiled. She was glad of company, even if it was that of a couple of snotty children.

'Come in then,' she said. 'I was thinking of going to

the park today, but the wind's turned so bitter. I think we'll have to blow the cobwebs away another day. We'll settle by the fire instead, shall we?'

Aggie could think of nothing more blissful than to spend a cosy afternoon with Mrs Southgate and Lily. She knew that lately she'd been rather neglecting her friend Babs. But Aggie adored Rose Southgate: she was pretty and kind. Mom was forever keeping on at her, do this, do that but Rose had a soft, musical voice and she didn't shout. Aggie wanted to be exactly like her when she grew up and to have a little girl with long flaxen hair and no other children, just one to dress up like a princess and buy her the prettiest shoes she could find instead of charity boots from the *Mail* newspaper like the ones Aggie had to clump about in, blistering her feet.

And she loved the house as well. There was a calmness and order in Mrs Southgate's house. She thought it was beautiful and found it soothing.

She looked around cautiously as they went inside. Sometimes a lady called Mrs Wood was there too. And was Mr Southgate in? He was a big, gloomy, mostly bad-tempered man and Aggie was scared of him. Mom said he was like the other men who'd 'come back'.

'Even the ones with all their arms and legs are no use to anyone half the time,' she'd say sorrowfully. Her own husband, Tommy, had stayed, having failed every medical for the army.

'No one else is here,' Rose said, seeing Aggie's unease. 'Just Lily – she's having a little sleep. I expect she'll wake up soon. Come and get warm.'

It was such a relief to be in out of the gritty wind. There was a fire in the iron grate in the front room – oh, so nice compared with their house! – and Aggie and May settled shivering on the soft little rug by the hearth. In the Greens' front room the only thing on the floor was a peg rug, ancient and worn to a brown, grimy colour from all the traffic of feet passing over it mixed with soot. There was nothing rich or fine about the Southgates' front parlour. Nearly everything they had was old and worn, but Rose kept it very nice and she was good with her hands. There was a modest-sized table and chairs near the window and the little wool rug was woven in lively patterns of crimson, white, blue and black. The sight of the colours made Aggie happy. The curtains were dark red, patterned with white and grey flowers, and Rose kept everything well polished and dusted. On the mantel there were china animals and jugs and a picture of Lily. There were a few brasses at the side of the grate and a gleaming copper coal scuttle. Most special of all was the piano, standing against the back wall, also polished to a sheen. Sometimes Rose would open it and show Aggie middle C and how to pick out an octave.

'What's up with you, little May?' Rose knelt beside her.

'Oh, our mom wanted us out from under her feet. Mom's feeling a bit any'ow – and our nanna,' Aggie said, stroking the soft rug under her as if it was a dog and basking in the fire's heat. It was making one side of her face hot and prickly.

'Oh, I see,' Rose said. 'But May seems a bit poorly too.'

Aggie nodded absently. One or other of them was

22

forever streaming with snot – this didn't seem anything worth remarking on.

'And how's your poor father?'

Aggie shrugged. She didn't want to think about it. 'Can I see the book?' she asked eagerly.

One of the treasures Aggie loved at Mrs Southgate's house was something she called a commonplace book. She wrote things inside which caught her fancy: snippets from the newspaper, poems, sayings, even recipes and all sorts. And she had the most beautiful curling handwriting that Aggie had ever seen. She had told Aggie she'd been in service once to some nice people who had taught her a lot of things. Aggie thought Mrs Southgate was a magical person being able to write like that and embroider so beautifully as well.

'All right – if you like.' There was a sigh in her voice as Rose got up, though Aggie didn't notice it and it had nothing to do with her.

The precious notebook was bound in dark red leather. Rose handed it to her and May came and craned over Aggie's shoulder as she turned the pages, the blue-black ink looping graciously along the lines.

'Stop that sniffing, May,' Aggie said irritably, covering her ear for a moment. May was like her shadow, forever there. She just wanted a few moments to herself. But May leaned against her shoulder, wriggling. Aggie, tensed against her sister's weight, tried to ignore her. She read from the first page, immediately caught up in the words,

There is no place where Earth's Sorrows
are more felt than up in Heaven,
There is no place where Earth's failings
Have such Kindly Judgement Given . . .

Then further down:

The Kiss of the Sun for Pardon,
The Song of the Birds for Mirth,
One is nearer God's Heart in a Garden
Than anywhere else on Earth.

At the bottom of the page it said:

Cure for Chilblains:
½ oz sulphur of zinc
½ oz sugar of lead
½ pint of Water, hot or cold – Not to be Taken.
   Bathed.—OR Turnip Poultice.

Leafing through she saw page after page of long poems, all very neatly copied, and all, Aggie knew, containing sentiments of love and hope which had the power to make her heart feel like a bird fluttering about in her chest. But she skipped over them to the page she was really looking for, at the back where Rose kept her clippings.

It was where she had first heard about Mata Hari. There was a picture postcard of her stuck into the book and Aggie drank in the sight. Mata Hari was dressed in a luxurious gold gown, low-cut at the front and sweeping the ground. The outfit was topped by a headdress which made her appear to have jewelled gold horns. She was half turned towards the camera with her arm across her body, bowing slightly, a purple sash draping from her waist. Aggie stared back at her dark, teasing eyes. Dancer, circus performer, spy – all the things Aggie thought the most exciting in the world and this woman had done them all! But beside the picture postcard was a clipping, headed: *Mata Hari Put to Death by Firing Squad in Paris.*

The first time she had found the picture she had stared entranced. She had never seen anyone in her life who looked in the least like Mata Hari, and her name made her sound so foreign and mysterious!

'What's a spy?' she had asked Mrs Southgate.

'It's someone who finds out other people's business,' Rose said. 'Who goes poking their nose in, I suppose you'd say. The French thought she was trying to find out their secrets for the Germans and that because of her, a lot of French soldiers died.'

Aggie could barely imagine such big actions with their terrible consequences. She just knew that she felt very small and rough in her cut-down clothes and boots, and Mata Hari looked like something out of heaven.

'That's bad,' she said finally. 'Ain't it?'

'If it was true, it is, yes.'

'But . . .' Aggie had stared and stared. How could anyone so gorgeous have done anything bad? 'Is there good spying – as well as bad?'

Rose laughed. 'Well, I suppose there must be – it depends whose side you're on and what you're finding out.'

'What d'you have to do – to be a spy?'

Rose shrugged, seeming amused by her agog interest. 'I don't know. I think you have to keep your eyes open, find out things. A bit like one of those detectives – Sherlock Holmes. You have to look for clues.'

Aggie's eyes widened. This was the most exciting thing she had ever heard! And if there was one thing Aggie longed for in her life apart from a pair of pretty shoes, and for Dad to be better, it was excitement.

Now, every time she came to Rose Southgate's house

she asked to see the picture of Mata Hari and wondered how you started out if you wanted to be a spy. Rose said you had to find out things. So Aggie spent a lot of time peering out of windows (listening at doors being almost unnecessary in her house as you could hear most things through the floorboards without much special effort). She told her friend Babs about Mata Hari so that they could spy together, though Babs wasn't as keen as her.

There were a few details she had already found out. Watching the street, the first things she noticed were the movements of Mary Crewe. She was called Mad Mary because she *was* mad. She smoked like a chimney and went about with a shawl swaddled up in her arms and rocked it as if it was a real baby. She lived in one of the two courts at the Mansions at the end of the road, opposite the Eagle, Dad's favourite watering hole. Babs lived in one of the six houses in Number One Court, at 4/1 The Mansions, and Mary Crewe in the next yard, at 6/2 with her elder sister Eliza, a thin, worn-out-looking woman. Aggie had started to notice that quite regularly, early in the mornings, Mad Mary left Eliza's and her humble house in her grubby clothes, her hair a greasy mat as usual, and came lurching and puffing and muttering hurriedly along the road, carrying the 'babby'.

She had seen day-to-day things: all the little businesses opening up along the street, and the way Dorrie Davis, a matron in her forties with her shop at number one, who was always 'so mithered it wears me down', seemed to be out in the street an awful lot, spreading gossip, even though she was forever complaining she was 'chained to that shop'.

And she had seen other things. Sad things. Across

the road at number six was a lady called Irene Best. Mr Best had been gassed in the war and hardly ever came out of the house, only just now and then, to be pushed along to church. Mom went over to call on Irene sometimes. When she came back she'd be shaking her head. It would make her gentler with everyone for a while and she'd say it all made you know when you were well off. A few days ago Aggie had seen Irene Best, a tall, painfully thin lady, come out of her house to go shopping. She closed the front door and, just for a moment, leaned her head against it. Aggie, young as she was and ignorant of adult feeling, could sense the despair and exhaustion in every line of her and almost wished she hadn't witnessed this moment.

And this morning, Dolly Taylor had come sneaking home early in the morning, her head down, hurrying along as if she didn't want to be seen . . .

What good any of this information was to her, Aggie had no idea. But everything she saw, every action, had taken on a heightened importance, as if everyone in the street was on a mission or scheme and it was up to her to find out what it was.

That afternoon though, all she wanted to do was revel in the loveliness of being in Mrs Southgate's house. She and May settled in for a cosy afternoon playing with Lily and eating bread which Rose cooked on the fire to make delicious toast, and for the first time that day, she was warm.

Five

Phyllis spent the rest of the morning doing battle.

She stormed down to the shops, and somehow managed to get round and gather up fish and bread, spuds and fruit and veg, returning with a big leafy cabbage sticking out of her bag. All the while in her head thumped a livid refrain: *She wants a damn good hiding, that girl, that she does . . .*

Her rage was almost uncontainable. All that she'd done to raise herself and bring up a decent family; all that she'd put behind her never to see the light of day again. And this little bit, little *hussy* flouncing in, threatening to tear it apart, to throw her mother's struggles and efforts down the drain like so much slop! The way she felt she could have ranted and shrieked in the street fit to be dragged off to the asylum.

But that wasn't all she'd been thinking – not by a long chalk. In between selecting apples and carrots and greens, all the time another part of her mind had been in a fury of activity, surging this way and that, forming plans, discarding them, making calculations. *No one must know . . . Ever.* They would not be disgraced. Not Phyllis Taylor or her family. Not after all she had won for herself. Gossip and sniggering and pointing fingers; she'd do anything to avoid that.

It came to her halfway along the Ladypool Road. The sounds died around her, the other shoppers, shoulders hunched against the weather, were all invisible to her. She stopped dead, oblivious to the cold, the smells of smoke and dung and butcher's offal. Even the woman who cursed when she all but slammed into the back of her, Phyllis barely noticed.

She didn't remember the walk home and arrived at her front door surprised to see it suddenly before her. Steeling herself, she pushed it open, preparing for the sight of that girl . . .

Dolly was slumped on the table, asleep, head resting on her arms next to the willow pattern milk jug. She had very dark chestnut hair which was plaited and coiled up in a loose bun. Phyllis could see everything very clearly, every hair of her daughter's strong, dark eyebrows, where they burrowed into her pale skin, the dull gleam of kirby grips in her hair. Dolly was wearing a cream blouse with a cardigan over the top and against the black wool her face looked very pale and young.

Dolly seemed to sense, rather than hear, her mother standing over her and opened her eyes. She sat up slowly, pulling a face at the feel of her queasy innards.

'Mom!' she said, alarmed, seeing the expression on Phyllis's face and trying to lean away from her as if expecting a blow.

Phyllis set her bags down and with a menacing air, pulled out another chair and sat down.

'Right,' she said. 'Now you're going to tell me whose it is.'

Dolly hugged herself miserably. She kept her gaze fixed on the table. 'I don't know what you mean.'

Phyllis slammed her hand down, grabbing Dolly's.

'You come with me.'

'Mom, don't! I don't feel well!'

She dragged Dolly into the front parlour, her pride

29

and joy with its solid, elegant chairs, its deep rust-coloured curtains and all the ornaments Phyllis had collected over the years, saving any spare penny for them and, heaven knew, there'd been precious few at times. She pulled Dolly over to the fireplace with its shining coal scuttle, tongs and poker, the china ornaments – animals and little children – the clock and the pretty bowl at one end. At the other, lavishly framed, stood the photograph of her and James Taylor on their wedding day.

'See this? That was the best day of my life, that was. And everything that came after.'

There they stood, arm in arm outside the Methodist church, both dark haired and tall, smart and magnificent looking, she in cream tulle; oh, yes, they had had a good wedding. James lived very carefully, but his family were not poor. Her husband was a tall man, striking to look at with his prominent cheekbones and that blade-like nose which Susanna had inherited. People noticed James. And she had entered into all that, into his kind of life. Meeting him had changed everything about her, and she had risen fiercely to the change, all of which she wanted. She had learned to speak differently, to lead the most upright of lives; to try and be all that he required. She had won his mother over, the way she had fitted in and become so devout. And James Taylor had gained the woman he needed to satisfy the vigorous, hungrily passionate side of him, the side for which God was not enough.

'You looked nice, Mom,' Dolly said carefully.

Phyllis put the picture back and turned on her daughter. 'I'm not having a little bit like you drive a cart and horses through everything we built – *I've* built, since he was taken from me. You've no idea, that's your trouble!

Don't you want your father to look down and be proud of you?'

Dolly nodded miserably.

'Now – you tell me. It didn't get there by itself, did it? Who spawned the little bastard?'

Dolly bit her lip, tears welling. 'Don't talk like that, Mom!'

'Answer me, wench!'

There was a long silence, then Dolly half whispered, 'I'm not saying.'

'Not saying!' Phyllis roared, before remembering to lower her voice. She pushed Dolly through to the kitchen again and she sank down at the table. 'Don't give me that. You spit it out, Dolly Taylor, this minute, or I'll—'

Dolly's eyes turned up to her, shining with angry defiance. 'You'll what?'

'I'll put you out on the streets like the little whore you are, that's what!' Phyllis hissed at her. 'You can fend for yourself – it's no more than what you deserve. *Tell* me who it was – was it the son? Is there a son?'

She realized she had very little idea who Dolly had been working for. A Mrs Lewis, that's all she knew. She could have had ten sons or none.

'Or was it someone who called at the house? Some lad off a delivery dray?'

'I'm not saying who it was.' Tears rose again in Dolly's eyes. 'One thing's for sure – I'm never going to see him again anyway so what use is there?'

She put her hands over her face and began to sob. Phyllis was taken aback by this. Don't say the silly girl had fallen for someone and entered into it willingly – oh, dear God!

'I only came back here 'cause Mrs Lewis told me to

go straight away – I had nowhere else to go. I didn't want to bring this to your door, Mom. I'm sorry. Only I dain't know what else to do!'

Phyllis could feel herself softening just a fraction as the whole sorry state of things began to sink in. She sat back and let out a long sigh.

'God in heaven, Dolly, how can you have been so *stupid*?'

'I never meant – I dain't know what was . . .' Dolly had gone a queer colour again and a few seconds later she ran out to the privy.

When she came back in, Phyllis had been upstairs. She had something in her hand; a tiny bottle.

'Here – take this. Do you good.'

Phyllis had the lid off and was thrusting the bottle of smelling salts at her. Dolly's head jerked back.

'Aagh – no!' she cried as the pungent fumes knifed agonizingly up her nose. She gasped and moaned, grasping her nose, her eyes streaming. 'Oh, that hurts so bad – it's horrible!'

With an air of satisfaction, Phyllis replaced the stopper in the little bottle.

'Who was he, Dolly?'

'I can't . . .' Dolly hung her head.

'Why are you protecting him – the bloke's not standing by you, is he? I don't see him at my door begging to marry you . . .'

'I can't tell,' Dolly sobbed. 'I can't, because I don't *know* who he was – he just jumped on me.' She got up tragically. 'Just let me go to bed, Mom – I want to sleep. I feel so rotten and my life's ruined. I want to sleep and never wake up!'

Her feet thumped up the wooden staircase and Phyllis heard her fling herself on to a bed, crying her heart out. Eventually it went quiet.

They were all gathered round the table, the curtains shut at the front even though no one was in the room. Phyllis felt as if she was sealing them all in against the world. They sat in the light of an oil lamp, in front of plates of boiled fish with cabbage and spuds, her son and her three dark-eyed beauties of daughters. Their father, James Taylor, who had been both an engineer and a lay preacher, had taken sick and died of pneumonia in 1914, leaving their mother in straitened circumstances.

Susanna, nineteen, was the quietest of the three sisters, the most biddable and responsible, as the eldest girl. Of the three, looks-wise, she had the most of her father in her. She had James Taylor's tall, slender build and strong, distinctive nose and, like her brother Charles, his dark brown hair and grey eyes. Rachel, eighteen, and Dolly, sixteen, were swarthier, like Phyllis, more curvaceous and very alike, though Rachel had a dark mole on her left cheek. They had plenty of spirit, yet along with Charles, who was twenty-one and training to be a lay preacher like their father, they had always been in awe of their mother, wanting to help and please her. The older three children had also seen more of her struggles to keep them all after she was widowed, the way she'd worked, two, even three jobs at a time to give them the best life she could, not to lose ground.

It was Dolly who had always been the rebel, who had had to be almost dragged to church – 'It's so *boring*, Mom!' – who refused to be moulded exactly as Phyllis demanded, into material for an upright, Methodist wife who would climb the social ladder. She had constantly fallen out with Charles over the years.

'Why d'you have to say those things to him?' Susanna would scold her, in defence of her pious brother.

'He's such a stuffed shirt,' Dolly complained. 'The minister this, the Bible that . . . Always quoting chapter and verse at me . . . He's so stiff and starchy!'

'He's just trying to take after our dad, that's all,' Susanna told her. 'It's his way of honouring his memory – and he is the man of the house now.'

'I know – but he's nothing like our dad. At least Dad smiled now and again,' Dolly argued. They both knew that it had been more than now and again. James Taylor had been a lively, fulfilled man and they missed him dreadfully. 'With Charles it's like living with Scrooge . . .'

'Just try and see things from his point of view,' Susanna said. She knew her brother was a boring fellow, but that he also had a tender side. 'He's doing his best – you know that really, don't you? And he's fond of you.'

'I s'pose so,' Dolly conceded sulkily. It was true – however much she goaded Charles, he had always had a soft spot for his youngest sister.

At this moment, it was obvious that he was having difficulty staying in the room. There was no hiding the situation.

'So,' Phyllis told them. 'That's the long and short of it.'

The Facts sat in the middle of the table like some grotesque creature that had crawled in. Charles had put down his knife and fork and was staring, stunned, into his lap. Phyllis could see that he was close to tears. Dolly couldn't look up from her plate.

It was Rachel who said, 'But Dolly – what happened?'

At this Charles pushed his chair back with a cry of distress and ran from the room and out of the house.

The women sat silently for a long while.

'If I don't tell you, you'll keep on at me till I do,' Dolly said at last. She raised her head. 'All right, then. If you must know. Mrs Lewis gave me an afternoon off a fortnight. She was a mean old witch – she didn't need me all the time but she just liked stopping us going anywhere. Lizzie was no company – I used to have to wait till she was asleep.'

Rachel gasped. 'That must have been late at night!'

'It was quite late sometimes. We used to sneak out – me and Viley, one of the maids from up Maney Hill – just now and again. There was nowhere much to go – it was just for the fun of it, doing something they didn't know about. It made me feel really happy seeing Mrs Lewis in the morning when I was "yes, madam, no, madam," and thinking, *There's things you don't know about me, Mrs. You don't own me.*'

Rachel and Susanna were both looking shocked. Phyllis tried to keep her face neutral. Dolly's story sparked memories that she didn't want to go into.

'One night I was just going back to Mrs Lewis's . . .' Dolly's face crumpled. 'I swear I never really saw him. He was just there all of a sudden and he grabbed me. He was quite big and his breath stank of drink . . . He pulled me down to the railway, behind a wall there . . . It was so dark – there was no one about, not that I could see. I couldn't stop him – it was horrible! I didn't

35

know what he was trying to do. I thought he was mad, like a mad dog . . . I never knew . . . And he tore my clothes, my bloomers . . . He hurt me . . . And then he'd done it and it was too late . . . I never knew that's how you got a babby! Even when I was being sick I never knew . . .'

Susanna leaned across and put her arm round her little sister's shoulder, her face full of pity and horror.

'Oh, Dolly – you poor, silly girl!'

This made Dolly sob even harder.

'It wasn't my fault – I never asked for it. And he ran off straight after – I never even saw his face. He was just a big, stinking shadow!' She looked up, her face distraught. 'I don't want a babby, do I? Can't I do away with it – somehow?'

'No!' Phyllis snapped, then recovered herself. 'No,' she said more quietly. 'Not that. You're not going to do anything of the sort.'

There was a silence.

'Mom,' Rachel said eventually. 'Whatever *are* we going to do?'

Phyllis leaned forwards. Very solemnly she said, 'I'll tell you what we're going to do. And you're going to have to obey it to the letter. All of you. So you listen to me, and you listen very carefully.'

Dolly lay awake that night. Her body felt limp and wrung out from being sick, but though she was exhausted, she could not sleep. She lay staring up into the darkness, hearing her two older sisters breathing. She was sharing the bed with Susanna; Rachel was across the room by the window.

She laid her hands on her stomach: it was flat as a

board. Could it be true – was she really expecting? But she knew she was now. The sickness, day after day. It was not so bad at night, and this left room for all the other feelings to rush in, all the anger and fear and resentment.

Curling up on her side she let the tears come, quietly, so as not to wake the others. Here she was, back here, to be bossed around by Mom, when she thought she had been so grown up, leaving home and going into service. Showing them all she'd do as she liked – even though it was nothing but drudgery when she got there. Even that seemed all right now compared with this. What she'd give to be back in Mrs Lewis's drab house, with all this just a bad dream! Her lips moved silently.

'I don't want this! I don't want a babby! Please God, please take it away. It wasn't my fault – not really. I'll do anything you want – you can do anything, God ... I'm so scared! Just make it not be happening, *please*.'

She hugged her arms round her thin body and sobs shook her. Soon the pillow was wet with tears. For the first time in her young life she knew, really knew, what it was to be a woman. *He* wasn't having to suffer any of this. *He* had gone off without a care. His life would go on just the same. None of what happened with Jack Draper had been quite what she told Mom. The way she had flirted with him, sneaking out to meet him while he wooed her with his charm. Oh, she'd enjoyed her power as a woman then, all right, had been drunk on it. Until that night. She hadn't lied to Mom, not exactly. Jack had turned into someone else, someone terrifying and cruel who came at her out of the darkness, dragging her down near the railway, forcing and hurting her. Even after she'd staggered home in her torn clothes, she hadn't stopped shaking for hours. She'd asked for it, he said. 'You want it – you've made me do it,' he kept saying and it hurt so much, this thing she had imagined was being in love.

She hadn't known that was how babies were started. At first she thought something she'd eaten had disagreed with her. And now the idea of the baby was terrifying, yet she still didn't know what was to happen. Something involving muffled screams behind doors, blood, pain. None of it seemed real. It was something much older ladies did, nothing to do with her . . .

She saw her life stretching ahead of her, chained to this screaming brat, her young life snatched from her. There'd be no fun, no *anything*. She'd never be able to get married now or have a normal life.

'It's all your fault, Jack Draper,' she raged. 'No one'll want me,' she sobbed. 'Why can't I get rid of it – this *thing*? I just want everything back how it was before!'

Seeing her mother's fearsome face in her mind, Dolly curled up even tighter, pulling the covers almost over her head. Mom was adamant – she had to have the baby, there was to be no arguing. She boiled with rage and resentment. *I hate her*, she mouthed. *Hate her, hate her* . . . Her face contorted at the thought of those terrible smelling salts, like daggers up her nose. That was Mom – you never knew with her. One minute she was harsh and cruel, the next, soft, sentimental, comforting. Dolly knew Phyllis would always fight for all of them and what they needed, like a tiger. And though she raged against it, the hardest thing for Dolly to admit was that she couldn't manage now without her mother – or her sisters. She was back here whether she liked it or not.

'I don't want to be a woman!' she cried to herself wretchedly. 'I don't want any of it! Just let it all stop!'

Six

Sunday. Lie-in morning. Downstairs, Dad was coughing again.

Aggie could hear the rain being blown in rattling gusts against the attic window. A dripping sound had started in the corner near the window as well. Aggie thought all the others were asleep, but then there came movements from behind the curtain followed by the sound of a jet of another kind of liquid streaming into the bucket. She rolled her eyes in the darkness, trying to guess which of her brothers it was. Silas, by the clumsy sound of things. At least now he was six he didn't kick the bucket over all the time. A whiff of it reached her. Soon it went quiet again.

All the Green children slept in the attic, the girls in a three-quarter-sized bed at the window end, the boys on a straw-stuffed mattress at the other with a curtain between. Until recently Aggie and Ann, who was now eight, had luxuriated, just two of them in the bed, until Mom decided it was high time May stopped sleeping down with them and she had arrived in the attic as well.

At this moment, May's warm head was nuzzled into Aggie's left armpit and Ann, a funny, twitchy little thing, was arranged in her usual fashion on her front with her knees bent under her and her bottom sticking up. Which was all very well but she thumped about and let a lot of cold air under the bedclothes and Aggie had to cling to them to keep them over her.

Lily Southgate didn't have anyone else crashing about in her bed, Aggie thought. Lily had a neat little bed with white sheets and a pink counterpane that Rose had made, not the ragbag of bits of blanket and coats that had somehow to be patchworked into one piece to cover them all. And she had such nice brown leather shoes and pretty clothes. Aggie felt no rancour towards Lily, although she envied her. She was a sweet child and looked up to Aggie as a 'big girl'.

Behind the dark blue curtain were the two boys: John, ten and still small for his age, and Silas.

There were two kinds of child in the Green family: 'gingers' and 'brownies' as they called them, each taking unambiguously after one or other parent. As a family they looked like two contrasting packs of cards shuffled together. The gingers – 'like Mom' – had all come in a run – Aggie, John and Ann – until Silas and May arrived, all dark curls and liquid brown eyes, looking as if they were quite unrelated to the others and, Aggie often thought, able to get away with murder because of those pleading eyes.

She was just drifting back to sleep when the coughing started again. Mom said Dad was down with bronchitis and it was taking him a long time to get better.

Then came another sound, more coughing, retching. After a time, her mother's voice, riding on a groan, came distinctly through the floor.

'Oh – what've you gone and done to me, Tommy Green? I might as well go and throw myself in the cut.'

Aggie's heart started to pound at Mom's terrible words. She remembered before May was born – a long time before, it had seemed at the time – Mom had been sick day after day. And after, she'd declared, 'If I have to go through that again I'll do away with myself!' She didn't mean the children to hear, but sometimes they did.

What did this mean? If Mom had 'caught' as she called it, what might happen? Dad said something back but she couldn't hear what and it set him off coughing again.

Aggie lay suddenly cold and full of dread.

May started squirming. Her eyes opened. Aggie's heart sank. There'd be no peace now, but at least it took her mind off her grim thoughts.

Tommy Green, even when in good health, was a small, wiry man who had the melting brown eyes inherited by his two youngest children and a winning, face-crinkling grin. This grin and his kind heart had won Jenny Adams's affection as they grew up together in Balsall Heath – only a few streets away. They had fallen in love in their teens.

Tommy had always suffered with his health. By the time war was declared in 1914, Tommy and Jen had Aggie, a year old, and Tommy had tried to do his bit and take the King's shilling. He was turned down – on grounds of being a family man, but even more on being too small of stature, weak chested and unfit for service.

In one way he was in luck. Tommy's father had been a 'white' cooper, who ran his own business, with a barrow, mending barrels and maiding tubs for washing by replacing the iron hoops holding them together. Although Tommy was his third son, Ollie Green, having seen that with his weak chest he would be the one least able to hold down a job for another employer,

41

trained him up in his own line of work. When he was fit, Tommy went out with his barrow and tools, and worked hard. But the work was patchy. He couldn't be sure of earning every day. To make ends meet, most days Jen cooked dinners for the workers in local factories and workshops which were too small to have a canteen. They could come and collect a plateful to stoke them up for the day. Most mornings saw the house full of the steam of cabbage and potatoes cooking, and pots of stew. When there was no school – and sometimes when there was – Aggie was expected to pitch in and help. Now Nanna had come to live with them, she helped most of the time instead and the two of them chatted and squabbled their way through the work.

Later the rain stopped, but the road was dotted with shiny puddles. Jen sent the boys outside.

'And don't go getting soaked!' she shouted after them.

Jen was hand washing more clothes – Aggie's and Ann's this time – and issuing orders: 'Take yer father up a cuppa tea – and yer nan!'

Aggie was wearing Mom's scratchy old grey coat that trailed on the floor and Ann was wrapped in a blanket, to keep warm until their clothes were dry again. The coat only had two buttons left and Aggie did them up to cover her modesty, but as she went upstairs in her bare feet, she had to try very hard not to trip over the coat's hem and spill the two cups of tea she was carrying. She put them down on the top step to open her grandmother's door and took one cup to put on the chair by Freda Adams's bed. The room was bracingly cold. Nanna always slept with the window open. It kept the germs at bay, she said.

The old lady's eyes snapped open, then narrowed humorously. 'Oi, oi,' she said. 'I can see yer.'

'Brought you some tea, Nanna,' Aggie said, smiling.

'What it is to have servants.' Freda winced with pain as she moved to sit up. 'Ooh, my blasted rotten old joints. Just leave it there, bab – I'll take my time getting up.'

Aggie went out and took the other cup to her father. The door squeaked as she opened it and she went into the sour-smelling room. She didn't know if he had heard. His body looked so thin and small under the blankets, his old coat on the top. Aggie was full of dread. It made her feel bad seeing him like this. She wanted him to get up and be the lively, humorous dad he'd always been. She'd always been close to her dad – she found him easier and funnier than Mom.

He stirred as she put the tea down on the chair by him and started to raise himself on one arm. First his matted hair appeared, then his ravaged face.

''Ello, Aggs,' he said, but then got stuck with coughing. He spat up into a bit of rag then laid it aside, looking exhausted. But he managed to force a smile on to his face.

'Cough it up, kid,' he rasped. 'It might be a gold watch.'

Aggie smiled. She felt shy of Dad now he was so sick. It put him at a distance from them.

'I brung yer some tea,' she said.

'Thanks, our kid.' He reached for it and she hurried round to hand it to him. Every time she moved a cold draught wafted over her bare body under the coat. She gave him the tea but after a couple of sips he had to lie down again, exhausted.

'Can I sit with you, Dad?' Aggie asked.

She wanted to snuggle up beside him and keep him warm, but she felt a bit too old to do that and she also felt funny without her clothes on.

Dad was shaking his head. 'Best go down, bab, and keep away from me. You don't want what yer old man's got, that you don't.'

Reluctantly she turned to go. At the door she looked back at him, hoping he would change his mind, but his sallow face was already sunken into blankness again and his eyes were closed. Sadly, she shut the door.

Jen was sitting at the table, the bits of clothes drying by the range, and Ann was on the chair across from her. Ann had bobbed red hair, a little paler than Aggie's, and a freckly face. She was often in a world of her own and now she sat, her face twitching every now and then, and tapping a teaspoon on a saucer to make 'music'.

'You can pack that in for a start,' Jen said. 'It's going right through me.' This was followed by a sharp sigh.

Aggie looked at her mother's pasty face and wondered how she'd know if Mom was about to 'do herself in'. What did that mean exactly? Was it like Mrs Pate down the road, who'd drunk something bad and never recovered? They said it burned all her insides. Aggie had pictured them smouldering, like the fire. But she knew what the cut was, all right, the murky canal water, and the thought of it made her shudder. She wanted to ask Mom – 'You won't, will yer? Don't leave us. Promise me?' – but didn't dare.

'Ooo-hoo!' There was a tap at the back door. 'Jen – it's me!'

'Come in, Dulce – it's open,' Mom said listlessly.

Dulcie Skinner, Babs's mom and Jen's best friend, popped her head round the back door. Babs looked very like her; both were skinny, long faced, brown haired and toothy, so that they looked forever cheerful. Babs was the only girl among seven children and Dulcie was run ragged, but she always seemed to ride it all.

'I've sent 'em out to play in the road,' she said with a grin. Her lanky figure came into the room and she plonked herself down at the table. 'They'll all be soaked to the skin but at least it's got 'em out from under my feet. Thought I'd pop in and see you, bab. How're you keeping? Oooh, dear!' She laughed. 'I only 'ave to look at yer!'

'Don't flaming ask,' Jen said with a groan. 'I've been heaving my guts up all morning.'

'Oooh,' Dulcie said again, but still smiling. She put her mouth closer to Jen's ear. 'So . . . When's it due, d'yer think?'

Jen looked at her daughters all round with their ears flapping.

'Go on, you lot – leave us in peace for a bit.'

As Aggie left the room, she heard Dulcie say in a low voice, 'So have you had the doctor in for him yet?' She heard her mother give a troubled sigh before saying anything.

Aggie took May's hand and led her into the cold front room. Ann followed in her dreamy way, still playing some game of her own with a teaspoon that she was talking to earnestly. All of them were barefoot and soon they were shivering.

'Come on, May – we're going to have a look out.' She didn't say anything to May about actual spying. May was too little. She went to her post behind the nets, picking May up so she could see. Peering out, she was soon rewarded by the sight of Mrs Southgate and Lily crossing over the road on their way to St Paul's Church. Lily had on her lovely brown shoes. May pointed.

'Yes – it's Lily, May. I wish we could go to her house again, don't you? But Mom'll want us to go to Sunday school so she and our dad can have a nap.'

Aggie's breath steamed the window. She drew a face to keep May happy and May started blowing and scribbling on the glass as well.

Soon after, the door directly across the road opened. Aggie watched carefully, forgetting May's weight dragging on her hip. She saw Mrs Best pushing Mr Best out in his wheelchair. Her thin frame had to lean hard on the chair to manoeuvre it over the step. The sight made Aggie's heart clench, then thump fast with the horror of it. Mr Best's face was a deadly white and his head was thrown back at an odd angle, as if he was struggling to breathe. His eyes were half open. He was well wrapped up with a blanket tucked round his knees. He looked very poorly. Aggie hated to think he was inside that house, day after day. Mrs Best leaned on the chair and they made their way slowly along the road. For a moment Aggie felt like crying. It would almost be better not to see him at all.

Seven

Aggie wanted to like Sunday school but, in truth, she didn't, even though Babs and her brothers went and it might have been fun. But fun it was not. She didn't like the musty smell of the church hall and they were always on about the Bible and Jesus. She found herself bored to squirming point and the only good thing about it was the drink of milk and the biscuit they were given in the middle. Ann quite liked it because you could win prizes and, with her good memory, she had done so once or twice. Babs was good at drawing pictures and could manage shepherds and camels when she put her mind to it. Aggie never won anything because her attention drifted. She desperately wanted to escape it. She had much more exciting plans.

Before dinner, she managed to get John on his own. They sat on the stairs, whispering.

'I don't want to go – do you?'

John, a skinny wraith, with pale skin and knobbly knees, was as red headed as Aggie, and he was made especially striking by having thick blond eyelashes. He looked up at her from under them.

'But Mom'll make us.' He slumped down with a sigh of one beyond his years at the thought of the crushing boredom of the afternoon to follow.

'But if we promised,' Aggie persuaded, 'just you and me. If we stay upstairs and we promise to be *really* quiet, our mom might let us. My clothes ain't dry, any road.' Jen had sent her out to the backyard to mangle the clothes and they were hanging by the range but Aggie's brown skirt was thick and took a long time to dry.

John looked doubtfully at her. 'Nah – bet she won't.'

'I'll *beg* her,' Aggie said passionately. She would really have preferred to carry out her plans with Babs, but Babs would never be let off taking her younger brothers to Sunday school, so John would have to do.

At first Mom was up in arms. 'I'm not having you all under my feet all afternoon. I need a lie-down and your dad needs some peace . . .'

'But the others can go – Ann *likes* it there, and May 'cause they let her do a picture but me and John don't like it – and you said when you were little you never liked it neither . . .'

'I'm not having Ann taking May by herself—'

'I'll take 'em!' Aggie had a sudden inspiration. 'And I'll go and get them but just let me and John stay in. You won't know we're here. We'll stay up the top and we'll be as quiet as mice – *please*, Mom!'

Jen Green, who was only just getting over her morning queasiness and trying to cook the family's dinner, was bowled over by the force of her daughter. She wiped steam and sweat from her forehead with the back of her arm, then made a dismissive gesture.

'All right – just this once. Just so long as we don't know you're there!'

'Yer little heathen,' Nanny Adams observed teasingly, as Aggie panted up the stairs.

She had walked Ann, Silas and May to St Agatha's

on the Stratford Road and having safely ushered them inside, she tore home again in the cold as fast as her legs would carry her.

Aggie stood in the doorway of her grandmother's room. Freda Adams had only come to live with the family a couple of years back, to save on rent and help out, and it was the first time in her life that she was not living off a yard. The children had all been put in the attic together to accommodate her in this tiny upstairs room. There was only just space for a bed and a wooden chair, and in the corner, by the window, was a small wooden chest in which Nanna kept her few possessions. On the wall hung her wedding photograph to Granddad Sid, who'd been dead a good while now. Aggie liked Nanna's room. It smelt of lavender and mothballs and of what Nanna called her 'mother's ruin' – the warming liquor she made sure of having in her little hip flask that she liked to take sips from.

Nanna was having her Sunday lie-down, and so were Mom and Dad, in their room opposite, with the door closed. Nanna had on the old black dress she always wore: she would mourn her beloved Sidney for the rest of her days. He was taken from her young and tragically. He had suffered a blow to the head at work in a foundry, from the end of an iron girder. After it, as Nanna would say, 'he was never the same again'. At the age of thirty-eight he had taken his own life, leaving Freda Adams with Jen and three boys to bring up, two of whom the Great War had taken from her as well. The only remaining brother, Uncle Bill, lived not too far away.

Nanna had a head of thick yellowish white hair that in her youth had been a fierce red like her daughter's. In the morning she would lean over and brush it out, sweeping it all up to the top of her head where she fixed it with pins into an elaborate pile so that she always looked rather grand. Her face had the pale, papery look of someone who was once pink and freckled. She was leaning back now, her hair still up, but she had taken off her little black lace-up boots and they were standing by the bed as if about to perform a dance, though with her sore hip joints, she wouldn't be doing any dancing herself.

There was a twinkle in the old lady's eye.

'Well, you ain't going to get to heaven, are yer?' she said softly as Aggie stood at her door, wiggling her bare toes against the cold.

Aggie grinned back at her. 'Have a nice sleep, Nanna.'

Nanna raised the hip flask jovially from where it had been tucked under her skirt. She had inherited it from her husband Sidney's father and it was a classy-looking thing with a silver top. It was Nanna's most prized possession. Every so often she limped off to the Outdoor at the bottom of the street and had it topped up with something strong and cockle-warming, 'to keep me going'.

'You behave yourselves. I know you're up to summat, you two. I don't know if I want to know what it is.'

'We're not, Nanna – honest!' Aggie said in a tone of hurt innocence. 'We just felt like staying in, that's all.'

'Hmmph,' Nanna said. 'Well, you'd better close up my door as you go.' She tucked the flask back alongside her. 'Then I shan't be any the wiser, shall I?'

*

50

Aggie pulled the door to and tiptoed up to the attic, where John was waiting. The curtain separating boys from girls was pulled back to let in a grey light from the window. John's skinny form, dressed in baggy shorts, was lying face down on the boys' mattress looking at a dog-eared copy of *The Champion* comic. But he sat up as soon as Aggie appeared. He was all knees. Like a lot of little boys, his shorts were concertinaed up at the right side because instead of unbuttoning when they needed to pee, to save time they rucked up the leg of their shorts and did it like that, leaving distinctive folds. Silas was starting to have the same cock-eyed look.

'What're we doing, Aggs?'

Aggie was two and a half years older than John and they had always been playmates. Even though he was getting big now, sometimes he still looked up to her and she had always been good at thinking up games and pastimes to entertain them.

She knelt solemnly on the mattress beside him.

'I've got a plan. But you've got to promise me, *swear* you won't tell anyone.' From up her sleeve she produced a round-ended knife from the kitchen. John's brows puckered.

'D'you swear?'

John raised his blond lashes to stare at her, then nodded.

'You've got to do everything I say to make the plan work.' She leaned close to him, talking in a fierce whisper. Close up, John smelt of gravy, which was spattered down his jersey. 'You listening to me?'

He nodded hard.

'We're going to do some spying. See this?' She held up the knife. 'We're going in there.'

She nodded her head towards a rough, rectangular hatch in the wall half obscured by the blue dividing curtain. It was there to allow access to the adjoining attic, in case the stairs in either house caught fire.

'Through there?' John said. 'Why? There ain't nothing in there. It's just Mrs Larkin's attic.'

'How do you know? You been in?'

'No, but . . .'

'See – you don't know *nothing* unless you find out.'

'But our mom'll *flay* us!'

'How's she going to know, if we don't tell 'er? I heard them both snoring down there. Come on – if we're quick . . .'

'But what's the point?' John grumbled, still drawn back to the comic's derring-do adventures.

'It's spying,' Aggie said witheringly. 'I thought you were going to be my assistant – I thought you were brave. You're worse than a *girl*!'

This pricked John's pride. He clambered up and stood on his bony legs and tried to pull the right leg of his shorts down straight. 'No, I ain't! Come on – give us the knife then. Bet you can't get it open without me.'

The walls of the attic were painted bright blue and the paint had also been washed across the plywood hatch. Aggie knelt down and peered at it. It seemed strange to her now that they had never tried to open it before. She tested the edges of it with her fingers. A gaggle of silverfish fled out of the way of this intrusion.

'It's a bit loose – I can get the knife in here,' she said excitedly.

'What if there's someone in there?' John stood behind her.

'Who's gonna be there? Mrs L can't get up the stairs.'

'What about *him*?' John said.

Aggie hesitated. She'd forgotten completely that Mrs Larkin had a lodger, a pale, ill-humoured man.

'He can't be in there – we'd hear him. He dain't live up here.'

All the same, her hands began to tremble as she inserted the knife's tip into the frame of the hatch and jerked it back and forth. It was all quite easy in the end: there seemed to be nothing much holding it all together. A few moments later, with a crackling noise which seemed deafening, she was able to push the thin hatch door open. Behind her she heard John gasp.

They were looking through into another attic room much the same as theirs, but with more light coming in from somewhere. There was nothing in the room – no furniture or sign of anyone living there. All they could see was mess. The floor was scattered with bits of stuff and a thick layer of dust and dirt. Some of it was a pale colour and there was a strong, bitter smell. Aggie realized the white stuff was bird droppings. The walls were a filthy colour and the corners full of dark spider's webs.

'Uggh,' she said.

'Go on, then,' John said, nudging her from behind. 'You chicken?'

'Course not!' She was the spy, not him, she thought crossly, and with a lurch of fear, made herself step through the hatch. John immediately followed.

They saw then why the next-door attic was lighter than their own. At the back of the house there was a ragged hole in the roof, slates teetering at the edge, through which they could see the grey sky. Aggie realized that they were walking on damp, squelchy stuff.

Right beneath the hole was the dried-out body of a dead pigeon. It had been there a long time. Aggie recoiled from it. She wanted to go back.

But John was the one excited now. He moved round the room, exploring.

'Sssh!' Aggie scolded. 'Don't thump about – she'll hear you!'

'Look.' John was squatting down at the far side of the room. 'There's another'un here.'

She thought he meant a dead bird, but tiptoeing over she saw that in the grimy darkness of the wall there was another fire hatch, identical to the one from their own attic except in one respect – it was already loose and flapping half open.

'We can go in there an' all – let's open it up!' John was the one keen on spying now. Aggie was beginning to wish she'd never started it. What if someone found them?

'Don't, John – you can't go in there. That's Mrs Southgate's house!' Because there was no number thirteen, the next house was number fifteen, Rose Southgate's.

John turned to her in the gloom. 'So what?'

'What if Mr Southgate catches us?'

'He won't – what'd he be doing up here? If there was anyone in there we'd be able to hear 'em. Look –' He was pushing on it and Aggie could see that the flimsy partition was beginning to give way. John gave it another shove in the bottom corner and almost fell into the next room.

'Oh, Johnny –' Aggie moaned softly. But she was excited and curious too, and edged forward.

The roof of the Southgates' house was not in such a bad state as Mrs Larkin's, so no light was coming in and she had to wait for a few seconds for her eyes to adjust. As with their house, there was just a high gable window. She looked around.

The floorboards, though dusty, were clear of mess and there was nothing much up there. On its side, along the length of the room, lay a narrow cupboard, too tall to stand upright. There was a tea chest by the far wall under the window and Aggie tiptoed over and peered into it. There were a few items at the bottom – an old saucepan, some boots which she thought must be army boots and something made of cloth, like an old curtain. She saw a fishing rod with its end snapped off lying close to the wall near her. Other than that, there appeared to be nothing to see.

John was creeping across, trying to open the door of the cupboard but it was awkward as it was lying on its side.

'Leave it, John,' Aggie said desperately. 'Let's get out of here.'

But he ignored her. There was no key for the cupboard and he could not get it open with his fingers. He gave up and moved to its top end. Something caught his eye in the corner of the room, behind the cupboard. Aggie was in an agony as he stepped round the piece of furniture. Supposing Mrs Southgate came up and found them. She'd never forgive herself. The shame of being found poking around in her house!

John was bent over, rifling through something. Aggie's eye wandered. There was nothing to see here – they must go, get out before they were found . . .

John gave a small, startled cry and stepped abruptly back, tripping over the corner of the cupboard and sprawling across the floor.

'You stupid!' Aggie hissed.

Both of them froze, eyes fixed in horror on each other.

But John was on his feet in a second. 'Look –' He grabbed her and pulled her to where he had been standing, though she was struggling to go the other way.

'Stop it – we've got to go!'

But he forced her. He was all a-quiver. All she could see was a dusty old canvas thing – a kitbag.

Then her whole body seemed to turn to ice. There were feet advancing up the lower flight of stairs.

'We've got to go!' She yanked at John's arm.

'Look – quick!' He pushed something out of the way and she glimpsed, in the fold of the bag, a metal thing with a dark handle.

'I'm going . . .' Running on the balls of her feet as fast as she could, she dashed to the hatch. To her relief, John followed. The footsteps below stopped, as though the person, who Aggie knew must be Mrs Southgate, had stopped to listen.

'Pull it shut!' Her lips were right by his ear.

They closed the hatch as best they could and hurried across the attic of Mrs Larkin's house until they were back in their own bedroom, yanking on the board to make it right, as if no one had ever even thought of passing through it. To Aggie's relief the hatch from their room lodged itself back in place. They threw themselves on the boys' mattress and lay hardly daring to breath. It was already as if those other attics were another world, not real, from a fairy tale.

Nothing happened. They began to breathe more easily, to giggle.

'Did you *see*?' John squirmed on to his stomach, his face serious, full of drama. 'That were a gun!'

'Don't be daft – course it wasn't.'

'It *was* – I'm telling you, I saw it!'

'You never – it was a . . . a . . . One of them tools . . .'

Aggie started to question what it was she'd seen. She'd barely had a second in the dark room.

'It was a hammer – for banging in nails.' She meant a chisel but couldn't think of the word.

John sat up, full of it. 'P'r'aps *he's* a spy. That Mr Southgate. P'r'aps they're looking for him!'

'Who?' Aggie frowned.

'I dunno – the peelers . . .'

They were silent for a minute. 'I dunno what it was,' John said after a minute. 'I thought it was a gun – that was what made me jump. Gave me a fright.'

'It was a hammer,' said Aggie. 'D'you think I don't know what a hammer looks like?' Her indignation expanded. 'And all that noise you made – you nearly got us caught. Real spies ain't s'posed to make a sound – you and your silly ideas! And don't you dare tell a word about any of this – to anyone.'

'I won't,' John said, crestfallen.

'Oh!' Aggie leapt to her feet. 'The others – I've got to go and get 'em!'

Eight

'Oh, thank goodness,' Rose groaned, closing the front door behind her. 'Take your wet shoes off,' she told Lily. 'Don't go walking them through the house.'

It was even more wet and blustery today and Rose had been out for her bits of shopping, wishing she could have left Lily behind with someone as she struggled along trying to carry her bags and keep the pair of them covered by the umbrella. By the time they got back home they were half soaked.

But she had no one to leave Lily with, no family of her own close by, and while Harry's family were only a few miles away, it was no good looking to Harry's mom for any help. She was a mean-spirited woman if ever there was one.

After she'd fed Lily and put her to bed for a nap, she went to her chair by the fire in the kitchen and sank into it with a deep sigh. Everything was in place – she worked hard to keep her house as neat and spotless as she could and now she could relax for a few moments – but if only there was someone to talk to!

Toasting her feet by the old black range, as the rain ran down the window, she thought about her acquaintances on the street. She wasn't really close to anyone but she did quite like Susanna Taylor. She was not too far off Rose in age and a very straight, pleasant person. They had a friendly chat from time to time, but the

Taylors seemed very tight knit as a family, keeping mainly to themselves. And Mrs Taylor was a strange woman, she thought. For all her airs she looked the sort who might turn and punch you and Rose kept out of her way.

She found herself thinking about Aggie's mother, Jen Green along at number nine. Everyone seemed to like her and she was bosom pals with that chatty Dulcie Skinner from the Mansions. They'd known each other since they were at school and Rose envied their easy friendship. Apart from that, Jen Green hardly had time to draw breath with all that family and her husband poorly. The thought of all those children made Rose shudder. The song floated through her head, 'The rich get richer and the poor get children...' Not her though – not if she could help it. She'd done all the childbearing she was prepared to do.

Jen was a good soul, and mostly cheerful with it. Rose saw quite a bit of Aggie, bless her – she had a soft spot for the child, all eyes and knees. She reminded Rose of herself at that age. But she felt that Jen Green was wary of her, as if she thought Rose was above her – or rather as if she thought that *Rose* thought she was above her ... Which wasn't true at all, but because Rose was pretty, with a striking combination of dark eyes and blonde hair, good with a needle and with a gift of dressing herself well on next to nothing, and because she was shy and unsure what to say to people, they often took her for being stuck up. Really, she would much rather have made friends but wasn't too sure how to go about it.

Looking for comfort she went to fetch her commonplace book and sat leafing through it, in search of all the lovely things she had written. Even holding the book made her feel better. The inner pages of the deep red Morocco cover were so pretty; a very pale green covered with a pattern of tiny gold leaves and blue flowers. The book had been a present from her employer, Professor Mount, years ago, when she left service to get married.

She read her curling hand, one of her favourite hymns,

Not now, but in the coming years,
It may be in the better land,
We'll read the meaning of our tears,
And there, some time, we'll understand.

By the time she had softly sung her way through it and reached the lines, *We'll catch the broken thread again, And finish what we here began*, Rose had tears running down her cheeks and could no longer sing or see the words to read. She put her hands over her face and gave vent to her feelings for a few moments, until she could control the sobs which shook her. Even she was surprised by the force of her own anguish. Eventually she sat straighter, wiping her eyes.

'I must stop this,' she said to herself crossly. 'Letting go like this. Where's that ever going to get me?'

Picking up her book again, she turned to the back, to the few items she had stuck in. Mata Hari's smouldering gaze met her on the next page. Rose drank in the sight of her gorgeous golden dress, the folds hanging down around her body as if she was a goddess, and she gave a sigh. She had stuck the picture in because of Mata Hari's clothes and also – though she could hardly admit it to herself – because of her desirability as a woman. Deep inside her, though she barely recognized it, was a longing to be desired and desirable. For with Harry, all she had ever done was try and avoid relations with him. All the more so now.

Turning the page she came upon her cutting about the British Empire Exhibition, last year. Her face twisted bitterly. Even now, the thought of how much she had longed to go made her burn with anger and resentment. She'd begged and begged Harry – as she never had for anything else.

'If we save we could afford it,' she'd said. 'And it'd be good for Lily – there'll be so much to see. It's going to be enormous!'

'Waste of bloody money,' Harry said, looking up from by the fire where he was polishing his boots. 'What's there to see that you can't see 'ere?'

Rose stared at him. The ignorance of the question aggravated her beyond words. *See here?* What did they ever see here, in their little house, in these same old streets, going to work, coming home, keeping house? She stared at her husband as if he was a stranger – and things were bad enough already by then. In fact, she had her own secret little store of money, but she didn't want to own up to that.

'But Harry –' She tried to control her resentment and speak persuasively. 'There'll be things from all over the world, from the Empire, like it says. And people going from all over, to see things, learn something new . . . Something big that you can be part of . . . We could take Lily on a train, get out for a bit. I mean, when have we ever . . .'

She had to stop speaking in order not to break down and weep with frustration. Harry kept brushing the boots with a hard, rhythmic stroke. She looked at his profile with his black, wiry hair and stocky body, so alien to her.

'I thought,' she recovered enough to say, 'it'd be something we could do together. Something to look forward to, as a family – the three of us. That'd be nice, wouldn't it?'

He looked up again, his eyes full of a sullen indifference. 'When've you ever wanted to do anything with me, eh – tell me that? If you think I'm spending a penny on carting down there to some fancy load of muck they've dreamed up to empty yer pockets, you've got another think coming. I'm not interested. Load of flaming claptrap.'

'Oh, Harry, *please* . . .' She longed to go so much, she almost sank to her knees. 'Just this one thing – it'd mean the world to me!' It felt like a tipping point in her life, something she had to do, whatever it took, something to treasure and to enlarge her existence. And he could see nothing of this.

Harry stood up, a boot stuck on his left hand. 'I've said no. You're not going and that's an end of it! Think you can just do what yer bloody like, don't yer? Well, I'm not having it.' There was a smirk of triumph in his expression. 'Now you can see how it feels.'

She knew it was hopeless. Harry would never change his mind. Once he went out she wept in bitter disappointment. She wasn't going to do it in front of him and let him see how much he had hurt and frustrated her. It felt as if some door of hope had been slammed in her face for ever.

The King had opened the exhibition on 23 April and she followed everything avidly in the paper. Muriel Wood at church, a kindly person, had said she would love to have gone too and take her boy but she couldn't run to the train fare. So they talked about it and shared their wistful longing to be there. Someone Muriel knew did go and kindly brought her back a souvenir. That tin of Sharp's Super-Kreem Toffees was the closest Rose came to touching the exhibition and all it had meant to her.

Like the other setbacks of her life, she had had to fold it away and try to forget it. Far worse things happened, she knew full well, yet the bitterness had stung for a long time. Turning the page today tore it open again, the feelings of longing and the deep loathing and disappointment she felt in her husband.

For the umpteenth time she asked herself how she could have been so stupid, so hasty and misguided as to marry him. Leaning forward to warm her hands by the fire she reflected gloomily that there was no point thinking like that. She had married him: they'd both made a bed for themselves and now they had to make the best of lying in it.

Nine

If it wasn't for Lily, Rose sometimes thought, she would have felt that her life was over. Though she was only twenty-five, her own mother died at thirty-seven of childbed fever and it had coloured Rose's sense of how long life might be.

And if it hadn't been for Mom dying – well, everything would have been different.

Rose, born in the spring of 1900, was the third child of David and Alice Spencer. Her big sister Bessie was six years her senior, her brother Peter four years. Their father ran a small photographic studio on the Stratford Road and Bessie had taken to working for him when she left school. Their mother's health was never very strong and above all she suffered with childbirth. Peter's birth had left her with an injury to her back, so that often she was in pain and found it hard to move about.

After Rose was born no more babies appeared for a long interval, but Rose had to learn very young to help her ailing mother about the house. Then, in 1911, Alice found she was expecting again.

Rose remembered those months with a poignant clarity. Her mother had been a gentle, kind presence in their little house in Sparkhill. She had had a genteel upbringing herself and was able to teach her girls all they needed to know about keeping a good home and about sewing and mending. Alice played the piano for as long as the pain in her back would allow, and Rose could recall her mother's sweet voice singing as she played. It was one of her dearest memories.

Rose could sense her mother's terror of childbirth and there was a feeling of cold foreboding during those months. As the pregnancy advanced, the pain in Alice's back also grew worse and she had to spend a lot of time lying down on her side to try and ease it.

On a muggy spring day in 1912, Maud came into the world. Bessie was kept back at home to help. Rose was very relieved not to be in the house and hear any of the disturbing noises of childbirth. She ran home from school at dinner time, anxious but excited. The baby had already arrived and she was allowed to go up and see. Her mother looked exhausted, her long brown hair lank from the effort of it, but she was full of relief and smiled when Rose came into the room.

'You've got a little sister, Rosie,' she said.

She had given birth to a healthy little girl. It was over.

But it was not over. Still in pain from her back, Alice found it hard to move and get out of bed. Within a week she was delirious with fever and they had to take it in turns to hold little Maud to her to feed as their mother scarcely even knew them. Bessie and Rose stroked cold water over Alice's limbs with a rag as the doctor instructed, to cool her down. Gradually her left leg swelled. Her thigh was a disturbing sight, all hard and pale. They propped her leg up on pillows but the swelling grew worse. Soon, the whole of her leg was like a dead, white log.

David Spencer, their father, was distraught, kneeling beside his wife every spare minute he had, stroking her hand, his greying head bent over her, caressing her palm and begging her to speak to him. Once, as she was watching at the door, Rose saw her mother open her eyes and a look pass between them.

'Oh, my sweet, my dearest lamb,' her father said tenderly, leaning to stroke Alice's forehead.

Alice gave a slight smile, whispered something, and Rose saw her father lower his head and rest it gently beside her, still holding her hand.

It was so loving that it brought tears to Rose's eyes. Whenever she thought of it, even years later, it caught at her throat. It was what love was supposed to be.

Mom slipped away slowly. Her heart gave out in the small hours of a May morning.

They were all left bereft. Life was never the same again.

Her father lost heart. In all the fear and grief of the time, this was the most frightening aspect of all. With their mother gone, Bessie, Peter and Rose felt exposed and frightened, missing her care. They needed their father to stand firm and safe, to provide for them and help them learn to carry on. David Spencer was able to do none of these things.

Up until then he had been a good enough father, but his wife, weak as she had seemed, had been his mainstay. Without her he was lost. He became a shadow who disappeared to work early in the morning and returned to eat, then slipped away to his room, heavy with sorrow. It was as if he couldn't even see them in front of him.

Most of the burden fell on eighteen-year-old Bessie, who was forced to give up work and stay home. Somewhere along the line it was decided that baby Maud should be given over to be brought up by someone else.

Rose only discovered this when she came home one afternoon to find her gone.

'Where's Maudie?' she asked Bessie, looking round. There was no sign of her or of her little things and the house looked bare. Bessie's eyes were swollen from crying. As Rose questioned her, Bessie broke down again, tears coursing down her good-natured face.

'A lady came and took her this morning!' She fell back on to a chair and wept. Rose sank down at her feet, clutching at her sister's knees for comfort, not taking her eyes off her.

'Our dad said it was the only way, that she'll have a better chance in life. But it feels wrong – he should never've done it. I told him I could look after her and he kept saying all of us could get on better without a babby in the house. He never liked Maudie 'cause he thinks she killed our mom, but it wasn't her fault . . . And oh, when the lady came . . .' Bessie wept, her shoulders heaving.

Rose licked her lips, tasting the salt of her own tears. 'What was she like?' she whispered.

'She was all right. Quite nice. Looked kind enough. She was wearing ever such a nice coat with a fur collar. But they live over in Knowle. She said to me that Maudie'll have everything she'll ever need and they'll give her dancing lessons and a good life and I s'pect she will – but they aren't our family, are they? Maudie doesn't belong over there with those people. She's not going to know who we are and we'll never see her now. Oh, Rose – I *hate* our dad for giving her away . . . I'll never forgive him!'

Rose felt as if she might explode. Sobbing, she rested her head in Bessie's lap and Bessie hugged her and they wept together. It was a long time before Rose could take in that Maudie had really gone and she wouldn't hear her crying any more or feel her little hand grab a finger and cling on, or see her little clothes hanging on the line. Although she was only three months old, it felt as if Maudie had been with them for ever and they couldn't imagine life without her.

Within a year of their mother's death, their father was taken gravely ill and went into the Fever Hospital, never to return home. The children scattered. Peter, then nearly seventeen, announced that he was going to go to sea – 'or anywhere but here' as he put it – and set off to look for a merchant ship. Bessie hurried into marriage with a much older man who was a widower and went to live in Acocks Green. There was talk of Rose going to live with them but she didn't take to Edwin Fisher, Bessie's husband, a large, loud man. She did the only thing she could think of to make sure she had a roof over her head, and went into service.

The first sight she had of the house in Oxford Road, Moseley, was on a summer day in 1913. Even in bright sunlight, the house looked gloomy and neglected. Rose felt a shiver go through her as she turned in at the front gate and saw the peeling paint and dark, forbidding windows. There was a look of everything being covered in dust, even on the outside, especially when contrasted with the neighbouring houses in this genteel street, which looked in much better repair. A discouraging smell seeped out from under the door and the steps were still clogged with last winter's leaves.

She hesitated before knocking. She had answered an advertisement for a maid of all work, preferably to live in. But could she really face living in this house? For a moment she was tempted to run away and look for a post elsewhere.

As she stood, dithering on the step, the door slowly opened and she saw an elderly man, dressed in clothes that appeared to be intended for someone several sizes bigger – perhaps the younger version of this man. He was little and birdlike, with pale blue eyes. The kindly way he looked at her was at least reassuring.

In a high, fluting voice, he said, 'You must be the young lady we're expecting? Miss Spencer?'

'Yes,' Rose whispered.

'We were looking out for you. Do come in, my dear.' He held out his hand. 'I'm Professor Mount.'

Startled, Rose reached out and shook his blue-veined hand, which was cold as a dead bird.

'Come along –' He beckoned her into the hall and closed the front door. Rose's nostrils were immediately assailed by an even stronger version of the heart-sinking, vegetable smell and in the gloom, following Professor Mount's stiff–hipped progress, she made a face. 'My wife and I are very pleased that you have come. We really are in rather a predicament.'

Rose was not entirely sure what one of those was, but she could tell from the smell and general state of the place that it badly needed attention.

'Our last maid left a few weeks ago and we haven't had much luck in finding anyone suitable – or who's prepared to take us on.' He stopped abruptly so that Rose almost crashed into the back of him. Without turning, which seemed to be a dangerous operation for his balance, he said, 'D'you think you're up to it?'

'I don't know – sir.' She hardly knew what she was supposed to be 'up to' yet. However, compared with some of the stories she had heard about the treatment some maids had in big houses, she was encouraged by Professor Mount. 'I hope so,' she added, trying to sound confident.

'Good, good,' he said. 'Now come and meet Mrs Mount, my dear.'

They had passed what must have been the front parlour, though the door was closed, and Professor Mount led Rose into a room at the back crammed with furniture, a couch, several tables and more chairs than could reasonably be needed by two people, all looking ragged. Each side of the chimney breast and along the back wall was completely taken up by bookshelves which reached the ceiling, crammed with books. Rose had never seen so many books anywhere. The fire was lit even though it was high summer and the room was stifling. Rose took a deep breath through her nose, then wished she hadn't. Then she sneezed. The place was thick with dust.

'Hester, my dear?'

It took a moment for Rose to work out that what seemed to be a pile of bedding on the couch topped by a lace-edged muslin bonnet was a person, until Mrs Mount's fleshy face bobbed up to look at them both.

'The girl has come.'

'Ah –' A tremulous voice came from the mound. 'Help me up a little way, Benjamin.'

Professor Mount did as he was asked. But he had such a job hoisting his large wife into a more upright position, with grunts and 'oh, deary me's from him and 'ooh's and 'oh, dear Lord's from her – all quite cheerful on both sides, Rose noted – that she almost felt she ought to offer to help, but was too timid. The woman's left arm seemed limp and useless.

Mrs Mount, once upright, had greyish-white hair spilling out from under her old-fashioned white bonnet. Her face was round with very pink cheeks and eyes almost as vivid as her husband's. Her gown was of a pale sugar pink, with a frill down the front. Quite breathless after her arduous ascent to a sitting position, she waved a handkerchief in front of her face for a few moments. But she was smiling.

'Well,' she observed at last. 'You do look young. How old are you, child?'

'Fourteen, ma'am,' Rose lied, adding an extra year. Fortunately she was well on in height for her age.

'She looks a strong young thing,' Professor Mount said. 'Like a useful little sapling that won't bend or break.'

'And so fair of face!' Mrs Mount added. 'Do you have any experience about the house?'

'I learned from my mother, ma'am.' Rose wasn't quite sure where to look as she was talking, and kept her gaze on the floor until she realized this might seem rude, and looked across at Mrs Mount. On the table beside the couch, Rose saw skeins of embroidery threads. The bright colours lifted her spirits. 'Her health wasn't good. After she passed away we all had to manage.'

'Oh, my dear,' Professor Mount said, perching on the chair beside his wife's couch. His jacket rose up round his neck as if he might disappear into it completely.

'We have a cook,' Mrs Mount went on. 'She comes in every day and makes sure we are suitably fed and thereby kept alive. But we are crying out for some domestic help – for someone who will *stick*. We are not the most orderly of households, but we shall so *appreciate* you.'

She went on to explain that there were only the two of them there unless their son came to visit, so that once Rose had 'refreshed' the rest of the house as she put it, her tasks would not be too onerous.

'We should like to have someone sleeping in,' Mrs Mount said. 'Just in case. And it does so add life to a house.'

After she had explained the duties in more detail, the two of them sat looking expectantly at Rose, who had no idea what to say.

Professor Mount leaned forward, bony hands palms up.

'So – are you to be she?'

It felt impossible to say no, although the house already oppressed her. Slowly, Rose nodded.

March 1925

Ten

'Where's Mom?' Aggie asked, worried at seeing her grandmother downstairs and no sign of anyone else. Nanna hardly ever appeared this early. Her joints were very painful to move first thing. 'It takes a while for me to get my turbines going,' she'd say. And Mom was always shooing her out of the kitchen. But Nanna seemed quite lively today.

'Your mother's bad this morning – and your pa. So I thought I'd better get myself down here instead of lying up there like a lump of lard. Now come on – get yourselves ready for school.'

She winked at Aggie. The two of them always had had an understanding. 'I was the oldest girl,' Nanna said to her once. 'A lot falls to you.'

She had brewed up a pot, which was standing under its cosy on the grey oilcloth covering the kitchen table, along with the milk bottle and the carved-up remains of a loaf. There were a few lumps of sugar and a scrape of margarine on a saucer. May was still asleep, but the other four of them who had to get to school, Aggie, John, Ann and Silas, all stood round hurriedly eating and for once not squabbling. Things felt different.

'Sit yourselves down,' Freda Adams chivvied them. 'You're not a gang of navvies.'

There were only four chairs so they made do with a

stool and a couple of orange boxes when extra were needed.

'Where's our mom?' Silas asked, wide-eyed.

Nanny Adams ran one of her gnarled fingers over his round cheek, her watery eyes affectionate.

'Yer mother's feeling bad,' Nanna told him.

'Are we getting a new brother or sister?' Ann asked solemnly.

But then they heard a door open, feet on the stairs, Dad coughing, then spitting up, halfway down the stairs. He always had a rag with him for the purpose. Surprised, they all turned to the door. Dad had been confined to bed for more than a fortnight. They had not been expecting to see him up. When his emaciated figure appeared, he was dressed to go out, his belt pulled as tight as it could go and knotted.

'Dad!' John said happily.

'Son . . .' they heard him whisper, then coughing folded him over.

Aggie and the others watched as, walking stooped over as if it hurt him to stand upright, he crossed the floor in his socks, toes and heels poking through like potatoes, and waved John off his chair so that he could sit. He took a heaving breath, going red in the face with trying not to cough again.

He was a wiry, undernourished-looking man at the best of times, but now his usually amiable face was sunken in, the cheekbones standing out sharply. They could see his collarbones standing out through the neck of his shirt. His dark, usually wayward hair lay greasy and lank against his head and a sour smell came from him. He stretched his back, put his head back and gasped, 'Oh, God!'

'You better, Dad?' John asked hopefully.

Tommy let out a sound which curdled somewhere between a laugh and a groan. 'Do I sound better, son?' His face was deathly pale, though there were hectic pink patches on his cheeks.

No one knew what to say. Silas went up to him, hungering for his company. No one could resist dark-eyed, beautiful Silas.

'Ey up, feller – what's this, eh?'

Tommy leaned to him and put his fist to Silas's nose, pretending to pluck it off. He poked his thumb out between two fingers. 'Look – got yer nose!'

It caught Silas out every time and startled, he put his hand up to check. The others laughed happily, even though it was an ancient joke. But Aggie had gone all tight inside. Dad looked shockingly poorly. She was frightened by the noise his chest was making.

'It's all right, son,' Tommy grinned, ruffling Silas's hair. 'Don't fret. It's still on yer face. John, son – fetch us me Woodies, will yer?'

Tommy's hands shook as he struck a match. He inhaled, then coughed until tears ran down his face.

Aggie watched. Everything felt wrong.

Her father took another drag, then sat back, seeming happier.

'Ah – that's the ticket.'

'Come on,' Aggie urged the others, sharp with them. 'We gotta go.'

'I'd best get off myself,' Tommy said. Talking made him heave, trying not to cough.

'You going out, Dad?' John asked.

'Tommy?' Freda Adams said, horrified. 'You can't – not in that state . . .' But he waved her away.

They could all see that this was wrong, but he wasn't having any argument.

'I'll take the barrer out for a bit. Your mother's bad today. Someone's got to bring in a bob or two.'

'I can't stop yer, Tommy Green,' Nanna said quietly, her eyes burning with concern. 'But I never thought I'd call you a fool.'

Ignoring her, he stubbed out his cigarette and struggled out to the back to get his barrow of cooper's hoops and tools. As Aggie chivvied the others out of the front door for school, they could hear him coughing in the yard.

Aggie was full of a sick dread. She'd never seen Dad look that bad before. But in seconds she was distracted by the sight of her friend Babs tearing along the road from the Mansions, dark plaits bouncing as she ran and her brothers straggling somewhere behind. A grin spread over Aggie's face.

' 'Ello, gingers!' Babs called out, seeing them coming out of the house. 'Oh – and Silas! Hey, Aggie –' She seized her friend's arm. 'I thought you was coming up ours to get me!'

'I never had time,' Aggie said as they all set off together, dodging brooms when some of the housewives swept off their bit of pavement into the gutter. Others were already out scrubbing their front steps, gossip puffing out white from their lips in the cold. Irene Best smiled at Aggie and Babs as they passed.

'Never mind,' Babs said easily, then shrieked, 'Ow! There's summat sticking in me foot!'

She bent, tapering brown plaits falling forward as she pulled a tack from the sole of her shoe. 'Cor – look at that. No wonder that hurt! Look – my toe's bleeding.'

One of her bigger brothers, Freddie, caught them up and gave Babs a teasing shove which sent her sprawling on her side and then ran off laughing, calling, 'What're you looking for down there, Babs?'

'Oi!' Babs leapt up, furious. 'I'll get you later, Freddie, you stupid pig!' She got up, cursing at the graze on her leg, then grinned. 'When school's out, I'm gonna go and find something *disgusting* and *put it down his neck*!'

They were both straightening up, giggling, when they saw two of the Taylor sisters coming along the road, walking heads lowered and close together, almost as if they were trying to keep each other warm. They were wearing matching coats, one in grey, one dark brown.

As they passed the two little girls, one of the Taylors raised her head and said rudely, 'What're you staring at? It's rude to stare.' When they didn't reply she added nastily, 'Cat got your tongue, has it?'

Aggie and Babs waited until they'd gone by then stuck their tongues out.

'Mardy cow,' Babs said, limping along. 'Which one was that? They all look the same to me.'

'That was Rachel.' Aggie looped her arm through Babs's again, relieved to see that her own brothers and sisters had gone on ahead. 'Rachel's the one with the spot on her face – you know, a mole thingy.'

'But they've both got a mole,' Babs said.

'No, they ain't.'

'They have – I saw!'

'You're seeing things.'

'I *swear*. The other one . . .'

'Dolly . . .'

'Dolly, if that was Dolly. What's the other one called?'

'Susanna.'

'Well, whichever it was, *she*'s got one.'

Aggie didn't argue. She was a spy – it was her business to know things and she knew perfectly well that Dolly Taylor had no mole on her cheek.

'So – are you coming to play out later?' Babs asked as they went in through the school gates. She was a sunny girl, always thinking about the next thing to look forward to.

Aggie's spirits lifted. Maybe Mom would be up when she got back and Dad would get better today and everything would be all right.

She nodded eagerly. 'Yeah – all right.'

Jen Green dragged herself into a sitting position. Her abdomen lurched inside with nausea and the back of her head was pounding. A second later she reached for the bowl by the bed and vomited a bilious stream into it, then sat panting, holding her throbbing head. She hadn't the strength at that moment to get out of bed.

Thank God Aggie and some of the others were old enough to see to a few things now. And, she reluctantly had to admit, she wouldn't get far without her mother these days. She owed her. A tower of strength she was really, Mom, even if they did clash at times. Somehow between them they'd have to get everything done.

She felt guilty that she had scarcely noticed Tommy getting up. He'd coughed and drenched the bed in sweat beside her all night but all she'd heard this morning were a few creaks of the floorboards, she was that far gone. Where the hell had he gone to? Perhaps he couldn't stand lying in bed any more and had gone to sit downstairs.

As she turned to put the bowl down on the bed, a

jolt of shock went through her. Along the old, greyish slip on Tommy's pillow, there were streaks of red-stained phlegm.

'Oh, my God.' It was like being punched. Her heart was pounding. The shock made her feel stronger and she climbed out of bed on unsteady legs.

Everyone knew what coughing up blood meant. That was it, she thought, her heart pounding. She was going to go and see Dr Hill and talk to him, whatever Tommy said. She was too frightened to go on without help. But she sank back on to the bed for a moment. She felt too weak to make it downstairs, never mind along to wait in the surgery.

Jen had managed to start getting dressed when she heard her mother call from the bottom of the stairs.

'Jen? You up? Tommy's out. He never should've gone . . .'

'I'll be down in a tick,' she called.

As she stood upright, another wave of nausea passed through her and she bent over the bed until it passed. It was days since she'd kept anything much down. She was so weak that the thought of even moving out of the room felt like climbing a mountain. But it had to be done. She stood up and forced herself.

When Jen got downstairs, her mother was stoking up the range in the cramped back room, in her old black dress and boots. Freda had a way of standing, getting her feet firmly planted a distance apart as if she was about to tackle a heavy job like digging a pit in the ground. Thus anchored, she was a strong woman who could manage a range of tasks with her gnarled hands so long as she was

81

not required to move far or fast from that spot. So wielding the coal scuttle was well within her compass, but bringing coal up from the cellar was not.

'Well, you look like death,' she observed as Jen came in. 'D'you think it might be twins?'

'Oh – don't say that!' Jen moaned, sinking on to a chair. 'That really would be the death of me. I feel half dead now!'

'Only, of all the ones I've known to carry more than one . . . Let's see now, Maggie Edmunds and that other wench, now what was her . . .? Doesn't matter . . . Ooh, no – that were triplets, come to think of it! Any'ow –' She poked the coal vigorously for a moment. 'Both of them were sick as dogs at the beginning . . .'

'Mom, don't,' Jen groaned. She didn't even have the energy to get cross. 'Pass us a bit of that bread. I'll see if I can keep anything down.'

Jen started to nibble the bread. Her mother made tea.

'Where's Tommy gone?' Jen asked anxiously.

Freda Adams peered out into the yard. 'His barrer's gone.'

Jen kept quiet. Her innards felt horribly unstable.

'What about the dinners, then?'

'I've got nothing in,' Jen said faintly. 'I just don't think I can get down there, not in this state.'

'I'd better go,' her mother said.

'No, Mom! I don't want you having to carry all that back.'

'Get one of the neighbours to go for yer,' Freda said. 'They'll help you out. We've got a few spuds already – I'll get going on them.'

Jen wrapped her old black shawl round her and shuffled over to gather her pennies. She felt like an old woman. What would she do without neighbours? But who could she catch to ask? Dulcie was too far away. Going to the front she stood with the door open a crack to look out.

First of all, she saw Dorrie Davis coming along, bony and ramrod straight with her sour, gossip's face. Dorrie's gossip wasn't the sort of general interest in the human circus that makes the world go round; it was sheer, probing malice. Jen closed until Dorrie had passed, then cautiously peeped out again. Mrs Taylor loomed into view. She shut the door again. For all her religious airs she wasn't the sort to do you a favour: Phyllis Taylor looked after her own and sod everyone else. On the third attempt she was met by a much more appealing sight: Rose Southgate with her little girl. Jen hesitated. She was shy of Rose. The young woman was so pretty and nicely dressed that Jen felt rough and awkward beside her. She'd moved to the street about a year ago but Jen had never got to know her very well – didn't think she was her sort. But she knew nothing bad about her and she was kind to Aggie . . .

''Ere!' Jen called to her. 'Can you come 'ere a mo', bab?'

Rose stopped and looked round, startled. Lily pointed. 'There – that lady . . .' But still she hesitated.

'Yes, you – can you come over?'

Rose Southgate, to Jen's surprise, seemed quite eager and came to her door smiling. Jen thought how lovely and fresh-faced she was, and that blonde hair was a picture.

'Hello,' Rose said. 'I didn't know you meant me to start with. Did you want something? Oh, dear, you do look poorly.'

'It's a cheek, I know,' Jen said. 'But . . .' Dizzy, suddenly, she leaned against the door frame.

'Oh, dear,' Rose said again. Jen thought how nice she was. There were no airs about her.

'I . . . It's . . .' But she really was feeling very queer. 'Can you come in a minute?'

The only thing to sit on was the old sofa with its tufts of horsehair sticking out and she collapsed on to it. She indicated that Rose and Lily should sit. Jen leaned over, too nauseous to worry what her visitor thought.

'Mom!' she called weakly, feeling she couldn't get another word out.

Nanny Adams limped through from the back, wiping her hands on a rag. She nodded at Rose, who gave another lovely smile.

'Tell Mrs Southgate what we need, will yer,' Jen said, half fainting.

'She seems terribly ill,' Rose said anxiously. 'Should you call a doctor?'

'Oh, there's no call for that – it's just another 'un on the way,' Freda Adams told her. 'She's specially bad with it this time. Get your head down, bab, that's it.'

She explained about the groceries required and Rose said she'd be glad to help and would be back as soon as she could.

When she returned with the bag of food, Jen was looking a little more lively.

'You poor thing,' Rose said as they paid her for the goods. 'I hope you'll feel better soon.'

She said it with such genuine concern that Jen looked up at her and managed a faint smile. 'Ta. Well, there's one thing for sure. It'll be over in a few months.'

Rose laughed sympathetically. 'I was a bit sick with Lily,' she said.

'While you was out,' Jen said, 'you dain't see my . . .'

She had been about to say 'old man', but corrected herself. '. . . my husband about, did yer?'

'Oh – yes,' Rose remembered. 'I did. He was coming along Turner Street – just by the corner. Did you want him? We could probably go and find him if you like? Couldn't we, Lily?'

The little girl looked at her with huge blue eyes and nodded.

'Oh, no – you're all right. I just wondered whereabouts he'd got to, that's all,' Jen said, relieved. She thanked Rose again and Rose said if she ever needed any help she should just knock.

When she'd gone, Freda Adams said, 'Well, they're a lovely-looking pair, ain't they?'

'Yes,' Jen said. 'She's nice enough.' But she had been warmed by Rose, cheered somehow, especially as she'd seen Tommy in one piece. 'Any road – sitting 'ere canting won't get the dinners done.'

Eleven

'Everyone's staring at us, Mom, I know they are,' Rachel complained, glaring across the table at Dolly. 'This is your fault. Now we all have to suffer!'

Dolly stared mutinously at her plate, feeling as if she was going to explode. But she was feeling queasy and, in any case, knew she didn't have a leg to stand on. The worst thing of all was knowing she was going to have to eat humble pie for ever now.

They had closed the curtains at the front again even though they were all round the table in the kitchen, the dim lamplight only illuminating the bare essentials of their faces, the rest in shadow.

'Don't talk daft, Rachel,' their mother snapped. She stood over the table, slamming plates down in front of them. 'Why should they be staring? There's nothing to see, is there?'

'That Mrs Davis just stopped and gawped at us when we went down the road this morning,' Rachel said, prodding at the ox liver on her plate with distaste. 'Even the kids – those redheads, Aggie and that, they stared at us as if we'd grown two heads!'

Phyllis sat down, still an imposing, matriarchal figure at the head of the table.

'I think we should remember to give thanks to the Lord,' Charles said in a stiff voice, as if it pained him now to be there at all.

Thanks? Dolly was about to argue. *What the hell do I have to give thanks for?*

'Quite right,' Mom agreed, shooting her a look.

'We need all the help we can get,' Rachel muttered.

Susanna dug her in the ribs.

Dolly lowered her head and squeezed her eyes shut, her rage turned this time on her brother. Would you believe it? Couldn't he, just for once, say something that wasn't religious and *stupid?*

They all put their knives and forks down and shut up for the 'what we are about to receive's, though all except Charles appearing less thankful than it had just been requested they might be. Dolly couldn't hold back any longer.

'I'm never going to get a job!' she burst out emotionally, once they had started the meal. 'Not in this state. I'm never going to be able to do anything ever again!'

'Don't talk silly – of course you are,' her mother said. 'Just 'cause Mrs Dunne doesn't want anyone else . . .' Dolly had been with Rachel that morning, pale and sick, to see if by any chance the milliner might take on another assistant. The answer was no. She felt sure by the way the woman looked at her that she had guessed her shame. That it was written all over her.

'You can go with Susanna tomorrow,' Phyllis said.

'They won't have her,' Susanna said. 'I know they won't.' Susanna was courting with a nice young manager called David Kay, in the curtain material department. Dolly knew that the last thing she wanted was a disgraced sister trespassing on her territory. 'She should go in a factory where no one'll know her.'

Dolly felt full of that tight bursting feeling again. She was just going to be pushed around from pillar to post, with no one ever asking her!

She saw Mom silence Susanna with a glare, even while taking in the fact that Susanna was right.

'You'd best stay away from there and take anything you can get.' Mom turned to Dolly with an intense look. She folded her arms across her massive bust, leaning forward on the table. 'Now, so far as everyone else is concerned, you've left service because the lady of the house died and they've sold up. It's far enough away – no one'll know.'

'God sees all our actions, however many lies we tell,' Charles pronounced gloomily.

'Oh, shut up Charles,' Rachel said irritably. 'That's no help, is it? It just makes us feel worse.'

'Thank heaven, God and Dorrie Davis aren't one and the same,' Phyllis said. 'I'm damned if I'm having that interfering tittle-tattler crowing over me and my family.'

Dolly picked at her food. None of it tasted right and she didn't know how long it would stay down. Even eating was unpleasant these days.

'I should never've come back,' she said, in barely more than a whisper. 'I should've done away with it. Got rid of it . . .'

'That's enough from you, you wicked girl!' Mom roared at her. 'No more talk of that! Now eat up, all of you!' She had piled their plates with potato. 'You've got to eat for two – all of you.'

They were all living on their nerves.

'But I'm not going to stay looking like this, am I?' Dolly wailed, laying down her fork and putting her hands over her face. 'I'm going to get all big out the front and everyone'll be able to see clear as anything! And then I've got to have it and I don't want to!'

'You should've thought of that before you went out gallivanting,' Susanna said furiously.

'What do you know about it?' Dolly cried, bursting into tears. 'You weren't there – you don't know what happened and it didn't happen to you so don't preach to me about it!'

As she put her hands over her face she caught sight of her brother's. His expression was full of pain and she realized that for all his piousness, he was suffering with her. This made her cry all the more.

'I'm sorry, Dolly,' Susanna said stiffly. She barely sounded sorry and only touched Dolly's shoulder for a moment. 'It's just making things very difficult for all of us. You must see that.'

Dolly nodded, wiping her eyes. 'I never meant for it to happen,' she said. 'He just—'

'Enough, Dolly,' Mom said. 'We don't need to hear any more about it.' She finished chewing on a rubbery mouthful of the liver and looked round at them all. They could tell she was thinking; calculating everything out.

'What Dolly needs,' she said, 'is any old job. A factory – nowhere near here – so she can leave and no one'll give it a thought. Tomorrow, Dolly, you'll go out round the factories . . .'

She pushed back her chair and stood up to stack the plates. They all listened, Dolly among them, a kind of relief washing through her. Mom knew what to do.

'Now listen to me. You've all got to do everything I say, to the letter. Let's go over it again. For now, all you girls've got to do is put yourselves about. Dolly, Rachel – make sure you don't keep wearing the same coat. Keep switching them over. You're not that different in size. Susanna – you could swap yours with them sometimes too. All we can do at the moment is sow the seeds for later. And keep painting that mole on your face, Dolly.

The only other thing is, you must keep on about how you feel the cold. Understand? You feel the cold, you dress up warm – keep mentioning it. And *eat*.' She picked up the mashed potato spoon like a threat.

'But . . . ?' Rachel tried to interrupt, but Phyllis held up a hand.

'Charles,' she ordered. 'All you've got to do is to keep your mouth shut. I should have thought you could manage that.'

Charles had his eyes fixed on his plate with the air of someone who may be bodily present but is mentally somewhere else. Dolly felt a pang of pity for him. But he managed a nod.

'For a couple of months, everything'll be as normal. After that we're going to have to get very clever. We'll have to be cunning as serpents. And – I'm going to have to write to Nancy.'

The four children all looked at each other in bewilderment. Dolly's eyes met Susanna's frowning ones.

'Who the hell's Nancy?' Rachel said.

'Language, Rachel,' Mom scolded. 'Nancy,' their mother, who to their knowledge had no living family in the wide world, announced, 'is my sister. The youngest of my sisters.'

Twelve

'Hello, Rose, dear, and little Lily – now do tell me what sort of week you've had.'

Muriel Wood said almost the same thing in greeting every Sunday after Holy Communion. Rose found it comforting. Muriel took a genuine interest in other people's activities, perhaps as a way of diverting herself from the sadness of her own life.

She was a slender, old-fashioned lady in her early thirties. Her clothes were simple, never anything frippery. At any time except the deepest of winter, she was almost always seen about in her favourite straw hat with a blue band. She had a round face with a pink, scrubbed complexion and pale, innocent-looking blue eyes.

Rose both liked and admired her, for her cheerfulness and for the way she devoted her life to her son Oliver, now six. He could not remember either his father or elder sister Elizabeth, having been barely a year old when both of them were taken by the Spanish Influenza in 1920. Rose had seen a photograph of little Lizzie Wood, a sweet, dark-haired child like her brother. The thought of the loss of her little girl was something Rose found almost unbearable to think about.

They always chatted once the service was over. Rose looked forward to Sundays. Harry never came to church, of course, had no time for all that sort of 'eyewash' as he called it. He thought all vicars were 'a load of poofters' (Rose had never got over being shocked by his language), and wouldn't have anything to do with them. So it was a pleasant, sociable time for her.

Of course she never told Muriel what sort of week she had had. Not in any deep way. She would never have said what Harry was really like or what she felt. It would be rude and disloyal to discuss the mixture of awe and contempt with which her husband seemed to regard her. Muriel always put on a brave face and almost never mentioned her struggles or grief but tried to count her blessings. And Rose, admiring her, tried to do the same.

Last week, Muriel had approached her, this time in her sober winter hat in dark green felt and her black coat, her face a pale smile between the two. They stood in the church porch out of the wind, the organ still sounding faintly in the background.

After the usual exchanges about their week, Muriel said, 'I was wondering if you had progressed at all with the piano, dear?' She touched Rose's arm for a moment. 'Not meaning to flummox you. Not at all, dear. I know what a lot you have to do. But I am ready and willing when you feel the time is right.'

Rose had been thinking about it. She had sold another embroidered cloth and had some money saved. Anything they did with the piano would have to be when Harry was out.

'I saw an advertisement for a piano tuner in the paper,' she said. 'From the works in Ombersley Road, you know, where they make the pianos.'

'Oh, well, that's marvellous,' Muriel said. 'Then we can make a start once you're ready. I can pop over while Oliver is at school. And you can come to me sometimes if you like. That'll be nice, won't it, Lily?'

She beamed at Lily and Rose saw the soft light in the other woman's eyes as she looked at her daughter and it wrung her heart. She could see that this meant a lot to Muriel. She was too delicate to mention that the two shillings Rose would pay her for Lily's lessons would also come in very handy.

Rose thought quickly. Ideally it would need to be when Harry was out, and his work was unpredictable. But surely he wouldn't be rude enough to turn away someone who was prepared to give his daughter tuition at a reduced rate? She'd have to try and get him in a good mood, and she knew the one way to do that.

'I think if we give it another week,' she said, 'we should be ready by then.' She gathered herself up. 'I'd better get back – see how our dinner is doing.'

Harry was in when they got back, waiting for his Sunday dinner, after which he was planning to go fishing.

'Hello, love,' she said brightly as they got in. At least he'd kept the fire going; the house was warm and full of the mouth-watering smell of beef and Harry seemed quite relaxed, sitting dozing by the range.

He grunted a greeting as she came in. Some of his fishing tackle lay by his feet and he had obviously been fiddling with hooks and lines. He was a doer, Harry, not a reader or a thinker. Rose had never seen him read more than the headlines in a newspaper and scan quickly over the sports pages.

'Have a good pray, did yer?' he enquired as she

quickly set the table while the cabbage water bubbled away on the range. But he spoke lightly, joking.

'Yes, thank you,' she said evenly.

Lily sat close to her father, longing for his attention, but wary of him. Dark moods sat in him like coils waiting to spring. Lily always seemed ready to leap out of his way and Rose felt just the same.

Only Rose knew that some of it was her fault, that she frustrated his manly tendencies. She was not as he thought a wife should be.

''Ere – look –' Harry leaned over towards Lily suddenly and thrust something in front of her.

Lily took one look, then screamed and almost fell trying to get away. 'Don't like it!' She was beginning to cry. Harry was chuckling.

'Soft little ha'p'orth!' he said scornfully.

Rose raged inside. Could he not be nice – just for once? Instead of sticking a tobacco tin full of squirming maggots in his little girl's face? His idea of a joke, of course, but why did he have to be so rough and nasty?

'Never mind, babby,' she soothed Lily. 'Your dad's just having his little joke.'

Swallowing her fury she carried the crisp, golden potatoes to the table. Lily came and clung to her skirt, her eyes red, and snivelling half-heartedly.

'Come on, bab – you sit down with your father.'

'Smells good, that does,' Harry said, rolling his sleeves down. 'You're a good cook, wench, I'll say that for yer.'

It was true, she was. That was something Rose could do to please him. She had learned from her mother and from Mrs Plummer, who had cooked for Professor Mount.

They sat eating in the steamy room. There was a plum pudding simmering in the background and the window was misted up. It felt warm and cosy and for some minutes as they ate they were almost friends. Rose looked along the table at her husband's swarthy face, heavier now than when they had first met. She remembered him as a cheerful lad, back in those days, full of jokes. Thinking what a different man he was now, she felt sorrow for him and for herself. His war wounds were on the inside. And there was her guilt . . . Always that.

'Where will you go this afternoon?' she asked pleasantly.

Harry chewed on a mouthful of beef with evident enjoyment, and caught up a gravy-soaked lump of potato ready on his fork.

'Dunno yet. Down Hall Green way, p'r'aps.' He was looking down at his plate so that she could only see his brows.

Look at me, she thought. *Please at least look at me.* She knew he didn't love her, nor she him, not now. It was as if they lived on opposite banks of a river which they found it impossible to cross. They moved back and forth, parallel and distant. But she longed for it to be different, for love. They might spend the rest of their lives together – couldn't they make it better somehow?

After dinner, he set off into the thin afternoon light, his bicycle waiting at the back. She stood up to see him go and touched his arm.

'Tonight,' she said softly, looking into his face.

This made Harry look round, startled, taking her meaning. He hesitated, in a moment of confusion at her forwardness, her unusual willingness, as if he might stay now and lead her up to the bedroom.

Rose stepped back. 'I hope you have a good catch,' she said, smiling.

She was frightened of intimate relations with her husband right from the beginning. It was not the act itself so much: what she was really terrified of was childbirth, haunted as she was by what had happened to her mother. To deliver children meant pain, fear and death. In addition, from what she saw around her, having too many children meant crowding and poverty and sickness.

When Jenny Green had beckoned her over a few days ago, looking so faint and sick in her doorway, Rose had been touched and glad to help. She had been glad to feel she could be asked to do something good. She had always felt rather alone in the world and wanted more friendships and people around her.

Jenny Green had made no secret of the fact that she was expecting and the situation filled Rose with horror. She could hardly bear to think of the seething number of children in the Greens' house, the poverty and daily struggles of it all. Jenny Green's husband had been sick for ages and he looked absolutely terrible. And there was that old lady in the background in her widow's weeds like Queen Victoria. Everything about the household filled Rose with panic. It gave her the feeling that life could quickly disintegrate into squalor and chaos . . .

Harry had been her rescuer. They had married barely knowing each other when she knew he had survived the war. She was in love with the idea of love, was desperate to get out of service, and there had been such a shortage of men. Marital relations seemed just a vague, far-off part of it all then. She hadn't known what it was all about – barely had any grasp of it. Nor did she realize how much the young man who had once courted her had changed.

The wedding night had been a shock, but they had expected that. It was later that things went sour.

'You don't want me, do yer?' he would rave at her. 'You married me false – you're a cold fish, Rose, that's what you are.'

All the way through she had tried to avoid catching for a baby. Turning away, rejecting him, asking him to withdraw at the last minute – which he only sometimes managed and resented her for. One way and another, for the first couple of years she managed not to have any children, but of course, in the end she did catch for a child.

All through her pregnancy with Lily, Rose was certain she was going to die, if not from the pain, the horrifying delivery, then of the fever afterwards. In fact, both the pregnancy and birth had been healthy and normal. But it was still agonizing and so frightening. Harry found the business of having a child burdensome. And Rose couldn't believe her luck would last. Her mother had had three before she died, hadn't she? In the end she would be damaged, gored in some way by a baby, and die. It felt like her fate. She resolved never, ever to carry a child again.

'If we just keep it to one,' she would say, 'we can give her a good life – a better one than we've had. That'd be the best thing, wouldn't it?'

While Harry agreed in theory that it was better not to have many mouths to feed, he wanted his pleasures without the consequences. So often, their relations were an awkward fumbling in the dark, his thickset form on top of her, pushing so urgently after overcoming her resistance that he was all ready to explode inside her.

'Please, Harry, don't!' she would beg. 'Take it out, please – quickly!'

Sometimes he would lose the impulse and she would hear him curse bitterly in the dark, pumping with his hand to give himself the finish he needed, and the next day they could never quite look each other in the eye. At those times he seemed to loathe her and she resented him passionately for having such needs.

Once she had met Muriel Wood, through church, Muriel had made a remark, just in passing, as if she thought Rose would know what she meant – something about people confining their relations to the 'safe' time.

Rose could not stop herself blurting out, 'What d'you mean by that? Safe time?' She had never heard anyone talk about anything like this before.

Muriel, who was both down to earth and shy, blushed thickly but did explain – vaguely anyway. She told Rose that the week before your monthly period was due was supposed to be a time when you would not fall pregnant. 'You need to keep a count, dear,' she advised.

And because of Rose's determination, her strict counting of time and date, she had managed to keep them 'safe'. There were times, she knew, when it was all right. She would not catch for a baby.

And today was one of those times.

She lay in bed in her white nightdress. Her hair was down and for a moment Harry turned from where he was sitting on the side of the bed, to look at her. The oil lamp was still burning on the chest of drawers.

'Yer a damn pretty wench, d'yer know that?'

He sounded puzzled, defeated in some way. Her looks had bewitched him, yet he could not find in her all he needed. It was the same for both of them – such a mismatch and disappointment.

He was undressing and when he stood up his . . . She never did know what word to use, even to herself. The only words she could think of were 'male thing' or 'manhood' . . . was half erect, pointing stiffly across the room. Her eyes were drawn to it. She found it fascinating as well as alarming. Before she married she had never seen a man naked, not even her brother Peter. Well, Professor Mount, once, but that hardly counted and he'd been a very old man and had had his back to her.

Harry threw off the rest of his clothes quickly. She wriggled over in the bed as he pulled back the covers on his side. For a moment they lay facing each other, avoiding each other's eyes, then, for a second, seeking each other out, uncertain. Once again she saw that he was in awe of her. She made him feel like a rough diamond he had said, once or twice. Her being so pale, so pretty and ladylike.

He laid his arm across her and started to lift the hem of her nightdress so she obligingly raised her body. Harry pushed himself up to a kneeling position, to take it off her. His manhood was stiff and ready between his legs.

'Let's be 'aving yer then,' he said, not roughly, but he had no other thought than plunging into her, his mouth sucking at her breasts for as long as he could manage it, until the surge in him became too strong. He liked her to lay her hands on his buttocks.

Her hands moved down his thickset back, to press on his pumping, muscular backside. The sheer power of him always amazed her. *I should be grateful. He earns his money and he's scarcely ever laid a finger on me.* Only once or twice in real frustration when he had lashed out. That was a good man, wasn't it, who earned his wages and didn't resort to his fists? Like her father. Only he and her mother had really loved each other.

Harry was close to the end. She could tell by the way his breathing changed. She would not make him come out. It was safe . . . Now and again she had had glimmers of desire for him, in the early days. Until they ended up on opposites sides of the river and there was nothing between them. No thoughts, words, interests that they could share. Her body did not light to his. And as he grew frantic, then coursed into her inside, she closed her eyes. Over. Pray God don't let it come to anything.

He withdrew from her, without a word, and leaned over to blow out the light.

Thirteen

Rose spent six years in service to Benjamin and Hester Mount in Oxford Road, Moseley.

Now and then she thought of leaving and looking for another post. But despite the musty, claustrophobic atmosphere, the boredom and loneliness of living with two such elderly people, she stayed. The only other regular visitor was Mrs Plummer, who came in and cooked in the middle of the day and left a cold plate for later. She was a widow, and pleasant enough, but no real company for Rose. The Mounts' son Ernest hardly came near the place.

Before too long, the war broke out and there was a crying need for servants. Rose could have left easily for a position elsewhere. She often dreamed of doing something different – women were doing all sorts by the end of the war. She could be a clippie on the buses. During the last summer of the war, Professor Mount told her that there had been a strike by women working on the buses and trains because, they said, their pay should be equal to the men's. The strikes had spread to other towns including Birmingham.

'And d'you know what the wily government have done?' Professor Mount was talking to his wife as Rose arranged their breakfast: she on her couch, he at the little table beside her.

'What, dear?' Mrs Hester asked, whacking her boiled

egg with the back of a teaspoon. Rose had to help her slice the top off.

'They've fobbed them off with a five-shilling war bonus, as if that's in any way the same as equal pay!'

'*Honestly*,' Hester Mount said furiously. 'Of course, it takes a particular male aptitude to hand out a bus ticket or steer a train. No woman could *possibly* manage it . . .'

'I know what your mother would have said,' Ben Mount chuckled, peering at her over both his half-moon glasses and the newspaper.

Hester Mount chuckled grimly as well. 'She'd have said they were a bunch of young upstarts. She never did like seeing a woman admit to having a brain in her skull.' She bit with some spirit into a slice of toast.

'What do you think, young Rose?' Professor Mount asked amiably.

Rose froze, in the middle of scooping out Mrs Mount's egg so that she could eat it with her good hand.

'Equal work for equal pay, eh? Does that seem fair to you? If you're doing the same job, does it make a difference whether you're a man or a woman? After all – supposing some young chap came in to work here and was doing all your work and was paid half as much again?'

'Well –' She straightened up, not in quite the panic she would once have been at being addressed like this. Over these years she had had all sorts of odd scraps of conversation thrown at her and had learned that she was allowed to think about it herself, not guess at some stock answer.

The very idea of women and men being seen as equal – it made your head spin! But Mrs Mount was always on about those women asking for the vote, saying that if it wasn't for her bad health she'd be marching with them. And putting it the way Professor Mount had just put it . . .

'It doesn't seem fair, does it?' she said tentatively. 'Not if you're all doing the same thing.'

'That it does not – well said!' Professor Mount squeaked. 'There we are, my dear – a young suffragette in the making.'

She often ached to get out and do something else. Mrs Mount had suffered a stroke which left her numb on her left side and though able to stand, she found it very difficult to walk. Thankfully she was now able to speak well again. They spent virtually all their time there, sleeping and eating, since it was so hard for Mrs Mount to move anywhere. Professor Mount wheeled a commode in for her when necessary. It was Rose's job to empty it. At first the heat and sickroom aromas of the Mounts' back room had appalled her. But she had done such things for her mother when she was sick too. And she grew used to it.

Rose was young and timid, and after all the sadness and upheaval of her family life at that time the last thing she wanted was more change. At least with the Mounts she had a secure roof over her head.

But the main reason she stayed was that Professor and Mrs Mount were so very kind to her. Much as she longed for another life and people her own age, she became attached to them. They would have had a terrible job finding someone else.

Benjamin Mount had been a Professor of Ancient History at the university and a keen amateur archaeologist. The place was full, upstairs and down, with dusty old leather-bound tomes – all of which it was part of Rose's job to make *less* dusty. In his study were glass cabinets from which looked out carved figures – 'All replicas, alas,' Professor Mount told her, 'but a comfort all the same.' He talked a good deal about the Hellenistic Period and how without the Greeks 'we shouldn't have anything approaching a democracy – although of course what we have here is really an oligarchy . . .'

When she looked blankly at him he would explain with sweet patience. 'You see, a real democracy is a place where all the people have a say in decision making and are equal before the law. In fact, a government which is in place for the needs of its citizens. An oligarchy, however, is rule by an elite group – a privileged group. So wouldn't you say that's closer to our state now?'

After a while she came to enjoy these conversations, the way he explained things she would never, ever have thought of. She did not realize it at the time, but she was learning to use her mind. To know that there could be more than the everyday scrubbing, the cycle of eating and washing and cleaning.

And part of her job was to help Mrs Mount with her embroidery. She had been a very fine needlewoman and could still sew well, but without the full use of her left hand she needed someone to hold the embroidery frames still for her. And she would talk to Rose as well.

The only time she saw other people, apart from delivery boys, was on her one afternoon off a week, when she would sometimes take the tram along the Moseley Road out to Bessie's house. Bessie's husband, who was in any case not young, had a reserved position in a factory that had gone over to making shells, so he did not go away to fight. As the war went on their family grew. Bessie was immersed in her children.

Despite the shortages she had grown quite plump and by the end of the war she had four children: two boys and two girls. She was always glad of a helping hand, though Rose did not feel they were close.

They heard nothing from Peter, not all the way through the war. And neither of them knew where little Maud was. After a time they stopped mentioning her.

Life in the Mounts' house kept Rose busy enough, but often, when she was alone, she sat on her bed, sadly wondering what would become of her life. Her room was on the second floor at the back, overlooking the neglected jungle of the garden. The windows fought it out with a wisteria gone wild. Rose imagined that one night it would push through the pane and she would feel it wagging in her face.

Something about the house, everything in it so old, decayed and neglected, made her feel old and sad before her time.

When the war's over, she thought, *I'll get out of here. Go and work in a factory – anything so long as it's different.*

In 1916, Professor Mount took what for him seemed a revolutionary step. For once he raised his head, stepped outside his house and took a long look at the state of it.

'Age and decay in all around I see,' he pronounced. 'Rot – that's what we're looking at, pure and simple.' And decided to have the woodwork painted.

Within days, a Mr Southgate arrived with ladders and brushes. He was a small, stocky, very dark man. Rose first saw him outside at the back, staring in dismay at the wisteria-choked house.

With him was his assistant – his seventeen-year-old son, Harry.

'Oi, come on, lad, get back to work – I need yer!'

This cry went up from Mr Southgate increasingly often as the days went by. Young Harry took to hanging around the back door and Rose took to hanging around it too.

That first morning, as they stood squinting up at the house, Rose spied on them through the tiny window of the pantry, standing on a stool. The boy she saw outside was a head taller than his father, and with the same solid build, broad shoulders and black hair. His face had a cheerful look and as he talked, creased in a jocular way.

They started at the front, as if defeated by the state of the back.

'Have you offered them a cup of tea?' Mrs Plummer demanded as she shelled peas from wilting pods. She was a plain, down-to-earth woman with swollen ankles.

'No. Should I? I dain't know what was right.'

'Well, it wouldn't do any harm, would it?' Mrs Plummer said. 'If I was tackling this place I'd want more than tea, I can tell yer.'

So Rose ventured outside. At the sound of the door opening, both men turned from scraping the hard remains of paint from the lower windows.

'' 'Ello 'ello,' the older Mr Southgate said. 'Look what we 'ave 'ere.'

Rose blushed, feeling them both staring at her. She never remembered that she was pretty since no one ever told her so. And now she had grown up, she had a well-proportioned, curving figure, kept lithe by domestic work. The younger of them had his eyes glued to her.

'Mrs Plummer says to ask if you want a cup of tea?'

The men looked at each other, seeming very pleased.

'Ar – we would,' the older Mr Southgate said. They were both still staring like mad. 'You the maid then?'

'Yes,' she said, and turning, fled back inside.

'Will you take it out to them?' she asked Mrs Plummer once the tea was brewed.

'Me? I've got quite enough to do, thank you, miss. I'd've thought you could at least manage that.'

Rose put the biggest cups and saucers on a tray and went outside. She didn't know why she felt trembly all of a sudden, her heart pit-patting as hard as if she'd been shaking out the rugs.

The men stopped work again at once and came over, both lighting up for a smoke.

'What's your name then?' the younger one asked.

Bending down to put the tray on the ground, she murmured, 'Rose Spencer.'

'This is Harry,' the older man said. 'My lad.'

Rose passed them the tea. Harry was staring at her with naked interest.

'What's it like working 'ere?' he asked.

'All right,' she said. She had barely spoken to any boy since Peter left home. It felt exciting.

Harry looked up at the house and across at the neighbouring ones, and made a face. 'Looks terrible,' he said. 'How long've you been 'ere then?'

'Three years,' Rose said.

Harry jerked his head, to indicate inside. 'They all right, are they?' He seemed to find it hard to believe that she could be working in such a place.

'Yes,' she said simply, not knowing what else to say.

'Nice tea,' he said.

'Always tastes better when it's made by a pretty wench,' Mr Southgate added.

Rose blushed again. She was enjoying Harry's obvious admiration but didn't know what to do with it.

'Mrs Plummer made it,' she admitted.

'Well, ta, anyway,' Harry said with a cheeky grin, handing her the cup. As she took it from him, for a moment he pressed his fingers hard over hers so that she could not pull away, and looked laughingly into her eyes. Then he released her. 'Best get on,' he said.

Soon, Harry was making excuses all the time to knock at the back door. Could he have some water, a rag, some tea, some soap? And Rose was always listening out, lurking in the pantry as if she was busy with something. When she saw him standing there in his paint-streaked clothes, his dark eyes searching her out, nearly always with a glint of laughter in them, she was filled with excitement. Harry was a jokey, cheerful lad and they developed a bantering sort of friendship.

'That were a nice bit of cake you gave us yesterday,' he might say. 'Don't s'pose there's any more going?'

'Huh – you've got a cheek,' Rose would reply in an arch tone. 'Coming round here, eating all our food. Mrs Plummer'll be after me if I give it all to you!'

'Oh, go on – you can spare it. I bet those old people eat like sparrows.'

In fact, the Mounts had remarkably good appetites, considering Professor Mount only ventured out once a day for his 'constitutional', occasionally pushing Mrs Mount out for some air.

'That doesn't mean I can just give it to you.'

'Oh, go on, Rosie – I'm a hungry man.' And then one day he added, 'And it's my birthday today.'

'You should've said!' Rose exclaimed.

'Why – would you've made me summat special?'

'Maybe,' she teased. 'But we'll never know now, will we?'

Life felt so much better now it included these snatched conversations. She thought about Harry constantly. So much so that she hardly realized he had almost become the air she breathed. When they packed up to go home in the evening, it was as if the life had gone out of the place and she could barely wait until they came back the next morning. It was as if for the first time, in Harry Southgate's admiring eyes, she had a mirror to see herself, and what she saw was someone pretty and worthwhile because he was obviously so taken with her.

Bit by bit they told each other about their families. Harry's mom and dad, from the sound of things, didn't get on any too well. He had a brother and sister, both older.

'My brother's in France,' he said. 'We get a card from him now and again.'

One day he said to her, 'Don't you ever get any time off from this place? Would you walk out with me?'

A couple of days later, Mr Southgate senior arrived at the house alone. He and Harry had been in the middle of disentangling the back wall from the stranglehold of the wisteria so that they could get at the window frames. Seeing him alone, Rose was very disappointed. No Harry today? Was he ill?

She stood at the back door, so glum that Mr Southgate came over immediately.

'I'm sorry, love.' He looked more sombre than she had ever seen him. 'Now he's turned eighteen, he's had his call-up papers. He's had to go. He said to say goodbye and he's very sorry he hasn't come himself. I don't think he could face it – 'e just wanted to get it over with.'

Rose swallowed hard. 'Oh.' She could barely speak. 'Will he be all right?'

'I hope so, wench,' Mr Southgate said. 'That's all I can say.'

Fourteen

'Lily, love – go and run that duster over the piano again, will you?'

Rose, who was on tenterhooks waiting, watched from the doorway as the little girl started earnestly on her task.

One day her daughter would be able to play like a lady, Rose thought. Whatever Harry said. Once it was tuned to sound right. She had done her best to keep him sweet over the past couple of weeks. And he'd be out all day today. Spring was coming and a mild one at that. He had a job on out at Olton – a big house to paint, he'd said.

A note had arrived yesterday from the piano works in Ombersley Road. The tuner would come at ten-thirty today.

Rose glanced nervously round her little front parlour. Did it look tidy and respectable? They didn't use the room much and everything was in place. Her heart was thudding with nerves.

He was absolutely punctual. Just as the clock on the mantel in the parlour let out a soft 'dong' on the half-hour, there was a polite rap at the door.

'Put the duster away!' Rose hissed at Lily. She touched her hair to make sure nothing was hanging down, took a deep breath and went to the door.

She had expected someone older, official looking,

bossy. Nothing prepared her for the sight in front of her.

The first thing she took in was his strange, fixed gaze, which seemed to be directed at her feet, or past them, or at nothing at all. Then she saw the white stick held in his right hand. Only then did she take in the young man himself, the brown trilby, the neat look of his brown coat and polished boots, the well-proportioned face.

'Good morning,' he said, shifting the stick into his left hand to lift his hat. Rose caught a glimpse of coppery blond curls. 'You're expecting me? My name is Arthur King. I'm here to tune your piano. I do have the right house?'

'Oh, yes – you do,' Rose said, flustered. Lily had come to peer out round her. She hoped the child wouldn't say anything that would cause offence. 'You'd better come in – please.'

'I'm sorry,' the man said very politely. He was softly spoken. 'But you may have to guide me, to begin with. I've got used to the streets, bit by bit, as much as one can, but in strange houses it can be difficult. I'm only quite recently without my sight, you see.'

'Yes – course I will.' Rose stepped out towards him, then stopped, at a loss. 'What exactly d'you want me to do?'

'Just take my arm – that's right. Once I'm at the piano, all will be well.'

Rose was aware of a few passers-by watching curiously as she took the young man's arm.

'This way – there's just a little step. It's straight in – there's no hall.'

'Much obliged,' he said.

Rose motioned to a round-eyed Lily to move out of the way as they shuffled on together.

112

'Now here we are – there's the piano. The stool's here.' For a second she felt ashamed of the decayed green material covering its seat, but then realized the young man couldn't see it.

He thanked her again with dignity and removed his coat and hat while she closed the door.

'Let me hang that up,' she said, going to the hook behind the door. The hat felt soft, and good quality. A smell lingered around the coat, sweet, like pipe tobacco. He seated himself at the piano, which was open, ready for him, and stroked his hands gently over the keys.

Rose looked curiously at his face, then away. It seemed wrong that she could just stare at him without him being able to look back. But as he befriended the instrument, her eyes were drawn back to his face. She could not seem to look away. Though his hair was cut quite short, it was tightly curled. His skin was smooth and his colouring healthy, except for the puckered burn marks on the flesh round his eyes. His nose was large and well defined.

He's beautiful, was the first thought which came to her. And his voice was lovely to her, gentle and smooth.

Lily crept closer, beside her, watching. He was running long-fingered hands over the yellowed keys.

'Nice,' he said. 'Is it a little Broadwood?'

Under the lid the name was embossed in gold letters: John Broadwood.

'Yes.' She was impressed.

'How did you come by it?'

'It was my mother's. She played a bit. I think her father gave it to her. My sister passed it on to me; she said it was taking up too much room.'

Arthur King stood up suddenly and opened the top

of the piano. He leaned over, seeming to breathe it in, then she realized he was feeling for something.

'D'you see – in here?'

Rose moved closer, conscious of the fact that their cheeks were almost touching.

'See along here – the hammer rest rail – maybe it's easier to feel. Give me your hand.'

He guided her fingers and she peered in at the same time, glad he couldn't see her blushing. There were a number of initials carved in the wood.

'Oh – yes, I see,' she said. 'Or at least, I can feel. What are they?'

He released her, smiling, though he was still looking straight ahead of him feeling the piano's innards.

'That'll be the other tuners who've been here before me. It hasn't been tuned in rather a long time.'

'Not in as long as I can remember,' she admitted. 'My mother might have had it done – I don't know.'

'The last date here,' he sat down again, 'is 1871.'

'Oh,' Rose said. 'Oh, dear. That's before she even owned it!'

To her surprise, Arthur King laughed, a full-hearted, infectious sound, and she found herself laughing too. 'Ah, well – we'll have to try and put the old girl right now, shan't we?'

He reached into his breast pocket, brought out a tuning fork and started work, playing different series of notes.

'Would you like a cup of tea?' Rose offered.

Her visitor stopped, looking surprised. 'Well – that would be very nice. Thank you.'

As she stood in the back room, waiting for the water, tidying, folding washing from the rack squeezed in next to the range, she could hear him working his

114

way along the keys, the sounds, as he adjusted, becoming clearer, brighter somehow. She loved having him in the house, this handsome, refined man. For a moment she stood with her arms folded, hugging herself, just listening. It was a like a door opening to something wider, and genteel and good. She realized she missed the Mounts.

She put the cups on a tray along with the toffee tin which Muriel had given her from the British Empire Exhibition. Lily kept her bits in it – little toys, pegs and cotton reels, treasures she had found, to amuse herself.

'Not long now,' he said as she came back in. Lily was sitting rapt, cross-legged on the floor. They waited, as the tea brewed and he finished off. It took some time, but then he stood again and closed the top lid.

'There – that's a lot better, the poor old thing,' he said. 'If possible it wants doing every six months.' He laughed again, gently. 'More than every half-century anyway!'

'I'll see what I can do,' she said, handing him a cup of tea and asking about sugar. As he stirred, she said, 'I don't want to delay you.' Although that was exactly what she wanted.

'A few minutes won't matter in the least,' he said. 'Thank you – I could do with this.'

Rose handed Lily her toy tin and she became absorbed on the rug.

'So do you play?' he asked. It was peculiar talking to someone who looked straight through you, or only in your general direction. Rose found it strange, but also freeing, knowing that she could not be seen.

'Not me – well, not much. My mother died when I was quite young, you see, otherwise I think she would have taught me a bit more. No – I want Lily to learn.

115

She'll be five this year, and we know a kind lady who said she would teach her.'

'Excellent,' he said. 'That's quite young, but she could start with a few basics.'

'Do you play?' she asked.

'Oh, yes. It was meat and drink in our house. I have to play mostly from memory now. Luckily I had a lot stored away before the war.'

'Will you play something? Please?'

His face turned fractionally more towards her, as if drawn by the longing in her voice.

'Really – you'd like me to?'

'Please – let me take your cup.'

He arranged himself, easing his shoulders for a moment, then began. Whatever it was he played, she was drawn in at once, enraptured. He swayed back and forth as he played, so at home with it, and the feel of it. By the time the rise and fall of the notes was over, Rose had tears running down her cheeks. As the last chords sounded she wiped her face on her sleeves, trying to pull herself together.

'Oh,' she said, knowing she sounded tearful. 'That was *lovely*.'

'Beethoven,' he said. 'Poor man lost his hearing – dreadfully young. I have a special feel for him now. And I've always enjoyed that piece.'

She could still hardly speak. She got up and passed him his teacup again from the top of the piano.

There was a silence. He raised his head to her, beside him.

'Cosy little houses, these. Have you lived here long?'

'A few years. Since the war. I'm a widow, you see.' What made her say it? It just came out, naturally, the way lies seemed to pop out of her mouth in times of greatest need. And just then it felt true.

'Ah,' Arthur King said sorrowfully. 'I'm so sorry.'

Another silence fell. He finished his tea and handed her the cup, with thanks. Rose went to the door to fetch his coat.

'Oh – I must pay you.' she said. 'How much will it be?'

'Well, as you're so very local, it'll be seventeen and six,' he said.

He didn't see her face fall.

'I'm so sorry,' she said, blushing to the roots of her hair. She hurried to fetch her pot of savings. 'I didn't realize it would be quite so much. I've saved fifteen shillings. I can get the rest – soon. I'll drop it into the works, shall I? And it's all in coppers and small change – I should have thought. Oh, dear, look – take the jar, I've nothing else to put it in for you!'

'Not to worry,' he said, tucking the jar under his arm. 'I'm sure we can trust you. We can send a boy round if it's a help – it's not far, after all.'

She helped him into his coat, gratefully, holding the jar as he readied himself.

'I'm ever so sorry,' she said again as she handed it back.

'Not at all. I'm just glad your nice little instrument is sounding in better health. And you, young lady –' He spoke generally to the room, unsure where Lily was. 'Make sure you do lots of practice.'

'Yes,' Lily said, awed.

Rose led him to the front door and out to the street.

'Will you be all right?' she asked. It seemed terrible just to leave him, not to go with him and help.

'Just point me in the right direction,' he said. 'And thank you for the tea.' He raised his hat. 'Goodbye.'

'Goodbye.'

Rose stood at the door, watching him feel his way carefully along. She could not bear to leave the doorway until he had passed the Mission Hall and was out of sight.

Fifteen

That dreadful afternoon, Aggie was sitting crouched on the front step after school. With her inky fingers she kept tugging at her skirt, trying to pull it down further and cover her bare feet. The soles of her pumps were worn right through and while she was at school, what was left of one had parted company with the top so she couldn't wear them any more.

Her old black charity Mail boots had been handed on to John. She could just squeeze into them, though they pinched and gave her blisters. John was busy clacking up and down the street in them now, dashing about with the other boys.

'All we've got's that old pair of wellingtons of your mother's,' Freda Adams said, seeing Aggie's miserable face when she got home from school. 'We'll have to cut them down for yer, for the time being.' There was no spare money for shoes – not at the moment.

'But they're too big,' Aggie protested. 'And they've got holes in already!'

'Look, if I could do spells I'd get you some golden slippers,' Nanny Adams said. 'But those'll have to do for now. Go and mind May – we'll see to it later. Your mother's not well.'

Aggie felt thoroughly miserable. It was cold and she didn't want to get up and run around with the others, with no shoes on. She didn't want to be outside at all.

And the thought that the only shoes she was going to get until they could get some more charity boots, which was not until Christmas, was that mouldy old pair of rubber ones which already had holes in was even more demoralizing. She thought of Lily's lovely brown shoes and the little red slippers she had as well. *One day, I'm going to have shoes like that*, she vowed.

But she was also waiting for her dad. Even though Mom and Nanna had tried to stop him, he'd gone out with his barrow again looking for work. And now they were all back from school and he still hadn't come home. To distract herself she looked round, scouring the gutter for dog ends for Dad, so that he could roll new cigarettes out of the nubs of tobacco. But there were none in sight. Where was he? Her heart thumped as she peered along the street.

Before Dad got so poorly she and the others used to wait for him when he went to the Eagle at the end of Lilac Street. They'd play out or huddle under the street lamp if there was anything they wanted to look at in the gloom. Dad'd come out after a pint or two, mellow and smelling of ale and say, 'Come on then, yer little buggers!' And they'd all traipse home after him. If he had any change left they'd get some chips from Price's. It was something she'd done since she was small, that made her feel happy and close to him. But he hadn't even the strength for the Eagle now. He shouldn't be out, she fretted.

'May!' she called crossly to her sister.

May was staring at a skipping game that some of the other girls were playing along the street, chanting their rhymes, the rope swinging.

'Don't go so far away – stay where I can see yer!

Look – I've got Silas's marbles – come and play over 'ere!'

She felt weary today, like an old woman, and cold to her bones. Why did she have to watch May all the time? Why couldn't John take a turn for once? But she was also worried, frightened. She told herself she was sitting waiting for Babs to come and play out. But she knew really she was waiting for Dad. She wanted him to come home, not be walking the streets, coughing like that.

Tommy Green had gone out to look for work for a few hours the day before yesterday. When he got back, he was four shillings better off but he could barely stand. He stumbled in through the back door, shivering, bent over, coughing up stuff from his lungs. It was all he could do to get upstairs and collapse into bed.

It was afternoon and Jen was feeling a bit better by then. Morning and evening were her sickest times. She carried some broth up to him, with bread with a scraping of margarine, and sat on the edge of their bed. Other than a broken-down chest of drawers, it was the only thing in the room.

'What the hell're you playing at, Tommy Green?'

Her voice was harsh with anxiety. *Look at the state of him*, she thought, a cold terror filling her. He looked terrible, his already thin face pinched, his breathing very shallow. There were pink spots on his cheeks and he looked feverish and weak. He managed to open his eyes. *It's consumption, I know it is*, she thought, and that freezing hand of fear gripped round her heart again.

'Don't . . .' He managed a whisper. 'Don't nag me, wench.'

His shirt was unbuttoned halfway and Jen could see the bones in his chest as he breathed. His face was all stubble, hair slicked to his head. Silently they stared at one another. Then he mustered one of his grins, the cheeky-boy face that had always won her over.

But not this time. Instead, she started to cry.

'Tommy, don't. You're sick, really bad – I can see. Don't try and hide it. I'm going to go and talk to Dr Hill. He's all right – he's a—'

'No!' he held his hand up. Tommy had a horror of any kind of interference from outside. It was doctors killed his mom, that's what he always said. 'I'll be all right,' he rasped. 'Let me sleep.'

She didn't mention the blood. How could she have missed that? Had he hidden it from her? The thought of life without him passed through her mind, terrifying, desolate. She had known him almost all her life. She pushed the thought away.

'Drink your broth,' she said, getting up. 'It'll do you good.'

She turned at the door, unable to hide her tears. 'If anything happens to you, I don't know what I'll . . .'

But his eyes were closed. He was already asleep.

Downstairs, Nanny Adams was dozing by the fire, a faint aroma of hooch around her. She found a lot of strength and comfort in her little flask and it helped dull the pain in her hips. She and Jen had cooked the factory meals together, the men taking a plateful, covered with another plate and wrapped in newspaper for their dinner. Always some kind of stew.

Jen sank by the table, unable to stop her weeping now it had begun. Everything was such a struggle, as if life was piled on top of her. She was exhausted, the

babby taking everything, it felt like. And Tommy ...
Her Tommy looked like a death's head.

Freda Adams opened her eyes.

'What's ailing yer, wench?'

'Tommy needs the doctor – but he won't hear of it.
He looks so bad. Oh, why did I 'ave to catch for a
babby now? What if he dies – we'll all end up in the
workhouse!'

Her mother pushed herself up straighter, almost
grandly, in her chair. Impeded as she was by her joints,
she had survived losing her husband at a young age and
being left with four children, two of whom had been
taken from her by war. Freda Adams had always
worked and struggled her way through. At one
especially desperate time she had had to turn to the
parish for help and the experience was burned into her
soul. She had fought her way back from it – she was a
survivor, and big-hearted with it.

'Don't you go talking like that. Over my dead body
we'll fall on the parish – those heartless, interfering
harridans! Not while you've got me, wench, with breath
in my body. I may not be up to much but I ain't dead
and buried yet. We'll think of summat. Give Tommy a
day or two. Then he might be glad of a doctor.' She
kept the thought to herself that there might not be much
anyone could do for Tommy now. He should have had
a doctor weeks ago, if he was going to have one at all.
'But we'll keep going. That's what you have to do
somehow or other – just keep going.'

Yesterday Aggie's dad had stayed in bed all day. But
this morning, still shaking with fever, he had gone off

with the barrow again. Aggie had heard Mom pleading with him, crying.

'D'you want to kill yourself – just for a few bob? Don't go, Tommy – stay for my sake . . .'

'A few bob's the difference between eating and going without. Just a few bob and I'll be home,' he'd said. 'It's a fine man can't feed his family!'

Jen had been too ill herself to stop him. It had shaken Aggie and the others up badly – they'd scarcely ever heard her mom cry the way she did when Dad left the house this morning. But they'd all had to go to school.

From her perch on the step, Aggie sat shivering, keeping half an eye on May, and on Silas and Ann. She decided Babs wasn't coming to play out after all. As the only girl in the family she was another one who ended up with a lot of jobs. Babs's dad, Mr Skinner, kept hens out in the brew house, or wash house, in their yard. They were in a little pen made out of crates and had to be moved in and out of the brew house, depending on the weather and who else needed it. On wash days when the coppers were lit – which was most days – they had to keep shifting the creatures in and out. And Mrs Skinner was always after Babs for something.

Aggie drew her knees up and sat hugging them, looking around her. The step was a good place from which to get a view of the street, with its rows of chimneys, the smoke all leaning to one side in the breeze today. From there, she could see the bulk of the Mission Hall at the far end to her right. When you went past you could hear them singing sometimes, especially on Sunday evenings.

This side of Price's was 'Auntie's', or Tippet's pawn-brokers, to give it its formal name. It was a busy shop, especially on Mondays and Fridays when the Sunday-best clothes were being taken in and out. Aggie liked to look in the window and see what was new. There were always medals in there now, old soldiers fallen on hard times. John Best's medals had disappeared into Tippet's. They were still there in the window, a heartbreaking sight.

There was always something going on out there. *I should be watching properly*, Aggie thought. She imagined her card, with its copperplate lettering: *Agnes Green: Spy*. The street was busy as ever at this time of day, children playing, swinging round the lamp posts, games of hopscotch and tipcat going on; two women talking by a front door. Over the other side, a man with a white pot of paint in his hand was redoing the number at twenty-five. A dog ran past, a brown mongrel, limping. It would be nice to stroke something. She held her hand out.

''Ere – come on, doggie – come and see me.' But the dog ignored her and hurried on with a hunted look.

When she glanced up again her attention was caught by the sight of a man next to the Mission Hall, walking along tentatively, somehow different from everyone else. Then she saw his white stick, feeling his way in front of him. He wore a brown coat and hat and had a nice face, Aggie thought. She didn't remember ever seeing him before.

As she sat watching, Rose Southgate came into view, walking from her house, holding Lily's hand. Aggie looked wistfully at Lily's nice little shoes.

'Af'noon Mrs Southgate!' Aggie called to her.

But Rose Southgate didn't answer. She was staring ahead of her. When she and the blind man were about to pass each other, Aggie saw Mrs Southgate stare hard at him. She must have spoken to him, because he stopped, and so did she. They talked for a few minutes. Mrs Southgate was shaking her head. The blind man held out his hand as if to stop her, then he turned back and walked in the same direction as Mrs Southgate. Aggie watched them disappear, frowning.

'Aggie!' May came running up to her, jigging about. 'Get out me way – I need to go!'

'Go round the back way,' Aggie tutted. But May didn't fancy the dark entry.

'Let me in – you come with me, Aggs!'

'No,' Aggie said grumpily. 'You're a big girl – you can manage.'

May was too desperate to argue and ran into the house.

Then Aggie's attention was caught by another unusual sight. A policeman was coming along Lilac Street. He was very big, a head taller than most other people, and he was walking fast, looking at the house numbers.

Ooh, Aggie thought. *I wonder what's happened?* Her heart beat faster. Was this something *Agnes Green: Spy* should know about?

Loping along, he was soon very close, then standing over her.

'Nine – that you?' He leaned down.

Aggie cringed, frightened of the big man in his uniform.

'I'm looking for a Mrs Green – that right?'

'That's my mom,' Aggie whispered.

'Right.' The policeman drew himself up straight again. 'Well – you'd better let me in then.'

Sixteen

'It's all right, Mrs Green,' the constable kept saying. 'He's being looked after.'

Aggie watched, clinging to the door frame between the front and back. Mom was sitting ashen-faced at the table, Nanna standing close beside her.

May appeared suddenly from the privy and stood round-eyed at the back door, awed by the sight of the constable, looking so big in their little room.

'I knew this'd happen,' Mom kept saying, too shocked to cry. 'I knew he should never've gone out there . . . I told and told him! He wouldn't listen . . .'

'His barrow's been taken in by someone – I was to tell you it's at number twenty Tillingham Street.'

'Our John can go and fetch it,' Mom murmured. 'Thank you.' It wasn't far off.

Once Nanna had shown the constable out, May ran to Mom and buried her face in her shoulder. Jen picked her up and sat her on her knee, absent-mindedly rocking back and forth. Aggie went to her grandmother for comfort.

'Your father's been taken bad,' Nanny Adams told her. 'He collapsed in the street. They've taken him to the hospital.'

'I knew I should've got him a doctor!' Jen cried.

Aggie searched her grandmother's face, unsure from

the way she was talking whether the hospital was a good or a bad thing.

'Will 'e be all right?'

'I expect so, bab.' She patted Aggie's arm. 'That's what hospital's for – for making poorly people better.' Half under her breath, she added, '*Or so they say.* Now, you run along and take May back outside. Keep an eye on the others, Aggie – there's a good wench.'

Once the children had gone out, Jen's pretence crumpled immediately.

'I don't know what to do . . .' She got up and moved about, agitated as a lost child. 'I've never been in one of them places. I don't want 'im in there – it's all wrong!'

Hospitals may have been for caring for the sick, but to many people they were terrifying places. The hospital and the workhouse seemed almost one and the same; enormous red-brick buildings with gables like frowning eyes and, inside, long corridors reeking of grief and disinfectant.

'You can visit,' her mother said. 'There'll be days when you're allowed – Sundays I expect.' Sounding unsure, she added, 'I don't s'pose he'll be there long. But he was bad – you could see that. P'raps it's for the best.'

'How do I get there?' Jen was working herself up, wringing her pinner in her hands. 'How do I know anything? I mean he might've . . .' She looked wildly at her mother. 'He's got consumption, I know he has! What if he . . . ? We'll never manage!' The words rushed out of her. 'Oh, why did I have to catch for a babby now? We'll have to go on the parish – we *will*!'

'What've I told yer?' Freda Adams came back at her,

bolt upright now, and so fierce that Jen jumped. 'I don't want to hear you talking like that ever again! Over my dead body will we fall on the parish. I'll go out collaring myself! I don't mind hard work – but we're not putting ourselves at the mercy of those wicked people ever again. D'you hear?'

Rose Southgate had reached home again that afternoon, breathing so fast she might have been running a race. What in heaven's name did she think she was doing?

Harry was in, where she had left him, sitting in the back by the fire. Trying not to show any of her seething emotion in front of him or Lily, Rose took her hat and coat off and set a kettle on to boil. Lily lingered in the front room. Before she could stop her, Rose heard the child lift the lid of the piano and gently tinkle on the keys. Lily had been sworn to secrecy about the piano tuner, but she was unable to resist looking at the instrument.

Rose screwed her eyes tightly shut, knowing what was coming next. Harry lowered his paper furiously.

'You can stop that racket, yer noisy little bugger!'

The lid of the piano closed abruptly. Lily stayed in the other room rather than come and brave her father. Rose could imagine the hurt on her face. She wanted to scream at Harry, at his rough, ignorant *brutishness* – that's how she saw him now. Dear God, how had she come to marry him? But she didn't want to fight, to have him storm out, so that she'd have somehow to make it up to him later. It just wasn't worth it.

Swallowing down her feelings she busied herself in silence, making tea and putting away her few groceries. But her mind was spinning. Thank *goodness* she'd gone out when she did, by pure chance! If she hadn't . . . Well, it would have been disastrous. She trembled to think of it.

When she had set off to the shops earlier that afternoon, she had been thinking of the piano tuner, Arthur King. In fact, since his visit she had not been able to stop thinking about him. For one thing she still owed him half a crown. That had to be scrimped for. But it wasn't that. She just couldn't get him out of her mind, his voice, the terrible sadness of losing his sight. He must have been gassed, she thought. Those scars round his eyes – weren't they burns? His blindness made him remote, but also added an intimacy that would not have been there otherwise. And it moved her to tenderness. She had had to take his arm, and she had been able to look closely at him without him seeing. And then there was the way he had played to her, the way they talked . . . She would have liked the conversation to go on for hours. She had felt like a plant, drooping with need of water, and he had offered her a running stream.

Then, this afternoon, he had appeared right in front of her! As he felt his way along the street towards her, her pulse had taken off so fast she felt quite faint. He drew level and she almost let him go past. But she just could not bear to let him go without their speaking, without hearing his voice.

'Oh – hello,' she said shyly. 'It's – I'm the lady whose piano you tuned the other day . . .' In seconds she realized that this was not much help. How many pianos did he tune in a week? 'Mrs Southgate, Rose Southgate – number fifteen, Lilac Street.'

'Yes,' Arthur King said. 'Of course. I know your voice. And in fact I was just on my way to see you.'

'Me?' Her heart rate picked up even more. Harry

was in today. Oh, thank God she'd stopped Mr King on the way! 'Why? I mean, it's me that should be coming to see you. I still owe you . . .'

He was shaking his head. 'No – that's just it. I was coming to say that I miscalculated. It won't be necessary. You're fully paid up. I thought you should know, that's all.'

'Oh . . . Are you sure?' She wondered how this could be.

But he wasn't going to explain. 'Quite sure,' he nodded. For a moment, he smiled. 'It's perfectly all right.'

'Well, thank you,' she said. Which didn't seem enough. 'That's very kind.'

'Not at all.'

There was a silence, after which Rose said, 'I'm just going to the shops, otherwise I'd ask you in.'

'Oh, no – that's quite all right,' Arthur King said. He made a humorous face. 'I'm really on my way to another customer. But of course I don't get anywhere very quickly.'

He turned back and they walked side by side.

'Would you . . .' She couldn't bear to let him go, not now she had seen him again. 'I mean, you could come and have a cup of tea another day?' Did this seem wrong and forward of her? Why did his being blind make it seem less so?

'I'd like that. But of course I am working in the week. So unless you have a selection of instruments for me to tune . . .'

'No – hardly.' Rose laughed. 'What about Sunday?' She seized on the idea. Harry would be out. He was always out fishing. 'The day can be long and lonely with just myself and Lily,' she added.

131

'Yes.' He seemed surprised, and pleased. 'Sunday it is then. About three? Or would that be too early?'

'No . . .' *Come at two, come at one*, she thought. *Just come.*

She trembled now, in her kitchen, unpacking the bargain cut of meat she had bought, at the thought of him turning up here with Harry waiting inside. She eyed her husband as he sat by the fire. There was an acrid smell of the stuff he cleaned his brushes with. She saw his strong, straight hairline at the back, his thick neck, so alien to her. She thought of Arthur's slender one and a pang of longing went through her. Already she felt she had begun on something unstoppable.

I must try not to feel like this, she thought, standing by the table, her hands clenched. *This is madness. What am I doing? I haven't even been straight with him. I've told lies.* Yet she did not want to think about it, or to let go of the sense of delight at the thought of seeing Arthur King on Sunday. Wasn't she just being kind to a casualty of the war, a lonely blind man? Where was the harm?

Turning to Harry she said in a bland voice, 'D'you want some tea?'

'This is the first time me and Tommy've ever been apart,' Jen said to her mother that night. 'In thirteen years.'

Exhausted and miserable, she crawled upstairs, barely able to make it to the top. She thought she would fall into bed and sleep immediately. But the bed felt cold and bleak without Tommy. She kept turning this way and that trying to get warm. Her tears came at the thought of him, sick and probably frightened, in a

132

strange bed in the hospital. If only she could go there and lie beside him. Tommy wasn't the sort of man who could stand being away from home and everything he knew. He was like a child in a way, bless him, she thought. He hadn't been away in the war. He had tried to volunteer again in 1915, even though they had Aggie, and John a babe in arms by then. He'd been ashamed, with all the other blokes joining up. But they turned him down once more. She had been so relieved, but Tommy was shamefaced.

'I can't even do that right,' he said. He saw himself as the runt of the litter, not much good for anything.

But he wouldn't have survived the war, wouldn't have lasted five minutes, she thought fondly. Her Tommy, the daft thing.

Tommy's mom had died when he was only five. A weak heart, he was told later, but all he knew was that doctors came and she was taken away and he never saw her again. He'd never go near a doctor if he could help it. His big sisters, Cissy and Flo, did their best to look after him. Their dad, Ollie Green, then took up with a foreign woman called Marta. Jen never really knew where she came from or if they ever married. Tommy never liked her much though she seemed to be doing her best.

The Greens and the Adamses all lived in Kyrwicks Lane, one of the old districts in Balsall Heath. So she must have seen Tommy all her life but he lived up the other end, near the livery stables. The first time she could really remember him, she'd have been seven, Tommy eight. She could see him in her mind now, flying along the road on his knobbly-kneed little legs, face alight and full of mischief. He was going full pelt and kept looking behind him as if someone was chasing him and a moment later a bigger boy appeared, looking furious, but Tommy had already flicked off along an entry and vanished. Jen had been at the kerb with some girls. She could remember wanting to laugh at the sight of him, of thinking, *He looks nice . . .*

At fourteen and fifteen they started courting. Not seriously then, but it grew. They'd been together ever since. Hinged together, she thought, like the top and bottom of a box. She couldn't imagine anything else.

Tommy's health had never been very good. He had trouble with breathing, often went down with bronchitis and other chest problems. Despite that, he had always had a lot of energy in the bedroom department and ways so winning she could hardly ever resist him. Tommy loved it – all of it – making babies, the sight of her carrying them, all the faces at the windows. She knew it drove him to despair when his health let him down and he couldn't earn. But it didn't stop him wanting to make another one – and Jen enjoyed the making too, if not the rest of the whole exhausting business, and by the time she minded it was usually too late.

Wiping her tears away she smiled for a moment, thinking of his exuberant lovemaking when he was well. She reached out and stroked his side of the bed.

'You're a rogue, Tommy Green,' she whispered fondly. 'You'll be the death of me. But you'd better not go and die on me yourself . . . Because I love you, damn you . . .' More tears came at the thought. Gradually she fell asleep. *I'll come and see you, soon as I can*, was her last waking thought.

Seventeen

That Saturday evening, as dusk was settling over the city, Phyllis Taylor stepped off the tram in Digbeth. Instinctively she looked around her as if checking for danger, then made her way up Digbeth towards the Bull Ring.

She could have sent one of the girls in for Saturday night bargains in town, and sometimes did. But every so often she felt restless, wanting to get out of the house and the neighbourhood. Her neighbours there didn't much like her. She'd never learned the trick of saying quite the right thing to people and she got their backs up. She was as good as any of them – what was wrong with them all, turning their noses up at her, *her*, James Taylor's widow? It was damn nice to be free of them all for a bit.

She also enjoyed walking the streets in the darkening evening. It gave her a feeling of excitement, though with an edge of dread, with memories of old times. But she liked the shops as evening gathered, the lights from the windows and naphtha flares brightening the market stalls, the festive feeling of everyone milling around, vying for the knock-down meat and fruit and veg.

Phyllis was dressed as ever in her heavy green coat and an extravagant hat with a wide, floppy brim fitting snugly over her magnificent head and coiled black hair. She had sat on the tram with her bags in her lap, turned towards the window to show that she didn't intend to get into any conversation. She wanted to let her thoughts roam, like a guard checking a building for points of entry.

Dolly had stopped being sick and was looking more normal. She had found a job in a toy factory, though this was not something about which she was especially happy.

'It's so *boring*,' she complained. 'And it doesn't half make my back ache, bending over that bench.' She had a job painting the black spots on white tin dogs. She moaned about the smell of the paint as well. She'd been carrying on about it just before Phyllis left the house.

'You, madam, aren't in a position to create about anything,' Phyllis told her. 'You're lucky I haven't turned you out on the street to fend for yourself. That's what most mothers would've done.'

She heard Dolly mutter something in the scullery.

'Dolly, don't talk like that!' Susanna reprimanded her from the table. 'You're a bad girl! And you're bringing all this trouble on all the rest of us as well. What am I s'posed to say to David? You're making me tell lies.'

There were more mutterings from the scullery. Insurrection was breaking out. Phyllis swelled with anger.

'What's that you said, you wicked girl?' she demanded.

'I said,' Dolly poked her head out, bristling with defiance (she wasn't grateful – not a bit!), 'then at least I could do away with the thing. I know where to go. I'd go to Mrs Horn.'

Mrs Horn, who had once been a nurse but was no longer, for some reason no one was ever sure of, lived in the next street and was well known to have an abortion business going on in her attic.

Phyllis lunged towards Dolly, but the girl darted back into the corner.

'You'll do no such thing!' Phyllis was fit to explode with rage. 'You don't know what you're saying – don't you ever go anywhere near the likes of Mrs Horn!'

'What do you know about it?' Dolly was muttering again.

Oh, she knew. Phyllis sat on the narrow tram seat, still seething. She knew, all right. And what was more, to go to Mrs Horn meant that all the neighbourhood would know by sunset the next day.

'You'd better damn well behave yourself,' she'd cautioned Dolly, in such a forbidding tone that even Dolly looked cowed at last. 'You keep up your end of the bargain, my girl – or you're out. And out for good – d'you hear?'

'Yes,' Dolly fumed into the sink.

The bargain was no one was to know – ever. So far Phyllis's plan was working – but then Dolly wasn't showing yet. They were putting it about that she had left service because her employer had died and the house was to be sold up. A perfectly respectable reason. The full challenge was yet to come and Phyllis was terrified that Dolly would ruin everything, blow her cover by sheer petulance, or clumsiness or spite. Phyllis lived in daily terror of it. But they were going to see this through. She'd make sure of it, with every fibre of her being. She wasn't having that little strumpet put at risk everything she'd striven for.

She worked her way through the Bull Ring, up to the bustling Market Hall. Whenever she went into the Market Hall, it filled Phyllis with memories of her children, and especially of the bleak, terrible months after her James was taken from them. The little ones didn't want to be left when she went shopping and she would sometimes bring them as a treat on a Saturday, even if they had to walk all the way. Those days had been bitter hard and she was glad they were over, but she still treasured the memory of the sight of their little faces when they saw the pets in the Market Hall, the cats, rabbits and birds. She gave a half-smile, thinking of it. Even Charles, her solemn boy, had lit up at the sight of the rabbits' wiffling noses. Phyllis sighed. God, she'd loved having her babies. She'd felt like a queen, with James so proud of her and she feeling she was Someone at last. She'd been a powerful, fertile woman and she'd gloried in it. She enjoyed her big, powerful body, developed a flamboyant dress sense. For the first time in her life she felt she was really living. Had he not died, they would have had more and more babies. She'd always wanted one at her side and one in her arms.

But it was no good looking back. It never got you anywhere. Phyllis was good at closing her mind to things. She turned her thoughts to her shopping.

After the long day's trading there was a mush of trampled vegetable leaves and stalks underfoot all round the markets. The air was full of the smells of fish from the stalls with their shrimps and oysters and jellied eels, the delicious whiff of roasted beef from the eating houses as she emerged into Spiceal Street. She'd bought her fruit and veg, and a pat of butter from the man who lifted it with his wooden paddles and made a packet of it for her. Jamaica Row was the place for some real bargains, for cheap joints and bags of offal, chickens and cagmag – bags of cut-off bits for stewing.

It was one of the busiest times for the market. Making her way down through the lively throng, she passed the statue of Nelson, the memorial round which was gathered a crowd so dense it made it hard to get past. Phyllis slowed, winding through it. Suddenly a long tongue of flame darted up at the sky and there was an 'oooh!' from everyone around. Phyllis paused at the edge of the crowd. She'd seen it all before; the man sold cough lozenges after his fire-eating display – 'Lozenges to clear the throat!' – but it was always a draw. It made her feel like a child again, the thrill of it. The nerve of the man – how did he do it!

The crowd gathered round were a merry lot, some munching on hot chestnuts and potatoes in their jackets. The smell made saliva rise in her mouth. *None of that*, she told herself. *No giving in to temptation: hold on to your pennies.*

As she eased through the crowd outside St Martin's church, she felt someone elbow her in the ribs. As there were so many people crowding towards Jamaica Row, she thought nothing of this, until it happened again, and a voice, horribly close to her ear said, ''Ello, Het – well, well, after all this time! Fancy seeing you!'

Phyllis thought her heart had stopped. The breath refused to go in and out of her lungs. Here was this voice from the days before she passed through and out the other side into a new life. Before James. She forced herself to turn to the person who had spoken to her, with a look of snooty contempt.

'What're you doing, elbowing me?' she said in her most correct voice. 'Who d'you think you are?'

The woman, who was about the same age as her, had narrow eyes and a head of sickly coloured hair piled under a hat. She was leering at Phyllis with apparent relish and her gums showed several gaps between her top teeth. She let out a scornful laugh. Other people were jostling past them.

'Don't you give me that. I'd know you anywhere! You're Hetty Barker. I'd stake my life on it, even if you are trying to sound like you ain't common as muck any more. Come on, Het, you remember your old sparring partner – it's me, Ethel.'

Oh, God, yes, she remembered, all right. Ethel Sharp. The sly, slitty eyes, the way Ethel would do anything to get her way, to survive.

'I've no idea what you're talking about,' Phyllis said, turning away. Her heart was now pounding alarmingly. 'I've never heard of a Hetty whatever-it-was. You've got yourself confused. Now let me get along . . .'

'Oh, come on, Het – with that conk of yours – it's no good thinking you can pretend, not to me. I *know* you . . .' The woman had hold of her arm and while Phyllis was trying to get along, to escape her, she was clinging on like a parasite.

'You look as if you've gone up in the world, Het,' she said in a whiny voice. 'Not the girl you were in Spon End now, are yer? Where're you living these days then? You can tell yer old friend Ethel all about it.'

'Let go of my arm!' Phyllis stopped abruptly and spoke in what she hoped was a commanding voice. 'I don't know who you are and I don't want to! Get away from me, woman, and leave me alone!'

'You having trouble?' A muscular man in a cap came up close, hearing Phyllis's voice, and looked from one to the other of them.

'This woman won't leave me alone,' Phyllis complained.

'I wasn't doing any harm,' Ethel whined. 'She knows me – she's just saying she don't.' But she released Phyllis's arm and Phyllis moved swiftly on while the man barred Ethel's way.

'I know you, Hetty!' Ethel roared after her. 'I'll find you out – you'll be seeing me again!'

Panting, full of a sense of horror, Phyllis ducked round the church and hurried towards Digbeth. Sod the meat. All she wanted was to get as far away from there as she could. She kept looking behind her, certain Ethel would be chasing after her. She even dived down a side street off Digbeth and waited at the mouth of an entry between the dark houses for a few minutes, to make sure she had thrown her off. Her heart was hammering.

On the tram, clutching her bags, she found she was trembling all over. Seeing Ethel Sharp was like waking the dead. The dead of a past she had done everything in her power to rise above and forget.

Eighteen

Phyllis was born in 1884, named Hetty Barker, the sixth child of Fred and Eileen Barker.

They lived in Spon End, Coventry, in a street comprised of scruffy, cramped courts and run-down terraces. The Barkers lived in a front house, facing the street. Except on the warmest days of summer, the walls inside were wet to the touch and sprouted black and green mould. Although there was a small attic they couldn't use it because Fred Barker had torn up all the floorboards for firewood.

Fred was a violent drunk and a loud one. Many nights they would hear him approaching along the street, falling about on the cobbles, yelling, and Eileen would say, 'Oh, Lor' – 'ere 'e comes.' Those words seemed mild compared with the fear and dread in her eyes. If the young ones were not already upstairs, the whole host of them crammed together on the floor in the bigger of the two rooms, they would scatter immediately. Upstairs they did anything they could not to hear the shouting, the cries of pain, things being thrown – not that there was much to throw. It was usually the poker or the coal bucket. Fred would be too hungry to throw his dinner. Hetty's elder sister Nancy would sing to them all – hymns, as they were the only songs she knew. They went to every church or Sunday school they could where they might get something to eat. The

Methodists were good. They had biscuits and sometimes offered bread and butter. *Happy the Souls to Jesus joined . . .*

Mom was a pale, emaciated woman, always worn out. Hetty didn't remember her being any other way, nor did she know what colour her mother's hair had been because in her own lifetime it had always been a sludgy grey. Eileen's clothes hung on her as if she was a wooden frame, there was so little flesh on her bones, and she had lost all her teeth, through childbirth and having them knocked out of her head. She had no false ones and could not chew meat. On the rare occasions when they had any, she would ask the children to chew it for her. She fainted often. Her movements were slow, without vitality. Sometimes there was food, sometimes not. Sometimes Fred worked as a labourer when he could stay sober long enough.

Eileen had grown up in an orphanage, shackled herself to the first man who came along, when she was sixteen, and had one baby after another. By the time Hetty was eight, there were eleven of them, eight boys and three girls. No distinction was ever made between them – they were all thrown in together and wore whatever came to hand if anything did.

So far as possible, their father was someone to be avoided. The children soon learned. He was a short, thickset man with black hair. Hetty looked very like him. Most of the time he was at home he was the worse for drink and in that state he drove his fists into anything that got in the way. Sometimes even Eileen hid in the coal hole with the children, or upstairs, leaving him food if there was any, in the hope that he would eat it and fall asleep. Often it worked. Fred would come in, yell the house down and then if they were lucky, there would be other noises – the chair, the only chair (the other had gone the same way as the floorboards) scraping the boards, then quiet. Sometimes he made it upstairs to sleep, other times they would all creep past him laid out on the floor by the last burning shreds of fire, mouth open, snoring.

Between Nancy and Hetty there were four boys. Nancy was the only one who ever looked after Hetty and the sisters really only felt they had each other. Hetty did her best to look out for the younger ones, but Mom was wrung out, outnumbered and sick. She was not cruel – had not enough energy to be so. For her father Hetty had not a grain of pity or fellow feeling. Never once in her life at home did they speak kind or reasonable words to each other. From a young age she felt superior to both her parents. Nancy was more of an adult than either of them ever were.

Why doesn't she kill him? Hetty used to think, on nights when he came raving home and Mom was cowering, waiting. There was the poker – why not just get rid of him? Her dark thoughts never shocked her. It just seemed a practical solution, like ridding the house of rats.

Nancy was five years older and had long, pale brown hair. Hetty thought that was how Mom must have looked once. On the bare boards of the room where they slept – there were no bedsteads in the house and only one thin mattress on which their parents slept – Hetty would always sleep beside Nancy and her older sister often wrapped an arm round her and they fitted their bodies together under the rags of bedding to keep warm. Sometimes they whispered together at night. Nancy would tell Hetty stories, or they would make up fantasies about the food they'd like to eat as they usually went to bed hungry. Once, Hetty remembered, there was some sugar in the house. Nancy crept down and came back with her fingers damp and coated with sugar. She let Hetty lick off some of the rough sweet grains.

All the Barker children learned young how to obtain food any way they could. They would hang round the market in Coventry picking up anything that fell, however bruised. They would swipe things from stalls when the stallholder's back was turned, ready to run for their lives with an apple or a fat, sweet carrot. Hetty once managed to steal a whole loaf from one of the baker's shops without them seeing. She tore home with it, convinced the police would be on her tail. When no one seemed to be after her she stopped, her chest heaving, and tore a lump off the end. The crusty, stretchy dough was the best thing she had ever tasted. She took the rest home and shared it with the others.

'Better not do it again, Het,' Nancy warned. 'You don't want to go to prison.'

But some days they would do anything for food. They picked sprigs of lavender and tried to sell them. They begged and wheedled. They tried to get work. Nancy left school and worked packing ball bearings. At least as the older ones grew up there was a bit more money coming in.

Everyone in their street was poor, but the Barkers were the family everyone looked down on. Hetty burned with rage. The cold she could stand, she could tolerate being hungry, ill-clothed and shod, often not shod at all. But the contempt of the other children cut deep.

'Your dad's no good – my dad says 'e's a waster ... Your dad fell over outside our 'ouse last night ...' And on more than one occasion, 'Your old man tried to

145

come into our 'ouse last night!' And cruel, humiliating laughter.

One day, Hetty thought, seething with determination, *I'm gonna be better than you . . . You just wait and see . . . Better than the whole lot of yer . . .*

It was a November evening in 1897, a Saturday, the year she turned thirteen. There weren't so many of them at home now. Some of the older ones had gone off – they never said where – and Nancy, who was eighteen, was going steady, planning to get married as soon as she could. Hetty couldn't stand the thought of being there without Nancy.

'Can I come with yer – when you get wed?' she begged.

'Oh, I dunno, Het,' Nancy said. 'I dunno how it's gonna be. There's Wilf and all 'is brothers on the farm – I can't just take you with me . . .' But she felt guilty going off and leaving, Hetty could see.

That evening, Hetty and her brothers were at the market. She loved it, the Saturday night bustle, with everything being sold off. She liked the business, the women in their bonnets, the bright colours and the noise. When all the crowds were there was often a good time. Things got dropped. If you kept a sharp eye out you could chase a fallen plum or hot chestnut, an apple or potato rolling under a stall, and be away with it before anyone noticed. She didn't want to be hanging around for long. She had nothing on her feet. It wasn't as cold as it might be yet, but cold enough. She could move fast as a mouse when she had to. She was all bones, her eyes big in her head.

Her gang of brothers had gone off somewhere. Hetty

was sloping past a stall with oranges on it, their happy, exotic colour glowing in the light of the evening flares. She was so busy eyeing the fruit, praying that someone would drop or discard something, that she didn't notice the man standing to one side, a little way from the stalls, looking at her. He moved closer.

'How would you like one of those, little miss?'

Hetty jumped, as if she had been caught doing something wrong. She saw a man with a cheerful pink face, mutton chop whispers and a black trilby hat. He seemed large, a fulsome tummy pushing out his thick tweed coat.

'It's all right – there's no need to be scared,' he said. He had an awkward way of speaking. 'Look – I'll buy a bag of oranges and you can have some too. How's that?'

Hetty nodded, never one to turn down an offer of food.

The man purchased the fruit and then turned to her again. His expression had altered. He was more solemn now and seemed to be thinking hard about something. Hetty thought he had probably changed his mind about the oranges and she felt angry as her mouth had started to water in anticipation.

'Tell you what,' he spoke more brusquely. 'Come over here . . .'

He led her to a quiet spot, then bent down, looking around him. He reached into the bag and pulled out an orange, offering it to her. Hetty went to grab it and run away, but he held on tightly and pulled her closer to him.

'You look like a nice, handy wench. How would you like to come and work for me?'

Nineteen

His name was Josiah Gordon. He worked for the bank and lived with his mother in a tall, thin house full of stairs and narrow corridors in Fleet Street, Coventry. He wanted a maid. He also wanted the body of a young girl.

Hetty never went home again. Later, when Ethel or anyone else asked where she'd come from, she'd say, 'I dunno. Can't remember.'

And the truth was, she couldn't. She could barely read and did not know the name of the street where her mother and father lived, although on days when she went to the market, she could have found her way there, but could state no address. At first she missed her brothers and sisters, especially Nancy. She went back once or twice, but although her younger brothers and sisters were pleased to see her for a short time, they didn't take much notice, and her mother wasn't any better. When she said she had gone into service, Eileen Barker said, 'Well, you won't need to stop 'ere now then, will yer?' She was one less mouth to feed.

Every so often she saw Nancy at the market. Nancy was affectionate, but she was on her way out too, getting married and moving further away. She told Hetty where she was going, to the farm out near Brandon, and said to come and see her, but it seemed like another world to Hetty. She told Nancy her employer's name but she didn't know his address either. So a new life began.

It was sad, but she got more to eat with Mr Gordon. And his mother was harmless enough, a timid, bonneted, black-clad widow who, truth to tell, was cowed by her selfish son.

Josiah Gordon was neither kind, nor cruel in a violent way. He simply took what he wanted and expected other people to fall in with his desires. He was doing well at the bank and he expected to be king of the house. In return, Hetty slept for the first time in her life in a bed, with a black iron bedstead. A bed! It was the greatest luxury. And there was so much food. She had never had so much to eat in her life. Meat almost every day except Friday when he sent her to buy fish. Potatoes and gravy. At first, in eating terms, she thought she had gone to heaven. She soon discovered that food is not everything.

Mrs Gordon sat on a chair with her in the kitchen and in her whining voice, taught Hetty to cook. And what she didn't cook, they bought already made. Food was even delivered to the house. Puddings and pies. In the first year there, Hetty changed so much that her family would not have recognized her. Flesh thickened over her bones, she grew several more inches in height and budding breasts appeared on what before had been a chest as flat as a washboard. And she was full of life and energy.

She swept, polished, dusted and scrubbed. She toiled over the wash tub and mangle and made up the fires. She learned to cook. And she did this other thing that they never spoke about.

*

149

That first night, Mr Gordon had taken her back to his house and showed her where she would live. Hetty felt as if she was living in a dream. He led her to the top of the house, up a curving staircase.

'There we are – this is for you.' He said it in a sing-song voice, as if offering her a treat.

And it was a treat. She looked in amazement at the bed, which had a soft eiderdown on the top. It also had sheets and blankets and when she came to go to bed, it took her some time to decide where and how to get into it.

The house even had a bathroom! Pans of hot water had to be carried up to fill the bath. She learned that it would be her job to stagger up the stairs with these. Mr Gordon told her, that evening, to pour a bath for herself and he even helped carry up some of the water. She had her first ever bath all to herself. At home they had only ever had a lick and a promise from the scullery tap and on very rare occasions, had gone to the public baths. As they prepared the water, Mr Gordon kept looking at her strangely. She wondered when he was going to start hitting her, but he never did. He gave her a candle, and he left her alone that night.

As days passed, she found that his manner with her was sweet in a way that deceived her into thinking he was kind rather than manipulative, which was the real truth. She wasn't used to much kindness and was hungry for it. He never raised his voice. His face was hairy, the mutton chop whiskers almost meeting at his mouth. He had slightly prominent teeth, rabbity, which made him look less imposing and slightly ridiculous. All of it was frightening at first but she got used to it. In any case, from the start she was less scared of him than she was of her father.

The second night he came in after she had gone to bed. She heard his feet on the stairs, the door squeaked open, and light came in. He was holding a candle and stood there for a time while she kept her eyes shut and heard him breathing fast. Then he stepped in and quietly closed the door.

Hetty felt the candlelight draw nearer. He put the candlestick down on the chair beside the bed and his weight descended on to the bed, making the springs groan.

Hetty's heart was pounding so fast she could barely lie still. Keeping her eyes closed, she thought wildly. Had he come to kill her? She had some knowledge of what men and women did together, but only from things overheard, a few noises which sounded like fights – nothing in detail.

'Little missy, open your eyes – I've come specially to see you.'

Again the sing-song voice, cajoling her.

There seemed no choice but to look at him.

'Ah, now that's better . . .' He sounded pleased and immediately moved closer to her. Suddenly he lifted the edge of the bedclothes, flicking them back and exposing Hetty in her ragged drawers and vest. She gasped, hugging herself as the cold air nudged against her.

'Oh, dear me – we must buy you some new clothes, must we not! We can't have you going round as a ragamuffin. I'll get Mother to see to you. But my dear, you are very lovely . . . We are going to be good friends, aren't we? Because you see – I do like you very much already.'

Hetty was gratified to hear this, although quite unsure what it meant.

'Do sit up, will you?'

She pushed herself up, feeling very small and scruffy.

Mr Gordon's eyes were looking all over her, almost as if he was going to eat her.

'Oh –' He sounded overcome. 'Do let me hold you . . .'

She was clasped in his arms and she could feel his heart thumping loudly. He seemed suddenly very excited and was fumbling at his clothes.

'You see, I have to have you . . .'

He pushed her back a little and used both hands to unfasten his fly buttons. Hetty shrank back. What she caught a glimpse of was a sight she had never seen before. She had known plenty of little boys in her life, but she had never seen a grown man down there before. She gave a cry of surprise, but Mr Gordon became stern suddenly.

'Now – none of that,' he ordered. 'Quiet, miss.'

He started fondling round her flat little bosom. Hetty's chest was so tight that she was struggling for breath and for a second he stopped.

'Don't be afraid. I'm going to teach you things you need to know, my dear. It may be a bit uncomfortable for you at first, but you'll grow to like it. You'll like it very much. Now sit back . . .' His voice sounded strained. 'That's it – now we're going to take those off . . .'

'No . . .' she protested. He wanted her to undress in front of him! She was horrified.

'Do as I say,' he said sternly. As she obeyed, trembling now, he pushed her down on the bed with one hand and with the other was feeling into her privates, his face intent.

'Oh!' she gasped. 'No – you can't!'

Without knowing the facts she understood what he was going to do.

'It's all right,' he said, soothing, hypnotic. 'This is for you. This is how it's meant to be . . .'

He was panting, very excited, trying to push up into her. She was so skinny and small and felt he was breaking her open. Then his weight was on top of her. She grabbed at handfuls of the silky eiderdown, screwing her eyes shut as he moved in a frenzy. All she could feel was the hardness of him poking inside her and his heaviness on her, until he stopped as if running abruptly out of steam.

'There,' he said as he pulled away from her. 'Not much to ask, is it?'

She turned on her side, and he flung the bedclothes back over her.

Hetty stayed in Mr Gordon's house for a year and a half. He was right, she did get used to it, to the things he wanted at night. He came up to her two or three times a week. It never took very long and in the day she shut all thoughts of it away. In that time she filled out so that she grew large and buxom, which he found exciting. She could eat and eat and he encouraged her to. He called her 'splendid' in size.

Josiah Gordon's mother lived an enclosed, monotonous life. She only went out to visit the shops sometimes and to one friend. Otherwise she stayed in the house, sewing, and for a lot of the time, so far as Hetty could see as she cleaned the house around the woman, just sitting. Hetty found it strange after her own mother, who seldom had a moment's rest. Mrs Gordon was a subdued, colourless person who scarcely ever laughed and was not much company. But she was not unkind and she taught Hetty a good many things.

One morning, when she had been in the house over a year, Hetty woke up and found blood between her legs and stains on the sheets. She sat up, shocked. Whatever was it? There was a low gripe in her stomach. He had come up to her last night. Had he injured her? Or what about the stewed rabbit they had eaten yesterday. Could that have made her poorly?

For a moment she was full of panic. Then she remembered the rags that Nancy used to wash out every month. Of course – that's what it must be! Nancy had called it 'her monthly' and said it would happen to Hetty as well one day.

She found some rags and saw to herself, washing them out at night and hanging them in her room to dry. In any case, the bleeding was not very heavy.

Six months later she became sickly. Then her belly started to grow. It was Mrs Gordon who noticed one morning when she came into the kitchen and showed the first signs of energetic life Hetty had ever seen in her.

'So that's it!' she cried out of nowhere.

Hetty jumped, taken by surprise.

'You stupid, wretched, filthy girl!' She picked up the jug of milk from the table and hurled it towards Hetty's head. Hetty stepped back in time and the jug hit the front of the range and smashed, sloshing milk up Hetty's legs.

Hetty had no idea what she was supposed to have done wrong.

*

She would never forget the terror, the gruelling agony of that evening.

Mrs Gordon walked with her, grim faced. They set off as the sun was going down and they soon reached the place, down an alley. Mrs Gordon was looking round as though she was afraid they were being followed. She had Hetty by the arm, in a vicious grip.

They were shown into a front parlour. Hetty remembered seeing china dogs on the mantelpiece. The woman, a Mrs Dickins, was middle-aged, and rather fat with a plain, bacon-pink face.

Money was exchanged and Mrs Gordon let herself out. Stopping at the door, she turned and said to Hetty, 'You can come back and get your things. We'll leave them out at the back for you.' And she was gone.

'Well – you'd better come upstairs,' Mrs Dickins said.

Hetty couldn't stop herself crying. Did that mean Mrs Gordon had dismissed her? And what was going to happen? Why was it her fault?

'What am I here for?' she sobbed. 'I don't know what's happening.'

'You're here to get rid of the child, of course,' Mrs Dickins said. 'You can't keep it, can you, a bastard and you nothing but a child yourself?' She looked Hetty up and down. 'How old're you?'

'Fourteen,' Hetty said.

'You're a big girl for your age, I'll say that. Now come upstairs. It won't take long and it'll hurt a bit but then it'll be all over. One minute – let me get the kettle.'

Hetty followed behind her, the woman's thick ankles showing beneath her skirt as she lumbered up carrying the kettle of boiling water. There was a smell, of sweat and mothballs and something else, stinging and unpleasant. At the top of the stairs she led Hetty into a back room with a rough little table right in the middle. The floorboards were bare and round the table there were dark stains on the floorboards. To the side, on another table, were long sharp things and cloths.

'No . . .' Hetty began to see what was afoot. She started shaking and her teeth began to chatter. She backed away towards the stairs.

'Look, child,' the woman said matter-of-factly. 'It's this or the workhouse. You'd best do it and get it over.'

Mention of the workhouse struck fear in anyone. Never go there, never.

Hetty stared desperately at her. The woman's pebbly eyes stared back.

'Get your underclothes off, and get on the table.'

Twenty

From that day to this, she could not remember how she returned from Mrs Dickins's alley to the back door of the Gordons' house. But she could not forget the feel of the stone step under her as she lay faint across it, blood seeping from under her skirt, sticky and unstoppable, and the tearing agony in her innards.

Her belongings had been bundled up and were set beside the step.

'Let me in,' she sobbed weakly, rapping on the door.

After a while Mrs Gordon opened up a crack. Hetty was slumped with her back to her, so Mrs Gordon could not see the red stains spreading down the back of her skirt. In any case it was almost dark.

'You get away from here,' she hissed. 'Your pay is in with your things. We don't owe you anything.'

'I can't,' Hetty started to say, but the door clicked shut. 'Help me,' she whispered. She was too weak now even to cry.

Soon after that, everything went dark and she knew nothing about what happened until she woke in her bed up in the Gordons' attic, the pain still writhing in her guts. There was something wrapped round the lower part of her body and it felt heavy and clogged with blood. She desperately needed a drink, but was unable to move and soon she passed out again.

The days disappeared into pain and fever. She was

dimly aware of someone caring for her – either Josiah Gordon or his mother. She heard their feet on the floorboards, the mutter of voices. They lifted her head to drink. Someone else came, a doctor, she realized later.

Later, once she began to recover, she understood they had taken her in out of panic, not concern for her. They had found her unconscious by the back step. What if someone else had stumbled upon her?

As she came to, she lay in a haze of weakness. Mrs Gordon was doing the cooking for now and they brought her food, saying very little to her, as if she was a dog that needed food and water but could have no other sense of itself.

Hetty was a strong girl and began to gather her strength. After two weeks Josiah Gordon came up to her. He sat on the edge of the bed and smiled his toothy, self-obsessed smile. Hetty had never felt as if he looked at her. When he spoke it was as if he was looking in a mirror, talking to himself.

'Now you're better, Hetty,' he said, 'it's time for you to move on. Your time of usefulness to us has come to an end . . .'

It felt terrible. This house was all she was used to now. Where was she supposed to go? But as she tried to protest, he held up a finger to admonish her. 'No – no playing up. There's nothing to be said. You can't stay now. I've found another little girl to replace you. Her name is Alice.' He put his head on one side then and in his silly sing-song voice he said petulantly, 'You should have told me about the blood, Hetty. That was a naughty girl. Keeping a thing like that from Daddy.'

Hetty stared at him. She shrugged. All her feelings were a shrug.

The next morning, still bleeding, she was out on the streets.

Coventry's cobbled streets were choked with carts and barrows doing morning deliveries. It was a warm midsummer day and at first Hetty enjoyed being out in the air, watching the sights, the ladies out shopping and carters bustling about. She soon found herself in the familiar streets of the middle of town, Butcher Row, with its wiggly fronted houses, then Hertford Street and down to the corner where a cluster of men were standing around outside the Peeping Tom pub. Peeping Tom had looked out as Lady Godiva rode naked through the streets and Hetty looked up and saw the little man, the statue that commemorated him, in an upstairs window of the pub.

She turned back and walked on, not knowing what to do. She was soon very hungry and reached into her bundle for the few shillings that were in there from her final pay from the Gordons. She bought a meat pie and went and ate it sitting on a bench outside a church. It tasted delicious. Then she went to a coffee shop and drank a coffee dash – milk with a dash of coffee – having put plenty of sugar in it. She felt quite the lady being able to buy her own food.

But she was utterly alone. The sky seemed vast above her. For the first time in a very long while, she thought of her mother. She had nowhere else, so maybe she should go home. She wondered if she could find Nancy. Her sister had said she should, if she ever needed anything. But she could not even begin to think how to get out to where Nancy lived. She would try to find her family home.

She headed for the market square to get her bearings, then set off towards the street where she had grown up, with its narrow, cramped houses. It felt as if she had not been there for many years, rather than twenty months, which was what it was. It was at once painfully familiar, yet like a foreign land. She stopped a distance from the house. In the doorway sat a bristly-faced old man with a rug draped over his knees. She didn't know who he was. He stared at her vacantly as she came closer and she thought he must have lost his wits, but at last he said, 'Who d'yer want?'

'I'm Hetty Barker,' she said. 'Where's my mom gone?'

'Barker?' he mumbled wetly, having no teeth. 'Ain't no Barkers 'ere now. Been gone six month or more. Dunno where, before you ask.'

She asked a couple of the other neighbours, but they shrugged contemptuously. Hetty turned away. So that was that.

Hetty knew she should look for work, but while she still had a few shillings to call her own, she didn't have the will. A great numbness had come over her, even more than before. She felt unclean and uncomfortable and it was hard to find anywhere to have a wash. For a few days she wandered out towards the countryside, through Stivichall and beyond, sleeping at the edges of fields and in barns. The weather was warm and dry. When she needed food, she went to a farm or village shop. She managed to have a quick wash in streams and ponds, rinsing out the rags she was using and drying them in the sun before moving on. Sometimes she sat for hours under a tree, or lay by a hedge, just staring, her mind almost blank. It felt impossible to think about the past or future. She seemed to have no energy.

Only once did anyone challenge her, a man she met on the road with a cart.

'Where're you heading to, young wench?' he asked.

Hetty's heartbeat thudded fast. A man. She knew now what men wanted, even though his tone was jovial.

'Going to see my sister,' she said and walked on purposefully.

Eventually when she was down to her last couple of farthings, she walked back into town. She was alone in the world, so far as she could see, with almost nothing. But still she didn't weep, or let herself ask for help.

She wandered for hours, until it grew dark, then quietly went into the grounds of the cathedral and tucked herself into a dark spot up against the side of the building. As usual she settled with her bundle under her head. She was used to the hard ground by now and soon fell asleep. It seemed only seconds later that something hard was nudging at her ribs.

'Come on – wakey wakey – that's it, up you get. You can't stay here.'

The hard thing was a police constable's boot. He shone his bullseye lamp in her face. Muzzily Hetty got up, too sleepy to care what happened next.

'Right – you come along with me.'

Gripping her arm with his free hand, the constable led her out to the path, to the light of the dim gas lamps. He was young, his face pinched and mean, like a stoat.

'Name?'

'Hetty Barker,' she muttered.

'Address?'

'Ain't got one.'

'What?'

'Ain't got one,' she said louder. It felt shameful, like a dirty admission.

'Right.' His grip tightened. 'You're coming along with me.'

He dragged her roughly so that she was pulled off balance and, in the darkness, she staggered back and forth.

'You're too young to be in that state,' he said with disgust, and for a moment Hetty couldn't think what he meant. Then she realized: he thought she was the worse for drink. Slyly she kept moving her feet unevenly and stumbling, and let out a hiccough.

'Bleedin' vermin,' she heard him mutter.

She walked beside him, docile while they were still between the railings each side of St Michael's. He was holding up his lamp and in its meagre light she peered at him sideways, hardly moving her head. He had his lips clenched tightly together in a look of weary contempt. Hatred for him seethed inside her, but she stayed obediently beside him. After a few minutes, thinking her surrendered, she felt him relax a fraction. She twisted abruptly out of his grasp and was running as fast as she ever had in her life before.

'Oi – get back 'ere, yer little bugger!' He sounded pompous, like an older man.

Hetty tore down a side street where the shops were closed and deserted now. When she sensed a gap had opened between them she hurled herself into a black doorway and flattened herself against the wall. There was an odd, bloody smell: a butcher's, she realized. A moment later she heard the constable go charging past.

Go on, you bastard, keep running, she thought.

She slipped out, back the other way, and ran for it, choosing another route, she hardly knew where. Warm trickles of blood were running down her legs. She began to slow, stopped running in sheer weariness. Her triumph seeped away and a bleak feeling of despair came over her. Where was she to go?

Then someone was there, suddenly, blocking her path, and she slammed right into them. For a second she assumed it was the young constable, but immediately her senses contradicted this impression. There was no serge uniform, no stoat-like face in the gloom, instead a smaller, bonier person altogether.

'Watch it!' a gravelly female voice protested. 'You nearly knocked my sodding teeth out!' Hetty felt her arm grabbed, the girl's fingers digging in hard as she dragged Hetty close to her. 'Let's see yer . . .'

A narrow-eyed face peered at her.

'How old're you?'

'Fifteen,' Hetty said.

'Who're you running from?'

'The peelers.'

The girl relaxed her grip. 'You got somewhere to kip down?'

Hetty looked down miserably, shaking her head.

'Right – you'd better come with me then.'

Which was how Hetty found herself waking the next morning in the attic of a shabby house in Spon End that felt all too familiar, and how she came to meet a girl a few months older than herself, a devious troublemaker called Ethel Sharp.

April 1925

Twenty-One

'Aggie? Come in here a tick – I want yer.'

Aggie heard her grandmother hiss at her from her bedroom. The door was unlatched and she pushed it open. Nanny Adams was sitting up in her bed partially dressed. The bones of her corsets poked out through her half-buttoned blouse. Aggie caught a glimpse of her grandmother's wrinkly chest above it. Nanna's lower half was covered by the faded green eiderdown. Her white hair was plaited, not piled on her head as it was in the daytime. Aggie liked seeing Nanna in bed. She looked softer somehow and welcoming and there was something reassuring about her musty, lavender, 'mother's ruin' smells that were so familiar. The house felt so sad and strange with Dad in the hospital, but at least with Nanna there, they could still feel safe.

'That's it,' Freda Adams said, with an air of mystery. 'Shut the door, bab. Now – I've got a little job for yer.' On the chair by the bed stood her precious hip flask with its well-polished silver cup. Beside it were a number of scraps of paper. She handed one to Aggie, folded over.

'See this? Now, you take this along to Sawyer and Hewlett's – you know where it is, don't yer? Other side of the Stratford Road. You go in and say to the man, "This is for Mr Martin" – he's one of the gaffers there

– "it's from Mrs Adams and she wants me to wait for an answer." '

Aggie nodded, uncertainly.

'He'll know who it is – I've known Joe Martin since 'e were in short trousers. He'll find some work for us. Now you've all broken up for Easter, you can make yourselves useful. And I've asked him a question on there – you bring me back an answer.' She nodded at the paper, reaching over for her hip flask. 'Go on, bab – and come back quick. Tell May and the others to come up to me if they want anything. And Aggie – mind the horse road while you're at it.' She raised her flask as if in a toast, then took a sip. 'Aah. There – go on. You still here?'

It was eight in the morning. As she went downstairs, she heard her mother call, 'Aggie – that you?' from the back.

Jen was sitting by the table, looking queasy. She'd got the kettle on and looked as if she was gathering her strength.

'I've got to go out – for Nanna,' Aggie said, holding the note behind her, though she didn't know why.

Mom frowned. 'Come here – what's going on?'

'Nothing,' Aggie said. 'She asked me to go and see a Mr Martin, that's all.'

'Oh, did she now,' Jen said, even more suspicious. 'And what is it you've got to see him about?'

'I dunno,' Aggie said truthfully.

'What's that you've got?'

Aggie held out the little note and Jen took it. When she'd read to the end of it, she gave a small groan and leaned forward, resting her head in her hands. She seemed to be thinking, but then, shaking her head and without looking at Aggie, with a resigned look she held the note out to her.

'All right. Run along then, if you have to. And mind the horse road.'

It was drizzling outside. At least, Aggie thought, looking down at the dreaded cut-off boots, they wouldn't look so horrible in this weather. Mom had trimmed down the mouldy old pair of wellingtons so that they came to just above her ankles. They had once been black but the colour was almost leached out of them, and they were all rough at the top. They looked terrible and they weren't a bit comfortable. The insides were perished and Aggie didn't have any socks to wear. She hated them. They were the ugliest things she'd ever seen, much worse than the *Mail* boots. But she knew if she said anything to Mom about them at the moment she'd get short shrift.

All the same, she liked being out with an errand to run, especially without May tagging along. She could go at her own speed and not have to worry about whether May was keeping up or running out into the road just when a horse and cart was coming. And the street was full of people – already a lot of children were playing out because the schools were on holiday.

It was a good chance for spying, too. Just as she left the house she saw the shambling, unmistakable figure of Mary Crewe ploughing along the street, cursing at anyone who got in her way. She never looked where she was going as she was mainly talking to the bundle in her arms. The boys often called out rude things to her but she took no notice, just cursed everyone through the cigarette which drooped at the left side of her mouth. 'Damn you!' was one of her favourites. 'Damn you and blast you!'

Aggie fell in behind Mary. She was a very stout woman with stringy brown hair, darkened by grease and hanging loose and matted on her shoulders. She always wore a coat buttoned tightly round her and big brown boots, summer and winter. A thin trail of smoke always followed her. Aggie thought she looked like an old woman and a little girl all rolled into one. It was impossible to hear what she was mumbling in the noisy street.

I wonder where's she's going, Aggie thought. And the idea came to her that *Agnes Green: Spy* would follow Mary Crewe one day, on a proper spying mission. But not today – now she had Nanna's mission instead.

Crossing the Stratford Road, she walked along until she could see the premises of Sawyer and Hewlett, a firm making buttons, hooks and eyes, snap fasteners and hairpins. Aggie's stomach felt jumpy with nerves.

As well as the main entrance to the works there was a side door, standing open. Timidly she went in and to her left there was a counter, about level with her nose. She thought no one was there for a second, and then a man shot up behind it, crying, 'Ooh! 'Ello, bab. Didn't see you down there!'

Aggie nearly jumped out of her skin. The man was mousey haired, gangly thin and wore a brown holland overall.

'Not after a job at your age, are yer?' he joked. 'What d'you want?'

'I've to give you this,' Aggie said, passing the note over.

He read it, squinting. 'Mr Martin, eh. Well well . . . Hang on a tick, bab, you're in luck – I think he's about.' And he vanished through a door at the back.

Aggie looked about her but there was nothing to see except the counter and the wall. She could hear muffled sounds from behind the door. A moment later it swung open and a much smaller man with black hair slicked back each side of a bald pate leaned over the counter.

'Well,' he said. 'You Freda's little 'un? You're a chip off the old block, I'll say that!' He laughed as if this was the best joke ever told. 'So, she wants some outwork – you going to help, are you?'

Aggie nodded.

'I've know your nanna since her hair was the same colour as yours,' he said, laughing uproariously again.

Aggie smiled because he looked funny. She thought the man was nice but she still didn't know what to say.

'All right.' He stood up straight again. 'You wait there a minute – I'll get you a box to take home. You'll have to get your own needles and thread . . .' He leaned forward and said, 'Now, as for the other thing. You tell Mrs Adams to come in and see me in person and we'll see what we can do.'

Twenty-Two

The box was not very heavy, but heavy enough, and by the time she got back to Lilac Street Aggie's arms were aching and her feet were burning and sore. She had been hurrying faster and faster and she was in a world of her own. She was just turning in to the road when she realized someone was talking to her.

'You're in a hurry, Aggie!' Looking up, she saw Mrs Southgate with Lily.

'Hello, Aggie,' Lily said, beaming. She always looked up to Aggie.

'Hello, Lily,' Aggie panted.

'That looks heavy, dear,' Rose said. 'Are you going home with it?'

Aggie nodded, her arms feeling like lead.

'Let me take it – I'll come back with you. You look as if you're about to drop it. I know it's not far now, but it's a big box for a little girl like you to manage.'

'Thanks,' Aggie said, her arms suddenly feeling as if they wanted to float up now the box was gone.

They walked along side by side, though it wasn't far. Aggie prayed they wouldn't notice her horrible boots.

'Not a very nice day, is it?' Mrs Southgate said, noticing them and thinking it was a shame. 'When's spring coming, that's what I want to know?'

But she didn't really sound as if she minded. In fact, she sounded happy. Aggie glanced up at her. Mrs

Southgate was looking even more pretty than usual. She had on her blue coat and lovely cloche hat, and today her cheeks were pink and there was a glow about her. Under the hat's narrow, curved brim, her hair was arranged in little kiss curls along her forehead and Aggie thought it looked lovely. She'd seen her a few times lately and twice been to her house for the afternoon. Mrs Southgate had stuck a new picture in her book, of a beautiful ballerina called Anna Pavlova. Aggie had stared at her for nearly as long as she had at Mata Hari.

'How's your mother, dear? I hope she's feeling better.'

'Yes,' Aggie said. 'Well – no. Not really.'

'Oh, dear,' Rose said. 'And your poor father?'

Aggie shrugged. She couldn't look at Mrs Southgate. Her cheeks were burning and a lump rose in her throat. They had reached number nine and she hesitated.

'Oh, dear,' Rose said again. 'Well, look, just a couple of things, dear. I thought you and your little sister – May – might like to come and see us on Sunday again? Lily would like that, wouldn't you?'

Lily nodded, jumping up and down, and Aggie grinned. 'Yes, please, Mrs Southgate – if that's all right.'

'Yes, dear, quite all right. And the other thing is – about your mother – I should so like to help her if I can. D'you think she'd mind?'

Aggie hesitated. You never knew with Mom.

'Well,' Mrs Southgate said, sounding unsure. 'I suppose there's no harm in asking. Can you tell her I'm here?'

Aggie took the heavy box and put it on the table. 'Mom – Mrs Southgate wants you.'

Her mother was washing up in a bowl at the table. 'Who? Oh – what does 'er want?'

173

'She said she wants to help you.'

'Well, tell her to . . . No, don't, hang on . . .' Hugging herself defensively, Jen went to the front door. Aggie listened from behind her.

'Yes?' Jen said, rather forbiddingly.

'I was only thinking,' Aggie heard Mrs Southgate say timidly. 'If you're still feeling poorly – well, you've got an awful lot to do – more than me with me only having the one. I'd be glad to come and help if you'd like.'

Jen leaned against the door frame, stern with pride. 'Help with what?'

'With – well with, you know, the meals you do – the children . . .'

'D'yer think I can't manage then?'

'Well, no, but, what with you being poorly at the moment . . .'

'Tell yer what,' Jen said, backing into the house again. 'When I want help, I'll let you know – all right?'

Aggie felt a burning blush move up her cheeks. She almost felt like crying. 'Mom!' she protested. 'She was trying to be nice!'

'Huh,' Jen said, going back to the kitchen. 'I've had more than enough interference from your grandmother for one day without that one poking her nose in an' all!'

Nanna was in the back as well. She beckoned to Aggie.

'Well?' she whispered. 'D'yer get them? And what did he say?'

Aggie glanced at her mother.

'You might as well speak up,' Jen said wearily. 'I know what you're up to.'

Nanna made one of her faces at Aggie, lips pursed. *I'm in trouble now*, it said.

'Mr Martin said you're to go and see him and he'll see what he can do,' Aggie reported.

Nanna looked pleased. 'Hear that, Jen? At least someone thinks I'm not just fit for the knacker's yard yet!'

Jen shook her head despairingly and left the room.

Alone in the front room, Jen opened the box which Aggie had brought home. A dull metallic gleam came from inside, from thousands of wire hooks and eyes. She ran the contents through her fingers. Tucked to one side were the little cards on which they had to be sewn to sell in the shops.

Jen sat down with a sigh. Grudgingly she had to admire her mother, but it drove her mad the way she took over. Having her living with them was a great help in many ways but it was always going to be a battle of wills as well.

'Oh, Tommy,' Jen said, looking down at her stomach. Her body felt battered from being sick, as if someone in hobnailed boots had given her a good kicking. She had been so ill that she was thin as a rake and there was very little sign of any swelling yet.

Just for a second, in spite of it all, she smiled. Twins – imagine. What if it was? How Tommy'd love that! He'd feel it would make a proper man of him. Two of the little buggers running about! And it was true that she'd never had it this bad before. Her smile faded as another pang of nausea seized her. God, it didn't bear thinking about, none of it.

Last Sunday she had at last managed to see Tommy in the hospital. She'd gone the week before, carted all the way over to the Fever Hospital only to be told that they'd moved him to the hospital in West Heath. When she heard she'd been furious, but saved her tears of rage and frustration until she got outside into the rain.

'How was I s'posed to know they'd moved him?' she wept.

She hadn't been able to get to West Heath that day. It was too far away and too late by then, so she waited and worried for another week. At last she'd made her way over there. Standing outside the red-brick building she'd been full of fear and misgiving. But nothing would have stopped her from going in.

When she got to the ward and recognized his dark hair on the pillow and the smile that crinkled up his face when he saw her coming along, it was worth every minute.

''Ello, my little babby!' he said, delighted, trying to sit up and sinking back in a storm of coughing.

'Oh, Tommy!' She sat beside him, with no interest in the other beds and what might be going on in them. She had eyes only for him. 'Oh, look at you – so clean and tidy. What've they been doing to you!' She leaned down once he'd recovered, eager for a kiss.

'You might catch it,' he said, anxious. 'They said I should never've stayed near you all . . .'

'It's a bit late to worry about that,' Jen said. 'Everyone's all right. Go on, give us a kiss.' She touched his lips with her own. 'Don't know if we're s'posed to do that in here,' she said afterwards, perching on the chair.

'Never mind that, kid – how are yer? How's the little 'uns?'

'They're all right – all of 'em – even this little so-and-so!' She pointed at her belly. 'She ain't half giving me the runaround though.'

'She?'

'I'm always more bad with the girls.'

'Still sick, are yer?' he said tenderly.

'Sick as a dog.' She leaned forward and whispered, 'Mom thinks it might be twins. All your cowing fault, you devil, you!'

'No!' Tommy grinned sheepishly. 'Twins – that'd be summat. Soon have my football team, eh?'

She wanted to take his hand but felt embarrassed to, in here. But then she took it anyway. It was so thin and dry. She held it gently.

'Any road – we're all all right and our mom's keeping us in order.'

Tommy rolled his eyes. 'As usual.'

'What've they said – how are you? How long're they going to keep you in 'ere?'

His face fell. 'Well, that's the thing – they're talking about months. Could be quite a stretch. I keep telling them, I need to get home and keep my family. I can't be apart from you and all of them lot that long.'

Jen tried not to show the lurch of dread that his words had given her inside. Months! Surely that couldn't be right. They couldn't do without him all that long.

'They said you nearly died.'

'Ar, so they did.' His grin was back. 'You don't want to believe everything you 'ear, kid.'

'You've been very poorly, Tommy.'

'I'm getting better as fast as I can.' His face clouded and he reached for her hand. 'I miss you like mad. It feels all wrong in here – though I've not a lot to complain about, 'cept being away from you.'

They spent the rest of the time catching up on the children and how things were in the hospital, and then Jen had to go out into the wet and make her way home.

At least he was in good hands, she thought, waiting at the bus stop. It was terrible, him being away – like a prison sentence. But at least he was still alive. God knew, it could be worse. Somehow, in the meantime, they were going to have to manage. She felt desperate and ashamed that her old mom, who had struggled most of her life, had now gone back to beg a job at one of the factories where she'd collared for years. It was all wrong. She and Tommy ought to be keeping her in her old age. She wanted to stop her, but she knew the wages would be a godsend.

Much as her mother's interfering irritated Jen, she had a burning pride in her spirit. She wasn't going to have her family fall into the clutches of the parish, whatever it took to keep them above water. Jen had to admit, that old lady was determined.

Twenty-Three

Rose waited for her visitors that Sunday afternoon in a complete nervous flutter. It had been bad enough waiting for Harry to go out. The weather was cold and showery and she had been terrified that he would change his mind and decide that an afternoon sitting by a bleak stretch of water was not what he wanted.

But Harry loved the outdoors and nothing would keep him from fishing except inches of solid ice.

'Tararabit,' he said, heading off as soon as dinner was finished. 'See yer later.'

From the window she watched him disappear, his strong legs pushing eagerly down on the pedals. Saturdays, fishing or football and the pub; Sundays, fishing. They didn't see very much of each other really. She watched him with a pang. *I loved him once*, she thought. *I'm sure I did. Or I thought I did.* But the tension eased out of her. He'd gone – the afternoon was clear!

She was expecting Arthur King at three, but she knew the little girls would be along before then. Aggie had said that for once her brother John was taking the others to Sunday school. Rose realized that Jen Green didn't mind whether her children were in the hands of the church or a neighbour as long as they were out of her way for a bit. She was glad to be able to do Jen a favour, even though she could be a bit brusque, and at the same time, she hoped Arthur would be reassured by

179

the children being there. She didn't want him to think her a fast, desperate widow. And, truth to tell, she knew Aggie and May would help keep Lily occupied so that she could fix her attention on him.

She had baked a sponge, filled it with jam and dusted the top with sugar. It had risen well and she was pleased with it. She set out her cups and saucers on a tray. In the front parlour she lit the fire and laid the little side table with one of her embroidered cloths. Then she went upstairs to see to her hair. How strange it was, getting ready to greet a blind person. She still had to look right in her own eyes even if Arthur could not see her. She had on a soft blue woollen skirt and a white blouse and cherry-red cardigan. Turning this way and that in front of the mirror, she knew she looked nice. Catching herself out, she told herself, *You're a married woman – he's a friend, that's all.* But he thought she was a widow . . .

By two o'clock there was a little scrabbling knock at the door. As usual the two little girls appeared bashful, Aggie especially. The child looked thin, she thought. She must be missing her father. And she was still wearing those awful cut-off boots. Oh, how horrible and ugly they were. Rose's heart went out to her. Surely something better than that could be done? Rose greeted them kindly.

'Mrs Southgate,' Aggie asked, 'Babs says is it all right if she comes up here for a bit too? Her mom said she could today.'

Rose hesitated. Why not? All the more company for Lily and it wouldn't make any difference. And she was fond of Babs with her toothy smile and lively ways.

'Go on then – you can leave May here – run and tell her.'

The two friends were soon back and Rose was glad to see them giggling together as she opened the door. She managed to stop herself saying, 'What*ever* have you got on?' to the child.

Having no sisters, Babs often had odd hand-me-downs from her brothers and today she was wearing a skirt that had obviously been fashioned out of a pair of boys' flannel trousers with the legs cut off. Dulcie Skinner wasn't the handiest of needlewomen either and there was something cock-eyed about the whole thing. Had it not been that afternoon, of all days, Rose might have been tempted to get it off the child and alter it for her.

The four little girls settled down to play with some wooden bricks. Rose noticed that Aggie had taken off her ugly boots and pushed them under a chair. The wait seemed long and Rose grew more and more nervous. The fire was burning well now in the front parlour and the room was warm and cosy. Everything was spick and span and as she wanted it.

She had a fit of panic about one of the girls mentioning Harry, so she said suddenly to Lily, 'Your dad's out fishing – he won't be back till quite late.'

Lily looked up at her with a frown.

'Just in case you were wondering,' Rose said, and subsided into her nerves again.

At last she heard a knock.

'I wonder who that can be?' she exclaimed.

He was already holding his hat when she opened the door but it was raining and his curls, a little longer than when she had last seen him, were already spotted with drops.

'Oh, come in,' she said. 'Don't you have an umbrella?' She stepped out into the dull grey afternoon and took his arm.

'Well, if I do, I can't find it,' he said as they stepped inside. 'Of course I try and keep everything exactly in place so I know where to find it, but if I mislay it – well, there's not much hope. And no one to ask except my landlady – but on a Sunday afternoon I didn't like to disturb her. Oh, hello – do we have company?'

He had felt rather than heard that there were others in the room.

'Some children from up the road – company for Lily,' Rose said, taking his coat. She looked at Lily. *Remember*, her eyes said. There had been several conversations. *It's just better if you don't ever, ever mention to your father that Mr King has been round, all right, dear? Just better that way.*

She installed him in the most comfortable chair near the fire and went to make tea. She heard him say to Lily, 'So – have you begun your piano lessons yet?'

Lily must have nodded. Piano lessons were another thing she was not allowed to mention. *It just makes Daddy cross. I don't know why but that's how it is. So don't talk about it in front of him, will you, love?*

She served the tea from the little side table and cut cake for Arthur King and the children.

'It's suddenly gone very quiet!' Arthur said, laughing, after she handed the plates round. 'Mouths all full, I presume?'

The children chewed and stared but as soon as the cake was finished they went back to their play. Rose and Arthur chatted. She had been surprised, the first time he came, to discover that he lived alone. She had thought that, being unable to see, he must still live with his family. She wondered how he managed. He had a room in Oldfield Road, not too far from the factory, he said. That was what made life easiest.

'Is your landlady nice?' she asked.

'Oh, yes – not bad at all,' he said. Rose thought that any landlady would have her heart melted by Arthur. 'She's a decent sort. She'll help me sometimes, with a few extras like, reading the odd letter to me or where have I put my umbrella. But as I say I didn't want to interrupt her Sunday nap.'

'That's nice,' Rose said. 'Some of them can be proper old tartars.'

'So I gather – I've never been in digs before. Not here anyway ...' He hesitated. 'One or two French places – we sometimes put up in a *pension* if we were on leave. They were a mixed bag.'

'Must be nice, France,' she said, unthinking.

'In the right circumstances, yes.'

'Oh –' She blushed, mortified. 'I'm sorry – what a silly thing to say.'

'It's all right. You're right – it is nice. I'd have liked to see it in peacetime, you know, travel round, especially the south. But now – well, there's not a lot of point.' There was an edge of bitterness to his voice, well controlled, but still present. 'Still – no good feeling sorry for myself. I've seen a lot worse – before, I mean.'

Rose glanced at the children. They were happily absorbed, Babs leading the way, building a tower of bricks, chattering nineteen to the dozen.

'Was it gas?' she asked quietly.

'My eyes? Oh – no! No, the injuries from some of the gas attacks – well, you wouldn't even want to survive, I tell you. That's what I always thought, anyway. Utterly terrible – much worse than this. I was too close to a shell that went off. It blew a whole lot of rubbish into my eyes – shrapnel, grit – I don't really know but the light went out. And stayed out. I was barely conscious for a long time and when I really came round – well, I've never been able to see since.'

'I'm ever so sorry,' she said.

'Well – me too. But there we are. I had a lot of help. St Dunstan's, bless them. I was sent to Brighton for a good while for rehabilitation as they call it. And it was they who saw to it that I got my training. They're quite wonderful.'

'They sound it,' Rose said. There was a pause, before she added, 'Would you like some more tea?'

'That'd be lovely – and how about some music?'

She had got up and was saying, 'That would be lovely too!' when there was another knock at the door.

Rose actually jumped, clattering the cup and nearly spilling tea all over the tray. Surely to God that wasn't Harry home? Sense told her that he would never knock.

'Sorry,' she said, flustered. 'It sounds as if we have another visitor.'

It was Muriel Wood. Rose felt she had to invite her in, and in a moment Muriel had joined them, bringing in a rush of fresh air and her plain, kindly self in her old winter hat and coat. With her was her little boy, Oliver, who went over rather cautiously and sat with the girls. Babs was soon bossing him about.

Rose took her coat, then introduced them – Muriel, a friend from church; Mr Arthur King, who tuned the piano for us. 'Do sit down, Muriel,' she said. 'I'll top up the pot.'

'Oh, don't go to any trouble, dear – we were just passing and your window looked so warm and cosy we thought we'd call.' She gave her little laugh and said to Arthur King, 'Rose keeps such a lovely house. I do believe it's a gift.'

'I'm sure,' he said.

In the kitchen Rose was gritting her teeth. She was fond of Muriel, but why, of all days, did she have to come today?

By the time she returned with the pot they were talking about music and how Muriel was teaching Lily.

'I know she's very young,' Muriel said, 'but I tend to think the younger the better. After all, look at Mozart!'

'Oh, yes,' he was agreeing. 'It starts to get them used to it. I believe I was her age when I first had lessons.'

Off they went, and Rose could do nothing but listen. After a while, Arthur clearly wanted to involve her and he leaned forward a little as if to identify exactly where she was.

'It's very interesting, this area of town, isn't it?' he said. 'I mean, it's all built over now, but it's odd to think that only a hundred years ago – well, a hundred and thirty or so, where we are now was right at the edge of Joseph Priestley's estate. It was between Priestley Road and Larches Street.'

'So it was,' Muriel said.

'He had a laboratory there, didn't he?' Rose said. 'He was one of those Lunar Society people.' She thanked heaven, silently, for Professor Mount, who had told her about Priestley, about his house being burned to the ground because people didn't like his new notions.

'He did,' Arthur said. 'He was a very impressive person – one of those who can take on so many different ideas.'

'Extraordinary how much change there's been since then, isn't it?' Muriel said. 'If you think, this was just fields, mostly.' She was pink from the firelight and from being in company. But Rose couldn't help still wishing that she hadn't come, though she was ashamed of this thought. Muriel was so good and kind. And it was nice to have an interesting conversation. But she noticed, uncomfortably, that Muriel Wood and Arthur King must be about the same age. And Muriel really was a widow . . . Rose found herself thinking unworthy thoughts. *But look at her – she's so plain.* Almost without realizing it, Rose had been used to being usually the prettiest woman in any room. *If he could only see me . . .* But then Arthur King could not see how pretty she was – or for that matter how plain Muriel was. It was a strange feeling.

'Arthur said he would play something for us,' she said, trying to chase away these shameful thoughts.

'How about a song?' he said. 'Do any of you fancy singing? So that I don't have to perform on my own?'

Seeing him move to the piano, all the children got up and gathered round, looking up at the adults and waiting for something to happen.

'I expect you know this one . . .' He started to play 'The Ash Grove'.

'Oh, yes,' Muriel said. 'How lovely – my father was Welsh.'

Rose knew it as well and they both joined in singing. Arthur played easily, fluently. Muriel was tuneful enough, though her voice was a bit thin, but Rose felt hers soar into the high second verse:

'Twas there while the blackbird was joyfully singing
I first met my dear one, the joy of my heart,
Around us for gladness the bluebells were ringing
Ah! then little thought I how soon we should part.

She smiled down at Aggie's eager face and Babs's mischievous one, trying not to show how affected she was by the sight of Arthur, by the back of his slim neck as he played, by the lovely words. They played it again and got the children to join in as best they could. Muriel's little boy Oliver had the makings of a lovely voice.

Arthur played more songs and time rushed by, until Muriel said, 'Heavens, I'm supposed to be at evensong – I must fly! Come along, Oliver!'

Rose jolted back to the present. What was the time? It was certainly almost dark. Harry must be on his way back.

She said goodbye to Muriel and Oliver and the other children thanked her and trickled off along the street in different directions.

'I must go,' Arthur said. 'Or I'll have overstayed my welcome.'

'No – not at all,' Rose said, meaning it with every fibre of her but on tenterhooks now in case Harry were to turn up. 'But I do have to see to Lily. It's been so nice . . .'

'Yes,' he said simply. 'More than nice.' He paused. 'You have a lovely singing voice—' She made to protest, but he said. 'No – you do. Didn't you know?'

'No – not really.'

There was a pause, as he stood at a loss and she was about to move and get his coat.

'Damn it,' he said, with such force that she jumped. 'I do wish I could see you.'

Her heart pounded. 'It must be . . . Well, it must be awful.'

'It is. It's damnable.' He paused, as if unsure whether to go on. When he did it came out in a rush. 'The thing is, Rose – it's lonely. I've got my mother and father – not too far away, and my sister's in Wolverhampton, a few male friends. But most people don't want to know.

They're embarrassed, or – I don't know what it is. I'm a cripple as far as they're concerned . . .'

His face was full of tender emotion. Awkwardly, he stretched out a hand into the darkness in front of him. Rose reached forward and took it. She saw something pass across his face, a moment of wonder.

'Will you come and see me again?' she said. *I'm lonely too*, she wanted to say.

'If I may. D'you know – you're lovely, Rose. That's all I can say.'

She smiled and then, realizing this was no help, let out a little laugh. 'No one's ever said that before.'

'Well, it's time they did.' He squeezed her hand. 'Thank you – so much.'

They agreed that he should come again next week, at the same time. He took out his wallet and gave her a card.

'This is where I live. It's not too far. Let me know if it's no good, in the end.'

He hesitated as if he did not want to go out into the darkness. But then she realized that dark or light was all the same to him.

'Goodbye,' she said softly.

He turned, raising his hat. 'Till next time.'

Rose closed the door softly. For a moment she closed her eyes, bathed in happiness.

Twenty-Four

She had closed her eyes in such a way once before, behind the back door of Professor Mount's house after Harry came back and she had agreed to marry him.

Standing at her own door now, picturing Arthur King feeling his way along the street to his house, Rose remembered that day. She stood for a moment, recalling it, then heard Lily's voice behind her.

'Is the man coming back?'

Rose turned, trying to look casual, with a slight smile.

'Oh, I don't know dear, really. Now – we need to get you a bite to eat.'

As she sat with Lily in the kitchen her thoughts wandered. *Was I in love with Harry? Or was I so desperate for a way out that I'd have married anyone? Or was it just that he had seemed so keen on her that she mistook her own feelings?* But she had thought she loved him, back then. She had had no idea.

During the two and a half years that Harry was away, she only heard from him twice. He sent a card quite soon after he arrived in France. Then, in 1918, when she had almost given up hope he wrote again. '*Thinking of you*,' it said. Not much more. But it gave her such hope. He was alive! And if he was thinking of her that must mean something. The war had felt like a lid closing

189

everything in, making it unable to change or move. She felt completely stuck. But there were other reasons why she stayed where she was.

Professor and Mrs Mount had one son, Ernest Mount, who Rose had only ever seen once. Ernest had come to the house in 1916 when he had also joined up. He arrived in an officer's uniform, tall, not especially handsome and stand-offish even with his parents. He was more of his mother's build than his father's, solid and pink about the face, with thin brown hair. He looked through Rose as if she wasn't there. He clearly did not have much time for his father, called him 'Pa' breezily and did not stay long. He was a man of the world, was the message he gave off and when Rose was in the room he talked a lot about money and shares. He seemed to get on a little better with his mother and sat beside her couch.

'You want to get yourself some decent servants,' Rose heard him say as she was disappearing out of the room after bringing them all tea. 'That girl's a looker all right but she's barely out of the classroom. I can pay if you like – get some good staff on board.'

Rose did not hear the Mounts' reply, but nothing happened so they must have quietly ignored him. In any case, he was off to France.

More and more she became like a daughter to them and having seen Ernest she felt sorry for them. How had this rather unworldly pair managed to produce such a son?

Mrs Mount passed the time by doing sewing and embroidery, but could only do so with Rose's help, so Rose spent a lot of time with her, watching. Sometimes she sent Rose up to Moseley village to seek out more embroidery silks in lovely rich colours.

One day, Mrs Mount said, 'Show me your hands, my dear. That's right – don't be shy – come a bit closer.'

Rose stood in front of her, holding out her hands and embarrassed at how chapped they looked, the nails bitten down to the quicks.

'Hard-working little hands,' Mrs Mount observed. 'We must get you some Pond's cream for those.' She turned Rose's hands over and back. 'But they are rather fine – nice delicate fingers. I think it's time I started teaching you to sew.'

'I can sew a little bit, ma'am,' Rose said. 'Darning and mending.'

'Ah – but that's bread and butter. What about the cream of sewing? Would you like to learn to do this?' She held up the frame with her good hand.

Rose nodded eagerly. And so her learning began, an education more valuable than she could ever have realized at the time. Mrs Mount began teaching her basic stitches – chain stitch, herringbone, blanket. Rose made a little sampler and Mrs Mount was impressed.

'You're a natural, my dear. You've such good control of the needle and a fine eye. I believe you have a flair for colour too. That's lovely work.'

Rose blushed with pleasure, and soon, as the days and weeks passed, they moved on to more elaborate stitches: threaded running stitch, lazy daisy, French knots. She made a little tea cloth with flowers embroidered at each corner. She was in love with the process of decorating the pristine white cloth. It felt like spring coming, colourful flowers breaking out everywhere. Mrs Mount kindly supplied her with some materials but she took to spending some of her wages on silks as well.

By the time a year had passed after Harry left, Mrs Mount said, 'You know, Rose, I shouldn't be surprised if you could sell your work – it really is quite something.'

And that was how it began: the little gift shop in Moseley she had found agreed to buy one of her cloths to try out and sell it on. Soon they were asking for more. She had an independent way of earning her own money, which, she realized, was what Mrs Mount had perhaps hoped all along.

But that year, 1917, two things happened. A letter arrived from one of Ernest Mount's fellow officers. He had been in the Tank Corps and was killed at Cambrai. The two of them were overwhelmed with grief, and Professor Mount always said afterwards, 'That was the end of my Hester.'

Quite soon after, just before Christmas, Rose was in the kitchen clearing up the dinner plates one day when she heard a cry from the front of the house. She knew it was the Professor and he sounded very distressed. As she rushed along the hall the door of their room opened. The Professor, wild-eyed and utterly distraught, reached out and grabbed Rose's arm.

'Hester – my girl – oh, look at her!'

Filled with dread Rose approached the couch. She could already see the strange way in which Mrs Mount was lying, somehow both slack and contorted at once. She lay slouched to one side, her white cap askew, staring dumbly up at them.

'Hester!' Professor Mount seized her hand, stroking it. 'Don't go, my dear, oh, do be all right, please don't leave me!'

It wrung Rose's heart to hear him and she was full of panic, not knowing what to do.

'Run for the doctor – Belle Walk, you remember, don't you?'

But by the time Rose had run back saying that the doctor was on his way, Mrs Mount had already slipped away. The Professor was sitting beside her, still holding her hand and reminiscing gently about when they were young together. His little face looked so sunken and bereft that Rose's tears came, and then he began to weep too and they sat together crying until the doctor arrived and officially pronounced Hester Mount dead.

After the funeral, Professor Mount said quaveringly to Rose, 'You won't leave me as well, will you, Rosie?'

All she could do was promise that she would stay.

After Mrs Mount's death, Rose was left alone with Professor Mount because Mrs Plummer, the cook, said it was ridiculous her being here working for such a small number of people and that Rose had learned everything that was needed; she was off to earn more money in another household.

So for that year Rose was Professor Mount's sole companion. He seldom had visitors. He was kind, she was paid well and treated decently. He gave her extra money of the little he had to buy embroidery materials – 'I like to see you doing that, my dear. It's homely and makes me think a bit that Hester is still with us' – and with Hester gone, the work was not very demanding.

But she was an eighteen-year-old girl and he a man in his late seventies. She saw scarcely anyone else except for occasional visits to Bessie, who now had five children and in a vague, overworked way was pleased to see her. Rose felt more and more lonely, stifled and desperate. Sometimes she would stand in her room looking out at the sky over the back of the house.

Am I always going to be here? she wondered. There

were so few men now after the carnage of the war. There didn't seem to be anything to look forward to, just more drudgery and the sad words of an old man talking to her about his wife. How was she ever going to meet anyone else like this, stuck in the house? The days seemed to crawl by. Sometimes she wept with desperation and longing for more of a life.

And then, in 1919 as the winter began to melt away and snowdrops appeared in the grass, he returned. As before he came to the back door, a rap of knuckles that took her by surprise. When she opened it, she did not recognize him at first. She saw a solidly built man, dark haired, much older looking than the boy she remembered. There was a thin scar on his face now, at the top of his left cheek, aslant beneath his eye. He was wearing a heavy, military-looking coat. Rose stared, trying to make sense of this.

'Rosie? It's me.'

He didn't smile, in fact he looked rather stern, forbidding almost. She took in that he had a long face, a pronounced chin and jaw. She hadn't remembered him quite like that. He was very much a man now, not a boy.

'Harry?'

Everything was crashing round her body, her blood, breath, everything, punching with shock, with excitement.

'You waited for me then?'

'Are you really back?' she asked stupidly. 'Truly?'

He grinned then and held out his arms. 'What's it look like?'

But they knew each other so little. After that first

embrace she didn't know what to say, except for, 'Well – d'you want a cup of tea?'

Within a month he had asked her to marry him and she accepted. She was radiant, excited. A new life – a real life, not living in the shadows here!

Professor Mount was shocked and upset at first. 'D'you mean you'll be leaving me after all, Rosie?' Then trying to be less selfish he was pleased for them, then put in his offer.

'How would it be if you took the first floor as your married quarters? Then you'd still have work and somewhere to live, as well as a husband?'

By the time they married, in May 1919, Rose's brother Peter, who had survived the war, had emigrated to Australia. Bessie and her children were the only relatives on her side when they got married in St Agnes church in Moseley. Harry's mom and dad came, and his brother. Though Rose had always got along all right with Harry's dad, she and his mother never took to one another. Rose found Mrs Southgate senior a jealous, suspicious-minded woman and kept out of her way as much as possible.

The rooms they were to have upstairs in Professor Mount's house were already furnished and there was not much they had to do except get them ready. There was even the bed, long abandoned by the Professor and his wife when she became ill. He still liked to sleep in the back sitting room – he didn't have to bother with stairs and it made him feel close to Hester, he said.

Looking back, the wedding night and what followed

had been a disaster. Rose had chosen at the time to tell herself it was all shyness and ignorance on her part. But she knew now that it had been something much deeper. She and Harry really barely knew one another and she had not given the realities of their physical relationship much thought.

She had managed to hold him off until the wedding night, even though he had tried hard to persuade her.

'Look, come on, Rosie – I'm desperate for yer. We're all but married, ain't we? I've waited long enough!'

'But I want to save it,' she'd said, barely even knowing what they were talking about. She imagined kisses and something warm and dreamy, not the peculiar, moist, embarrassing reality that it was.

Before they'd even got up to their room that night, he was at her on the stairs, hands fumbling for her breasts, then up her skirt.

'Don't!' she hissed, shocked. 'He'll hear us.'

'No 'e won't, deaf old bugger. Come on, Rosie, let's have yer!'

They had two candles in the big main bedroom that the Professor had bequeathed them. Harry had been taken aback by the room, which although old and faded was grander than any other room he'd ever slept in. But now it was not the room he was interested in. He wanted Rose naked and ready and he started to fling off his own clothes.

That was her first shock. It was not just the obvious strange reality of maleness, Harry's hungry manhood stiff and ready – which in itself was surprise enough. It was the sense of revulsion she felt towards him in general. In the candlelight she took in his neck which had become thick and bullish, the dark hairs on his arms and chest and at his groin, his thick arms and thighs;

even the way his hair was cut round his neck and forehead felt alien. She just wanted to run away and never come back.

'No . . .' She started to back towards the door. She was half undressed, still in her under-slip and stockings.

He took no notice. He came up to her, the smell of sweat on him overpowering, his body all hardness, his arms, chest, cock against her. It was no good struggling. They were married and he was entitled, and too aroused to hear her. He rubbed his hands over her breasts, hard, his eyes rolling back so that he looked as if he was in a trance.

'Get on the bed . . .'

He reached under her slip and pulled down her bloomers. She had to help so that he didn't tear everything, all the pretty clothes on which she had embroidered her initials so carefully in curling white letters – as if he would notice such a thing!

As he moved her to the bed and pushed her back, a cold terror seized her. Babies – this was how you made babies, wasn't it? And oh, God, she didn't want that – not what happened to Mom. Her mind was racing as he forced himself up inside her like a broom handle, something hard and foreign invading her body, and he wasn't looking at her, he was carried away with himself.

Rose let out whimpers of pain as he thrust urgently into her. She screwed her eyes tightly shut. *I don't want this*, she thought, deep in herself. Never ever, not with him, and not if it means babies. She felt no desire, hardly knew what desire was.

And so began the long battle of their marriage.

*

But now – when she thought of Arthur King ... Even the thought of him made her feel fluttery and breathless. And when he was actually there – the tenderness, the longing to touch and be touched was like nothing she had known before. She was possessed by it, so that she could hardly look at Harry or think of anything else.

Now, she had discovered desire.

Twenty-Five

It was still the school holidays and Freda Adams had come into her own.

She'd gathered her grandchildren round her when Aggie got back from Sawyer and Hewlett's and given them their marching orders. And a few days later she made another announcement.

'Once you lot are off to school, I'm going to work. I've talked them into putting me back on a press at Sawyer and Hewlett's. Mr Martin didn't believe I could do it, but once I'm set in position it'll be second nature. I could turn out them fasteners with my eyes shut.'

Aggie watched her grandmother, amazed. Nanna, going back to work in the factory! But there was no arguing. Nor with her orders about who was going to do everything round the house.

'It ain't just going to be Aggie,' she said. 'Not on her own – it's too much for her. You others are going to have to help, 'specially you, John, and not think it's above you to turn a mangle or sweep up.'

She dispensed orders about who was to do what. John was looking rather put out.

'It ain't no good putting on that long face, lad. You're the man of the house now and you do what needs to be done, like it or not.'

John scowled, looking down at his feet. But they

199

were grateful. Their father's absence seemed to echo round the house. Nanna somehow put things in order.

'Right – now you listen to me, all of yer. Things are hard at the moment, what with your father in the infirmary and none of us knowing how long he'll be there for. And your mother's poorly. You're a good bunch of kids and now you've got to rally round. I'll be here till school starts again, but while there ain't no school, you can put your backs into it. You girls – your job's carding. Aggie's collected the things from the factory and the more we do, the merrier. Aggie, Ann, you can get started – and John, you could have a go . . .'

'*Sewing!*' John turned pink in the face with outrage. 'I ain't doing that – that's *girls'* stuff and anyhow, I don't know what to do . . .' He got to his feet as if he was going to run off.

'All right,' Nanna said, unable to suppress a smile at the sight of him, her skinny, ginger-topped grandson in his baggy shorts, fit to burst with indignation. 'Well, you can find summat else to bring in a bob or two.'

John racked his brains for all his money-making schemes.

'I'll get some horse muck – and jam jars . . .' Pennies could be earned by collecting horse muck off the road and selling it to people with gardens, and by taking empty jars back to the shops. 'And fag ends!' he added as final inspiration.

'Well, that's a start . . .'

'And Silas can help and I could get our Dad's barrow and take the stuff to Auntie's . . .'

John had collected his father's barrow and it was stored out the back. It would have been ideal for collecting neighbours' bundles to take for pawn every week and be paid for his troubles. But there was a problem.

'Ooh, I don't think you'd better start on that,' Freda said. 'Old Edna Hawkins has been at it for years – she'll be after you with the poker if you start working on her patch. You stick to your other schemes, John. And Aggie –'

Aggie jumped as her grandmother suddenly turned her attention on her.

'We've got to do summat about those flaming boots. You can't go about in them, like that!'

Aggie's rubber boots had split all along the bottom on the outer side of the left foot. They didn't even keep the wet out and although it was spring, her feet were burning with chilblains. She spent her life pretending to herself that her feet did not exist. But she knew what Nanna had in mind. It'd be another pair of charity boots, the leather as hard as anything, chafing the skin round her ankles. All the rubs in the world with tallow fat only made a bit of difference. The thought of more boots made her feel even sadder. Nothing like the beautiful shoes she dreamed of in her mind's eye, like Mata Hari's. Or red and sparkly, with a strap and a delicate heel.

The next morning, Mom was having one of her bad days.

'I knew I should never've gone up the shops for so long yesterday,' she groaned, after another bout of retching. 'I knew I'd pay for it.'

Aggie's spirits sank. She had thought maybe that yesterday was the start of Mom getting better, but today she was even worse, sallow and sick and so weak that she could barely stand. She sank down in the kitchen, face twisted with nausea.

'I've got to admit, Mom,' she said to Nanny Adams, 'I don't know where we'd be without you. At least it ain't the winter.'

Winter implied another range of chores like unfreezing the scullery tap and helping Mrs Larkin next door with a bucket or two of water as well as making sure the lavatories could be flushed if the pipes were frozen. They all had to help with that. But now the warmer weather was coming.

The others had gone out about their various businesses. Every spare moment they had they spent carding, sewing a dozen hooks and eyes on to a piece of card ready to be sold in the shops. It was fiddly work and hard to see at night in the light from the gas mantle. By the time they had finished last night Aggie's eyes had been red and stinging with tiredness. But even Nanna did it with her twisted hands. They all sat round the table, Aggie and Ann who they taught to do it, and Nanna and Mom, when she was up to it.

Now though, Aggie knew it was almost time to start on the dinners. May was occupied for the moment, running her hands through the box of hooks and eyes which, it seemed to Aggie, never appeared to go down, no matter how many they sewed.

She crept to the front window and pulled the curtain aside enough to see out. *Agnes Green: Spy* . . . A lot of children were playing out. She could see the brothers who had tried the knock-knock trick on Phyllis Taylor's door pushing a contraption along, an orange crate with some wheels fixed roughly underneath. The street was busy and she watched people walking back and fro.

A familiar pair of figures came into focus, walking towards the house. Aggie felt an inner leap of excitement. Mrs Southgate and Lily! She was still living on the memory of last Sunday's visit. When the blind man was playing the piano and they were all singing in the cosy room, with Mrs Southgate's pretty face looking so happy, Aggie thought she'd died and gone to heaven.

She watched carefully. Mrs Southgate was carrying a cloth bag – and she was coming to their door.

'Mom!' Aggie ran to the back. 'It's Mrs Southgate!'

The knocking came then.

Mom was still at the table, her head in her hands. 'Oh, Lord love us – what does *that one* want?'

Twenty-Six

'You open the door, Aggie,' Nanna said, so she hurried to do it.

As she opened the door a little way and peeped out, she saw Mrs Southgate in her hat and coat, looking nervously at her.

'Hello, Aggie – is your mother there?'

'She said for me to see who it is,' Aggie told her.

'Well –' Mrs Southgate was holding up the bag and seeming about to explain when Aggie heard her grandmother limping up behind her.

'Out of the way, wench – what does she want?'

Nanna pushed the door further open and stood on the step with her hands on her hips, a fearsome, stout figure with a thick apron over her black dress. Aggie thought Nanna seemed younger all of a sudden.

'Good morning,' Rose Southgate said. 'I was only wondering if – well, I've got these parsnips, you see. My brother-in-law grows them and he had some over. I've had all I want. And—'

'That's good of yer, ta,' Nanna said. 'If you can spare 'em.' Her face softened a little. Most people's faces seemed to soften at the sight of Rose and Lily, Aggie noticed.

Rose hesitated. 'How is Mr Green? Is there any news?'

'Not to speak of,' Nanna said. 'He's going along – in the infirmary.'

Rose nodded. 'The thing is, when I came the other day, I asked your daughter – Mrs Green – whether I could be of any help, what with her being poorly . . . I'd be happy to give you a hand. And I brought something else – for Aggie. Only I don't want to cause any trouble . . .'

Standing behind her grandmother's substantial body, Aggie began to feel excited. What had Mrs Southgate brought for her? Had she heard right?

'Well, it's true, Jen's feeling very poorly today. And I'm none too quick on my feet . . .'

'I'd be glad of the company to tell you the truth,' Rose said. 'With it just being me and Lily at home – it's company for her as well.'

'All right. I've got plenty to get done – you'd better come in.'

Aggie ran ahead of them. 'Mom –' she said in warning.

Jen Green looked up to see her mother leading Rose Southgate into her back room. A look of dismay passed over her face, but Freda said, 'It ain't no good looking like that. Mrs Southgate's come to help and you ain't in a fit state to do a thing.'

'It's nice to have some company,' Rose assured her, anxious to please. 'I'm happy to help.'

Aggie could see that her mother would soon be on the point of having to be sick again. She leaned forwards with a groan.

'You go up and have a lie-down while you can, bab,' Freda commanded her.

'Thanks,' Jen muttered and passed out of the room looking terrible.

'Poor thing,' Rose Southgate said. 'Is she always like that? I suppose I didn't have it too bad with Lily.'

'I've never seen her take so bad with it before,' Nanna said. She was rummaging in the bottom of the cupboard for potatoes. 'Those parsnips'll do nicely. It could be twins, I reckon.'

Rose gasped. 'Oh – d'you really think so?'

Nanna shrugged. 'Well, it does happen.'

Rose turned to Aggie, seeing her waiting on pins to know what was in the other brown paper bag.

'Here you are, dear. I found these for you. I hope they fit and you, and,' she turned to Nanna, 'that you won't mind?'

Almost reverently, Aggie took the bag. It felt quite heavy. Ann and May were all agog as well and tried to peep in. Aggie hugged the present to her chest, sparks of excitement lighting in her. It was a pair of shoes! Could it be pretty red ones – *could* it?

When she pulled them out, the shoes were brown, sturdy leather with laces, and obviously not new. Aggie stared at them, having to adjust to them not being the lovely shoes of her dreams. She stared at them, her excitement dying a bit.

'Your feet have been looking so sore, dear,' Rose said. 'And I knew how busy your mother and Mrs Adams were so I thought these might help – to tide you over, sort of thing. I gave them a little polish for you. Oh – and there's a little pair of socks in the bag as well.'

'Well, say thank you,' Nanna said, looking very pleased.

Aggie sat on the floor and pulled the socks and shoes on. They were in quite reasonable condition and gleaming with polish. Though they were on the big side they were well worn in and surprisingly comfortable. It was

206

a treat to have socks on too and her feet suddenly felt a good deal more content. They looked so much better too! The dream of red glittery shoes faded and she looked up, smiling.

'Thank you, Mrs Southgate. They fit ever so well.'

'Very good of you,' Nanna said. 'She could do with 'em, that's for sure. I don't know how we can repay you, though.'

Rose beamed, seeming really happy to have pleased everyone. 'It's nothing,' she said. 'I just saw them and thought of Aggie. I hope they'll be comfortable, dear. Now – what needs to be done?'

Aggie sat on a chair with May on her lap and Lily beside her and they watched as her grandmother and Rose Southgate cooked the stew for the dinners. Ann got bored and drifted off outside in a world of her own. Around midday, there would be a string of knocks at the door as the men came, handed over their couple of bob and went off with a hot dinner sandwiched between two plates and wrapped in newspaper. Aggie often helped to wrap the warm parcels of plates, which would be brought back later empty.

Nanna sat herself down on a chair and it was Rose Southgate who nipped about the place, fetching and carrying and helping chop and stir. She seemed very content to be there.

'I could come most days – any time you like,' she said.

Nanna looked up at her. 'Ain't you got enough to do, then?'

'I've got my own house to keep, of course,' Rose said. She was peeling one of the parsnips she had brought. 'But I'm very quick at it. I suppose I'm just a fast worker – and I used to be in service, you see.'

'Did you? I'd never've thought it,' Freda Adams said.

Rose laughed. 'Why not?'

Freda looked at her, in a considering way. 'Now you say it, I don't know. I s'pose I saw you as a bit of a lady – too good for service, for being someone's skivvy. Is that where you was till you married?'

Rose paused for a moment to push her hair back with her arm.

'And after. We only came here a year ago after the man died who I worked for and the house was sold. The old man – he was Professor Mount, a very clever person, and a widower. I'd been there years and he let us live upstairs and carry on working for him.'

'Oh, I see,' Nanna said.

'His wife, Mrs Mount, before she died, she taught me to embroider a bit. So I make a little bit of money selling things I make.' She turned to the girls. 'I could teach your Aggie if you like. Then she'd always be able to make a little bit, when she needed to. If she takes to it, that is.'

Aggie bounced with excitement. 'Oh, yes – can I, Nanna?'

Her grandmother looked hesitant. 'We've nothing to give yer, what with him being taken bad . . .'

'No, that's all right. I've got some spare bits and pieces. It doesn't need to be anything fancy at the beginning, just learning the stitches. I'll teach Lily as well.'

'Well – if you're happy with the idea,' Nanna said, smiling suddenly, 'that'd be nice, wouldn't it, Aggie? That's very good of you, Mrs Southgate. I used to be able to sew quite well – but now look at me.' She held out her swollen-knuckled hands.

Rose looked pained. 'They look like hard-working hands.'

'Ar – they've been that all right,' Nanna said. She did not mention that they were about to be again.

But she found herself telling Rose Southgate something about her life. Aggie sat listening, keeping very still, as they seemed to have forgotten the children were there. Nanna talked about her Sidney. 'He died in an accident,' she said, not divulging the whole truth to Mrs Southgate, that Aggie's grandfather took his own life. She talked about the struggle to bring up her four children alone and Rose looked very sympathetic and said she'd lost her mother young and how their father had not been able to manage and how her sister had been given away . . .

And suddenly without warning she was weeping over the vegetables, tears running down her smooth cheeks. She reached into her sleeve for a handkerchief.

'Oh, I'm sorry! I never meant to do that. I've barely even thought about little Maud for years but talking about it brought it all back.'

'That's a terrible thing,' Nanna said and she struggled to her feet. 'Come on – let's brew up a cuppa. We could all do with one now. You dry your eyes, bab, and we'll try and think about summat more cheerful.'

By the time the dinners had all been handed out, Rose and Freda Adams were getting along very well.

'I must be off now and get a bit of dinner for me and Lily,' Rose said. 'But I'd be happy to help any day if

Mrs Green's not well. It's been nice.' She spoke shyly. 'Nice to be in a proper family, I mean.'

Then she turned to Aggie. 'If you like, you could bring May over again on Sunday. I think Mrs Wood might be coming again and she could play for us.'

Aggie looked at her grandmother. 'What about Sunday school?'

But Rose had thought of that. 'If you don't want to miss it, you could come along afterwards, couldn't you?'

'Well, if you're sure,' Freda Adams said.

'Can I, Nanna?' Aggie said. 'If I take May?'

'Your little friend, Babs, isn't it? She could come too if you like,' Rose said. 'And one of these days we'll start on that sewing, all right?'

Aggie could feel herself prickling with excitement. How she loved Mrs Southgate! When she was grown up with a house of her own, she was going to fill it with children and feed them all cake.

'Well,' Freda Adams said. 'I don't see why not.'

Rose and Lily walked the two doors back to their own house. Rose was in a good mood, with a warm sense of satisfaction. It was true what she said to Freda Adams – it *was* good to be in a proper family. Her own household never felt like that. Old Mrs Adams had a reassuring, motherly way with her that Rose craved, having lost her own mother. And she had felt able to be helpful to poor Jen, with all her babies. Maybe Jen would feel a bit more friendly herself too, one day. She could see that it was pride that made Jen the way she was. And Rose, for all her prettiness, was not well practised in making friends. She had spent too many years in isolation with the Mounts to be used to it.

And it had been good to be in company because while she was alone with Lily, her mind was flooded with one thought – Arthur King. At least this morning had taken her mind off it a bit, pleasurable as it was, the gnawing, prickling hunger that filled her day after day, and the anxiety that accompanied it. Her thoughts were overwhelmed by this man. She saw his face everywhere, heard his voice. What on earth was she doing? Why could she not keep her feelings under control?

Twenty-Seven

The following day, Rose found a little note that had come through the front door. She was sweeping the hall when she saw it and stood her broom by the wall, bending to pick it up, her heart quickening.

Opening it, she saw handwriting that she did not recognize. It was looping, neat, but wayward on the page, the lines diverging away from each other. The address at the top was in Oldfield Road:

> Mrs Southgate – it has only occurred to me now
> that this Sunday is Easter Day and that you may not
> have thought of this when you kindly invited me to
> tea. I wondered if you might prefer to postpone for
> a week – much as I should be disappointed! But of
> course that would be quite all right and still leave
> something to look forward to if the following
> Sunday were more convenient.
>   Yours sincerely,
>   Arthur King

Rose clasped the note to her chest, her heart pounding. Of course she had forgotten about Easter as well. She could make something special – a simnel cake, perhaps?

She went into the parlour to find something to write with, then stopped, staring into the cheerless fireplace.

Would Harry decide to stay at home as it was Easter? It seemed very unlikely – she was scarcely able to interest him in Christmas festivities, let alone any other date in the church calendar. She had better check, though, just in case.

But he wouldn't be home until later – he was finishing off a job in Acocks Green. And she was burning to reply to Arthur's note now, would not be able to settle to anything else until she had done so.

'What're you doing, Mom?' Lily asked, as Rose sat to write. She could only find a pencil, but that would have to do.

'Nothing,' she snapped, jarred by the child's intrusion into her thoughts. 'Nothing you need to know about anyway. Go and find something to do for a few minutes.'

Lily went away quietly, looking glum. Rose tutted. There was never a moment's peace! Poised to start writing, she remembered that Arthur had said that his landlady had to read his post to him. She must be careful what she said. She wrote a polite note saying that she was almost sure that his coming on Sunday would be perfectly all right, and that if there was any problem she would let him know as soon as possible.

She managed to find an envelope, addressed it and sealed her note into it. She thought for a moment, then went and opened the front door and looked along the street.

It was wet again, a mizzling rain, and a lot of the youngsters were outside. She could see the younger Green children in a cluster, the two little lads, whose names she could not remember, with a bucket, looking as if they were setting off to scout for something, and their sister, Ann, tagging along with them, looking miserable.

213

'Ann?' she called as they came near.

The girl came to her, looking worried instead now, gripping the edge of her grubby cardigan.

'It's all right, dear. Is your sister Aggie about?'

''Er's indoors,' Ann said, wringing the right side of her cardigan between her hands. She seemed unable to stand still. She was like Aggie, with her carroty hair, only paler and somehow less well defined. 'Shall I get her?'

'If you could, please,' Rose said.

Ann looked doubtfully at her, then went to her house. A moment later, Aggie appeared, stepping along proudly in her new shoes. They did look better, Rose thought gladly. They'd cost her half a crown in the pawnshop, but it was worth it, the poor child.

'Aggie – would you like to earn yourself a twopenny piece?'

Aggie nodded eagerly.

'All right – well, I've got a little note to be delivered. Tell your mother where you're going. You'll need to go out along the Ladypool Road . . .' She gave directions and Aggie set off happily, glad to earn some money.

Harry, as Rose expected, had no intention of staying in and missing his fishing on Sunday, Easter or no Easter. This week she greeted his hobby with more enthusiasm than usual.

'The days are drawing out now,' she said. 'That'll be nice – you won't have to cut it so short, will you?'

'No – nor freeze my arse off neither,' he said, peering at some intricate piece of fishing tackle in his hand.

'Harry!' she scolded. 'Must you be so coarse in front of Lily?'

'Harry,' he mimicked her in a silly voice, tutting and mocking.

Rose bit her lip and turned away. Say nothing – what did it matter anyway? He was going out, that was the main thing. And soon, very soon, she was going to see Arthur King. These days, that seemed to be the only thing that did matter.

She baked the cake with great care, and by the Sunday, she had spread a thin layer of marzipan on to the top and rolled the remainder into little balls to place round the edge as traditional. She could remember her mother doing it, at the right season. While she was laying out the teacups, Lily asked, 'Is the man coming?'

Rose felt a chill go through her. She went tight and angry inside. What if one day the child said something carelessly in front of her father? It would ruin everything. She bent over her daughter, trying not to sound as tense as she felt.

'He might come, Lily. But Mrs Wood might come instead – I'm not sure. Now you will remember, we don't need to talk about the man ever, do we? Especially not when Daddy's at home?'

Lily eyed her cautiously. She could sense the wound-up mood her mother was in.

'D'you understand, Lily?' She spoke more sternly than usual and Lily's eyes filled with tears. She nodded.

Guilt surged through Rose then. 'Oh, look, it's all right, babby – come to Mommy.' She hugged her. 'Don't you worry. It's just better if Daddy doesn't know, that's all. You know how cross he gets sometimes. Now – never mind about that. D'you know who else is coming, for you to play with? Aggie and May and maybe their friend Babs – after they come back from Sunday school. That'll be nice, won't it?' Lily brightened up a little.

Rose knew this was wrong, all of it, but she couldn't seem to help herself.

He came very punctually at three o'clock, by which time Rose was in a total state of nerves. She leapt up at the sound of his knock, almost overturning the chair in the back room. She had a good fire burning at the front to make the parlour cosy.

Opening the door, she was struck once again by the fact that her sight revealed him to her in a way that was not possible for him. She took him in, neatly dressed, hesitant in his step and with something tucked under his arm. He smiled in her general direction, that lovely face of his, she thought. She felt a grief that he could not see her.

'A blessed Eastertide,' he said.

'Oh, yes, and to you too,' she said, glancing along the street. 'Come in, do. It's very nice to see you.'

Then she felt that was tactless and tried to apologize but he laughed it off.

'It's a figure of speech,' he said, taking his hat off. His hair had grown a little. 'I could say, "Good to hear you," which would be true. You have a very lovely voice.'

'Oh,' Rose said, thrilled by this. 'Well, that's nice of you. Shall I take your coat?'

'I brought this –' He held out the shallow, oblong box he was carrying. 'I thought Lily and her little pals might like it.'

Rose took it, seeing that it was a game of Ludo.

'My mother passed it on – I used to play with my sisters.'

'How lovely – look, Lily! We can show you how to play once Aggie gets here.'

Lily looked pleased, and took the box over on to the floor to look inside. Rose took Arthur's coat and hat from him, her pulse racing as they stood close. How she longed to reach up and stroke his cheek! It was because he was blind, she realized. They could not speak to each other with their eyes.

'Here –' She took his arm and led him to the chair. 'I've left everything in the same place, look . . . I mean . . .' Again she stuttered into confusion.

'That's good – I'm beginning to learn my way round. It doesn't take too long. I find I get quicker at it – like a sort of inner eye.'

'It's hard to think of it,' she said, hanging his coat on the back of the door. 'When you don't need to. But I'm learning.'

'Nice of you to try,' he said sweetly.

She made tea and came back in to find him holding out his hands towards the fire.

'It's a nice cosy room this,' he said. 'I get the feel of it, even without being able to see.'

'It is,' she said. 'I've got the curtains closed already – to keep the heat in.'

They drank tea together and he was very enthusiastic about her cake. Lily was still absorbed in the little counters and dice out of the Ludo box. Arthur asked Rose, gently, about her family. Rose told him what had happened to them.

'I suppose it was my mother who held us all together. Once she had gone – well, we scattered. My brother Peter emigrated after the war, to Australia. Bessie's still here, she's my only family really, though I don't see much of her now. I've never seen Maud since.'

'How dreadfully sad,' Arthur said. 'Should you want to see her, d'you think?'

'I don't know.' Rose sat forward, saucer on her knees, warming her hands on her teacup. 'Sometimes I'd just like to know what happened to her, to see that she's all right. She was such a little poppet. But she wouldn't know us – she was very young when the lady took her. I think it might just disturb things, for all of us.'

'That sounds wise,' he said. 'But I can see that you must wonder.'

She described the Mounts' house to him, but of course did not mention Harry. It seemed so natural and effortless to write Harry out, as though she were in a different life suddenly, where he no longer existed. She wondered at herself even as she did it.

She asked him about his own family. Arthur described a rather genteel upbringing: his family still lived in Solihull.

'There's just me and my two sisters, Edith and Connie. Thank heavens. That's how I look at it now. To have sons was really a curse in our parents' generation. I have – well, had – a school pal, George Sanders. He was one of five boys – after that lot there's only one left, Dickie, and he didn't fight because he was too young.' He shook his head, his face pained. 'I tend to remind myself of them, rather often, when I'm falling about over chairs or almost getting run down by a tram. I am still here, pretty much in one piece except for this.' He raised a hand to his face. 'Anyway, both my sisters are married and keeping my mother busy.'

'What are they like?' Rose asked. 'Do you look alike?'

'Oh, well, Edith and I are alike – Dad's curly hair. Conn, she's out of another drawer altogether – and bossy!' He sucked his breath in, shaking his head humorously. 'Oh, dear, oh, dear . . .'

Rose laughed. 'My sister Bessie's like that. Like a flaming sergeant major . . .'

'Ah, well, Connie's almost reached the lieutenant colonel's rank in terms of giving orders.'

They talked and laughed easily together. After a time Rose heard a timid knocking and let Aggie in, with May and Babs.

Once the children were settled by the fire with cake and the game, Rose said, 'I hope you'll play for us later, Mr King?'

'Arthur, please,' he said, seeming taken aback. He turned as she came and sat down again, as if still in the habit of glancing round, even though he could not see. Then he turned back to the fire. The children were laughing, but for a moment Rose and Arthur sat still and quiet.

'You know,' he said softly after a few moments. 'It means more to me than I can say, being able to come and visit you like this. To be able to walk here and be in such nice company.'

'Oh,' Rose said, feeling her cheeks burn. 'It . . . It means an awful lot to me too. I don't get many visitors. Do you see your family?'

'Now and again. They're all with Edith and her children today. I usually feel a bit of a spare part, to tell you the truth. Everyone tiptoeing round about my sight and acting rather breezily as if nothing has happened.'

She felt for him, seeing how the blindness must lock you inside yourself. 'It must be ever so difficult,' she said.

'It is. Well, can be. It's claustrophobic, especially at first. Like being shut in a box. It's another way of experiencing the world, certainly. You have to learn all about touch and smell, sounds, atmospheres – they all start to become sharper. And of course, with all the carnage that happened to others, one doesn't feel right complaining.' He gave a rueful smile. 'It's hard for other people to enter into it. But it only takes someone like yourself to take a bit of trouble to understand, and it makes all the difference.'

Still facing towards the fire, slowly, cautiously, he reached out his right hand to her. Rose's heart lurched. She was so moved by him, so longed to touch him, to hold him. Glancing at Lily, to see that her daughter was not watching, she reached out and their fingertips touched. He clasped her hand then, with strong fingers.

'Thank you,' he said, as if she had spoken. She realized that with her hand, she had.

'Come through to the back,' she said. 'I'll put the kettle on for some more tea.'

He stood with his fingertips touching the edge of the table while she filled the kettle and set it on to boil. He faced straight ahead as if listening, getting the feel of the room.

'It's all very small,' she said. 'But it does us.'

She saw Harry's cap hanging on the back door and glanced anxiously at Arthur for a moment, then realized she was being foolish. He would never see it. She stepped round and stood in front of him.

'Arthur,' she said softly.

He reached his hands out, his face tenderly hopeful,

and she stepped into his arms, putting her hands on his shoulders.

'Oh, you're lovely,' he breathed.

'I might not be,' she teased. 'I might have a face like the back of a tram.'

'But I don't think you have. I expect you're beautiful. You *sound* it.' He reached for her face, felt her features and her strong, thick hair.

'What colour is it?' he asked.

'Blonde – very light. Lily's is the same. Grey eyes – blue-grey.'

He ran the side of his thumb down her cheek.

'You're lovely – I can feel you are.'

She was full of trembling, longing emotion. Reaching up she stroked his face at last, and when she saw tears begin to run down his cheeks, her own emotions twisted and spilled and she was weeping too.

They drew each other close and stood holding on for comfort, and she loved the feel, the smell of him, this gentle man. It was if she had come home.

Twenty-Eight

Phyllis and all her brood went to church on Easter morning. There had been a few warm days in the week before, but the overcast weather had returned and they were wrapped up warm again.

'Well, that's no bad thing,' Phyllis observed, peering up at the sky. 'Get your coats on, all of you. Wrap up well – you feel the cold, and don't you forget it.'

'Oh, not again,' Rachel muttered. 'We'll be flaming stifled. It's bad enough getting fat.' She pinched her midriff with distaste. Phyllis was feeding them all up like turkey cocks.

Phyllis opened the front door to leave and found Charles already waiting out there, standing stiffly, facing away down the street as if disowning them all. He had a cold and a sore nose, and looked generally miserable.

'You go on ahead if you want,' Phyllis instructed him. And Charles was off as if sprung from a trap, desperate to be away from his sisters and all their alarming physicality.

Phyllis looked cautiously both ways along the street.

'What's the matter, Mom?' Rachel said with daring sarcasm. 'They're not going to come and arrest Dolly, are they? Not for that.'

'Oh, stop it, Rachel!' Susanna said crossly, adjusting her hat. She wanted to look her best for David, her fiancé, who would be at the service.

'Enough of your lip,' Phyllis said.

She had been full of unease ever since she ran into Ethel Sharp, expecting constantly that she would turn up again. But the girls didn't need to know anything about Ethel and her foul ways. Or anything else about her past for that matter. James had offered her a new life, and she'd seized it with both hands. Nothing was going to drag all that out again. That part of her was dead and buried.

But ever since she had seen Ethel, things she had long hidden away had been roused in her mind. Terrible images kept flashing across her memory.

'Come on – we'll be late.' She adjusted Dolly's collar, then ran her hand down her daughter's front. Her hand paused over her belly.

'Mom!' Dolly protested.

'Not much to show – but there soon will be.'

'Thanks,' Dolly said bitterly. 'For reminding me.'

'Come on,' Susanna urged. 'Or we'll be late.'

Phyllis revelled in the walk to church, which was a bit of a step away on the Moseley Road. The Taylors made a fine sight, and Phyllis knew it. There was she, massive and handsome, and her three girls were all good-looking in their varied ways, Susanna stately and straight backed like her father, Rachel splendidly curvaceous and dark haired in Phyllis's mould, and Dolly an even prettier version of her.

Phyllis nodded grandly to people along Lilac Street and called out a greeting. Dorrie Davis, scurrying along to the Mission Hall where she sometimes played the piano, twisted her sour face into something that was meant to be a smile and hurried on in her flat old shoes.

Sour bitch, Phyllis thought.

'She stared at me,' Dolly hissed at Rachel. 'I'm sure

she knows – she's guessed. If she finds out, we're done for – the whole flaming neighbourhood'll know in five minutes!'

Phyllis turned and glared her into silence as Rachel hissed, '*Button it*, Dolly.'

Susanna was walking slightly ahead, in a world of her own as if she, like Charles, wanted to pretend they didn't exist. Phyllis looked proudly at her. She'd turned into a fine woman and no mistake. There was her wedding coming up next year and a grand occasion it was going to be. A lot was at stake.

Old Mary Crewe appeared then, lumbering along in her usual distracted fashion, puffing away on her cigarette. The forefinger and thumb of her right hand were canary yellow. Every time she saw Mary Crewe, Phyllis felt a mix of pity and horror. *That could have been me*, she thought. *Could easily.* She had pulled herself out, struck lucky meeting James that night, the way she had, and she had looks on her side. But had things gone differently . . .

'Morning, Mary,' she said kindly.

'Damn you!' Mary said with some energy, clutching her bundle tighter. 'Damn and bugger you!' she continued on, muttering. Dolly giggled. Phyllis turned on her.

'Don't you *dare* laugh, you little madam! She'll've been like you once – young and foolish. And don't you ever forget it. Some mothers would've put you out, my girl – I might yet if you don't watch your step!'

Dolly at least had the grace to look sorry for laughing.

At the bottom of the street she met Dulcie Skinner coming out of the entry into the Mansions. Ignoring Dulcie's wry expression at the sight of her and her

224

extravagant hat, Phyllis boomed out, 'Morning, Mrs Skinner – a happy Easter to you!'

She stopped, wanting to make the most of this opportunity.

'Oh,' Dulcie said vaguely. 'Happy Easter, Mrs Taylor. Off to church, are yer?'

'Oh, yes, of course,' Phyllis said in her most refined voice. 'My Charles has gone on ahead – he has responsibilities as a lay preacher, you know. And Susanna is going to meet her fiancé there – a *very* nice lad. Aren't you, Susanna?'

Blushing, Susanna quietly agreed that she was. The other girls looked away and fidgeted.

Dulcie folded her arms. 'Oh?' she said, lips twitching a little.

'Yes,' Phyllis gushed. 'He's doing *very* nicely at Edwards' Drapers – *very nicely indeed.*'

'Oh, that's *nice*,' Dulcie said insincerely.

'Well, we must get along,' Phyllis said merrily. 'We do stand out rather if we all come in late!'

Quite oblivious to Dulcie rolling her eyes and muttering, 'Oh, he's doing *very* nicely, oh, kiss my backside,' behind her, Phyllis sailed off past the Mansions and round the corner.

One of her greatest pleasures was making an appearance at church: the five of them all along one pew not too far from the front, she resplendent in her Sunday hat. She had on her best one of all today, her Easter bonnet, a straw hat lavishly dolled up with flowers and a striking artificial bird she had found in the market with vivid green feathers. She liked to make a splash among all these dutiful, colourless little church mice. After all, she was the widow of James Taylor, who had been a much respected lay preacher in the congregation.

225

When James preached, she used to sit watching her man as he stood, tall and passionate, up at the front and she would be fit to burst with pride. She also knew she was the most striking woman in the congregation by far. If anyone thought her vulgar they would be far too polite to say so. And she had a strong, loud voice which could soar on the rousing hymns. Did she believe in it all, the words she was belting out? James certainly did but Phyllis seldom gave it much thought. Being a Methodist had brought her to where she was, with a certain standing, that was what mattered. In fact it was everything.

Twenty-Nine

'Right,' Mom ordered them all when they reached the church's pillared entrance. 'Smile – this is a happy day, remember. The Lord is risen.'

In the middle of the service, just after they'd blasted out 'Hail the Day that sees Him rise!' at a rousing volume, Dolly felt very hot and sick, lights danced at the edges of her eyes and during the following prayer, blackness came down over her. She crumpled, landing half on the seat and falling forwards, slumping over the back of the row in front.

The next thing she knew, she was being held up in her seat by Susanna and Rachel on each side of her.

'Dolly?' Susanna nudged her.

'Let me get out of here,' Dolly begged queasily. All she wanted was to lie down somewhere cool. The room was swimming round.

With all the eyes of the congregation swivelling towards them – the minister was already in the pulpit waiting to preach – the three of them stood up. As they squeezed past Mom, Dolly saw her making fierce faces at them which meant, *Stop attracting attention to yourselves* . . . But it couldn't be helped. Dolly was desperate to get out and afraid she might be sick there in the church.

'Oh, *Dolly*!' Susanna erupted as Dolly sank groggily on to the steps. It was such a relief to be outside.

'Sorry,' she muttered, head down. 'I didn't feel it coming on. It just all went dark suddenly. Ugh – I feel horrible.'

'I expect it's your condition,' Rachel remarked unsympathetically.

'Rachel!' Dolly heard her sisters bickering in hissing whispers over her head. 'For heaven's sake keep quiet.'

'You're just worried that David'll find out,' Rachel said.

'Well, of *course* I am! What the hell would his family think?'

Dolly, feeling sick and guilty, started to cry. 'I never meant for it to happen. You know I didn't. And now it feels as if everyone's staring at me and thinking I'm ... I'm dirty and loose ...'

To her surprise, Rachel softened, and Dolly felt her sister's arm round her shoulders. 'The one who wants seeing to is the dirty man who did this to you – it's not your fault, sis.'

'Well, not much anyway,' Susanna said impatiently. 'Going out on the streets at night ...'

'Stop it, Suz!' Rachel's voice rose a bit too high. They all froze. They could just hear the minister's voice now, rising and falling inside. 'Look, you stay here and see David – come back with Mom. I'll take Dolly home in a bit. You don't look too good.' She squeezed Dolly's shoulders.

'I don't feel it,' Dolly said. 'I feel really sick. I wish I could have a drink of water.'

But there was none to be had.

Susanna went back in to join their mother and when Dolly had recovered a little, Rachel helped her make her way home. It was a nice feeling, Rachel being kind.

'I'm really scared,' Dolly confided in her as they

went along. 'I don't want a babby, Rach. What am I s'posed to do with one at my age? I'll be chained to it for life then. But what if I tried to get rid of it . . . ?' She shuddered. 'Mom'd kill me. I don't think I could go through with it in any case.'

Rachel nodded. You heard stories, truly horrible ones.

'You will be with me, won't you, sis?' Dolly looked into Rachel's lovely dark eyes. 'I'm so scared, I can't sleep at night thinking about it. I don't know . . .' She spoke in a small voice. 'I don't know what's going to happen. And Mom keeps saying all these odd things . . .'

'I know,' Rachel said. 'I mean, who's this Nancy she was talking about? I kept asking and she clammed up, said we'd know soon enough.'

'She said she's her sister,' Dolly said. 'But where's she been all this time? Why didn't we know about her?'

'I think,' Rachel said, 'after dinner, we'd better get Mom to tell us exactly what she's got in mind.'

They were walking along the Moseley Road, talking over their troubles, when a stooped, scruffy figure who had been moving towards them stopped in their path.

'You look a pair of nice young ladies,' she said in a gravelly, insinuating voice. Dolly saw a face looking at them which it would have been hard to put an age to. The woman's hair, lank stuff hanging out around her hat, was of a sickly, greyish yellow colour. Her teeth, the few remaining, were brownish, and she peered at them through narrow, calculating eyes.

'Where do you two young lovelies live them, eh?'

She reached out a hand and gripped Rachel's forearm tightly.

'What d'you want to know for?' Rachel said. Dolly could see her shuddering, trying to pull her arm away.

'What're you doing?' The woman was staring horribly at her.

'You have a certain look about you,' she said. Her mind seemed to drift for a moment and she looked away. Then she went on, 'I'm looking for someone and you look the sort of nice young ladies who could 'elp me. No one else's given me what I want yet.'

'Get off my sister,' Dolly said sharply. She felt panicky. The woman looked a bad lot and even worse was the stink of her, a ripe mixture of long-unwashed clothing and drink.

'I'm looking for a lady by the name of Hetty – used to be Hetty Barker – lives round 'ere somewhere if I ain't mistook. Would you know anyone called Hetty?'

'No,' Rachel said truthfully. 'We don't. Now let go of me, please!'

'Can you spare a penny or two, you pretty young ladies?' the woman whined. 'Or a tanner if you've got it . . .'

'No!' Rachel said, pulling away abruptly. 'We've no money on us. Just leave us alone, please. Come on, Dolly.'

Dolly followed gladly and the woman slid away, cursing.

'Wants locking up, she does,' Rachel said crossly, rubbing her arm. 'Nasty slimy thing. What's she want to go asking us for? The woman could be anywhere, whoever she is.'

The girls cleared the meal away. Phyllis had had a nice joint of beef cooking slowly all morning and a mountainous number of potatoes. Dolly was looking a good deal better now she had some food inside her. She and

Rachel forgot about their encounter on the Moseley Road for the moment and over dinner they talked about church gossip and this and that.

'Mom,' Rachel said as they were clearing away. Rachel always seemed to be the one who had to voice things that no one else particularly wanted to. 'Look – what happened this morning . . . Dolly's scared – and the rest of us . . . I mean, what're we going to do?'

'Right,' Phyllis said. Any day now Dolly was going to start showing. She was four months gone already. 'Fill the teapot, Rachel, and while we have a cuppa, I'll tell you. I've said nothing before because the less said the fewer tongues will wag. No, Charles – it's no good thinking you can just disappear. You're part of this family too.'

'But what am I supposed to do?' he shrugged, sitting down again. During the service he had sat stiffly beside one of the other lay preachers, trying to look as if all the females of his family were people he'd never seen before. 'It's nothing to do with me. I didn't get her into the mess she's in and it's . . . Well, it's women's business.'

'No –' Phyllis said, leaning towards him with a look that made him sink back on to the chair again. 'It's *all* of our business.'

Rachel brought cups to the table and the teapot in its cosy. Dolly sat slumped, looking ready to go back to sleep.

'What we're going to do is this,' Phyllis said, lowering herself grandly into her chair and sitting up very straight. 'We're going to hide this child. No one is ever going to know . . .' She held up a hand as they all tried to ask questions. 'First of all, I've written to my sister, Nancy.'

They all stared, agog. Dolly was wide awake now they were finally going to hear something.

'Nance lives on a farm near Coventry. Come the time Dolly's due to have it – a bit before – we're going on a holiday visit down there. Dolly can have it there . . .'

'But does she know about the babby, Nancy – whoever she is?' Rachel asked. Things were going almost too fast for them to keep up.

'She does now. We haven't seen each other for years but she's written back saying she'll help me out. She's a good sort, our Nancy – always was.'

'I don't keep it?' Dolly half whispered, her face showing a terrible tension. 'I don't have to? I thought you were going to make me.'

'You'll keep it over my dead body,' Phyllis said. 'We can't have some bastard child in the family – not *this* family. Ho, no – it's going to be gone, well away from here. Now look – the important thing is what we do now. Very soon, Dolly's going to start getting bigger.'

She looked at her other daughters, pausing for effect. 'Remember what I told you? We're all in this together. You two – when Dolly gets big, you're going to get bigger with her.'

Thirty

A shower of rain sent the children tearing back to the house. The horse pulling the milk cart lowered his head against the deluge and the milkman tugged his cap further down as the road began to shine with water. Aggie ran, half dragging May, who was holding her hand.

'Come *on!*' she urged. 'We're gonna get soaked!'

When the soggy children peeped into the kitchen, Aggie saw that Rose Southgate was there by the table with Nanna and Mom. Lily was perched on a stool. There was a pungent smell of onions.

'Hello, Mrs Southgate,' Aggie said gladly, though she was still trying to swallow her disappointment that Mrs Southgate seemed to have forgotten all about her promise to teach her embroidery.

'Oh – hello, Aggie. I'm just lending a hand again today. I expect Lily'd like to come and play with you now.'

Aggie held her hand out to Lily. She felt happy – it was almost as if Mrs Southgate was becoming a member of the family. Even Mom seemed to be getting along with her.

It was almost the end of the Easter school holidays, and Jen Green was starting to feel a bit better.

Things had been made a lot easier for her by the fact that now, almost every day, Rose Southgate turned up of a morning saying she would help Freda with the dinners. Freda Adams was to begin her job at Sawyer and Hewlett's next week and Rose said she'd fill in until Jen was feeling better. The pair of them would order Jen to go back to bed.

'I can't just keep on going to bed!' Jen protested at first.

'Why not?' Rose said. She seemed so delighted to help and Jen, at first reluctantly, had to admit that Rose was not snooty like she'd thought.

Jen hadn't put up much of a fight because she was feeling so wretched. When she went up to bed, her head would be spinning with worries about Tommy. She lay picturing him in his hospital bed and aching for him to be home, for things to be different. Often she cried, desperate at the thought that he might never come home again. How would they make ends meet? And she was so ashamed at the thought of her old mother going back into the factory at her age, with her seized-up joints.

But by God, it was a relief to lie down; an unheard-of luxury!

And she had to admit that it was mainly thanks to Rose Southgate. Freda said she thought Rose was lonely.

'She ain't got no family – just her and the girl and that husband of hers, and by the sound of things he's as married to his fishing rod as he ever is to her.'

Now Jen felt able to be up and about again, they could manage without Rose, strictly speaking. But she had come to the door again that morning, with Lily, saying, 'Well, here I am – all ready to roll my sleeves up.' She looked surprised to see Jen. 'Are you feeling a bit better?'

'Yes, ta. I can manage now. Just in time. But it's been good of yer to help.'

'Oh,' Rose faltered. 'Only – I don't mind lending a hand. If you'd like?'

'Come on in!' Freda called from the back.

Jen shrugged. 'All right then – if you want.' There was still something about Rose that she didn't feel quite right about, but she couldn't put her finger on it exactly. Something closed and, she thought, hard to fathom. But the odd thing was Rose and her mother seemed to have become quite fond of each other. Rose had bought those shoes for Aggie, which showed a kind heart. And she had certainly lent another pair of hands – and that was saying something.

It wasn't long before the rain stopped and Aggie and the others were back outside. Soon she saw Babs, in among some of her brothers up the street. Babs caught sight of her and came running along, grinning as usual. She was dressed in boys' clothes, a baggy pair of shorts and a dark green shirt, but she didn't seem to care.

'D'yer wanna come and play tag, Aggie?' she yelled. Babs did most of her communication at the top of her voice. Aggie put it down to living with so many loud boys.

'What about May and Lily?' Aggie said. May had pottered over to a puddle and Aggie could see that at any moment she'd go and fall over in it and get them both into trouble.

Babs looked back at the careering, leaping, dodging

mass of Skinner brotherhood and screwed up her nose. 'Best not. They'll flatten 'em, that lot will.'

Aggie was just about to suggest some more sedate game they could play with the little girls, when something caught her eye. Lurching along the road was Mad Mary Crewe, with her sad little bundle in her arms.

'Hey,' she nudged Babs. 'You know what I was saying about spying and that? D'you wanna do some?'

'Yeah!' Babs enthused, then looked puzzled. 'What d'you mean?'

'What about finding out where she's going to?'

'Follow Mad Mary, you mean? What about May and Lily?'

In her excitement Aggie had forgotten about them. Lily had May by the hands, doing 'Ring-a-Ring-o'-Roses'. For a moment she felt a rush of bitter resentment. Why was she always the one lumbered with looking after the babbies? John hardly had to do anything. He spent his time crouching near the back of horses so he could sell buckets of muck! But she was too on fire with the idea now to give it up. She eyed the house. They were all busy: a whiff of stew was beginning to seep out from the kitchen.

'Let's take 'em with us!' she said and saw Babs's face break into an excited smile. 'Old Mary can't be going all that far.'

But that was where she was wrong. The two of them gathered up the little girls – 'Come on, Lily, May! We're going to do some exploring, have an adventure!' Lily and May looked up to Aggie and Babs and they followed without question.

'Now. We mustn't let her see us, all right? So if

Mary, that lady up there, turns round, we just act normal, or turn and look at summat else as if we're nothing to do with her, all right? We're being spies and spies have to be able to be invisible and not let anyone see 'em.'

May looked uncomprehending but she took Aggie's hand anyway and Lily gladly went with Babs.

Mary Crewe set off at quite a pace. She headed off up Lilac Street into Larches Street and turned left, storming along in her usual way, cigarette stub at the corner of her mouth, muttering to herself and almost shoving people out of her way. Larches, Kyrwicks Lane, where Mary stopped and lit another cigarette, laying her bundle down on someone's step for a moment. Then left along Highgate Place beyond the coal wharf and on to the Moseley Road. Already by this time the little girls were finding it hard to keep up and were getting hot with the effort. May was starting to whinge at having to trot to keep up and Lily, who had stepped off a kerb and into a puddle, wetting her nice brown leather shoes, was trying very hard not to cry. Babs tried to jolly her along, pointing out the trams, horses and shops along the Moseley Road. Even Aggie and Babs were starting to tire of this game already. Aggie hadn't had any breakfast and felt empty and bad-tempered.

Mary Crewe paused outside a big building on the Moseley Road and for a moment they thought she was going to go in, but she gathered speed again and went on. As they passed Aggie read, 'Society of Friends Institute.' She thought vaguely that it seemed odd to have a building especially for people who were friends. Did that mean she and Babs could go in? But she was getting too tired and fed up to think further about it. May was yanking on her hand now.

'Where're we going, Aggie? I don't like this game – I wanna go back!'

Lily was sobbing now and the sky had turned a terrible, threatening slate colour. The clouds were so low they looked as if they might tumble out of the sky.

'Where d'you think she's going?' Babs said glumly. 'She just keeps on and on. She must be walking all the way to town.'

Aggie knew they would have to admit defeat. It already felt as if they'd been out for hours. She'd never walked so far from home before.

'I dunno,' Aggie said. 'I s'pose we'd best go back.'

Even as she said it, the first fat drops of rain began to plop down on them.

'Our mom's gonna give me a proper hiding,' Babs groaned. 'I've already had a soaking once today.'

'Don't like it!' May started bawling, and Lily was snivelling with cold and fright at being taken so far from home and spoiling her shoes.

The rain came teeming down so fast and suddenly that within a few steps they were half soaked. They started running and were soon by the Institute again.

'Come in 'ere!' Babs yelled, leading them through the gate.

Over the windows of the grand building, to the left of the entrance, was a canopy and they all dashed underneath it. For a while May and Lily stopped crying, distracted by the sheer novelty of standing in this strange place. But they were all shivering and wet and soon the little ones were crying again.

Aggie and Babs tried to jolly them along, though Aggie's teeth were chattering and she felt utterly miserable.

'It's all right, May,' Aggie said, putting her arm round her sister's convulsing shoulders. 'And you, Lily. We'll soon get home.'

But it rained for about twenty minutes and her patience wore thin. 'Oh, just *shurrit* now, May,' she said. 'We've all got to put up with it so stop blarting!'

At last the clouds slouched away and the sun came out, dazzling in all the reflecting water. It felt as if they had been away for an eternity.

'Come on,' Babs said. 'Let's get moving.'

They set off, sloshing through the wet. 'Can you remember the way, Aggs?' Babs said.

Aggie looked around her, uncertain. Luckily she had a better sense of direction than Babs. 'We've got to turn left here somewhere . . . Under the railway bridge.'

'I'm hungry, Aggie,' May was whinging. 'And I need to wee.'

'Oh, flaming 'ell,' Aggie said, cursing the day she had ever had a younger sister. Even Lily was getting sorely on her nerves. 'Just hang on, May – I'll help you go under the bridge.'

This all took some time. Lily stood in silent misery. It felt as if getting home was going to take the whole of the rest of their lives.

Eventually they got to the end of Kyrwicks Lane. As they turned along Larches Street, Aggie suddenly heard Babs say, 'Oh, Lordie – look what's coming.'

Advancing along Larches Street, Aggie saw her mother, walking side by side with Rose Southgate. Jen spotted them immediately.

'Aggie!' her voice boomed along the road. Oh, Lord, Mom was feeling better all right! Aggie led the sodden little troop towards their fate.

Rose Southgate broke free and came running along to them, squatted down and took her wet, sobbing little daughter in her arms.

'Oh, Lily, where've you been? Where've these naughty girls taken you, eh?' Aggie could hear that Mrs Southgate was almost in tears herself.

'Aggie!' Her mother was steaming along behind, seeming frighteningly full of energy all of a sudden. 'Where've you been? We've been at our wits' end – up and down looking for all of you. What the hell do the pair of you think you're playing at?'

Reaching Aggie, she boxed her ears firmly. Aggie reeled with the stunning pain and tears sprang from her eyes. Babs stepped back just in case Mrs Green had any thoughts about trying it on her. Her own mother didn't seem to have noticed she'd gone.

'You've had Mrs Southgate that worried!' Jen scolded furiously. 'We've been all round, trying to find where you'd got to. As if we haven't got enough to do and Mrs Southgate being kind and helping us. You're a naughty, ungrateful girl, that's what you are! Now you say sorry for all the trouble you've caused.'

Aggie did feel sorry, and cold and miserable and her face hurt. She hung her head, crying herself.

'I'm sorry, Mrs Southgate. I never meant to take Lily so far. Only we was playing a game and we got lost . . .'

Rose Southgate looked appeased and now she had Lily back safely that was all that mattered.

'I know you're a good girl really, Aggie,' she said. 'But you must remember that Lily's only little – and May as well.' May, who no one had taken much notice of, was snivelling hopelessly to herself. As if remembering this Jen Green went to her and said, 'Come on, little 'un,' and took her hand. Aggie had a strong feeling that if it hadn't been for Mrs Southgate going out to look for Lily, her mom, like Mrs Skinner, wouldn't have noticed that she and Babs were not in the street. They both just had so much to do.

They all walked back to the house, where by now Freda Adams had handed out the dinners. Mrs Southgate took Lily home and Babs ran down to her house to dry her clothes for the second time that day and probably to receive a clip round the ear.

'So where the heck've you lot been?' Freda Adams asked, not sounding very concerned.

'Round the bleeding houses, that's where,' her daughter replied, sinking into a chair. Now Rose Southgate had gone she had climbed off her high horse a bit. All she really wanted was a cup of tea and some peace. 'God Almighty – kids!'

Thirty-One

After all the mishaps of the morning, Aggie was keeping out of Mom's way. Her cheeks were still smarting from the slapping Mom had given her. She and May took refuge up in Nanna's room. Nanna was sitting up against her pillow at one end of the bed; Aggie, cross-legged at the other, was carding, sewing on hooks and eyes. May was squeezed in by the wall, next to her. May was too young for carding and after all the airing and exercise she had had, she soon slumped down on the bed, eyes closing. As ever she looked gorgeous, with her pink cheeks and dark lashes. No one could ever be cross with May for long.

'That's it, little 'un, you have yourself a bit of shut-eye,' Nanna said fondly. She was also, painfully, carding with her crooked hands. She put the work down for a moment, reached under her skirt for her little hip flask and took a generous swig.

'Ah!' She winked at Aggie. 'That's better.' Screwing the top back on, she fixed Aggie with a sudden, sharp gaze.

'Where were you off to, this morning, the four of yer?'

Aggie looked at her grandmother, her saggy cheeks and piercing but kindly eyes. She didn't want Nanna to go to work next week. She wanted her here, always. And now, she wanted to tell her the truth but it all sounded a bit silly.

'We . . .' She looked closely at the hook she was sewing on. 'We went for a walk.'

'With Mary Crewe?'

Aggie's head shot up. How did Nanna know that?

'Not *with* her!'

'So Mary never asked you to come with 'er?'

'No! It was just . . . We . . .'

'Dorrie Davis said you was walking along behind her. I mean, I know that one's a nosey bint but she has her uses.'

Aggie sighed. She didn't have to tell Nanna everything, did she, not about Mata Hari and *Agnes Green: Spy*?

'We just wanted to follow her. She goes off, you know the way she does, and we were going to follow and see where she went. But she went so far, and she was walking so fast, we all got tired and May and Lily were mithering and then it started raining . . .'

Nanny Adams was chuckling, her substantial body heaving up and down.

'Oh, dear, oh, dear! Bit off more than you could chew, didn't yer? No, you'd never keep up with poor old Mary.'

She was silent for a moment, peering at her needle. The sky had darkened and the rain was pouring down again, spattering off the roof into the yard.

'I know everyone calls her Mad Mary these days. But shall I tell you where she goes, poor thing?'

Aggie abandoned the sewing and was all ears. 'How d'you know, Nanna?'

It was Freda's turn to sigh, a long, sad breath. 'Oh, everyone knows, who's lived around here for a bit. I've known Mary for years and years, since she was, well, older than you, but not by much. I saw her grow up.'

Aggie frowned. 'How old is she, Nanna?'

'Oh, let's see now – she'd be a few years older than your mother, maybe as much as ten years. Mary must be getting on for forty-five . . .'

Aggie was astonished. She thought of Mary Crewe as a really old lady, more like Nanna.

'Quite pretty she was then, though you'd never guess it now. She had good hair, long and thick, and a nice figure. She was well built, a strong wench, popular with the men. By the time she was seventeen or eighteen a husband came along for her and after they was wed they moved away. I don't know exactly where to – somewhere off the Hagley Road, I believe. Any road, soon there was quite a few children by all accounts, four or five. Now I don't know exactly what happened next, whether her old man died or ran off and left her, but soon Mary was left on her own, with a babe in arms and a clutch of others and not in good health. Old Mrs Jenks, her mother, had died and I don't know whether the rest of the family washed their hands of her or whether they never knew till it was too late. That sister of hers, Eliza, was too young then to do much, though she's made up for it now, bless her, taking her in the way she has. Mary was too poorly and down in herself to work and they were getting to a pitch where they was starving. She had nowhere to turn.'

Aggie listened, mesmerized. It was hard to imagine Mary Crewe as a pretty young woman. Nanna was looking across at the window and the steely sky, remembering.

'Sometimes, you look at other people you've known, and even when your own life's been terrible hard at times, you think, *Well, I could've been like so-and-so – things could be worse.* I lost my husband and two sons, but when I think about Mary Crewe, then I know life's cruel – bitter cruel for some, that it is.

'Mary did the one thing left to a destitute young woman with kiddies to feed: she turned to the corporation looking for help. She took herself to the workhouse door, hoping for a bit of kindness, that they'd be fed and sheltered and that she'd be able to get back on her feet. They even took the babby off her. Mary was too low in herself to have any milk left for it. Any road –'

Nanna became suddenly brisk, brushing bits of cotton off the front of her dress, as if she couldn't bear to think about what had happened next.

'One way or another, Mary never saw them kiddies again – not one of them, not even the babby. Now I reckon one or two of them must of died in there. What happened to the older ones, where they sent them, no one'll ever know now. Poor old Mary's never been right since. She never got wed again – no one'd have her, wrong in the head like that.

'Mary's been trying to get those kiddies back ever since. You've seen her, tramping halfway across Birmingham to the old Archway of Tears. Been seen there many a time, Mary has, begging them to give her back her children. Not that anyone listens, nor ever did. But that cloth you see her carting about done up in her arms – that's all poor old Mary's got left of that babby of hers, and all she ever did have after she trusted them to that place.'

Aggie stared at her, trying to take in all this adult tragedy.

'So you see – Mary may be crazy in the head, but all she deserves is a bit of kindness.'

'We never meant anything bad to her,' Aggie said,

stricken. 'It was just a bit of a game. We wanted to know where she was going.'

'I know you never meant no harm. And I don't s'pose old Mary ever knew you was there. But now you know. Some lives have that much sadness in them and that's one that's had more than most.'

Somehow after that, all Aggie wanted to do all day was to make up for it, even though really she had not done anything very wrong, or not intended to. She kept thinking about Mary Crewe and seeing her, with her scruffy old clothes and greasy hair, and chain smoking, through new eyes. Most bad things she had heard about in her life had been something to do with the war, like Mr Best in the house opposite and all the people like Nanna, who were left grieving for husbands and sons and brothers. But this was something else. What Nanna had told her stayed closely with her. But that afternoon something else happened that, for the moment, wiped all thoughts about that morning right out of their minds.

It was tea time and some of them were round the table for bread and a scrape of jam.

The rain had stopped and it had turned into a sunny, newly washed evening. Aggie noticed with relief that Mom seemed to be in a better mood now than earlier. John was jubilant, having sold a couple of pails of horse muck. At this time of year, anyone with a patch of land for growing veg was very keen to get hold of some.

'There was this bloke, waiting there with a shovel when one horse came along, but I nipped in quick and got there before him!' He laughed. 'You should've seen 'is face!'

'You never sold him it, did you?' Aggie asked.

'Nah . . .' John said.

'I was the one picked it up,' Silas said.

'No, you wasn't – you weren't even there!' John was outraged. He reached across and cuffed Silas. 'Fibber!'

They were about to break away and start wrestling on the floor.

'Knock it off, you two!' Jen scolded, bringing her tea to the table. She was just on the point of sitting down, and Aggie had a piece of bread halfway to her mouth, when they heard a rattling of the back door handle, then a cautious knock. Silence fell.

'That can't be Dulcie . . .' Jen said. She would have 'cooee'd and just come in.

'Probably kids, playing about,' Nanna said. They'd been too distracted to see anyone pass the window.

'Anyone in?' a man's voice shouted.

Frowning, Jen went to the door, opened it and then gave a huge gasp, her hand going to her mouth. 'Oh, my Lord!' she cried.

'I come upon 'im just along the road back there,' a voice said. Aggie didn't recognize the man's voice. 'Thought I'd better give 'im a hand.'

Jen reached out her arms. 'Oh, my . . . What've you gone and done? Get in here, quick.'

The family's gaze was fixed on the door as he came in. Their eyes widened all at once. It was a sight Aggie would never forget.

'Dad!' It was John who broke the astonished hush. 'It's Dad!'

Their father, thin as a skeleton but grinning from ear

to ear, dressed in a motley collection of pyjamas, coat, rug draped round him and some sort of old slippers, shuffled into the room, held between Mom and a man called Mr Purvis from up the street.

''Ello, everyone!' Tommy wheezed.

'Oh, my word, Tommy Green!' Nanna said, sounding amused, appalled and confused all at once. 'What in heaven's name're you doing here?'

'Dad!' Aggie kept saying, and they all did. 'Dad!'

'There you are, pal,' Mr Purvis said kindly, as he and Jen deposited the invalid on the chair she had vacated. 'Well, I'll leave yer to it.'

They remembered to thank him and then they were alone, all together as a family again. Jen could not contain her emotion. She put her arms round her husband's shoulders.

'Oh, my God, Tommy Green, what've you gone and done?' She burst into tears. 'Oh, just look at the state of you!'

Aggie found tears running down her own face and she could see that even John was struggling not to cry. They hadn't had any idea when they might see their father again and there he was suddenly!

Nanna poured Tommy a cup of tea. 'Here you are, lad, get this down you.' Tommy took it between his bony hands and drank desperately. He was shaking.

'What've you done?' Jen repeated. 'You must be soaked! They never sent you home, did they?'

Tommy shook his head, swallowing the sweet tea despite his shivering. The whole family were hanging on his every word.

'I walked out. Couldn't stand it there no more. Not that they weren't good to me. It was comfortable like, but I want to be here, with all of you, not stuck in some

248

hospital and left there to . . . Well, till I sink or swim.'
He swallowed.

'Oh, Tommy . . .' Jen couldn't seem to take her eyes
off him, held his shoulder as if he might vanish. 'The
state of yer! But you're not wet. How've you managed
to come all this way without getting soaked?'

Tommy looked down. 'I missed the worst of the
rain. I was on the bus when it came down . . .' He
stopped to cough and this took some time. Then he
went on. 'I had to sneak out, of course. Lucky they're
so keen on fresh air – always on at you to get out in it.
Bloke in the next bed gave me a hand, said 'e thought 'e
wouldn't be leaving the place standing up so he gave me
these old slippers . . . I had a few coppers with me for
the bus . . . And I was just coming along when I met
Mr Purvis . . . Any road.' Exhaustedly he raised his head
and smiled round at his children. 'Couldn't live without
the sight of your ugly mugs, could I, eh?'

Aggie felt a big smile spread across her face.

May 1925

Thirty-Two

'Mom?' Lily's soft voice insisted. 'MOM!'

'What *is* it, Lily? Don't shout at me like that.'

Rose was crossing Lilac Street holding Lily's hand. They had been to the Greens' house to offer help but Rose hadn't felt especially welcome. The old lady, Mrs Adams, was out at work now, the children, except for May, were at school and Jen seemed to be back on her feet, so Rose's help was not needed.

'It's nice of you to ask,' Jen said, politely enough. 'But we're all right. I can manage now, thanks.' Rose saw that Dulcie Skinner, Babs's mother, was there in the background, so she retreated, feeling sad and out of place. Jen already had her friends – she didn't need any more. Rose would miss her chats with old Mrs Adams.

She gathered that Tommy Green had discharged himself and come home. Standing at the front door, she had heard some muffled coughing from upstairs. Jen seemed very happy that he was here, Rose noticed. She loved her husband, it was clear. What must that be like, Rose found herself wondering, actually to love your husband – *really* love him? This thought brought her back, as all others did these days, to Arthur King. *Her* Arthur as she thought of him . . . Lily's prattling ruptured her thoughts almost like a physical pain.

'When's Aggie coming back?'

'I've *told* you,' she said as they reached their door.

'Aggie's at school – she's a big girl. When you're a bit older, you'll go to school too.'

As they went into the house, Rose found herself wishing guiltily that that day had already come. Up until now, Lily's presence had been such a joy to her. Harry was no sort of companion and her daughter had become her all in all, her affection and company. But now there was Arthur.

She could have spent every hour daydreaming about him, about his lovely face, the vulnerable expressions she saw registered there, the tender way he spoke to her and held her. Since that Sunday afternoon when they had first shown their feelings to each other, he had been to the house twice more and there was no hiding how they felt about each other.

'I find I can't think of anything else,' he admitted bashfully. 'Nearly all day, in my imagination, I'm here with you. Even when I'm in the middle of tuning, of talking to someone even, I'm with you, my arms round you.'

It was the same for her, all day, every day, that tension and longing.

But she was frightened and ashamed of how she had let this happen. As she cut some bread for Lily's and her dinner, her mind spun round. Arthur was starting to talk about coming to see her at other times.

'Lily – stop clattering that spoon!' Her nerves were in shreds.

How could she tell Arthur now that she was a married woman, when he believed her to be a widow? He would know her as a liar. But if she was really a widow, what reason could she keep up for him not coming round? There would be no bar to their relationship.

254

He had not insisted so far. She had tried to emphasize her own strict respectability.

'Coming round on a Sunday for tea with all the children is one thing, dear, but if you start coming over in the evening, the neighbours will talk – you've no idea what a collection of gossips we've got in Lilac Street – some of the worst anywhere, I think.' She made light of it, but it was enough.

'Oh, of course,' he said in his decent way. 'The last thing I want is to cause you any trouble. But is it really so shameful, since you're a widow, alone?'

Rose put her head archly on one side, before realizing that this gesture was wasted on him. 'There's Lily to consider as well. She's had so many changes – her father's death, moving here, and now you arriving in her life. Perhaps we should take things slowly, dear?'

And Arthur, being the honest, trusting darling he was, had readily agreed, even though she could feel his impatience, his need to be loved and to be with her. And despite the lies, the awfulness of it was that she loved him back and wanted him, in a way that she had never wanted a man before.

'But *whatever* am I going to do?' she cried, silently, in her head, day after day, never finding an answer that was both happy and true.

She had agreed that Arthur could visit on some Saturdays as well, so long as she was sure that Harry would be out. Both mornings of last weekend, she had been in a fever of nervous excitement. It was a revelation to her. Even when she first met Harry, she had never really experienced the feeling of true attraction. She had been so desperate for a new life, she had imagined that a few jokes and promises were all it took to make a proposal of marriage something she could gladly answer.

In her marriage to Harry, their physical relations had never been good. Rose understood now that she had never truly desired Harry. In reality, she had found him rough and unsympathetic. Adding that to her dread of childbirth had meant they never had a successful marriage. He had resented her from the beginning and in a way she did not blame him.

But now she was gripped by desire. It had taken her over, body, mind, soul, a gnawing hunger that would never leave her alone. During the long week, when she didn't see Arthur, the hours stretched out unbearably. For the first time she experienced physical desire, the aching, longing force of it, and she hardly knew how to contain it.

Now, when she and Arthur were together, it felt frustrating that there were always the children there. Sitting talking with Arthur was sheer pleasure, but a tension of longing had fast grown between them, a need to hold and touch each other, so that by the time he left, after snatched embraces in the back room, Rose was quite edgy and wrung out with it.

'Perhaps you could come to my place one day?' he whispered, that last time as he held her. He took a deep, emotional breath. 'God, I just long to be with you alone.'

She looked deeply into his face and felt he was looking back at her, even though he could see nothing.

'What about your landlady?'

'Well – she's not a bad sort, really. But if you came it might be better if we slipped in without advertising the fact. To start with, anyway.'

Oh, she thought, the idea of being alone in a room with Arthur, just him!

'What am I going to do with Lily though?'

Arthur shrugged. He was very good, she thought appreciatively. He never complained about Lily or tried to make things difficult and she said so.

'Listen –' He squeezed her shoulders to emphasize what he was saying. 'Have you any idea what it means to me to have found you? And Lily too? I've been so gloomy these last years, assuming that I'd spend the rest of my life alone. What woman would want a blind man – let alone a blind husband? And then I meet you and you're so kind and lovely. I still can hardly take it in. After that, everything is a bonus!'

She hugged him back. 'Oh, Arthur – I do love you.'

'That's not to say,' he whispered close to her ear, 'that I wouldn't absolutely love to be alone with you. But we have to be careful with each other and what we already have in our lives.' He kissed her cheek. 'Don't ever think I'm discontented. I'm full of wonder!'

Rose was almost counting the hours until she next saw him. Every day she kept having to drag her mind back to the jobs that needed doing, the cooking, cleaning, shopping, and Lily. She had gone over to the Greens' as a welcome distraction from her burning thoughts. Was she becoming depraved, the way her mind was full of thoughts that no married woman should be having? Her desire for Arthur King was all consuming. She could sit or lie in bed for hours at a time, dreaming of him, his face, his body. Over and over again she imagined him naked, and her naked with him, her undressing him, touching him, their coming together in a loving union.

She was so full of desire, that one night, when Harry had made advances to her, she had responded to him almost gladly. All the way through she had pretended to herself that it was Arthur in whose arms she was lying, Arthur whose lips were fixed on hers, who thrust inside her, and she became more excited with Harry than she ever had before, though she felt like a traitor – to Arthur and Harry both.

Harry noticed, with approval. Instead of rolling off her and turning away to sleep straight away as he normally did, he lay beside her in the dark, on his side, resting his heavy hand on her belly.

'That was nice, kid,' he said. He seemed uncertain suddenly. 'You're my woman, ain't yer?' He laid his hand roughly on her head for a moment. 'God, Rose, you're summat, you are.'

Rose made a small noise which she hoped was enough of an answer. She lay in a state of wonder, washed in warmth and temporary, sated contentment, feeling their shared wetness between her legs. When had she ever felt like this before? She didn't want Harry to speak, she wanted to carry on pretending that it was Arthur beside her and that they were going to fall asleep together.

'I wish it were always like that,' Harry said. And she certainly did not want to think about the fact that Harry had not withdrawn from her at the critical moment.

At least, she thought, she seemed to have done something right for him for once, even if he didn't know it was all a lie. Then she forgot about him and once again, all her thoughts were of Arthur, Arthur her love.

Thirty-Three

'Aggie dear!'

Rose stepped out of her house to waylay Aggie as she and the others were setting off for school, John running ahead, Ann and Silas trailing behind her. Aggie had the resigned, put-upon look of someone older than twelve years, but Rose was in far too much of a state about her own concerns to notice this.

Aggie stopped and Silas caught up with her and took her hand. The two of them stood looking up at Rose, Aggie with her clear blue eyes, Silas's a heart-melting brown.

'Just a quick word, dears,' Rose said. Her hands were clammy with nerves. The idea had come to her as she was falling asleep last night and she jerked awake, her heart pounding, and had hardly slept the rest of the night. If only it worked, she and Arthur would be able to have time alone!

'Aggie, Lily has been asking me if she might be able to come to the Sunday school with you. Would that be all right, d'you think?'

Aggie, eager to please, said, 'Yes. She can come.' Importantly, she added, 'I can take her, if you like.'

'Oh, *good*.' Rose found she was actually trembling. 'The thing is, Aggie, I need to go and see my sister on Sunday. She's not well, poor thing. So if Lily *could* come along with you? And –' Rose could hardly believe the way things were falling into place. And why not? She had done a lot for that child. What was the harm in asking her a favour? 'Just in case I'm not back once you get home from the church, could Lily stop at yours – just for a bit?'

Aggie was nodding but Rose added, 'You'd better just make sure it's all right with your mother.' But she knew it would be. Why would they refuse her?

Full of excitement, she knew she had one more thing to ask. She bent closer to Aggie. The child's breath smelt of stale bread.

'Now – if you come and see me after school, I've got a little errand for you. You could earn twopence – how about that?'

'All right,' Aggie said, looking pleased. Silas was yanking on her hand, impatient to be off. Solemnly, she added, 'I'll see you later, Mrs Southgate.'

She could not tell Arthur the news, not directly. She had said that there might be a possibility of him being able to come round on Saturday. Once the football season ended, Harry would most likely go fishing both days. If she could see Arthur on Saturday, she could tell him about Sunday, when they would have more time and could be alone together!

She couldn't stop thinking about it all day. That afternoon was when Muriel Wood came round to teach Lily the piano. Rose let her in, very pleased to see her, as she would take up all Lily's attention for half an hour.

The day was warm and spring-like and Muriel arrived wearing her summer hat and smiling with her usual tired bravery.

'Hello, dear,' she said to Rose. She looked carefully at her once they were inside. 'I must say, you do look well. Your cheeks are as rosy as your name today!' She gave her little laugh.

'Oh – thank you,' Rose said. No wonder she looked well, she was in love and brimful of excitement, but she could hardly tell Muriel!

Lily came running in eagerly, calling, 'Hello, Mrs Wood!' and Rose told Muriel she would go and make tea while the piano lesson got started. Soon she was in the kitchen, hearing the sound of 'Baa baa black sheep' being picked out on the piano. While the kettle heated she sat quickly at the table and composed a note.

'*Dear Mr King,*' she wrote. '*The arrangements for Saturday are quite satisfactory. I look forward to seeing you at three. Sincerely, Mrs Southgate.*'

His landlady had to read him any correspondence, since there was seldom anyone else to do it. Rose hoped that this would sound impersonal and that Arthur would not find it too peculiar. She was playing up her preoccupation with respectability. What else could she do, even though she longed to write an impassioned note saying all she really felt?

The afternoon crawled by and it was all she could do to sit and drink tea with Muriel and hear her talk about Oliver and the church and the little concert she had been to, struggling to keep her frantic mind on the conversation.

'Now, you remember the address in Oldfield Road?' she instructed Aggie. 'Just put it through the door and come back and tell me you've done it dear, all right? And Aggie . . .' She gave a conspiratorial smile. 'This is our secret. I don't want anyone else knowing my business, so you make sure you keep all this to yourself – and there'll be more errands you can run for me. We can pretend it's part of your spying work, can't we? Like Mata Hari?'

'All right, Mrs Southgate,' Aggie said, taking the note. She had had to tell Mrs Southgate about the spying after they took Lily to follow Mary Crewe. She felt a bit silly about it all now. But never mind – Mom would be pleased with the twopence.

'Have you got a pocket?' Rose asked anxiously.

Aggie pushed the note down into the pocket in her brown skirt. 'All safe,' she smiled.

'Off you go then – there's a good girl.'

By Saturday afternoon, Rose was in a terrible state of nerves.

The day dawned mild and sunny and Rose woke hopeful that it would be a fishing day. She even let Harry make love to her again, knowing that this would put him in a mellow mood. Her sense of control over things seemed to have deserted her. What if she fell pregnant, she thought, as Harry's dark head moved over her, close to hers. But it was as if she was a slave to fate, on a current that she could not stop. Her life now was balanced on so many lies – would punishment be hers, somewhere, sometime? Would a baby put a stop to all of it, be her mark of fate? But somehow she could not grasp what might happen, so borne along was she by her feelings. She would do anything, anything at all to make sure that one day soon – perhaps tomorrow! – she could be alone with Arthur King and in his arms. It was as if she could imagine nothing else beyond her absolute yearning for him.

But once they were downstairs having breakfast, she said lightly, 'It's a lovely day. Are you off fishing?'

Harry looked up, seeming relaxed as she had hoped. 'Nah – not today,' he said. 'I told our dad I'd go over and give him a hand with a couple of things.' Rose's heart rate picked up. At least he was going out, but would there be enough time for her to see Arthur, to make sure he had left again before Harry came back? Tension mounted in her to such an extent that she could hardly breathe.

Harry stood up. 'Just going to get a paper.' He was already halfway out of the back door when Lily piped up, 'Is the man going to play the piano again?'

Rose gasped. She forced herself to say dreamily, 'Umm? What, Lily? You mean the man in your story?'

The back door closed and her head whipped round. Harry was going down to the entry. He hadn't heard – had he?

'*Lily?*' She could barely contain her fury. 'What did I say about talking about the man and the piano? Those are two things we don't mention – is that clear? Don't *ever* say a word.'

'Why?' Lily's face crumpled hearing her mother's tone. Rose was angry with her so often these days. 'The man's nice.'

'I know – but . . .' What could she possibly say? She breathed deeply. 'Your father's not very good friends with Mr King, you see, Lily. And you know what he thinks about piano lessons. So – we don't want to upset him, do we? It's better if we just don't say anything, all right?'

263

Lily nodded, looking tearful and glum.

'Oh – come here!' She beckoned Lily to her and sat her on her lap, trying to quell her fever of impatience. 'Shall we have a story?'

Harry went out after dinner and from that instant Rose was praying for Arthur to arrive, not to be late. Three o'clock they had said. If only she had agreed on two o'clock! Lily was settled playing, so she took out the mats she was embroidering with flowers and butterflies.

Embroidery was yet another secret. Harry didn't know she still did any. Any pieces she sold, she kept the money for things that she wanted to do. Rose's pulse was racing hard and she jumped at the slightest sound.

If I go on like this I'll give myself a bad heart, she thought, taking a deep, ragged breath. She imagined Arthur leaving his house, feeling his way along the street, coming closer and closer to her, knocking . . .

Three o'clock came and went.

'Come *now*,' she was saying over and over again in her mind. 'Please, my darling, my love, don't keep me waiting, come now, for God's sake!'

At last, at almost ten past, there was a discreet knocking.

'I wonder who that can be?' she exclaimed, dashing to answer.

He smiled up at her, taking off his hat.

'Oh!' she breathed. 'You're here at last!'

'Hello.' He came in, more used to the house now and not needing her assistance, but she took his arm anyway, giving it a passionate squeeze.

264

'I thought you'd never come,' she whispered, before saying, 'Look who's here, Lily!'

'Hello, young lady,' Arthur said and Lily beamed.

'Answer Mr King, Lily,' Rose said. She had often repeated to her, 'Remember Mr King can't see you smile or nod, so try to say something instead.'

'Hello, Mr King,' Lily said obediently.

'I'm so sorry, Arthur,' Rose told him as they escaped into the kitchen, 'but you won't be able to stay long today. I'm afraid my sister in Kings Heath has been taken ill and I'm going to have to go over there quite soon. But . . .' She lowered her voice and moved closer to him, putting her hands on his upper arms. Delighted, he returned her embrace and they pulled each other close, his lips reaching for hers. At last, she was where she longed to be!

'Oh, my love,' he murmured. 'With you, finally!' He held her tightly, passionately.

'Tomorrow,' she whispered, lips close to his ear. 'I can come to you. In the afternoon. Alone.'

He listened attentively, his face solemn. 'To me? Can you?' Suddenly he sounded uncertain, as if he was afraid of wanting something that he couldn't have.

'I'd like to see your rooms,' she said a little more loudly. 'And Lily is going to Sunday school with Aggie . . .' Lowering her voice again, she added, 'Alone, at last. Oh, Arthur – we can be together for a while without all these other people.'

He lifted a hand and stroked her face. 'Oh, my Rose. If you can come that would be . . .'

'What about your landlady?'

'If you tell me when you will arrive, exactly, I shall wait. She takes a nap on Sundays and in fact, she's quite hard of hearing.'

'I shall have to go soon today,' she told him, trembling at the thought that Harry could come back at any time. 'I really mustn't delay. But I'll be there tomorrow – at two-thirty, on the dot.'

Arthur smiled. 'On the dot it is.'

Thirty-Four

He was waiting, just as he said he would be, behind the door, one in a long terrace of houses. She scarcely had to tap. He must have heard her step and the timid scrape of her fingers against the black paint. The door swung open and there he was, his face, his lovely self in the doorway.

'Take my hand,' he whispered, leading her to the stairs. 'She's right out at the back – there's a sunny window she likes.' Closer still to her ear, he said, 'Where's little Lily?'

'Sunday school.' Rose could have kissed Aggie, bless her, the poor grown-up little soul in her gigantic clothes! For a moment Lily had baulked at going with Aggie, had wanted Rose to go too. Aggie, holding May by one hand, held out her other to Lily in her good-natured way.

'You come with me, Lily,' she said. 'We're going to the church and we'll sing some songs and do some pictures. See, May wants you to come, don't you, May? And then you can come and play at ours after.'

Lily yielded and took Aggie's hand. Soon she was walking off along the street with Aggie, Ann, Silas and May with hardly a backward glance.

It seemed so wrong, so illicit, but neither of them could help themselves. Following Arthur up the thinly carpeted stairs, both on tiptoe, to the dark landing, Rose felt she was living a dream, but one more real than anything she had ever dared to hope. And then his room opened out to her, its window overlooking the back garden. She saw a bed, table and cupboard, a dressing table with a mirror. Otherwise, a bare room. After all, what was the use of him putting up pictures? But at least it was light and sunny, though he probably could not tell.

Arthur closed the door, very carefully, then turned, seeking her out.

'My dear?'

'I'm here – oh, my love, here!' She stepped so eagerly into his arms.

'We must be careful not to keep walking about,' he whispered. 'She's under us, but I really don't think she'll hear. If she does she'll think it's just me!' But however quiet they were it felt as if someone was listening.

But the sight, the feel of him close, rendered Rose helpless, her body pulsing, yet limp with desire for him. She had no rational thoughts, except, *Thank heavens I have been a married woman so that I know what physical love is, that it is not frightening and strange.* Because she knew – they both knew – that now they were alone they could not hold back. Never in her life had she experienced this kind of desire, like being washed over a waterfall and not caring, only knowing that they must be together and must physically possess each other.

As soon as they began to kiss it was hopeless. Rose caressed him, at first under his jacket, which she soon removed, undoing the buttons of his shirt as their lips and tongues met, playful at first but soon hungrily, forcefully. She heard his fast, excited breathing. She helped him to unfasten her dress, felt the air on her arms and shoulders as they took it off her and then she slid his shirt from him, seeing for the first time his fine, muscular chest and arms.

'Oh, you're lovely!' she said. So beautiful after Harry's thick body.

Reverently he reached for her breasts and she helped him, took his hand and trembled as he touched her, his head slightly tilted back almost as if listening. The pleasure of it coursed through her. Moved, she helped him undress further, until both of them were naked.

'Oh, my love,' Arthur said, holding her close, his hands stroking her back. 'How I wish I could see you – but there is nothing to compare with how you feel! You're so smooth, so lovely.'

Their touching became more heated. Rose found herself, again as if dreaming, leading him to the bed, where she lay and spread herself for him and led him to her and then he was in her, crying out with pleasure and love and gratitude. She held him with a tenderness she had never felt for a man before, taking him to her, her body answering him wholeheartedly.

The sun was streaming on to their bodies as they lay in each other's arms, their blood slowing. Their heads were in the shade so that they were both cool and warm at once. Arthur lay with her cradled in his arms, a hand on her breast, and every few moments he kissed the top of her head which lay close to his lips, her pale hair loose on the pillow. They murmured amazed, loving words to each other.

'You're here,' Arthur said several times, in wonder. 'You're really here with me!'

'I'm here . . .' She snuggled closer. 'I'm here, my love.' She reached up and ran her fingers gently over his face. 'Can you see anything?' she asked. 'The sunlight?'

'No. It's completely dark. But I can feel it.' He moved his hand in and out of the shadow. 'Where it begins and ends. D'you know what the worst part of being blind is?'

She thought about it. 'Having to have people help with everything?'

'No – that can be very trying. But the worst is, that it's so *boring*.' His tone was matter-of-fact, not self-pitying. 'It's hardly like living in the same world as everyone else any more. There's no colour. One of the things about enjoying life is being able to see it, to look forward to things that you can *see*. You don't realize, you take it all for granted when you can always see. But now I can't see my food, so eating's not so much of a pleasure. I eat because I have to live of course, but it's not the same. Imagine going to post a letter – I'll never see a pillar box again – never see red! No trees, no sky . . . And worst of all, I can't see you, all your colours, your shape, the light and shadow . . .'

Releasing her, he pushed himself up and kneeled over her. 'I want to learn every part of you – with my lips.' He kissed her tummy button, tracing a necklace of kisses round it until she squirmed.

'That tickles!' she giggled. 'You don't want me to scream, do you?'

'No! The bedsprings have made enough noise already. We'll have Mrs T rampaging up the stairs.'

'From the sound of her she's not a rampaging sort.'

'True.' Arthur considered. 'But I expect she could rampage should an urgent need arise. And this would probably count as one, don't you think?'

'Ooh, *don't*,' Rose said with a thrill of fear. 'There's not even a lock on the door!' She pulled on his arm. 'We should have put the chair there.'

Arthur got up and did as she suggested.

'Come and lie with me here again,' she begged. 'Don't go so far away.'

She was in a heaven that she didn't ever want to end. She didn't want to think about anything outside that could spoil these moments.

'Arthur,' she said seriously as he took her in his arms again. 'I've never, ever done anything like this before. I mean, I don't want you to think . . .'

'Nor me!' He laughed, suddenly so youthful sounding, so happy. His lovely voice throbbed with it. 'You are the most wonderful woman, Rose – you just bowl me over with desire.'

His words thrilled her. Desire. The way things *should* be, love and passion between a man and a woman who love each other, like it said in the stories.

'My darling,' he said earnestly. 'I know you have Lily to consider, and that when it comes down to it I'm not much of a catch. A blind man round the house is not ideal. But I do at least have a living, thanks to the firm and good old St Dunstan's. But I can't imagine a life now without you in it. Dearest one, I want to be with you, to be your man – your husband, of course, I mean – and live with you always.'

'Oh, my love!' Rose said, stricken to the core. It was all she wanted to hear, all she longed for. But she had told so many lies. There were so many difficulties! She was so deep in untruth – what could she possibly say about Harry, about how things really were? He would never see her in the same way again.

She lay silent, caught in a trap between truth and

dishonesty, like a drowning island between two rivers. Surely one day she must tell him everything, about Harry and why she had acted as she had. But supposing Arthur rejected her in horror? He seemed such a straight, truthful person. If only she had not lied in the first place! But if she had not, surely she would not have had this now, here, this miraculous lovemaking, with him?

'Darling?' He sensed it, her hesitation. Had he guessed there was something wrong? She spoke quickly, stroking her hand over his belly, loving the place where the smooth skin met an edge of wiry hair at his groin. With Harry she only ever felt a degree of revulsion. With Arthur the love was complete and for every part of him.

'It's all I want as well, my love,' she said. 'You are . . . Well, I can't really say what you mean to me. You're everything. But this is all so fast, and there is Lily to consider, as you say. We must take things slowly.'

'Of course.' Arthur sounded happy enough. He lay back slack and contented. 'Look, Rose, the fact that you are here, that you're part of my life – it's more than I ever dreamed of. When I came back here with no sight – well, I thought that was an end of it. Of any sort of life where a woman could want me. There's no need for any rush – I love you. That's all we need to know. God I do –' he added with vehemence, turning to her. 'Oh, my sweet – hold me –' Gently he took her hand and guided her to him, ready to love her all over again.

Thirty-Five

'Morning, Mrs Taylor!'

Phyllis jumped violently as her neighbour called from the next doorstep. Phyllis was leaning out of her front door, arms folded, watching as Rachel and Dolly departed along the street. Did they look all right? Would anyone notice anything?

'Oh!' She came to herself, laying a hand on her pounding heart. 'Morning, Mrs Paige.'

'Bit warmer today – at last.'

'Er, yes – very nice,' Phyllis said vaguely. *Yes, it is a bit warmer, confound it*, she thought. If there was one thing they didn't need it was hot weather, with her sending her girls out padded up to the hilt.

'Your girls are looking bonny!'

Phyllis forgot to breathe for a moment. Her pulse started thudding. What did the woman mean? Groping for words, she managed, as casually as she could, 'Oh, yes – they're all very well.' But her neighbour was already turning away. She'd meant nothing by it.

Phyllis hurried back inside. She had been about to set to on the washing, but found herself in the back room, clutching at the table, her legs almost unable to hold her up.

'Come on, Phyllis Taylor – this is not like you,' she rallied herself. She was about to sink on to her chair, but she muttered, 'Let's have a cuppa – that'll put me right.'

Kettle on, she sank on to the chair. Holding her plump hands out in front of her, the flesh swelling round her wedding ring, she saw there was a tremor in them. Her head ached along one side. Her sleep had been broken by bloody, nightmarish, dreams.

I'm a bag of nerves these days, she thought. She took in a deep, shuddering breath, feeling the bite of her corset at her waist. She wore a traditional whalebone corset, what she considered 'proper' as clothing. It was what respectable women wore. It held her in, made her walk upright and straight. But it felt too tight today, hot and constraining, and that only increased her anxiety. She shifted uncomfortably in her chair, breathing in and pushing out her chest and ribcage to try and get her fingers under the edge of it and ease the tightness. It didn't help much. Her wool dress was too warm for today and she felt trapped in her clothes, in her own body, as if she wanted to fight her way out. Sinking down again, she had a sudden desire to weep. If she could have put her feelings into words she felt worried and small and vulnerable. And Phyllis Taylor didn't want to recognize vulnerability. It was something she had closed the door on years ago, something she never wanted to feel ever again.

She was worried to death about all the ways her girls might give themselves away, especially Rachel, with that mouth on her.

'Mom – we're not wearing *those*, are we?' was Rachel's horrified reaction as Phyllis outlined her plans. Dolly was getting on for five months gone now. From a small, almost imperceptible bulge, the girl was beginning to stick out distinctively at the front. A fat belly and a babby didn't look the same. Most women would be able to tell, those who knew a thing or two. It wouldn't do – Phyllis had put the first part of her ideas into action.

Rachel was staring in horror at the object in Phyllis's hand, a sort of cushion affair she had stitched out of old ticking and stuffed with sawdust. She gathered the girls round her (Charles had fled at any mention of underwear) and gave them their marching orders. Susanna already wore a girdle – a more up-to-date thing, not like Phyllis's 'dreadnought' as they called it. Susanna thought it the right thing and that it improved her figure. Rachel, who disliked anything constricting round her, was appalled.

'We're already putting on flesh – look,' Rachel said, feeling round her thickened waist. Usually she was supple as a sapling. Phyllis had been making them eat and eat: potatoes, dumplings, suet puddings, piling their plates full.

'Well, you can wear one of these instead if you don't like it,' Phyllis snapped, running her hands over her ribs and the whalebone corset.

'I'm never wearing one of them!' Rachel cried.

The elasticated girdle was the lesser of two evils. But now Rachel was baulking at the next step of the plan – that she and Susanna should slip these sawdust pillow things underneath the girdles to pad themselves out!

'Go on,' Phyllis instructed them. 'Stick it in, spread all round the front of you, see? That girdle's a big size – it'll all fit in.'

'Mom – what'll we look like!' Rachel said, chin jutting obstinately. 'I'm not going about in *that*! I'll be flaming boiled alive!'

'Yes, you *are*!' Susanna's tone was tight and angry. 'Look, Rach, it's not just you. We've got to get through this somehow, without anyone finding out. It's all right for you – you don't even have a man friend, or anyone else to worry about. What am I going to say to David? If he comes anywhere near me or touches me he's going to feel it!'

Rachel had sulkily removed the top part of her dress to reveal her white, slender arms and was wrapping the girdle round over her camisole.

'Don't you want it underneath?' Phyllis asked. Dolly's eyes were wide with a mix of anxiety and astonishment. She had become quieter lately, as if resigned to her fate.

Once the padding was inserted, the girdle fastened and Rachel's dress back on, she looked a rather more substantial young woman at the front. Susanna began to do the same.

'Well, what am *I* supposed to do?' Dolly said quietly.

'What d'you mean, "What am I supposed to do?"' Rachel advanced on her, hands on her hips. 'Why do you need to do anything when you're the one with a babby sticking out and making the rest of us dress up as if we're expecting a cowing snowstorm?'

'Shush, Rachel!' Susanna snapped. 'And stop that language.' Her eyebrows tugged into a frown. 'We'll have to let our dresses out, Mom.'

'We might as well wear coal sacks,' Rachel muttered.

'Just stop keeping on!' Susanna exploded. 'We've got to do this and it's no good mithering on about it. You're getting on my nerves!'

Phyllis sat thinking about them. Usually in family disputes her word was law and that was that. But this was different. She knew her girls were trying to pull together. Susanna and Charles cared as much as she did about keeping it secret. She was less sure of Rachel and Dolly. They were doing their best, but one false word and it'd be out – scandal, gossip, how the mighty are fallen . . . She knew what people thought of her – Mrs High and Mighty, putting on airs. That somehow she was not quite the thing, whoever she had managed to marry. Phyllis didn't care. In fact she revelled in it. She hadn't dragged herself up in life to care about a bit of neighbourhood tittle-tattle – not of that sort. She could hold her head high, whatever they might say. But this sort of gossip about one of her family getting caught out, playing fast and loose – *bastard brat, bun in the oven* – was another thing altogether. Gossips never took into account the circumstances – and she did believe Dolly's account of what had happened. Phyllis knew what men were like. But God, how they'd love it, Mrs Paige, Mrs Green, that Mrs Davis – no first names for Phyllis, she was always 'Mrs Taylor'. They'd love showing her up! She'd never live it down – nothing in her carefully built life would ever be the same again. And she wasn't having that – oh, no, not at any price.

So the girls had been going off to work with their first lot of padding on. She'd have to thicken it up as the months went by. And she'd have to pad Dolly up too in due course, to hide the shape of it. A steady gain in weight all round and as much clothing covering it as could be born. It had to work – *had* to.

'It's going to be hell all summer,' Rachel had stormed once the girdle was fastened in place. 'I'm going to be so hot, I'll *die* of it.'

But the girls were not the only reason Phyllis was in such a state. There was another fear, more uncertain and threatening, which broke into her rest. When she did manage to sleep, horrors slithered through her dreams.

In the light of morning she told herself she was being ridiculous. But it ate away at her, had done for the past ten days, since Easter when Rachel had suddenly come out with it about that rough-sounding woman who was looking for her.

By a stroke of luck, when Rachel and Dolly started talking about it that evening, Phyllis was standing with her back to them at the range, waiting for the milk pan to come to the boil.

'Oh, I'd forgotten about her!' Rachel said when Dolly brought it up, about that horrible old hag who'd collared them on the way back from church.

'Ugh,' Dolly said. 'She didn't half stink! And she gave me the creeps – did you see her teeth? They were like a dog's, what was left of them, all yellow, like fangs . . .'

'What was she on about?' Rachel said. 'Some woman she thought we could tell her about – Hetty or someone?'

Goose pimples prickled all over Phyllis. She found herself breathing very fast, aware that she needed to control her face. The girls were giggling and shuddering as if discussing a pantomime goblin.

'Ooh, I'll have nightmares about her, I should think!'

But it wasn't Rachel who was having the nightmares.

'Who was this?' Phyllis turned, pouring milk on to the cocoa, trying to sound unconcerned.

'On the way back, this morning,' Dolly said. 'She came up to us on the Moseley Road – she even grabbed Rachel's arm in her claws!' They both laughed, enjoying this now. 'She wanted to know if we knew some lady called Hetty something . . .'

'Baker?' Rachel said.

'Barker, wasn't it? Any road, she had Rach by the

278

arm and she stank of booze and . . . Ooh, she frightened me half to death.'

'How peculiar,' Phyllis said casually, handing them their cocoa. 'What was she like?'

'She was a hag,' Rachel said. 'Horrible. There was something threatening about her. As if she might . . . I don't know what. It was just a feeling.'

'She had funny hair, with a nasty yellow tinge, sort of sulphur colour and eyes like slits.' Dolly was enjoying this now.

It was her. Just how she'd been when Phyllis saw her: Ethel Sharp.

'Oh, well,' Phyllis said. But her heart was pounding and her corset had started to feel tight then, and she hadn't been able to breathe properly since. 'There's all sorts of funny people about.'

She didn't think Rachel or Dolly had noticed anything, but since that evening she'd had no rest. Ethel Sharp was in her neighbourhood, or close, asking for her. Not by a name that anyone would recognize, but still. It might not take long. All the time now she was looking out, almost afraid to go to the shops, checking the street before she stepped out, jumping if anyone called her name.

Ethel loomed in her mind, not as the real, dissipated old woman she obviously was, but as a fearful creature, symbolic of everything about the past, something squelching its way out of a dark swamp and lurching towards her, dripping ancient slime. The past was when she had been Hetty – another person who, with every fibre of herself, she had done her utmost to bury.

And now Ethel Sharp was looking for her. She had come menacingly close. *What did she want?*

Thirty-Six

That first morning in the broken-down house in Coventry, Hetty woke to the sound of the babies crying with hunger. The room was so like the one she had once lived in with her brothers and sisters that when she opened her eyes she thought for a moment she was back there, all of them asleep on the floor round her. A pang went through her, of both longing and dread.

She was on a hard, lumpy mattress that she could dimly remember collapsing on to the night before in her relief at being able to lie down. When she sat up, dizzily, she saw that at the foot of it the red-haired girl was crouched, watching her, and her heart began to pound hard. The girl seemed more animal than human. She was very thin, with prominent cheekbones pushing out her pallid skin and narrow, glinting eyes. She reminded Hetty of a rat. Her dress, barely big enough to stretch over her, was made of a rough, black material, and had stains all down the front. There was something severe and hard about her, her hair pulled loosely behind and tied with a scrap of rag.

'Come on then, if you're awake,' she said, standing up to reveal puny ankles, the skin mottled. There was nothing on her feet, which were very dirty and defaced by sores and cuts.

The sound of crying infants from downstairs had not

abated at all and Hetty could also hear coughing. It sounded as if there was a woman down there.

'Where're we going?' she said, struggling to her feet. A tight, clogged feeling resulted between her legs. She was caked in dried blood. 'I want to wash.'

'Ethel?' A thin, nasal voice came up to them. 'Get down 'ere and get 'em out before I finish the pair of 'em!'

Ethel jerked her head to indicate that Hetty should follow and the two of them climbed carefully down the splintery stairs. Halfway down there was a jagged hole in one of the treads.

In the downstairs room, Hetty was surprised to see a bed, which she had not noticed in the dark last night. It took up almost half the space and there were a couple of rough blankets on it, rumpled, as the woman was clearly not long out of it. She was perched on the edge of the one wooden chair, a sickly-looking creature in a dirty skirt, of a dark plum colour, and a grey blouse which may once have been white. Her mousey-brown hair was half piled on her head, half tumbling down, and against it her skin seemed tinged a sickly yellow and was marked with red, angry-looking blotches. She might have been quite pretty had she not looked so faded and sick. There was a stink of booze in the room, all too familiar to Hetty.

By the dead fire sat the two distraught infants. Ethel went and picked up the younger one, whose head appeared too big for his body – if he was a boy. It was not easy to tell. Perched on Ethel's skinny hip, he roared even more loudly. The older one, who clearly was a boy, got up and took Ethel's hand.

'Take 'em, for Christ's sake,' the woman said in a slurred voice. 'You can make the fire up when you get back.' She looked dully at Hetty. 'She'll have to earn 'er keep if she's staying. 'Ere . . .' She reached down the front of her blouse and pulled out a twisted piece of rag. Hetty heard the chink of coins. Ethel went to her and the woman dropped something into her hand.

Ethel jerked her head again. 'C'mon.'

'Go on – get out,' the woman said, without energy. They left, to the sound of her coughing. Hetty had a strange, floating feeling in her head and she felt cut off from things. She didn't even bother to ask where they were going. The baby quietened for a time when they got outside, distracted by the change of scene. The other child walked silently, as if he already knew that crying would not gain him anything. A woman along the street darted them a hard, hostile stare as they walked past. Looking round, Hetty realized, with a force that hit her hard, that she was in a familiar place. Somewhere in the surrounding streets was the house in which she had first grown up. But they were long gone, her family, she knew that. The one person she ached to see was Nancy: the rest of them seemed to have faded from her mind. But she wouldn't think about it. She pushed away all thoughts of them.

They came to a tall, imposing brick building, and from an arched side entrance they could see a queue assembled along the building's flank. It seemed made up all of children, rather subdued in manner, some in hats and caps, others bareheaded in the drizzle, some with boots and others barefoot, and most looking unkempt and dirty. As they waited, they stared without curiosity at the newcomers.

When Hetty and Ethel had been in the queue for a couple of minutes, two ladies appeared through the doorway, wearing long navy blue skirts and bonnets tied under their chins in a big bow. Each of them had their fingers threaded through the handles of a number of white china cups. With a kindly but brisk and distant air they came along the line.

'Here's your cup. Have you got your farthing?'

Hetty saw Ethel nod to these questions. She and Hetty were given a cup and as she gave Ethel hers, the woman leaned closer to her and murmured, 'How is she? Any better?'

Ethel looked back distrustfully and gave no answer. The woman moved back a fraction and patted the younger of the boys on the head.

'How're your little brothers?'

Ethel made a small sound but still said nothing and the woman moved on, seeing she was not going to get a reply.

'Are they your brothers, then?' Hetty hissed.

'Course they ain't – but she don't need to know that,' Ethel said, her voice hard and aggressive.

The queue moved slowly into a big room in the building where there was a long table and they were given sweet tea and a chunk of white bread each, after they had handed over their money. One of the ladies stood making sure that no one took more than their fair share. Ethel handed over the coins and was given four pieces of bread, one of which she put in her pocket. The other three she shared between the four of them, softening little pieces in the tea to feed to the baby. The other boy ate eagerly and solemnly. The tea and bread brought Hetty round a bit and she started to feel better.

'I want to wash,' she insisted again, feeling very uncomfortable.

Ethel scowled at her. 'Well, you'll 'ave to 'ang on a bit. We got to go back first – and we've got to get to work.'

At the house, they boiled water and at last Hetty was able to have a proper wash. She took a bucket upstairs and stripped off. But even as she rubbed herself over with a rag, feeling cleaner than she had in days, she was very uneasy. From downstairs she could hear one of the children crying. She had learned that the worn-out looking woman whose house they were in was called Ada. As Hetty and Ethel waited for the water to boil, Ada sat listlessly on the edge of the bed.

'Ask 'er how old she is,' she said suddenly, in no one in particular's direction. She had an odd way of talking, not looking at the person she was talking to but turning her head from side to side, looking out of the window, or anywhere, her fingers restlessly moving in her lap.

'How old're you then?' Ethel said, from where she was squatting by the range, holding Alf, the younger boy. The other, Eddie, sat beside her, staring at Hetty.

'Fifteen,' Hetty told her.

'You look more,' Ethel said. 'You're the same as me.'

'You're not very big,' Hetty said, disbelieving. 'Bet you aren't really fifteen.'

Ethel gave her a sly look. 'I say I am. That's how I got out of the reformatory – I told them a few fibs when they took me in. Changed my age, no home to go to, all that . . .' She put her head on one side. 'Where's your mom and yer old man then? Passed on?'

'Yes.' Hetty couldn't think what else to say.

When the water boiled she filled the bucket and went upstairs, grateful to be alone for a few minutes.

She didn't feel at ease with Ethel, and Ada was a strange, unsettling presence. But where else was she supposed to go?

Thirty-Seven

Hetty soon began to make sense of the strange household she had come into, and what 'work' meant. Ethel, having got out of the reformatory (into which she said she had been consigned, aged eleven, for 'thieving'), had met Ada one day in town. Ada had given her a roof over her head in return for help with the babies, and so long as Ethel earned her keep.

By the first afternoon, it all became clear. There came a rap at the door and Ada suddenly sprang into life and ordered Ethel and Hetty upstairs with the boys.

'And keep 'em quiet,' she hissed from the bottom of the stairs. ''Ere – take these.'

Hetty, nearest the bottom, reached out and found that Ada had put four sugar lumps in her hand for pacifying the little boys.

'We 'ave to keep 'em out of the way while she's with the punters,' Ethel said matter-of-factly. 'Most of 'em come at night time but there's one or two turn up afternoons, if it takes their fancy.'

They heard a male voice downstairs, followed by other sounds. Hetty tightened with dread. It was Mr Gordon all over again. It brought back the night, only a few weeks ago, when she was lying on Mrs Dickins's table as she did away with the baby. She tried and tried not to think of it, even though the bleeding had not even stopped completely. The memory was so raw, of the pain, the horror. Never, ever was she going to have that happen again.

But Ethel was looking at her strangely. 'You can't just live 'ere and do nothing, yer know. Some of 'em like young meat.'

'No!' The word sprang out of Hetty's mouth before she could think at all. 'I ain't doing that – not ever again!'

A sly look came over Ethel's face. In a soft, sneaking voice she said, 'Oh, so you've been on the game before then, 'ave yer?'

'No. *No!* ' Hetty was appalled. That hadn't been it! She wasn't one of those women! It had all been in a respectable house.

'Well – what then?' Ethel said avidly, quietening the boys with their second sugar lump, which they sucked on hungrily.

'It wasn't like that. I was a maid in the house. But the master, Mr Gordon . . .' Hetty stuttered out what had happened, all of it. 'And I never told him I was bleeding and . . .' For the first time, tears began to run down her face and she was sobbing, unable to stop the memories that were washing through her. 'He . . . I . . . It was just last month . . . I had to do away with it.'

'Blimey –' Ethel's eyes were wide with surprise, and a nasty kind of triumph, as if she was seeing Hetty through quite new eyes. 'I thought you was new to all this! Well – Ada *will* be keen on yer! Give 'er a bit of a rest!'

'No!' Hetty pleaded. 'I'll do anything. I'll earn my keep somehow. But don't make me do that!'

Ethel looked dispassionately at her. 'Well, we all 'ave to take our turn or she ain't going to want you 'ere. If

287

they ask for a young 'un, you'll 'ave to do what Ada
says.'

They never knew exactly when the men were going to
come. There was one who turned up after work, twice
a week, regular as a factory bull blaring out. But sometimes one would arrive first thing, straight out of bed.
They'd hear a knock at the door, Ada would roll her
eyes and if they had already come down, she'd hiss,
'Get upstairs, all of you – quick.'

Hetty and Ethel would each seize hold of Eddie or
Alf and go up to the attic where they had to try and
pretend that none of them existed. It was a hard task
with two infants to be entertained, especially early in
the morning when they were hungry. The older boy,
Eddie, was very quiet anyway. He would sit staring
with wide eyes and at any sound he ran to one or other
of the girls and buried his face against them. Alf was
more difficult; he cried a lot and was hard to pacify.

The girls would hear the deep rumble of a male voice
through the floorboards, and Ada saying things back
faintly, then those other noises, grunts and shouts, all
the men, nothing from Ada except now and then – and
this made Hetty's heart pound in horror – a shriek of
pain, her crying out and moaning. There was one man
who came who she was very frightened of, a Mr
Lavender. They never knew his other name. He always
came late and the worse for drink and Hetty never once
saw him. He blacked Ada's eyes and sometimes there
were rings of bruising on her thin, sallow arms. Hetty
would lie, tensed, horrified when they knew he was
there. Hetty was surprised how agitated it made Ethel.
She would lie, writhing, cursing. 'The bastard, the

filthy . . .' But at least he came late enough so that it was very unusual for Eddie and Alf to be still awake. If a punter came when the boys were still up, they struggled to keep Eddie happy with little games, tickling his tummy and making faces. But if Alf started crying there was a terrible ordeal of pacing the floor with him, trying to distract him and stifle his cries.

As they never saw the men, except in small glimpses as they hurried up the stairs, the only way they could tell them apart was by the time they turned up and sometimes the tone of their voices. Ada didn't say much about most of them. It was as if once they had disappeared through the door they were shut out of her mind. Only occasionally did she make passing comments. When the girls came down once after terrible sounds the night before, Ada was sitting with a bowl of water, dabbing at her face with a piece of rag. There were bloody, swollen cuts across her left eyebrow, her lips were thickened and gashed. For the first time Hetty saw in Ethel a moment of real emotion, of vulnerability, and that there was some sort of bond of pity between Ethel and Ada. She stood in front of Ada, hands on her hips, and as well as her raw fury, there were tears in her eyes.

'Which of those bastards did that?' she demanded in a tight voice.

Ada looked up, the bloody rag pressed to her eyebrow. Her eye was half shut. 'Mr Lavender,' was all she said.

Otherwise they only heard the regular comings and goings of the noisier men, and Ada mentioned a 'very quiet gentleman' who would appear now and then with no warning, usually in the early afternoon when the girls often took the little boys out.

Ada said little most of the time. She almost never ventured out of her wretched little house. Sometimes she grew agitated and quarrelsome, but a lot of the time she spent lying on the bed in a limp, listless state.

Hetty guessed that Ada was about thirty, though she looked older and worn out. Her brown hair was thin and lank, though she did her best to pin it up and smarten herself. Her face was yellow and sunken. If Hetty asked Ethel about her, Ethel would shrug.

'Where did you meet her?' she asked, and Ethel said, 'Oh, round the back of the market. 'Er wanted help getting some stuff home so I went with her.'

Somehow this arrangement had come about and Hetty could see that it suited them both. Ada was saved the effort and shame of going out and Ethel had a roof over her head as she did now, herself.

Once in a while it was Ethel they wanted. Ada would call up the stairs for her. When she came back, Ethel would fling herself down on the mattress, curled up with her face to the wall. Later she would get up and carry on. She never said anything about it. How the men knew where to come, Hetty never knew. Ethel just said, 'I dunno. I s'pose they sniff it out, like dogs.' The last time it had happened, she looked at Hetty and said, 'Next time, it's your turn.'

No, Hetty thought. *Not me – never.*

Hetty immediately told Ada she was going out to get a job – that she would bring in money that way. She soon found work in a laundry. At first Ada seemed pleased.

'Well, I s'pose you'll bring in a wage,' she said. She couldn't spare Ethel to go out and work because of the boys. And Ethel seemed to thrive on a life of ducking and diving. When she did go out it was usually to hang around the markets, to see what she could pick up or steal in the way of odds and ends of food. But Hetty would bring in some actual, regular money.

As it was the summer, the laundry was a horrible place to work because of all the steam and the heat when you were ironing with a heavy flat iron or hauling on the handle of the huge mangle. But it was work. She at least learned how to do something. When Ethel talked about the reformatory, pouring scorn on all the things they had been forced to do, learning about domestic chores, sewing, cooking and laundry, she felt almost envious. *If I'd been in there*, she thought, *I'd have learned everything, and got out and got a decent job somewhere.* At least she had been taught things by Mrs Gordon and had some idea how to cook. Sometimes a powerful longing filled her to be someone, to have a better life. She could see what Ada was and that Ethel was destined for that as well. That life was so close to her, sucking at her. The thought of it filled her with dread.

Sometimes at night she lay beside Ethel and the boys in the poky upstairs room and wondered why she stayed there, with the sordid sounds from downstairs. In her head she made plans. She had lied to Ada about how much she earned, keeping a bit back. She would save the remainder, which she kept on her at all times. As soon as she felt she had enough, she would get out of here.

One afternoon, when Hetty was coming back from the laundry, a cooling breeze blowing through her sweaty clothes, she saw someone walking towards her. The woman seemed familiar, even in the distance. As she drew near, Hetty grew more sure. The woman was a young, tired and preoccupied-looking matron, carrying a plump baby on one arm. She did not look twice at Hetty.

'Nancy?' The word slipped out of her mouth, almost unbidden.

The woman turned, eyebrows rising in surprise. The baby jiggled on her arm in pleasure as if a game had begun.

'You are Nancy Barker?'

'I was – I'm Nancy Pearson now. Who . . . ?' She peered closer. 'Are you . . . ? Is it . . . ?'

A smile broke across Hetty's face. 'It's Het, Nancy. Your sister Het!'

'Well, I . . .' Nancy seemed quite affected. She laid a hand on her chest. 'Look at you, you're all grown up. Where're you living now?'

'Not far,' Hetty said evasively. She felt her face grow serious. 'Have you been to our mom's?'

'*No*,' Nancy said. 'Mom passed on a year ago or more now. She had a growth. And the old man – well, 'e was nowhere to be seen.' She saw Hetty's enquiring expression. 'You were best out of it, Het. I couldn't do much, out there on the farm. They took 'em all away in the end. The young 'uns went to the Industrial School and some of them've fended for themselves.' She half turned away for a moment and when she turned back, Hetty saw tears in her sister's eyes and felt them fill her own as well. They each blinked them away.

'This is Susan,' Nancy said, hitching up the child on her hip. She was a healthy-looking little thing with a cap of brown hair. Hetty took her hand and made a fuss of her.

'I only come 'ere once in a while, to see Mrs Brannigan.' The name brought back a dim memory to Hetty as one of the neighbours. 'So it's surprising I should see you. How've yer been, Het – did they treat you all right?'

It seemed aeons to Hetty since she had left home. She couldn't think where to begin, so she just nodded.

'Look – I've got to go, Het. But come out and see us, eh? It's not far. Come to Brandon – ask for Leofric Farm, anyone'll tell you. You're always welcome.'

Hetty could see that Nancy was caught up in her new life, but she meant well. Smiling, she came and embraced Hetty with her spare arm. 'Look at you! You've grown up nice,' she said with sudden fondness. 'You always were a good kid. Come any time – Leofric Farm – remember? We're sisters, after all.'

Hetty stared after her as she left, with a sudden feeling that her chest was going to split open with the need to weep and weep. *Grown up nice*, Nancy had said. If only Nancy knew! Hetty didn't feel 'nice' at all. She felt dirty and spoiled and she wouldn't have told Nancy where she was living now, not for anything.

Thirty-Eight

Gradually, after Hetty found her job at the laundry and was out of the house all day, she noticed that when she was back indoors with Ada and Ethel, things had changed. The two of them seemed to have drawn closer. Sometimes, Hetty got back to find them sitting together, often with a bottle of hard stuff on the go, and giggling. When she came in they'd go quiet and look at her, as if they'd been talking about her. As soon as Hetty got paid, Ada and Ethel were keen to lift her money off her. Hetty had a little rag tied under her clothes with the money in that she was keeping back and she never let go of it and made sure she kept it well hidden from Ethel.

They started ordering her about more, making her do all the work in the house when she was there. Ethel, on the other hand, seemed to be doing nothing very much these days, now there was another source of income.

'If you're too good to work on your back,' Ada said nastily, 'you can at least give us a reason to keep you. You're only here because we let yer.'

So a lot of the cooking fell to Hetty. Ada lived in such chaos of odd moods and drink and sickness that she was hardly ever in a state to do anything.

One hot, still afternoon she came home to find the two of them, Ada and Ethel, sitting at the table, thick as thieves, a stronger than usual stench in the dingy little room. Along with the harsh-smelling drink, she recognized the odours of men, of bodily intimacies, which made her screw up her face in disgust. As she came in, Eddie ran up to her and threw his arms round her legs. He had grown fond of her and she liked the feel of his scrawny little body pressed against her.

'Got a pong under your nose, 'ave yer?' Ethel demanded. Her hair was hanging limply round her face. 'Don't like the smell of people earning their living then?'

'What d'you think I've been doing all day?' Hetty demanded. Not for the first time she asked herself why she was in this house with these women. She had been so lost and desperate that it had been a haven at first. She would have put up with almost anything and it had been easier to stay. But now she was working, maybe she could get a place of her own. She would bide her time, wait until it was right to go and she had enough pennies saved . . .

'Thinks she's too good to lie back and spread her legs,' Ada said. 'But I'll tell you summat.' She sat up, waving a finger at Hetty, the drink making her speak too loudly, slurring her words. 'Mr Lavender's been asking after you, Het. 'E likes the look of you, 'e does – and I've said 'e can 'ave yer, he's welcome!' She let out a nasty burst of laughter.

'No!' Hetty said. 'I'm not doing it . . . I'm not! Why can't Ethel . . . ?'

'Oh, Ethel's doing 'er share,' Ada said. Her hair was straggling all over her face and her eyes were moving strangely. Hetty looked at Ethel, who was smirking horribly at Ada.

'Don't think we can't make yer!' Ada said, and the two of them rocked with drunken laughter.

Hetty backed away. She was frightened by the way they were together. 'I ain't doing it. I'm doing my share. I ain't staying 'ere if you're gonna keep on about doing that. And then you won't have my wages neither.'

She was always on edge after that. The atmosphere in the house had turned. Ethel and Ada seemed to grow closer and the mood became more poisonous by the day. Ethel grew more mean and aggressive, always out to pick a fight.

''Ere comes Miss Hoity-Toity,' she'd say when Hetty got in from work. Sometimes she pinched or slapped Hetty, out of nothing but spite.

Hetty tried to ignore it, not wanting to get into a three-way fight with Ethel and with Ada, who could rouse herself to a flaming temper. But everything she did now was wrong. Ethel had been difficult enough before. Now she and Ada were ganged up against her. They kept on talking about her going with Mr Lavender. Hetty dreamed more and more of getting away from them. She would walk out of there, find somewhere else to go . . .

But it happened soon after that, one afternoon, the way she fled from there. The night before, a Saturday, Ethel had been to the market and scrounged or bought leftover veg which they cooked up into a thin stew.

Ada sat watching impassively from the bed, her legs drawn up under her. Even when there was food to be had she barely ate. She'd got a bottle from somewhere, fetched by Ethel from the Outdoor no doubt, and she drank steadily until her eyes were glazed over. She was in a nasty, snarling mood, her face drawn and sour in the candlelight. Hetty thought how little life Ada had in her for someone not very old. Even her own mother had been more alive than that. Ethel was starting to drink more and more as well.

The air crackled with resentment. Hetty held Eddie on her knee, rocking him. She'd grown fond of the neglected little boy, who reminded her of her own brothers. But she'd never taken to Alf and left him to Ethel.

'Well, don't just sit there,' Ethel snapped. Her scrawny form was bent over the pan, stirring it on the fire.

'I'm not just sitting here – I'm nursing Eddie.' No one else ever bothered.

Ethel muttered curses, her rat face tight and resentful. There were only two plates in the house so she dolloped out the food on to them, took one to Ada, who put it on the bed beside her and looked indifferently at it, and the two girls shared the other one, feeding the babies from their own helpings. Whenever Hetty went to help herself to a mouthful, Ethel spitefully pushed the spoon away with her own.

'Stop it!' Hetty said. Ethel was like a five-year-old sometimes. 'Leave me be!'

Then Ethel punched her shoulder, hard. Her eyes were narrow with spite.

'What the hell's got into you?' Hetty got up and moved away, barely fed. 'You can sodding well feed 'em then.'

She went upstairs and lay down on the mattress. It was the last night she was to spend in Spon End.

Sunday was a hard-working time for Ada, so Hetty took herself off the next day, even though it was a grey morning, spotting with rain. By now she knew a bit about some of Ada's customers. She'd see them coming

along the road, men who came ambling along pretending they were out to get some smokes. There was pasty-
faced Mr Lavender with his cap on, who made Hetty's
flesh creep, and the respectable Quiet Gentleman who
barely ever said a word. He was a dead cert for Sunday
morning. They knew he had a family somewhere, that
was all.

'Most likely packs 'em all off to church,' Ethel said
dryly once.

Hetty had nowhere particular to go. She had her little
stash of money tied into her waist, never trusting Ethel
or Ada an inch. It amounted to few shillings by now.
One day, she thought, she'd walk out to Brandon to see
Nancy, but today looked too grim and wet. She hung
about, went to the river, through the town and when
she thought it would all be over she headed back again.

There was nothing amiss outside, no indication then
of what had happened. As she went to the door, things
were unusually quiet.

She would never be able to burn the sight from her
mind. Everything was very still. The room, usually so
grey and drab, was daubed with red. There was blood
seeping across Ada's pillow and her pale, bare flesh. The
two little boys were on the floor, limp as dolls, both
with their red life seeping from their heads. The only
movement was the convulsive heave of Ethel's shoulders
as she knelt by Ada's bed, holding her hand, begging
and begging her not to die.

Possessed by panic and horror, Hetty had no thought
in her mind but to get out and as far away as possible.
She hurled herself out of the house and along the street,
only stopping for a moment by the Spon Arches to

check that her money was still in place at her waist, then tore onwards, at first not knowing or caring where she was going.

But somehow a plan was forming, one which had been a germ before: her way of escape. She made her way to the railway station.

Running to the window of the ticket office, she panted out the words. 'A single to Birmingham, please.'

Thirty-Nine

'Aggie, let Mrs Sissons in!'

Aggie had already run to open the door that Saturday morning as soon as she heard the knocking. Mrs Sissons, a rounded, soft-cheeked lady, well into middle age, was on the step in a clean pinner. Her hair was kirby-gripped into a loose bun and kindly eyes greeted Aggie from behind her spectacles.

'Morning, Agnes,' Mrs Sissons said. She was the only person who ever called Aggie by her proper name, but Aggie didn't mind. Mrs Sissons, who lived just round the corner on Turner Street, was well known in the district because for a modest fee, she helped people with laying out a body or birthing a baby. Mrs Sissons had once been a nurse and would help if called upon. When Dulcie Skinner told her that Tommy Green had come home in such a poor state, she had called round.

'I'll help you, bab, if you want me to,' she told Jen gently. 'I only wish you'd called on me before.' Jen wept with relief and worry.

'I should've got the doctor for him before,' she said, sobbing out her worries to the kindly woman. 'But he wouldn't have it – he's so set against them . . . I defied him, once he came home, and called in Dr Hill, but he says there's nothing more they can do for him now . . . I'm at my wits' end. I don't know how to manage. I've another one on the way – and we're relying on my old mom . . .'

'Don't you worry, bab,' Mrs Sissons soothed her. 'I'll help you. You don't have to pay me right away if you can't manage.'

'That's ever so good of you,' Jen said. 'But you've got to eat like the rest of us.'

Mrs Sissons chuckled. 'Oh, I don't think I'm about to waste away, do you? Any road, you think about it – everyone needs a bit of help and succour at a time like this.'

And Mrs Sissons gave it with practical generosity. Aggie beamed, seeing the woman's comforting shape on the step. It was lovely to have her dad home, but it was so frightening and sad to see him the way he was.

'How's your grandmother going along?' Mrs Sissons asked, as she came in. Her face furrowed with concern. Everyone seemed to know that Nanna was out at work now. She hobbled home exhausted every evening after a day turning out press studs. 'Someone's got to bring in some wages,' she kept saying. But the house felt wrong without her.

'The old girl's getting on all right, ta!' Nanna's voice boomed from the back. She was resting in the chair by the range.

Mrs Sissons made a comical face at Aggie, who couldn't help smiling back.

'Glad to hear it, Mrs Adams,' Mrs Sissons called to her.

Jen was coming downstairs. 'Mom's bearing up,' she said. 'I don't know how she does it. She's strong as a mule and stubborn as one too. I've tried to stop her going but there's no telling her anything . . .'

Mrs Sissons smiled. 'And how's the patient?'

301

'I'm glad you're here,' Jen said tremulously. 'Come up.'

Aggie crept upstairs behind Mrs Sissons. There were heavy creases in the back of her grey skirt where she had sat and her black shoes were distorted by her bunions. Aggie wasn't sure whether Mrs Sissons realized she was there, but at the top of the stairs she turned and put her finger to her lips.

'You stay by the door, Agnes,' she said kindly. 'There's not a lot of room in there.'

Mrs Sissons and Mom stood each side of the bed. Aggie watched, peering round the door frame.

Dad coming back home had been such a happy thing, making things feel more as they should be again. Except they weren't as they should be at all. Tommy had made a huge, final effort to get back to his own home, but it had drained him utterly and ever since he had been back, he seemed to have been going downhill. The doctor came twice after he got back. Dr Hill was a small chirpy man who Nanna said made her think of a budgie. But when he came to see Dad that time, he was quiet and grave.

'Just keep him warm and comfortable, Mrs Green,' he said. 'Do you have any more bedding?'

Mom shook her head, shamefaced. 'I could try and—' she began to say.

Dr Hill held up a hand to quieten her. 'I think I can help there. Someone will be round.'

True to his word, later that day he sent round the lady who worked at his surgery, with two rugs and a bundle of cleanly folded rags. When Mom saw them, more tears came.

'You're so kind,' she said.

Neighbours were coming in offering things as well

302

and it kept making Mom cry. Dulcie Skinner was in and out whenever she could spare a moment, with odd gifts – a milk pudding or a cake.

Aggie felt a tight, scared feeling inside her as she looked at her father. He had shrunk so thin now that the bones all stood out sharp in his face, which had turned a dull yellow, almost like Mary Crewe's fingers from all her smoking. When he tried to smile at her, which seemed to take all his strength, she could see the bones moving under his skin and his arms and legs were thin as sticks. He had a little jar that he had brought back from the hospital, to spit up into. Every time Aggie saw him it made her feel queasy and upset.

'How're you today, Tommy?' Mrs Sissons asked. Aggie heard her father give a slight groan in reply. 'Maybe the little 'un could fetch some boiled water for me,' Mrs Sissons whispered to Mom.

'Go and bring us some water from the kettle and one or two of them cloths, Aggie,' Jen said. 'Make sure it's not scalding.'

Glad of something to do, Aggie went back downstairs. Nanna was sitting with her head back, boots off and her feet up on a stool, drowsing. She looked exhausted but resolute as ever.

'There's a good wench,' she remarked, opening one eye as Aggie came in. But soon she was snoozing again.

Aggie poured the water into Mom's biggest mixing bowl, blowing away the steam, and added some cold so that it was comfortable to dip her own hand in, before carrying it up, the cloths tucked under her arm.

Aggie felt proud to be helping. The others were out playing. She wasn't sure if any of them understood how poorly Dad was, though she couldn't see how you could look at him and not know. All the time she felt peculiar, as if living on her nerves. Her body seemed to feel her sadness for her.

Aggie tried to steer her mind on to other things, and one of them was that Rose Southgate kept getting her to run errands. Mrs Southgate seemed to have changed and Aggie wasn't sure it was for the better. She didn't have her nice little tea parties on a Sunday any more and she seemed to have forgotten about some of the other things she'd promised, like teaching Aggie to sew. It was as if her mind was always far away. But at least twice a week now, Mrs Southgate beckoned her from her door and Aggie would run over to be invited inside.

'Now listen, Aggie,' she said, when Aggie had already delivered the first message to Mr King's lodgings. She called Aggie in when she got back from school. 'Sit down – I need to have a serious talk with you.' This was something new.

They were in the kitchen and Rose pulled out a chair for her, then came and sat opposite. 'Would you like a cup of tea, dear?'

Aggie shook her head. It was as if Mrs Southgate was treating her like an adult. On the table were some of her sewing things, lovely coloured threads catching the light through the door. Aggie fingered one, a bright, burned orange colour, hoping it might jog Mrs Southgate's memory of her offer, but she took no notice.

'The thing is, Aggie . . .' She stopped again. Aggie looked up. The woman's face looked tired and different somehow. 'I shall need you to run a number of errands for me like the last one to Mr King's house. Would you like that? I'll give you a penny or two of course, for your trouble.'

304

Aggie nodded. 'Yes, Mrs Southgate.'

'The only thing is . . .' Again, the hesitation, as if she didn't know what to say. 'I need you to be very careful. I am communicating with Mr King about piano lessons for Lily—'

'But I thought Mrs Wood was teaching her?' Aggie interrupted.

'Yes, well, she is,' Rose said hastily, 'but I thought, with Mr King being without sight the way he is, and him having to earn a living somehow, it would be the kind thing to do to let him teach her sometimes as well. But Aggie, the problem is, my husband's not in favour of piano lessons, not from anyone. So you see, I need to you be very careful and not tell anyone what you are doing for me or where you are going, do you see? In case it gets back to him because then I should be in dreadful trouble.'

Aggie nodded again, a bit bewildered.

'I know!' Rose said with a strange giggle. 'Why don't we make it into a game – just between ourselves? No one else must know.' She seemed to gather enthusiasm for this idea. 'You can be Mata Hari, delivering a secretly coded note across to the enemy . . . I mean, I know Mr King isn't the enemy, but we can make up our own story, can't we? You have to move back and forth in secret between here and Oldfield Road to complete your mission. Oh!' She stood up, pacing the room. 'This will be a good game, don't you think, Aggie? You could even take Lily with you now and then, as a cover story for why you are going out. Won't it be fun!'

Aggie grinned, borne along by her enthusiasm. *Agnes Green: Spy* had a mission! And it meant bringing home a few pennies for Mom as well.

'I can do it,' she said excitedly. 'No one'll know where I'm going – I shan't let on, I promise.'

'Well, that's settled,' Mrs Southgate said, laughing happily. 'Now – would you take on a little mission for this afternoon? I do need a message delivered . . .'

Aggie thought quickly. She could easily go there and back before tea and Mom wouldn't even ask where she'd been. 'Yes – but I might have to take May with me. I'm s'posed to be minding her.'

'Oh,' Mrs Southgate's expression soured a fraction. 'I see. Well, let's hope she won't slow you down too much. But I suppose, if you have to.'

'All right,' Aggie said. This was all a bit odd, but there was twopence in it for her. 'I'll go and fetch our May and I'll come straight back.'

Forty

Jen climbed the stairs that Sunday afternoon, her legs shaking with weariness. Her mother was lying down in her room, already deeply asleep. She came home from the factory every day white with exhaustion, yet determined to hide the fact.

'A cuppa'll soon set me right,' she'd say, spooning sugar in and drinking it down.

She's a tough old bird, all right, Jen thought. It wasn't enough just to say she was grateful. Stiff and tired as she was, Freda seemed to have a determination that would overcome anything. Jen was moved by her old mom, by what she was capable of. But sometimes Jen would be seized by terror. Her mother shouldn't be collaring away like this at her age! What if something happened to her? What if she was taken ill? The kids were doing their bit, bless them, but they could only earn a few coppers. She was struggling to keep up with the factory dinners. And there was her mother's miserly pension. But even so they could scarcely get by. Freda was the only thing now keeping them away from the hard-faced officials of the parish, those who could decide whether or not a family deserved to eat, and Jen knew that, at the moment, she owed her everything.

But this was only one of her troubles. She scarcely knew which way to turn for worry, about Mom, about the kids, including the ones not yet born. Mrs Sissons had persuaded Jen to let her examine her. She lay back on her bed next to Tommy as Mrs Sissons felt her belly and then listened for the heartbeat. After a few minutes she looked up, still listening.

'I've found a second one.' She spoke softly, with a note of awe. 'It *is* twins, I think, Mrs Green.'

Jen's heart leapt at this wonderful, terrible news. Her eyes filled with tears but she tried to joke. 'D'you 'ear that, Tommy Green? Two of the little so-and-sos!'

But once Mrs Sissons had gone she couldn't help herself. She lay beside Tommy and gave way to her tears. Both of them knew that he was not going to see these babies born.

He was her greatest worry and grief. For the moment, it was him she had to be with and thank the good Lord that whatever the rights and wrongs of her relying on her mother's labour, she had Freda there to help.

Now, on this quiet Sunday afternoon, the boards seemed to creak very loudly as she crept into their bedroom where he lay, on his back, his eyes closed, his chest crackling as he breathed. Jen eased herself on to the bed beside him, the rusty springs squeaking as her weight sank down. She felt queasy with tiredness and settled down with a long release of breath. Thank heavens for Sunday school. The kids were all out, at least for a couple of hours. Her hands moved over her belly. She was more than four months gone now and there was a definite bulge. Everything about carrying twins was more intense. She could hardly stand anywhere for long without feeling faint. At least it was not her having to stand on a factory floor all day.

Tommy shifted slightly beside her and began to cough, the shudders starting small then dragging out of him harder and harder until she felt he must split apart with the strain of it. Her heart seemed to turn over. However tired she was and longing for sleep, every part of her was jarred and overwrought with the distress of it all. Tommy was so weak that she knew he had to think for a long while just to move an arm or leg. How he had ever got back from that hospital she'd never know, not the state he was in. But he'd gone downhill a lot in the few weeks since. He had barely eaten anything for days. She knew she was watching death slowly take him, an agony that she could do so very little about. It was *his* death, a journey upon which she could not follow him, which he was undertaking far too young, and far, far too soon. Anger and grief went through her like a wave of bile. She could not let her mind go down the path of thinking about the future, about all their children, the unborn pair in her belly that Tommy would never see. If she started to think like that she would go mad with it.

He's here now, now this minute, she thought, and as his coughing quietened, she reached for his hand. *Here, now.* The hand was warm, dry and skeletal. His nails had changed, had turned pale and bowed out, so that his hands had a froggy look.

'Jen?' It was a hoarse whisper.

'Yes, love?' She turned to him.

There was a lengthy silence as he gathered strength, then he managed to say, 'Fancy a bit of . . . You know . . . ?'

'Tommy Green!' Startled into laughter she leaned up on her elbow and looked down at him. 'You are the very end, that you are!'

'Just kidding.' A whispery little laugh came from him.

309

'I'd never have guessed,' she said softly, kissing his sunken cheek.

He tried to say something else but the coughing came again. She had to help raise him so that he could spit out, a process which was such a racking, painful one that it was awful to watch. At last he could lie quiet again.

Jen lay tenderly stroking his arm. She was on fire with a sense of the preciousness of this moment, now, with Tommy still here. She pulled the pins from her hair, letting its faded auburn hanks loose so that she could lie comfortably beside him, burning, wretchedly full of love for him. It was bright outside, but the sun was not shining directly into the room, and the outside world felt far away, unreal to her. All her reality was in this room.

'Jen?' Tommy whispered. 'I can't see too well.'

A sense of horror seized her. His joke had lulled her into thinking he was still the old Tommy. But he was leaving, slipping away. Consumption, that's what they called it. And it was consuming him, inch by inch.

'What d'you mean?' she said, trying not to let the panic sound in her voice.

'There's . . . It's like a film over my eyes.'

'Let me look.'

She leaned over, and though he had his eyes open, they were yellowish like his skin and were taking on an increasingly foggy look, as if they were coated in sour milk. Moving her hand over his face, she said, 'Can you see that?'

'Barely. Summat moving.'

'Oh . . . Tommy.'

She lay down again, trying to warm him, wanting to weep, but the grief of it all was dammed up inside her.

And there it must stay, she knew, for the moment. He needed something better from her.

'Hey,' she said, 'd'you remember that time you and Frank Murphy and the others climbed up to spy on Mrs Evans? You were the one right at the top – I don't know how you didn't fall and kill yourself!'

Tommy and the other lads in the yard had formed a tree, scrambling up on to each other's shoulders one winter evening to peer in at the window of the most loathed woman in the street. They knew if she caught them she'd come roaring out ready to give all of them a good hiding. Jen watched, a hand over her mouth, as Tommy climbed the drainpipe like a monkey, over the first boy's shoulders as he clung on, grumbling, then the second boy who was already looking as if he wished they'd never started all this. Tommy's face moved above the sill of the upstairs window and Jen gasped, certain that Mrs Evans would be out with the poker any second. And then Tommy, in a hissing whisper, had let out the electrifying words: ''Er's there inside – in 'er nuddies!'

''Er's never!' The boy at the bottom started shaking with a fatal mix of laughter and fear and the whole structure started to look very shaky.

''Er is – honest!'

Everyone started to panic. Jen thrilled with utter terror as the stack of boys crumpled. Tommy slithered down the drainpipe, jumping from halfway up, and they all fled out through the dark entry, expecting Mrs Evans to be roaring behind them. The debate had gone on for many days afterwards as to what Tommy had seen.

'You never saw 'er with no clothes on,' the middle boy argued. ''T'ain't true – you never.'

After a time Tommy conceded that she might just

have had her bloomers on. But they'd never got the full truth out of him – what had he actually *seen*?

Jen lifted her head again. '*Was* she there – Mrs Evans, that day?'

She felt a light tremor pass through Tommy, a memory of laughter more than the thing itself.

'She wasn't, was she? You were having us on all the time!'

'Not saying.'

'Tommy!' she cajoled. She looked into his face. 'She wasn't there, was she?

Faintly he shook his head, grinning. 'No one there . . . At all . . .'

'You cheeky little bugger,' she said affectionately, lying down to reminisce some more, to bring back sweet memories of their youth. 'You always were a cheeky bugger.'

Tommy, her Tommy, just like the first day she'd set eyes on him in Kyrwicks Lane, on his mucky, cheeky, incorrigible face. She'd loved him ever since then, hadn't she?

She lay close, wrapping her arm very gently around his wasted body, the bones all that seemed left of him. But he was still here . . . Now. For the moment. And in this moment, whatever the future held for her, she wanted to love him with all her heart.

Forty-One

Tommy Green was nearing his end. Everyone knew Mrs Sissons and when you saw her going in and out of a house it was certain something was up.

Neighbours came and went, offering help. Dulcie, Jen's best friend, came as often as she could, and others called to see what they could do or just to exchange a few words.

Irene Best was one of them. She came over and stood at the front, saying she wouldn't come in. She kept turning and glancing anxiously at her husband as she was talking. John Best did not like to be seen outside but as it was a warm day she had wheeled him close to the door. He could just be seen, stiff and immobile in the front room.

'How is he, Rene?' Jen asked, even though she knew the answer really. Her heart ached for Irene, whose face, as usual, looked pale and strained.

'Much the same,' Irene said with a slight shrug. She appeared much too old for her age. The war had knocked the life out of both of them. They'd never had any children. 'Although –' She hesitated. 'I can't help thinking he's going downhill a bit. A dose of something – that influenza – it'd finish him. Anyhow –' She gathered herself bravely, as she had done so many times. 'We go along. I came to ask about your Tommy.'

Jen's eyes filled with tears but she wiped them away fiercely.

'Nothing to be ashamed of,' Irene told her sweetly. 'I must've wept that much I could've topped the sea up in my time.'

'But if I start . . .' Jen said, wiping her eyes on her sleeve. 'He's fading fast, Rene. You should see the state of him. His sight's gone. All that's left of him's skin and bone.'

Irene Best reached out and touched her arm. 'I'm always there if there's anything I can do, Jen. I know everyone says that, but it's true – you just let me know.'

Jen thanked her and she scurried back across the street. The sight of her made Jen's tears flow again. All this sadness brought out the tenderness in people.

She was surprised the next day to find Rose Southgate on the step, holding a plate with a Victoria sponge on it. Rose seemed shy and awkward.

'Aggie told me how poorly her dad is. I . . . Well, I thought the children might like a bit of this – when they get home from school. Aggie's been such a good girl, taking Lily to the Sunday school and . . . Well, I just wanted to say I'm sorry . . .'

'That's good of yer,' Jen said, feeling awkward, but genuinely touched.

'How is your husband?'

'Bad,' Jen said. Again, she couldn't hold the tears. She saw Rose Southgate's brow crinkle with sympathy as she wiped her eyes on her pinner.

'I'm sorry. Oh, you poor thing. But –' She stopped, as if feeling she was about to say the wrong thing.

'What?' Jen said.

'No – nothing. Here – take it, won't you?' Rose

handed her the plate. She didn't seem to expect to be invited in, was backing away. 'She's a good girl, your Aggie.'

Jen stared at her, then looked at the cake in her hand. It had icing sugar sprinkled on the top, as well as a layer of jam in the middle. Rose had gone to some trouble and she was touched. 'That's nice. Don't s'pose it'll last five minutes when this lot get in.'

Rose smiled. 'No, I don't s'pose it will. Oh – please give my regards to your mother, won't you?'

And she was gone. Jen watched her for a moment, puzzled, then took the cake into the house.

A few days later, Rose was giving Lily her tea, when she heard a knock at the door. Frowning, she went to answer.

'Oh!' She actually jumped, her hand going to her heart, and cried, 'Arthur – oh, Lord! What on earth are you doing here?'

He looked understandably taken aback and hurt. She had left him only last Sunday after another afternoon of love and closeness.

'I'm sorry, Rose – it's just that I'm on my way back from a job over this way. I couldn't bear to pass you by. I got off the bus a couple of stops early.' He added uncertainly, 'I so much wanted to see you.'

Rose looked despairingly along the street. It was teeming with children and people coming home from work. Everyone would see them! And she didn't know when Harry would be home but it could be any time.

'Come in, quickly!' She reached for his hand and almost pulled him inside, closing the door as soon as she could.

'Rose, love, whatever's wrong?' He could hear how flustered she was.

'Arthur . . .' She tried to make her tone more gentle but she was utterly wound up with tension.

'Who is it?' Lily wandered out from the back.

'Hello, Lily,' Arthur said.

'Go and eat your tea,' Rose ordered her sharply.

Lily looked very downcast and stumped back into the kitchen, resentment in every line of her body.

'I've done wrong in coming – I'm sorry,' Arthur said. 'Only I was longing to see you and I don't really see the harm. Why should you not have an admirer? No one expects a woman to stay alone for ever.'

Appalled at herself, Rose, said, 'Oh, Arthur, I'm sorry. It's hard to explain. But you really can't stay. I'll tell you everything properly one day, but not today. Listen – come to the back with me for a minute, but then you really must go, dear.' She reached for his hand, then moved close and kissed his cheek. 'Never doubt that I love you so. I'm just a foolish woman.'

He seemed a little reassured and followed her to the back room, but Rose was still in a turmoil of nerves. Had she time to offer him a cup of tea? How could she not? It would look so odd and offhand, cruel even.

'The kettle's on,' she said, trying to control her tone. Her heart was beating so hard she had to keep taking deep breaths to try and calm herself. 'Why don't you sit down beside Lily, Mr King?'

Arthur felt his way to a seat and sat, saying, 'Hello, Lily. How's your piano playing coming on?'

Lily looked solemnly at him, a tussle evident in the expression in her blue eyes. She liked Arthur but she didn't like the way his coming made her mother so sharp with her.

316

'All right,' she said, but she didn't summon up a smile.

Arthur, kindly man that he was, asked her some more simple questions, drawing the little girl out. Rose was just about to fill the teapot when to her horror she saw Harry walk past the back window, guiding his bicycle to where he left it in the backyard. She sprang across the room.

'Arthur – get up now – get to the front!'

Harry had not looked inside, thank God, thank God.

Her tone was so hysterical, so commanding, that he did not question it. She led him as fast as possible to the front.

'Here's your coat, hat – go, please.'

'But . . . ?'

'Just get out of the house. I'll explain – but not now. Just get out – please!'

He was stepping out as the back door opened.

'Rose!' Harry shouted.

She closed the front door as quietly as she could, her hands shaking. She felt utterly wretched.

'What're you doing?' Harry said, morose as usual. His clothes were begrimed with a day's work and many smears of paint.

'I thought I heard someone at the door,' she said. 'But there was no one there. Must be hearing things.'

'Huh.' He lost interest.

'I was just making tea,' she said. Lily watched them both warily, knowing better than to speak.

Harry went into the scullery to wash. Rose brewed tea and cut him a slice of bread to keep him going. She stood by the range, watching as he ate hungrily, biting off big hunks with his strong jaws, ravenous after a hard day's work. Neither of them spoke. Harry seemed so far from her, a stranger. All she could feel was distance and loathing. Yet she also felt terrible. He was her husband. She was a deceiver and was living off the fruit of his labours. He didn't know about the bits of money she earned, she'd made sure of that.

What kind of person am I? she thought, holding her own cup of tea with trembling hands.

But more than all that and far worse was the thought of the way she had treated Arthur. With her whole being she longed to run to him and put things right, hold him close in her arms and pour out to him how much she loved him and why she had behaved like that, pushing him out of the house so roughly as if he was nobody! She ached with longing and frustration at the thought that she would not have an opportunity to see him until Sunday. She was so appalled, so agitated that she had to restrain herself from letting out a groan of anguish right there in the kitchen with Harry and Lily at the table.

She had to get a message to Arthur somehow – *had* to! In those moments, all she wanted was for her family to vanish in a puff of smoke so that she could run to him, write to him, anything to relieve the terrible burden she was holding inside her.

Turning to the stove, she put the stew pot on to warm through and forced herself to speak casually. 'Will you be going down the road tonight?' Harry liked a pint or two whenever he could afford it.

Harry took this to mean resentment. He was in an aggressive mood. 'I've been collaring all day, woman. Don't flaming start on me!'

'I wasn't.' Keeping her back to him she swallowed down her anger, her urge to shout, *I don't care if you*

go out – go on, go! I don't care if I never see you again!
'I was only asking.'

'What if I am?'

'Nothing – you go.'

He put his head down, muttering about how he'd go out if he cowing well wanted. Rose closed her eyes. He'd be out. Thank God. Could she get Aggie to deliver the message before school tomorrow? No, that was ridiculous. What possible reason could she give? She'd either have to do it herself or wait until the school day was finished. No – she couldn't bear that. She'd have to take a note round herself – tonight.

Once Harry had put his cap back on and strolled off to the pub, Rose got Lily into bed with as much patience as she could manage. It seemed to take an eternity. At last she could settle down to write a note. But this held its own frustrations. Anything she wrote would be read by Mrs Terry. Although Arthur's land-lady must know by now that he was courting a young lady and there was no shame in that, she certainly didn't know what was going on in her house on Sundays. She also did not want the woman nosing into any personal details.

Dear Arthur,
    It was unfortunate that I missed you today over a slight misunderstanding. I shall meet you next time, unfailingly.
    Yours,
        Rose

It seemed a dreadful, stilted note, but she could hardly pour out all she felt for Mrs Terry's eyes. At

319

least, until she saw Arthur on Sunday he would know that she was thinking of him and that there would be an explanation for her behaviour.

She slipped out and along Lilac Street, praying that Lily would not wake while she was out. *I mustn't do this again*, she thought, feeling conspicuous even though it was already dusk. *People will see – they'll soon be talking. I must use Aggie.* But this time she just *had* to. She hurried as fast as she could to Oldfield Road and posted the note, standing back to look up at the house. But of course there was no sign of him. His window faced over the back and even then she doubted he put the light on. He had no need of it. It seemed so sad, to be sitting there in the dark, and she longed to push her way into the house and go up to him.

Walking home, she was talking to him, trying to explain. 'I'm sorry my darling, I'm so sorry. I'd never hurt you for the world. But you came when . . . My husband was coming home . . .'

Husband. Arthur did not know she had a husband. She had lied and lied to him. What explanation could she possibly give for that?

Forty-Two

Even when she was standing at the door in Oldfield Road on Sunday, Rose still had not decided what she was going to say to Arthur. She could not lie to him any more – but how could she tell the truth? How would she appear to him then: not just as a liar, but as a fallen woman? Round and round her mind went, never getting past her fear and shame.

Aggie had taken Lily to Sunday school and, at three o'clock exactly, Rose stood waiting. The door swung open.

'Rose?'

She could see him listening and for a second she longed to run away again. Pulling her cardigan more tightly round her, she stepped forward.

'I'm here, love.'

'Good, I'm so glad.' He seemed relaxed and was talking normally instead of in the usual whisper. 'I got your note – or rather, Mrs T did. She's gone out for the afternoon to see her sister,' he added jubilantly.

Rose followed him inside, relieved that he seemed so untroubled. Following him upstairs, she could see that he was just glad she was there. She wondered whether he would even ask about what had happened, or, in his discreet way, act as though her behaviour had just been a result of some mood of hers that need not be discussed further. What she did not know was whether Arthur could have heard Harry as he came in. Surely he must have done?

Arthur led her up to his room and closed the door. She did not look around her, so preoccupied was she with all that was spinning round in her head. She longed for someone else to decide what must come next.

And Arthur did just that. Closing the door he came and stood by her. Rose turned to face him.

'You're here at last,' he said. She could see that he was terribly nervous now, that he both wanted and did not want this conversation to begin.

'Yes,' she gasped. 'Of course.'

They put their arms round each other and held each other closely, with great tenderness, but still all the questions seethed between them.

His lips close to her ear, Arthur said, 'What is it, my love? What happened the other day?'

She hesitated. She could cover up, concoct something. But it was no use. Why lie to a man who was so good? In the end, how could he love her for a liar?

'I'm married,' she told him. Just like that. Simply and straight. And she stood in his arms and waited. She did not weep. She felt cold and dry and terribly sorry.

Arthur pushed her away, as if to look into her face, and it wrung her heart because he could not read her like that. Had he been able to see, would he have seen before that she was not true? He gripped her upper arms so hard that it hurt but she was almost glad of this.

'Is that who I heard?'

She nodded. 'Yes.'

Arthur released his grip on her and felt his way across to sit on the bed, slowly, like someone with an internal injury. He slumped forward, arms resting on his thighs.

Rose did not dare to break the silence. She folded her arms tightly across her, feeling suddenly as if all warmth had been sucked from the room. She could see that he was trying to take it in, to summon up how he really felt but he just looked bewildered and winded by the information. She stood very still, hardly knowing how to breathe.

Without turning his head, at last Arthur just said, 'Why? – *Why*?'

'I . . .' Rose drew in a long breath. Her words came out in a rush. 'I liked you. I wanted you. I was – am – so unhappy. I don't love my husband – I don't think I ever have. If I'd told you the truth we've never have –' Blushing suddenly she stopped.

'But –' Arthur's voice rose. 'You're married. *Married*, Rose! To a man – a real flesh-and-blood man. You can't just pretend he doesn't exist so that you can do as you like. You have a child – responsibilities. A *marriage*, for heaven's sake! You must have lost your senses, lying to me the way you have.' His voice was hardening into anger. 'What did you think you were doing? Playing – is that it? A nice little game of secrets, lies – do you have any idea what this has meant to me, what I feel?'

'*Yes*.' She almost roared at him, hoarse with emotion. 'I have an idea, Arthur. Do you have an idea what it's like being married to a man like Harry, who has no . . . No interest, no conversation . . . Who never . . . Oh, I can't explain. I liked you, Arthur, and then I loved you and I was so frightened that you'd leave. I've never met anyone like you, or known what it was like before to love someone properly. I couldn't help myself.'

Arthur had bowed his head wretchedly and she dared to go and sit beside him. She could sense that he was very close to tears and all she wanted to do was to give

323

comfort. She gazed at his face, full of love, wanting to put her arms around him but not daring.

'It's very, very dark in here,' he said slowly. He paused, swallowing. 'I try not to be some whining, self-pitying ninny. And then suddenly there you were, lovely – I know you're lovely – loving. Lighting everything up, making things hopeful in a way I never ever expected to feel . . .'

Rose laid her hand on his back, but Arthur flinched. 'Don't!' He turned his head and very calmly, said, 'Please go now. Just go.'

'Arthur, no!' Now she began to cry. 'You don't mean that – you can't! How can you just end things like that? We can't—'

'No,' he said, his voice cold and angry now. 'That's just it. We can't. That's an end of it. You're married. You belong to another man and you have been untruthful to me and to him. We can't have any sort of future together. What more is there to say?'

Rose had stood up, propelled by his words, but she could not take in the finality of what he was saying.

'But what about being friends?' she said, tears on her cheeks. 'We could—'

'D'you think I'm made of stone? How could we be friends after this? What, me coming round again for polite cups of tea with that Muriel woman and with Lily? Yes, I would do it to be with you because maybe it would make life more worth living. But how could I be in the same room as you and not hold you, bed you – after how we've been? I couldn't, Rose. Look, *please*.' He was half weeping now as well. 'Just go away.'

She walked draggingly to the door, then to the top of the stairs, glancing behind her several times, wanting him to get up, to call for her, stop her. One by one she took the stairs, each step a knell, hollow and final. Every fibre of her wanted to turn back, to beg him for mercy, but she didn't dare. She knew she had done Arthur a terrible wrong, but she could not help herself.

At the bottom of the stairs she paused, hand on the latch, listening. No sound came from the bedroom above. She turned the handle and let herself out, quietly closing the door.

The street outside, the lovely spring day, felt like another existence altogether, mocking her. She didn't want to go home, not yet, but the sobs forcing up inside her would not be controlled and in desperation she turned into an alley between two houses for a few moments to try and calm herself. Head pressed against the brickwork she gave way to the emotions tearing at her, but still having to be quiet, though she wanted to wail and scream. The future was a place of despair. She would have to go back to Harry, to act as if nothing had happened, just go on, in the bleak way she was used to.

'Oh, Arthur,' she whispered. 'Arthur, Arthur.'

Quietening a little she felt suddenly that she wasn't alone. Stepping back abruptly, dashing the tears from her eyes, she saw a little girl watching her from some distance along the alley. She was a sturdy little thing, about Lily's age, with plump, grubby cheeks and short brown waves of hair; barefoot and wearing only a long shirt. She was frowning slightly, in puzzlement.

'Don't cry, lady,' she said.

Rose wiped her face and tried to smile. 'All right,' she said kindly, 'I shan't. Don't worry, little girl.'

She went back out to the street and in a daze, somehow made her way home.

Forty-Three

Rose stood peering round the edge of the net curtains, at the busy street. She kept finding herself drawn back to stand and stare. She did not know what she was looking for, and sometimes did not remember even going into the front room. But there she was, watching, waiting.

'Mom?' Lily stood timidly at the door.

Rose turned irritably. Nothing was Lily's fault, the poor innocent little thing, but Rose was in such a state that she found it almost unbearable to have anyone there, breaking into her thoughts.

'I'm coming, just leave me a minute,' she said, turning back to the window.

'You said that before,' Lily said. Her mother who had always been so affectionate and available had changed into someone unpredictable and moody.

'Just go back to the table for a minute or two and finish your picture – then I'll be in.'

Lily squirmed, swinging back and forth, her weight mainly on one leg. 'But I've finished.'

'Well, just go and wait quietly!' Rose's temper flared. God, how she longed to be alone, to lie on her bed and give way to a storm of tears. 'Can't you just leave me alone for one minute?'

Tears came then anyway, as Lily went back sulkily to the kitchen. What had come over her, talking to Lily like that? But all she could think of was Arthur. She was consumed by longing and grief, by a gnawing physical need for him which she knew could never be answered. Many times that week she had thought of ending her life altogether. Throwing herself in front of a train or into the canal. Poison – anything to end this bitter, dragging pain and the knowledge that that was all she had to look forward to now: her pain and the shame and bitterness of knowing what Arthur thought of her and how she had hurt him.

Over and over in her mind she wondered how she could have done things differently and been more truthful. If she had been straight with him, they would never have become lovers, surely, and despite everything, her times lying in Arthur's arms were her most precious memories The thought of not having had that was truly unbearable. And now all she could think about was that she would never have it again . . . Her days were very dark, so much so that even Harry had noticed her low mood. It was only Lily who was keeping her now from doing something extreme, committing an act that would allow her to sink into deep, relieving darkness.

There were movements in the street. She saw Mrs Sissons making her way stiffly along with her little blue bag. Mrs Sissons had been going to number nine a lot – Rose knew from her frequent visits to the front window. That could only be a bad sign. She would have liked to pay another visit to Jen Green, to offer any help that might be needed. Aggie had called in a number of times, to bring back Rose's plate which had had the cake on it, and to ask if Rose needed any errands running. When she said no, Aggie looked puzzled and disappointed. Poor little waif, Rose thought. She ought to just go along now and ask after Tommy Green, but she couldn't seem to decide to do it. All she could do was stand in a stupor by the window.

That's all she wanted, she told herself, just to see him. If she could see him one more time, walking past, to know he was in the world somewhere, living his life, not weeping as she had last seen him, and all because of her, then she would feel better.

She composed letters to him in her head, and felt bitterly frustrated because he could never read them for himself. In her more distraught moments she agonized about asking for Aggie's help, getting the child not just to deliver the letters but to read them to him as well. Surely, if she paid her, Aggie would help? The child seemed pathetically eager to please, to be in her company. All the more so now her father was so ill. A number of times when Aggie had come to play with Lily she had almost been on the point of taking her aside and confiding in her, confessing everything. To a child! But who else in the world did she have to tell her heart to? She knew that as the days went by she was beginning to feel more and more unbalanced, but there seemed no way out – she was caught in a trap of her own making.

That night, Harry came home looking pleased with himself.

Rose heard him putting his bike away round the back and tried to pull herself together and arrange her face to look normal. He had already asked her a number of times what was eating her – as if she could tell him!

He came through the back door carrying something wrapped in a greasy-looking piece of brown paper which he planted on the kitchen table, and said with a grin, 'Have a look in there – and it dain't cost us a penny!'

Trying to look interested, and as if she was not in a state of agony, she peeled back the paper. Inside was a leg of mutton. She looked questioningly at Harry. Lily was by the edge of the table, peering at it.

'Some pal of the old man's – had a few going spare. Ask no questions like.' Harry grinned, tapping his nose. 'Nice, eh? Shall us have it tonight?'

Rose shrugged. 'It'll take a long while to cook – it's a bit late . . .'

'Well? We can't save it for long or it'll walk off on its own. Let's get it in the stove – it's only five o'clock and it'll be done in a couple of hours.'

She seemed to have no energy, her limbs and voice no force. 'All right, then,' she agreed.

At her lack of enthusiasm, Harry's temper switched.

'What the hell's the matter with you now, yer mardy cow?'

'Harry!' she protested. 'Lily's here . . .'

But he was livid, spoiling for a fight. 'You've done nothing but mope about for the past week, face as long as Livery Street and not a word for any of us. There ain't no pleasing you, wench. You're no sort of wife, you ain't – you can't even put a smile on yer face when I come in through the door. I've been collarin' all day and what do I get? You, you miserable bint!'

'Harry!'

'Don't "Harry" me!' He came up close and Rose saw Lily run out of the room. They heard her feet on the stairs.

'You're no good in the bed and you're no good out of it neither – I've had about enough of it.' He came round the table so that she was trapped, her pelvis

329

forced painfully up against the range. Rose was taken aback by the sheer speed and force of his change of mood. He took her face in one hand and squeezed painfully.

'I should never've married such a pretty bitch – I knew there'd be a drawback.' He squeezed harder, pressing his groin against her.

'Ow – that hurts, Harry!' She pulled at his arm, twisting her head to try and get away from him. She managed to free her face from his grasp but he still had her pinned. Her own temper rose to boiling point. 'Get away from me – don't you dare touch me like that!'

'Touch you!' He brought his face right up to hers. His breath was a blast of stale cigarettes and onions. 'Why shouldn't I touch you? You're my wife, or supposed to be! I've got my rights, you know. I've got the right to you – not this half-and-half wishy-washy offering I get. Rights – that's what!'

She looked aghast at him. Who had he been talking to? Had he been complaining to other men about their most intimate life? What was all this sudden talk about rights? It took the wind out of her sails. Not only was she trapped with him now, for life, but he had it in his head suddenly that there was no holding back. He had rights to anything.

'Get off me,' she said quietly, her voice full of venom.

'Get off yer!' He mocked. 'That's all I ever sodding well do – just when I want more. You're a cold bitch, you are. I wish I'd married someone with a bit of fire, a bit of summat for mc! I wish I'd never married you!'

'Well, that makes two of us,' she cried, hating him with a force that swelled in her, and he could see it. Grimacing, he drew back his hand, slashing it across her face, back and forth several times, stunning, stinging

330

blows, until she was limp at the knees, sliding to the floor, hands shielding her face. She pulled her knees up and buried her face in them, arms over her head to fend off more blows. She could tell her face was bleeding. Harry stood over her.

'Ah, you stupid, useless bitch,' he said contemptuously. He stood over her. 'I should finish you off for good, that's what.'

She heard him go out again, then the slam of the back door.

June 1925

Forty-Four

'Go *on*, Silas.' Aggie stood on the step with her hands on her hips like a miniature mother, watching as Silas trotted along trying to catch up. 'John – wait for 'im!' she yelled furiously.

Mom had made her stay off school today and she never really trusted John to get the others there on time and in one piece. She was about to shout after John again when she heard another voice.

'Aggie! Aggie!'

Lily came running along from her house. Even though she only lived two doors away, Aggie knew that Mrs Southgate hardly ever let Lily out on her own.

'What's the matter, Lily?' Aggie bent over her kindly.

Lily's pretty face was pale and she looked upset, but she was not tearful. There was something tight and mutinous in her expression.

'Mom wants you.' She pulled on Aggie's hand. 'Come quick.'

At number fifteen, Aggie found the door open a crack. Lily pushed it wide and dragged her inside. To Aggie's surprise, Mrs Southgate was standing in the front room as if she was waiting for her. Aggie froze, shocked. The left side of Mrs Southgate's face was all mauve and swollen and she could hardly open her eye. There were other signs of bruises and cuts on her face as well. She stood frantically rubbing her hands together as if she was washing them over and over again.

'Aggie . . .' There was a tremor in her voice. 'I wanted to ask you if you could take a message for me later, please – when you get back from school? I can't go,' she added faintly. 'Not like this . . .'

Aggie's heart was pounding. Mrs Southgate looked terrible! Whatever had happened? She knew instinctively that it was Mr Southgate who had done it to her.

'I ain't going to school today,' she admitted. 'Mom wants me at home. What with our dad being bad and . . .' Tears suddenly filled her eyes.

'Oh!' Rose Southgate clenched her hands over her heart. 'Oh, dear. I'm so sorry – but if you could take the message straight away . . .' She stopped, seeming to think. 'It's no good, he won't be there,' she muttered to herself. 'No, it's all right – take it later as usual. You promise me?'

Aggie nodded solemnly. She didn't know what else to say.

Rose Southgate touched the side of her face self-consciously and gave a strained little laugh. 'I do look a terrible mess, I know. I've been so silly – had a little fall. Didn't I, Lily?'

Lily stood stony-faced, without agreeing. What Aggie noticed more even than Mrs Southgate's face, was the change in Lily, who had always been a precious, sunny little girl.

'You will come then, later?' Rose insisted. 'You won't forget, will you?'

'I'll come,' Aggie said.

336

She left Mrs Southgate's house, for the first time ever feeling that she was glad to escape.

Aggie spent the day minding May and helping Mom. Now Mom was feeling better herself she was cooking the meals again. She said all she wanted was to keep busy, and the house felt quiet and bereft without Nanna. But Aggie could see changes in her grandmother. Although the work was gruellingly tiring, Nanna seemed more able to get going these days and there was a new light in her eye. Instead of sitting about trying to keep out of the way, she came home with news and chat and seemed suddenly livelier.

Aggie washed a few clothes in a pail outside, as it was a nice day. The backyard was paved with blue bricks and led out on to a narrow alley which ran along the backs of the houses, accessed by the entries every few houses along. Right outside the back door there was the brick privy. Dad kept his barrow just across by the wall, and on the back wall of the house beside the window, hooked on a nail, was the family's tin bath. The washing line hung the length of the yard, fastened to the back of the house and to a post by the gate.

The blue bricks were already running with water. Aggie had dragged the mangle out from the privy where they kept it under a piece of sacking to stop it rusting too quickly. It was a tight squeeze in there when you wanted to piddle. She squatted down to work while May splashed about in another pail of water beside her.

'Don't go getting your clothes all wet,' Aggie scolded her.

May decided her job was to take a scrubbing brush

to the clothes pegs and as this seemed a harmless pursuit, Aggie let her get on with it, even though she got soaked in the process.

Aggie was glad to be kept busy. She didn't like to think about the fact that only a few feet above their heads her dad was lying, wasted as a skeleton and so frighteningly yellow. From inside she heard the faint sound of voices when Mrs Sissons arrived to help wash and turn Dad and try to get him to eat or drink. It was days now since he had eaten anything.

'I don't know how he's still hanging on,' she had heard Nanna say. 'Must be tough as old boots.'

Mom was upset all the time. 'I can't stand seeing 'im like this,' she'd sob. 'I almost wish it was over for him – but I don't want him to go . . .'

Aggie felt a bit sick nearly all the time. Trying to push away any thoughts about what was going on indoors, she stood up and tipped the rinse water into the drain.

'Come and catch the clothes then,' she ordered May. 'Empty out your bucket now and you can put the clothes in it.'

May obeyed gladly; she liked this game. The washed pegs were all rowed up on the side wall like little soldiers, to dry out. As Aggie turned the handle of the mangle, pushing through the bits of hand washing, May waited the other side ready to catch the clothes as they came through like flattened snakes.

As she was about to mangle the second item, Aggie said, 'This is John's shirt. I'll have to put it through and then back to save the buttons – they'll smash, else.'

May watched solemnly as she performed this feat. Aggie caught sight of her sister's dark-eyed, squashy little face fixed in complete concentration the other side of the mangle, and for an unexpected moment felt such a rush of love for her that she almost started to cry. She felt bewildered. Everything seemed to be heightened at the moment, her feelings at times storming up within her, overwhelming her. She stopped and after a moment May looked up questioningly at her. Aggie struggled to control herself.

'Right. I'm gonna turn it back the other way now,' she said gruffly. 'So the buttons don't go through. Mind your fingers, May!'

After Mrs Sissons had gone, Aggie, May and Mom had a bite of dinner together, just bread and tea. Mom looked so pale and sad. Afterwards she slowly climbed the stairs and Aggie heard her speak. A few minutes later she came down. Aggie's innards tightened even further when she saw Mom had tears in her eyes. They were never far away these days, grief flooding out of her for the man who was leaving them and leaving life too young.

Softly, she said, 'Your dad wants to see you – and May. Take her up in a minute – before he falls asleep again.'

May looked at them, wide-eyed. Aggie's stomach clenched, but she became the grown-up one again.

'Come on up with me, May. We're going to see our dad.'

Full of both longing and dread, she climbed the creaking stairs holding her little sister's hand. May looked up at her more than once on the way up, as if for reassurance. Aggie could hear Mom weeping quietly downstairs.

They tiptoed to the bedroom door and looked in.

Dad was all bones and so shrunken, it was almost as if there was no one in the bed. They heard him make a faint sound, a papery rattle in his chest as if he needed to cough but hadn't the strength.

Aggie looked at May and pulled on her hand. She felt almost afraid, as if Dad had become someone else now his flesh had wasted away, as if death was stealing him, piece by piece. They walked round to his side of the bed and stood looking. There was that funny smell hanging about him, Aggie noticed, like pear drops. They didn't say anything but he seemed to sense them there. He couldn't really see any more, only shadows, he said, but he turned his shrunken face towards them. Aggie saw the bones and skin moving at his neck.

'Is that my wenches?' he whispered.

Aggie was almost afraid to speak and was nodding when he said again, 'Is it? Speak up.'

'Yes,' she said.

'Dadda . . .' May said in a frightened voice. They had both almost forgotten how he used to be.

There was a movement under the covers.

'Take my hand,' he whispered.

Aggie looked down and uncovered his hand with its odd, bulbous nails. She pulled May's warm little hand close and put it between hers and her father's.

'Here we are, Dad. It's Aggie and May. The others're at school.' Tears ran down her cheeks as he tried to tighten his grasp but hadn't the strength.

Her father's face convulsed and Aggie thought for a terrible moment that he was going to cry. She didn't know whether it was twisted by pain or grief. But the spasm passed. They stayed for a few moments, in an agony of feeling mixed with not knowing what to say.

There came the faintest of squeezes from his hand, then he whispered, 'That's my good wenches.'

Before long they realized he had drifted off to sleep, and traitorous with relief, they tiptoed away again from the man who was barely their father any more.

As promised, Aggie called in to number fifteen later that afternoon. This was also nerve-racking, because Mrs Southgate had become a stranger as well.

When she knocked, she sensed that Mrs Southgate had been looking out for her because she was not long coming to the door, which she opened a crack to let Aggie swiftly inside. Her face was still a dreadful mess, though her eye was a little bit wider open than it had been in the morning. She seemed pleased with Aggie for coming on time, but there was something frantic about her which Aggie found a bit alarming.

'Did you want me to take a message to Oldfield Road then?' she asked.

'*Yes*,' Rose said, almost gasped. 'But Aggie dear, this time I want you to do something different from usual, please. I haven't written a note to Mr King this time. He should be home from his work quite soon. What I need you to do is speak to him. If he's not there when you get there – his landlady will tell you – you must wait for him. D'you understand?'

Aggie nodded solemnly.

'When he comes, tell him who you are – remember he can't see you.' She spoke with great intensity. 'Give him your name and tell him that Mrs Southgate has a problem with her piano and she needs to speak to him about it urgently.'

'With her piano,' Aggie repeated.

'*Yes.*' She didn't enlarge upon this. 'He'll understand. And you bring me his reply. All right?'

Aggie hurried away, and trotted past the Mission Hall and along to the Ladypool Road, glad to have something to do with all her own pent-up energy. It took a little while to get to Oldfield Road and when she reached the house she was panting. She didn't feel much like ringing the bell and after a few moments she thought she caught sight of a figure walking along from the opposite end of the street, moving in a way different from everyone else. His gait was slower and more uncertain.

As Mr King approached she felt a bit nervous. Seeing him again though, she remembered what a kindly manner he had. But as he drew near the gate, she was startled to see that instead of having a sunny, amiable look, his features were now drawn and sad.

'Mr King?'

He stopped, startled. 'Yes?' he said wearily and not in expectation of anything that would interest him.

'I'm Aggie – Agnes Green. I've come from Mrs Southgate, in Lilac Street, to give you a message, like.'

'Yes?' His tone was wary, almost angry.

'She says she's got a problem with her piano and that you're to come and have a look at it.'

'Oh, *does* she?' He turned away slightly, preparing to go to the door, as if he wasn't even going to bother answering, but then his better nature had mercy on Aggie. Without turning back to her, he said, 'Tell Mrs Southgate that so far as I'm aware, her piano has had all the attention I can give it – there's nothing else I can do.'

Seconds later, he had let himself into the house and closed the door.

Forty-Five

Aggie was scared as she hurried back to give Rose
Southgate Mr King's message. This was not the answer
the woman had wanted, she could see, and she sensed
that there was far more going on than she could understand. She was not knowledgeable enough to realize
what it might be, only that there was something strange
and intense about it all.

Aggie thought Mrs Southgate might be angry and
blame her and she tapped the door of number fifteen
nervously. Rose opened the door a crack.

'Yes?' Her voice was faint.

'Mr King said to tell you that he can't do anything
more for your piano. And he's sorry,' Aggie added, not
quite truthfully but feeling something was needed to
soften the blow.

Rose Southgate stared at her through the crack in the
door, as if she couldn't take in what Aggie had just said.

'What?' Her tone was desperate.

Aggie repeated the message and Rose's face took on
an expression of such despairing misery that she almost
ran away. But there was something she needed first.

'Can I have that twopence, then?'

Mrs Southgate seemed to come to herself. She disappeared for a few seconds and then came back.

'Here. Thank you, Aggie,' she said faintly. 'Take this
– it's all I've got.'

The door closed. Aggie looked at what was in her hand. A silver joey! Three whole pennies just for a run along the road! Well, that wasn't bad going. She hurried home, hoping the sight of it would make Mom happy.

That night Aggie woke, hearing a kerfuffle downstairs, voices, feet hurrying back and forth. None of the others stirred, but Aggie slipped out of bed, and crept round the boys' mattress and down the attic stairs. She paused on the bottom step, feeling the rough wood under her bare feet.

A dim light came from Mom and Dad's room and she could hear whispering. A moment later, she saw her grandmother's shape in the doorway. Aggie could not see her expression in the shadows, but she had the impression from her bearing that everything was very solemn.

'Who's that?' Nanna caught sight of the little figure on the stairs. 'That you, Aggie?'

Aggie stepped on to the tiny landing. She felt Nanna's warm hand on her shoulder, and the lavender-scented shawl she was wearing over her nightclothes tickled Aggie's ear.

'It's your father,' Nanna whispered tenderly. ''E's on his way out, bab.'

Aggie looked up at her in the gloom, feeling as if something was pressing very hard on her chest.

'Why don't you go in and be with him, with your mother? We won't wake the little 'uns, but as you're up . . . Come on, bab, you're old enough . . .' She took Aggie's hand in her gnarled one and led her towards the room. 'I'm going down to get the fire going,' she said. 'We'll need a cuppa, sure enough.'

Aggie peered inside, finding that she was shaking, and not from cold. The night was quite warm. There was a candle burning on a saucer on the chest of drawers, and her mother was sitting on the edge of the bed, holding Dad's hand. Her other hand was clasped to her eyes and Aggie could see that her shoulders were shaking, but she made no sound. Afraid that Mom would snap at her, she moved closer.

But as Mom turned and saw her, she looked calm, almost as if she had been expecting Aggie, and she wiped away her tears with the back of her hand.

'I woke up and he was different,' she whispered, seeming glad that someone else was there. 'His breathing was different and I just knew summat'd changed ... Come here and sit with him.' She held her hand out and Aggie sat on the edge of the bed close to her father's head.

She could hear nothing from the bed at first and wondered if Dad was breathing at all. Then a tiny puff of breath escaped through his dry lips. He seemed so quiet and far away. It was as if he was still him, but only just. He was so thin and light, she had a fancy that he might just leave the bed and float, lying flat as he was, wrapped in a blanket, out of the window, past the curve of the moon and up to heaven.

Her eyes met her mother's for a moment.

'He's leaving us,' Mom said. More tears spilled from her eyes. 'Dear God – I don't want him suffering any more, but I don't want him to go.' She put both her hands over her face.

Aggie began to cry too, a feeling inside her like something tearing open. But they both wept very quietly, as if what was taking place on the bed beside them needed to be done in peace. Dad was there and

345

not there. He had withdrawn from them already. Aggie sensed that he would never speak again, he was too far gone. *Dad!* she wanted to say. *Tell me about ... Tell me about anything, just speak to me, don't go!* Sobs shook her.

A few moments later, each of them realized that there was someone else in the room. May had crept down and was standing at the door, two fingers in her mouth, looking at them with a glazed, half-asleep look.

'Oh, babby,' Jen said. 'Come here ...'

May came over to her and Aggie saw her mom pick the little girl up and cuddle her against her bulky tummy. May snuggled up to her mother and, still sucking on two of her fingers, began to fall asleep again.

They sat on, and sometime later they heard Freda's slow, heavy tread on the stairs and the faint clink of cups.

'Give us a hand, Aggie,' she called softly, as she reached the top. 'And go and get that chair from my room.'

Aggie helped her grandmother rest the tray with the pot in its cosy on the chest of drawers, then went and brought in the chair. Freda had brought up a new candle which she lit from the stub of the old one and stuck it into the wax on the saucer. Then she poured the strong brew into the cups, stirred in sugar and they all sat sipping quietly, their eyes fixed on Tommy – their father, husband, son-in-law – as he breathed out his last hours.

When she had finished her tea, Aggie began to feel sleepy. She lay down on the other side of the bed, quite close to her father, her foot just touching up against his stick-like leg. Jen settled May down too, between them.

Aggie put her arm round her little sister and felt Nanna lay something over the pair of them before she slid into sleep again.

She was woken by her mother's heart-rending sobs.

'Oh, Tommy! My Tommy!' Jen was curled forward, her head resting on her husband's emaciated chest. 'Oh, he's gone, oh, Tommy don't go – come back to me!'

Aggie scrambled to sit up as did May, looking bewildered at the sudden outburst. It was still not light, everything uncertain in the shadows. They each found their grandmother's hands resting on them from behind and she bent close to them.

'It's all right, babbies.' Her voice was trembling. 'Your father's gone to his rest – he's not with us any more.'

May twisted round to look up at her, not understanding. Aggie also could not take it in yet, but the fact that Nanna was in tears shook her to the core. She could hear her mother's grief, see her father lying there, just as he had been before, breathing almost silently into the night. She sat very still, trying to let her nanna's words sink in.

After a few moments she moved up the bed to look more closely. Her father's face was very still, even though the shifting candlelight gave it a look of life.

'Your dad's passed on,' her mother told her tearfully. As she said it, she seemed to be trying to understand it for herself.

Aggie reached out and felt his hand. It didn't feel much different from before, but leaning to look closely at his face, she knew then. It was her father as she remembered him, wasted by his cruel illness, but now, though his body was here, there was nothing of him, no life. He had gone.

'Dad!' She burst into tears and hearing her May started to cry as well. Soon, Ann and Silas appeared and finally John. As dawn broke over the rooftops, the family all said their goodbyes to their beloved Tommy, all round his bed where he had suffered for so long, but was free from suffering now.

Aggie would always remember that Saturday, not only as the one when her father died, but as one also, when he was still with them. Mom was distraught but gentle. There was an atmosphere of love and tenderness, of everyone in it together and trying to be helpful. Even John was a model son and brother.

Once the sun had risen that morning, after their father had breathed his last, Mom sent Aggie to fetch Dr Hill. Mrs Sissons came in full of help and reassurance to lay Tommy out. The girls boiled pans for washing his body and the kettle to make cups of tea. Just for once when Aggie asked anyone to do something they did it. No one played out. They all wanted to be in together. News spread and neighbours came round to pay their respects. Some of them sat in with them for a bit, talked to Nanna and asked Jen if they could be of any help. Aggie let people in at the front. It was nice to have something to do, and everyone tried to find comforting things to say. Irene Best came and Dulcie, with Babs.

'Ooh, there you are, bab,' Dulcie said kindly to Aggie as she opened the door. Wiping tears away she squeezed Aggie's shoulder. 'Poor babbies,' she said. 'Let me go and see your mother.'

Babs didn't know what to say to Aggie but she stuck around with the rest and it was a comfort to have her there. Everyone made a fuss of May because it was easier to cuddle a small child than to know what to say to the others. Aggie noticed that Mrs Southgate did not call on them and she guessed this was because her face was covered in cuts and bruises.

They knew Tommy had been very sick and was dead. What was harder to take in was that soon, they would never see him again. And today everything was so busy there was no time to start taking it in.

Forty-Six

The funeral carriage, with its pair of noble black horses, made its stately way along Lilac Street and came to a stop outside number nine.

Rose stood on her doorstep, the curtains of the house drawn closed as they were along the street out of respect for the occasion. Tommy had been a popular man in the district and everyone felt for his family. Rose didn't want to go any further out and attract attention to herself, but she wanted to pay her respects like anyone else. She had put her hat on, the brim pulled down low to hide the yellowing rainbow bruise that was working its way across her face.

The horses were shaking their heads, their black plumes swishing away the flies. One of them lifted its tail and left its steaming message on the cobbles and she heard a small boy laughing at the sight on the other side of the street. Many of the neighbours were outside, some other women with their hats on, all talking in low, respectful voices.

The family must have poured in every last penny for this, Rose thought, though it was quite a humble funeral as these things went: only one carriage. She watched as the undertakers carried out Tommy's coffin, laying it reverentially in the carriage, and the family emerged, dark heads and ginger heads, all dressed in the best clothes they could muster, with black armbands. They would walk behind, to the church. She saw Aggie emerge from the house, still in her old brown skirt but now, at the top, was a black blouse.

Aggie was holding May's hand and she looked along at Rose for a moment. The child's unwavering, blue gaze seemed to pierce through Rose, before she turned away. Rose felt unsettled by it, as if she had let the girl down in some way. She told herself it was her own sense of guilt needling her. Hadn't she always been kind to Aggie and invited her into her house? And at least Aggie had some decent shoes to wear, Rose thought, seeing the brown lace-ups, well polished again today.

Yesterday, partly out of sorrow for the Green family and partly to distract herself from her own agony, she had gone and bought a bag of sweets, walking along to the Stratford Road to find a shop where they didn't know her. Her face was still in such a state, she wasn't shopping at Dorrie Davis's.

She went along to number nine late in the day, when the other visitors had left, and it was Freda Adams who opened the door. She looked tired, a little more stooped, and no wonder, Rose thought. Working in a factory at her age! But she admired the woman and was moved by her.

'Oh, it's you,' Freda said. Her tone was not rude, just weary.

'I just came to say I'm so sorry to hear about Mr Green.' Rose looked Freda Adams full in the eye. Though she was ashamed of the state of her face, in a way she also wanted them to know, to say, *Look at me – this is the kind of husband I've got, my life's not so easy either!* – and to be given sympathy. But Freda Adams seemed too preoccupied to notice.

'And I bought these – for Aggie and the others. You know – a little treat.'

As Rose handed over the generous bag of sweets, Freda's tired face broke into a smile.

'Oh, now that's kind of you! Well, I know they won't say no to those. D'you want to come in . . .'

Rose shook her head before the woman had finished.

'Oh, no – thank you. I'm sure you've got more than enough to do. But please pass on my condolences to Je– to Mrs Green.'

Now, at last, everything was ready and the cortege moved off slowly. The few men in the street removed their hats as it passed.

Rose went inside then, and even though Lily was there, she wept and wept.

She didn't know what to do with herself. Tommy Green's death was one thing that pulled her out of her despair for a while, giving her the relief of thinking about someone else. But Arthur's dismissal of her, the ending of things, felt unendurable, as if a whole part of her had fallen away, leaving very little behind.

Her body was leaden. She found it so hard to get out of bed each morning, to do everything that needed to be done, to move, to think. She would find herself perched on the edge of the bed or on a chair downstairs, staring, and if left uninterrupted she would suddenly come to, not knowing how long she had been there. But she was not often left to herself. Lily could feel the change in her – another change which meant she was paying the child less attention, but this time she was miserable instead of charged with happiness as she had been before.

'Mom?' Lily kept coming to her, pulling at her. Her mother, whose world had revolved around her before, had withdrawn. Lily wasn't the sort of child who had been sent out on to the street to play and fend for herself. Used to attention, she would grab Rose's sleeve and tug on it, whining, until Rose was driven almost hysterical by it.

'Just leave me alone, Lily! I need some peace!' she'd cry in an overwrought voice.

'I hate you!' Lily was starting to shout now, stamping her way upstairs, crying with hurt and frustration and Rose had not the energy to do anything to put it right.

All she could think about was Arthur. What could she do? The worst of it was his anger, the contempt she knew he must feel towards her.

Whenever she thought about this it made her want to slam about in fury and frustration. What else could she have done but lie? How else could she find any escape from this death-in-life of a marriage? What if she were to fly in the face of everything and leave Harry? She had heard whispered conversations about divorce – it did happen. She would be the guilty party, *was* the guilty party. But how could that make things any worse than they were now? Wouldn't she do anything just to be with him, for her life to be different?

But how could she do anything or make any change if Arthur would not forgive her or let her see him? She would be stuck here now, for ever, when they could have made things different, gone away to live somewhere else, anything . . . And again she would weep with the pain and frustration of it all.

How was she going to go on like this, she wondered, after days of being unable to eat, to sleep or settle to anything. She cooked Harry's meals and looked after the house as best she could, but barely spoke to him and could not look him in the eye. He said nothing about his assault on her. He thought she was sulking, and he wasn't the apologizing sort. And he seemed to feel he had put up with enough. He moved around her with a sneer of contempt, grunting when she put his dinner in front of him. The very sight of him made her feel ill. Many times, day and night, she thought about finishing herself, or running away, anywhere, just to get away from this place and from Harry, from the unbearable violence of her feelings.

Last night, he had forced himself on her as soon as they got into bed. Without a word he had been there suddenly, his thick hands forcing her to roll over on to her back.

'No!' she cried, seeing that he was already half naked and ready, an ugly expression on his face.

He brought his face up close to hers. 'Don't say no to me, woman. Never again, d'you hear? I've had enough. I've put up with your games for years and I ain't having any more of it. I'm a man and I need what I need – and it's your job to give it me.'

Forcing his way in, he took with relish what he considered to be his full entitlement, not withdrawing, moving in her with sharp, aggressive little sounds. He had the upper hand now, and he was enjoying it.

Two days after Tommy Green's funeral, Rose was upstairs, stripping the bed to wash the sheets and tidying the room. She felt the need to wash them more often now that Harry had decided that almost every night he would have intercourse with her. She knew what he wanted: to put another child inside her. He was not interested in a child for its own sake, simply to prove his manhood and to have power over her in every way.

'That Jen Green along the way – that's what I'd call a proper woman,' he said as he prepared to mount her again.

'What – a widow?' Rose retorted, voice laced with sarcasm.

Harry raised his hand and made a motion of slapping her face, so that Rose cringed away from him. But he had stopped short of actually hitting her and stared down at her as if trying to dominate her with his eyes. She had stared back for a moment, then looked away.

She yanked the bottom sheet from the bed and bundled it up and still holding it, stood staring across the room. Those afternoons she had spent with Arthur – oh, the bliss of it! But could she be carrying his child? She didn't know, not yet. Sooner or later the way things were, she'd be carrying Harry's. Shame burned in her cheeks. To be carrying a child and not know whose it was! She wasn't that kind of woman, was she?

She sank down on the side of the mattress, dreaming that it was Arthur's bed, in his room in Oldfield Road, the sun streaming through the window. She stroked her hand over it, remembering his strong thighs, his face . . .

'Mom!' Lily's voice cut in, from downstairs. 'Mom!'

Rose ignored it, frantic not to have her fantasy disturbed. This, now, was all she had left. She pictured him lying there, the way he had caressed her, the look of sheer delight on his face.

'Mo-om!'

'What *is* it, Lily?' she shouted irritably.

'There's a letter for you.'

Rose frowned. 'All right,' she said distantly. She gave a deep sigh, closing her eyes. *Oh, God, save me . . .*

355

She'd never even been religious. But to who else was she supposed to cry out?

Lily was coming upstairs. 'Look, Mom . . .'

'I'll be down in a minute – you stay—'

But Lily was already there, a sheet of folded paper in her hand. She thrust it at her mother.

On the outside, in unsteady capitals, was written, *ROSE*. Puzzled, she opened it up, her heart suddenly thumping as she saw the copperplate script, wayward on the page, the lines wavering and some words running into each other. But it was not hard to make out. One hand at her throat, she read:

> *We may not meet and yet I am made glad*
> *because I know thou livest,*
> *That the sun that lights my pathway*
> *falls across thine own,*
> *That in the night the pale and patient moon*
> *watches thy way and mine.*
> *With all I do, the blessed hope is born*
> *that even you, friend of my former day,*
> *May hear and guess,*
> *that time nor ties, nor distance*
> *make love less.*

At the bottom, it was signed simply, with a curly *A*.

Forty-Seven

The house seemed so deserted without Dad coughing.

It took days and days before Aggie woke without expecting to hear him. Each morning she opened her eyes, with May and Ann beside her, and listened for it. Then in would rush the realization that Dad was gone for good and all the world turned grey with sadness.

Before the funeral, he had stayed with them for a time, at least in body. Mrs Sissons, kindly and reassuring as ever, laid Tommy out. Such a sad, shrunken figure he was, dressed up in his Sunday suit, lying in his coffin in the front room, and they filled with place with flowers.

'I don't want anyone saying it smells bad,' Aggie heard Mom say to Nanna. 'I want him to look his best, whatever that wicked illness has done to him.'

They kept two candles burning each side of the stand which the undertaker brought to keep the coffin on, with a dark green pall underneath.

All the time he was in the house the children were very subdued. Aggie could not forget he was there, even though they closed the coffin because Dr Hill said it would be best. Every so often she crept into the room and made sure the candles were burning, that the flowers had enough water, and whispered to him.

'You all right, Dad? Can I get you anything?'

One afternoon she went into the front room and found John in there by the coffin, his lips moving. When he heard her he whipped round, blushing furiously, but she didn't say anything. She'd come to talk to Dad too. Everyone was in a state. Mom cried a lot, and they could hear her at night through the floor. It made them cry as well, when they heard it. It was such a lonely, desolate sound and sometimes Aggie, Ann and May all clung to each other sobbing. John wouldn't cuddle Silas so he came and got in with them as well sometimes.

'D'you want a love, Silas?' Aggie would say, and his puppyish little body climbed in and curled up against hers.

For the first couple of days Aggie was haunted by the fact that they were going to come and take Dad away. It felt so final. But when Tuesday came, and the funeral, it was a relief because while at first Dad had been dead and still there, now he was about to be dead and not there. By then they had taken in the fact that he had really gone.

And while she felt sad at the funeral, and Mom was weeping and Nanna holding her arm, it was something far away that didn't seem to have anything to do with the dad she remembered who was full of jokes and barely ever went to church in his life.

She had said her goodbyes to him as they carried the coffin out of the house to the funeral carriage. Standing with her brothers and sisters in the street, waiting, in her head she said to him, *Bye, bye, Dad. I hope you feel better now and you ain't got a cough now you're in heaven.*

And as they all stood there, she had a strong feeling that he was about somewhere, that he could see all of them and he was looking down with that mischievous, crinkly smile of his.

*

But it was then that their troubles really began. A few days after the funeral, Aggie and the others came home from school to find that a calamity had happened.

'Your nan's had a fall,' Mom said almost before they'd all got in through the door. Aggie ran up to Nanna's room and found her lying on her bed, grey in the face. She looked different, her features drawn and aged. Her right cheek was cut and bruised.

'Oh, Aggie – I've been a silly old fool,' she said, sounding upset. 'I could curse myself, I really could.' Her right arm was bent across her body and encased in a white plaster cast. Her other hand also had a bandage on it.

'What've you done, Nanna?' Aggie asked. The others had come up now and were all peering in through the door.

'Hey, Nanna, you could knock someone out with that!' John said, making moves like a boxer.

'Thanks very much, young man,' Nanna said dryly. 'I wish I had the steam to knock someone out – that'd be summat, that would.'

'Shut up, John!' Aggie said. 'Let Nanna tell us . . .'

'Shut up, yourself,' John retorted, cuffing her.

'Pack it in!' Aggie was livid. 'When're *you* ever any help?'

'Right, that's enough, the pair of you,' Nanna said. 'I'll tell you what happened and a pretty poor story it makes. I fell off the kerb, that's all. I was crossing the Stratford Road and one minute I'm on my feet, steady as a rock, and the next I'm sprawled out for all the world to see my petticoat . . .'

Despite her pale, shocked look, she told the story with a twinkle and the children laughed.

'I put my hand out to save myself and lucky for me all that was coming was the milk cart . . . But I felt my hand go and then I fell on the other one –' She held out her left arm.

They all came up close, into Nanna's usual aura of mothballs and lavender with a lacing of booze, and examined the plaster cast.

'Careful, Silas, you'll hurt Nanna!' Ann pulled him back.

'Is it broke?' John asked.

'In two places, they reckon.' Freda held up her left arm. 'And this one – bruised a bit. They both flaming hurt, I can tell you.' She lowered her arms and gave a deep sigh. 'Truth is, I can't go out to work like this.'

As the children drifted away from her room, Freda called Aggie back.

'Here, bab – I've got a little job for you.' With her good hand she reached, wincing, under the bedclothes and brought out her hipflask, with its shiny cup lid.

'Go along to Auntie's, Aggie, and get as much as you can for that. Make sure it's at least half a crown.'

Aggie's face fell. 'Oh Nanna, no! That was Grand-dad's – it's your favourite . . .'

Nanna tutted impatiently. 'Your father's passed on – and now this silly old fool's brought us more expense.' She made a shooing motion. 'Go on with yer – do as I say. And don't tell your mother.'

Aggie swallowed. 'I'll run like the wind,' she said.

'Oh – faster than that, if you can,' Nanna said.

Jen was in a dreadful panic.

'What're we going to do?' she kept saying, pacing round the kitchen while the children were eating tea.

'Won't Nanna be better again soon?' John asked.

'Not for months! We'll be on the parish! No – not

that, never.' She was thinking aloud. 'The funeral's cleaned us out and the hospital – Tommy dain't 'ave the chance to pay in much. I'll have to go out and look for summat. Oh, heavens . . .'

Desperate, she sank down at the table.

'Should we move to the Mansions?' Aggie suggested. That was what people said when they were struggling: *They'll have to move to the Mansions . . .* Which round here meant any of the back-to-back courts at the end of the street, not just the two which were actually called the Mansions. Mom had always said that she'd move back into that sort of place over her dead body. Nanna and she and Dad had all grown up in decaying back-to-back houses and she was so proud of living here with her two rooms downstairs and a tap indoors.

For a moment Aggie thought Mom wasn't listening. She seemed to be staring straight through her. But then, in a serious voice as if Aggie was suddenly a grown-up who had said something of consequence, she replied, 'God knows, I don't want to leave this house. We need the room and it's where your father and I . . .' Tears welled in her eyes. 'I'll go and look for work, but how much longer'm I going to be able to do it – even if I can find anything?' She laid a hand on her swollen belly. She was nearly six months pregnant already. 'If it comes to it, we'll see if there's anywhere going in the Mansions. Anything but go crawling to the parish.'

Freda Adams was quite poorly for the next few days. Her fall really knocked her back.

'I don't bounce at my age,' she said groggily, when Aggie went to keep her company. She had had the accident on a Friday so there was no school the next day. 'If you live to sixty-four like me, you'll know what I mean. Your poor mother's going to have to find summat for the moment. I couldn't get up and move about for all the tea in China.'

'Never mind, Nanna,' Aggie said. She loved sitting in there with her. It was cosy and reassuring, and unlike Mom, Nanna had always had time for her. 'Mom'll find summat and we're all getting bits and pieces. John's out finding stubs and Mrs Southgate's paying me to run errands for her.'

'Yes . . .' Her grandmother turned, paying sudden close attention. 'What's going on? You're as good as the Post Office for that woman!'

Aggie shrugged, feeling a bit awkward. 'She just wants messages taken.'

'Well, where to?'

'Oldfield Road. There's a friend of hers lives there, only he's blind and . . .'

'A man, you mean?'

Aggie nodded. 'He tunes pianos.'

A little smile appeared on her grandmother's lips. 'Not the only thing he tunes, by the sound of it,' she murmured. 'What, and he sends messages back?'

'No. Just Mrs Southgate. She's got a problem with their piano, only I don't think Mr Southgate is s'posed to know that Lily's having piano lessons. He doesn't like it.'

'Oh, doesn't he?' Freda said musingly. 'I see. Bit of a dark horse that one, ain't she?'

As they sat talking they heard footsteps hurrying into the house, then coming upstairs.

'Mom?' Jen came round the door, panting with the

362

exertion, and sank on to the side of the bed. 'Well, that's summat. Mr Price says I can work for him for a few weeks, being as the girl's just left.' Mr Price owned the fried fish shop at the end of the road. 'It ain't much and I'll stink of fish but there might be a bit of extra grub in it for us. Oh, he is a *kind* man, he is.' She was quite tearful.

'On what he's paying me it still won't be enough. And then when I 'ave these two . . .' She looked down at her expanding belly. 'Oh, Tommy, you bugger, you . . .' Smiling and filling up at the same time, she said, 'And Dulcie says Mr Paine at number one in their court is on 'is way out. They're taking him into the infirmary. Seven bob a week cheaper than this.'

The two women looked at each other.

'We'd best have it,' Freda said. Then added gently, 'Can't be helped, bab.'

Jen shook her head. 'God knows, Mom, you shouldn't be the one keeping us. Not at your age.'

Freda looked at her arm with a shrug. 'I ain't keeping anyone for a while, not in this state. Don't mither, wench, we'll get by.'

Aggie saw her mother's eyes fill with tears again. There was silence for a moment, then Jen rallied.

'You know what? I've just seen them Taylor girls – the youngest two, I think it was, though I have a job telling them apart. They're getting ever so big, the pair of them – broad in the beam, you might say.'

'Like their mother,' Freda commented.

Jen shook her head. 'I dunno. That's the funny thing. When the little 'un – Dolly, is it? – came back I said to myself, *That one's got herself into trouble*. You know, bun in the oven. But I don't know now. They're all looking mighty bonny.'

'You must've got it wrong,' Freda said, grimacing as she shifted her position on the bed. Her face was drawn with pain but she wasn't one to make a fuss. 'They're just getting stout like their mother – it's bred in the bone.'

There was another silence.

'So,' Jen said desolately. 'Looks as if we'll 'ave to move down the road then.'

Forty-Eight

'Right, I want you all in this afternoon,' Phyllis ordered that Saturday. 'We need to sort your clothes out.'

The girls were all in the kitchen. Charles had escaped to a church meeting. Dolly was immediately full of dread. They all knew what Mom meant by 'clothes' and she knew what her sisters were going to say to that! Mom was like someone running a military campaign.

'Oh, no!' cried Susanna, who had been on the point of leaving. 'It's my afternoon off – I said I'd go to tea with David's mom and dad! What d'you think it's like for me, having to keep my distance from David in case he finds out I've got all this . . . *padding* round me?'

'I hope you're keeping your distance in any case, my girl,' Phyllis retorted. She came back out of the scullery with another bag of sawdust.

'I might just as well not be keeping my distance,' Susanna grumbled. 'I look as much as if I'm expecting as Dolly does!'

Dolly stared sulkily at the tabletop. All she could do these days was keep her head down and wait for it to be over. No one was going to have any sympathy if *she* complained. Mostly she tried to make herself numb and ignore the insistent little kicks that had begun in her belly.

'David must think I'm turning into a barrel,' Susanna

365

said. With the extra padding she looked definitely matronly. She peered in the little mirror on the mantel.

'Has he said anything?' Phyllis demanded.

'No, but . . . Oh, my face looks so blown up and fleshy. It's horrible!'

'That's all right then.'

'But I can see him thinking . . .'

'Thinking what?' Rachel asked, on a chair by the table. She yawned, scratching round the edges of her bulging belly. 'What can he be thinking?'

Even more aggrieved, Susanna said, 'When he asked me to come over today, he did say his mom and dad would make sure there's plenty of cake.'

Hearing Rachel snort with laughter, Dolly couldn't help creasing up. Even Mom started to laugh.

'I bet he thinks he's marrying a right pig!' Dolly giggled.

'It's not funny,' Susanna snapped. 'It's all very well but you're not walking about with a bag of sawdust strapped to you!'

'What d'you mean it's all right for me?' Dolly erupted. 'And I am wearing one anyway – remember!'

'Much smaller,' Rachel said. 'Have you any idea how flaming hot it is carting about with all this on? Why couldn't you've got a bun in the oven over the winter? Then we could've bundled up in all our winter coats. I'm sick of having to wear this great big cardigan to cover it all up. I'm going to pass out one of these days!'

'I feel like passing out half the time anyway,' Dolly said. 'You don't know what it's like! Not that I'm expecting any sympathy from you lot.'

'Good, 'cause you're not getting any,' Rachel retorted. 'If you think—'

'Anyway,' Susanna interrupted. 'I can't see why we

366

need to wear all this heavy stuff when we're not with Dolly. If we're on our own what difference does it make?'

Their mother cut her off, her voice low and intense. 'You *will* wear it and you'll wear it *all* the time, d'you hear? It may be embarrassing, my girl, and it may mean a bit of discomfort, but by God if it made any sense I'd be doing it too, make no mistake. You – *we* – are going to see this through. I'm *not* having my family dragged into the gutter with tittle-tattle from the likes of –' She jerked her head towards the window. 'Of them out there. Three more months – *that's all it'll take*. Stop mithering and get on with it.'

They were all momentarily silenced by her stern intensity. Then Dolly looked up at her. 'But what about the babby? When . . . After, I mean?'

'I've told you: Nancy will keep it. For a price.'

They all stared at her but something in her manner forbade any more questions. Dolly looked down again, full of confusion. Everything seemed to have been taken out of her hands and she was both upset by this and glad of it.

'Now,' Phyllis said, seeing she had them all where she wanted them. 'Dolly's six months gone – we're going to have to give you some extra padding.'

Dolly slept most of Saturday afternoon, exhausted. Phyllis sent Rachel along to the shops. When she came back with her bags, she hurried round the back and tapped urgently on the door.

'What's up with you?' Phyllis said, having hauled herself out of her chair to open it.

'I dain't want—'

'*Didn't*, how many more times?'

'Didn't then – I didn't want to come to the front. That horrible old lady was out there again.'

Phyllis felt as if her blood had stopped pumping for a few seconds. She mastered herself, to appear casual.

'What old lady?'

'That one we met on the way back from church – I told you. She keeps going on about someone called Hetty. I met her down at the end of the road, in Larches Street. Ugh, she's vile, and she stinks. I don't think she's right in the head.'

'Well, what did she say to you?'

'She didn't – she was talking to a man outside the pub, but I heard her say the name again, Hetty something. She saw me go past and I was scared she was going to follow me, so I came down as fast as I could.'

Her heart pounding with anxiety, Phyllis lifted a loaf of bread out of the bag.

'Hmm, strange,' she said, as if moving on to something else. 'Still, there's some queer folk about.'

Once Rachel had gone upstairs, she hurriedly slipped into a cardigan, pulled her straw hat low over her eyes and went out through the back. Standing in the shadow of the entry, she leaned on the wall just inside, trying to look as if she had just come out to take the air. Twisting this way and that, she took in the whole street, to see whether there was any sign of Ethel.

A slow, shuffling movement caught her eye at the far end opposite the Eagle – but no, it was an old lady who lived in the Mansions. Of Ethel there seemed to be no sign.

Phyllis ambled out into the street and took a turn up and down. She stopped for a word with Irene Best, who was sitting sideways on in the doorway with Mr Best behind her, helping him smoke a cigarette. Irene was one of the few people in the street Phyllis had time for. It would have taken the hardest of hearts not to feel for the creeping martyrdom of her life.

'Hello, Mrs Taylor?' Irene looked up timidly, squinting into the bright sun.

'All right, Mrs Best. How is he today? Enjoying a bit of baccy, I see?'

Irene gave a wan smile. 'He's going along, thank you.'

'Well, you know where we all are . . .' Phyllis passed on. She would have been perfectly willing to help if help had been required. At the present, things with the Bests seemed to go on much the same for month after month.

Poor cow, Phyllis thought as she ambled along in the shadow of the Mission Hall, then back home amid the milling children in the street. No sign of Ethel, any road. But she was filled with unease. How did Ethel have any idea where she lived? Had she managed to follow her from the Bull Ring that night after all? Whatever the case, it seemed guaranteed that Ethel would be back, and whatever it was she wanted, Phyllis was going to be ready for her.

Forty-Nine

That night, in the early days of 1900, when Hetty arrived in Birmingham, she had not the first idea where to go. Darkness was already gathering when the train pulled in. She walked with dragging feet along the crowded platform and out of the station. In her desperation to get away from Ada and Ethel she had thought of nothing else. During the journey her mind had been full of the horrifying scene she had left behind, the crumpled figures of the little boys, the wounds on Ada, the seeping blood . . .

And now, once again, she was on the streets with nowhere to go. A sense of despair filled her.

The city at night seemed even more frightening than before. Coventry at least was home, but now she was alone in this big, strange place. She found herself in a warren of dark streets not far from the station, among the other figures moving in the gloom. There was an occasional gas lamp round which were gathered gaggles of children, either sitting dumbly on the road or wrangling shrilly with each other. The street was narrow, and even in the enclosing darkness, had a grimy, threatening feel to it. People moved close to her in the dark and quite soon, to her discomfort, she began to attract attention. Men who passed stopped and stared, turning back to watch her walk on; some nudged her, and one man forced himself up against her, squeezing her breasts and making lewd comments.

'How much?' his moustachioed mouth hissed.

Hetty tried to ignore him and walk on, but he persisted beside her. His thin, rat-like face peered out from under a cap and his voice rasped at her.

'Too stuck up to speak, are yer? I said, 'ow much?'

Hetty shook her head and walked on.

'You don't wanna walk round 'ere if you ain't offering,' the man said crossly.

'What's up, Bert – trouble?'

Terrified now, Hetty found herself faced by a group of four lads, blocking the road in front of her. She could see they were some kind of gang as they all had a similar look, caps on their heads and what looked like colourful scarves at their throats. *Peakies*, she thought. She'd heard of these gangs who called themselves the Peaky Blinders, vicious enough to knife you to get what they wanted.

'What've we got 'ere, then?' the tallest of them said.

He and the one beside him must have been brothers, they were so similar. The two hanging behind looked very young. She kept her arms folded, one hand clutching her waist to protect her hidden bag of money.

'This moll's on our patch but she ain't coughing,' the one said who had first grabbed her. He was one of them too, she realized. She was surrounded now.

'Oh – is that so?' The tallest of the lads who was evidently the leader of all of them, placed his feet wide apart, challenging her with a swagger.

'And who might you be, then?'

'She's with us,' a voice said from behind Hetty. Someone elbowed in among the gang of Peakies. 'Come on, Susan – you're coming with us.'

Before she had even managed to see who her rescuer

was, Hetty found her arms being seized on each side and she was pulled away down the street. To her surprise the lads put up no resistance. She took in that she was being steered along by two girls. One, she could see, was a pale blonde, the other dark, both with their hair fixed up in elaborate styles with pins and coils round their ears.

'What the **** are you doing out here on your own?' the dark-haired girl demanded, in a thick Irish accent. 'You never do dis place on your own – not even in the daytime! And you don't do it anyways – this is Ma Hegarty's patch. You can't just move in on it, you know.'

'I . . .' Hetty could think of no lie she could tell that was any more help than the truth. 'I don't know where I am – I've just got here.'

The blonde girl let out a string of filthy curses which ended with, '. . . and what're we getting ourselves stuck with her for?'

'Oh, I think the old lady'll be pleased to have her, don't you?' the first one said. 'Listen now – what's your name? Not Susan, I don't suppose?'

'Hetty.'

'Hetty,' the Irish girl said. 'Well, I'm Mary and this is Dora. You come wit us. You'll not want to be out here at night – it's not safe. Those Peakies – halfwits and eejits dey are, every one of dem, but dey think they own de streets . . .' She jerked Hetty's arm. 'Come on – in here.'

They were at the mouth of an alleyway, a stinking, fetid place, and Hetty tried to draw back, the over-powering stench of sewage and rotting refuse stinging her nostrils. She could hear sounds from the warren of buildings around, shouts and crying children, and the air was full of smoke. Desperation rose in her again.

'Where're we going? What if I don't want to come with you?'

'Oh, you do,' Dora said, suddenly nasty, digging her nails into Hetty's arm. She could tell the girls were not going to let her go, now they had got their claws into her. She was frightened of them, even though they had rescued her from the Peakies. Both of them reminded her of Ethel, the ruthless, calculating natures she could hear in them. Getting caught up with them felt like going back to the life she had just tried to escape. But the streets were terrifying and she had no idea of where to go to find anywhere better.

'You're coming to meet Ma Hegarty,' Dora said. 'She'll decide what to do with you.'

They dragged her further along the alley and as soon as they had her there in what was almost total, engulfing darkness, Dora, who had suddenly become the leader, said, 'Right – let's see what you've got, then!'

The girls grabbed her even tighter and shoved her back against the wall, their spare hands that weren't pinioning her against the slimy bricks, rummaging among her clothes. It only took seconds for them to feel the promising lump stashed at Hetty's waist.

'Ah, now – what have we here?' Mary yanked the bag from her waistband. 'Treasure!'

'No! That's mine – it's all I've got!' Hetty fought back as savagely as she could, grabbing Mary's hand which she drew up to her lips, and sinking her teeth into the girl's wrist. She tasted blood.

'Ow! You filthy bitch!' Mary hit out at her, flailing and slapping in the dark. 'She's bitten me, Dora – get her.'

'We'll 'ave to learn this one some manners.'

Hetty felt the other girl move round her and seize

her by the shoulders. The two girls yanked her whole body forward, then shoved her forcibly back again. Her head cracked against the wall and she knew nothing more.

'The best thing,' Dora instructed her, 'is to make them do it between your legs. Some of 'em are so far gone they'll do whatever you tell 'em. But –' She jerked her head in the direction of where Ma Hegarty was enthroned in the back room. 'She'll give you a sponge – you dip it in the vinegar, then put it up. If the old lady finds you've got a bun in the oven she'll flay you alive. She don't hold with doing away with 'em – and it costs.'

Hetty had come round after her blow on the head, to find she was lying on a lumpy straw mattress in the back passage of the slum house, being observed by a bloated woman with bloodshot eyes. Hetty gave a whimper. Her head was pounding and moving sent shooting pains through her neck.

'Looks all right.' The voice came rumbling from a throat that vibrated with alcohol and pipe tobacco and the cadences of County Limerick. 'Looks a strong girl, not a bad face. I'll take her. See to her.' She started to shuffle away. 'She's coming round now.'

Hetty realized that the woman was addressing someone who turned out to be Dora. There were other distant sounds in the background and there was a strong smell of coal dust and smoke around her. Dora's face loomed into Hetty's wavering vision.

'So – you're awake. Get yourself up, then.'

Hetty sat up, groaning. Her bladder felt full to bursting and her head was pounding. She felt her waist.

'Where's my money? You stole it off of me! Give it me back!'

'Money?' Dora gave an exaggerated, innocent shrug. 'I dunno what you're talking about. There ain't no money here belongs to *you*.'

Hetty groaned again, defeated, drew her knees up and rested her aching head on them. 'I want some tea. And I want to pee.'

Ma Hegarty was a shrewd, rough, drunken, fearsome, occasionally sentimental businesswoman. Including Hetty, she was housing nine girls at that time. None of the ones Hetty got to know in the few weeks she was there had anything much in the way of family. They were waifs and strays, some orphans, some having left home because it was hell one way or another. Hetty heard tales that made her hair stand on end. Taking up with Ma Hegarty was a living which gave them a roof over their head. Some knew almost no other.

Mary had run away from home in Ireland, where she had had a baby by her father, hoping to make her fortune across the water. Dora had grown up in an orphanage and had no one in the world. Hetty quickly saw, with a sense of despair, that she was just like them. And here she was, sucked back into this again. All life ever seem to offer her was making a living with her body. She wanted to run away again, but now she had no money and no real idea where to go. Quickly she decided to bide her time. She'd look about her. And then, one day, she vowed to herself, she'd be off.

*

It happened even sooner than she expected and in quite a different way from what she envisaged. She dreamed of escaping to a different part of town, getting herself a factory job, trying to make herself respectable. Instead, she met James Taylor.

She was paired with Dora when they went out on the streets and they were working a particular patch in Balsall Heath. Most of the encounters took place in back alleys, often against the warm bricks of factory walls, unless the man had anywhere better in mind. Dora became annoyed quite quickly because she was not much of a looker. She had a narrow-eyed, malnourished look whereas Hetty was very handsome. With her wide, curvaceous body the men went for her instead.

So, after all her resistance at Ada's place, Hetty found herself back in the situation of letting men use her as Mr Gordon had done. She followed Dora's advice about how to protect herself. The feeling of a man thrusting against her brought back the most terrible memories. As soon as she was working, she took her mind somewhere else, anywhere, out into the fields and villages where things had seemed free. She thought about Nancy and dreamed of living with her on her farm. Most of the men were quick, and when they were finished she would come to as if from a dream.

But one evening, a warm, August night when it was only just turning dark, she was standing at the end of an alley on the Moseley Road, waiting for Dora. Dora had made her hide so that she'd have a chance, and she was the one working this time. Hetty still only had the dress she had arrived in and didn't feel at all grand or smart, but she knew she had a good body, a strong bearing and she leaned against the wall, dreamily glad that it was Dora the whiskery, portly man had chosen.

The place where she was standing was a short distance in towards town from the Methodist church. After a short time, Hetty heard footsteps approaching and a tall, well-built man appeared, giving the impression, in the gloom, of being smartly, if not expensively dressed. He was hurrying along, head down, seeming preoccupied, and only looked up at the last moment, sensing someone there on the pavement.

He raised his head to show a young, striking face, with a big, almost hooked nose, dark eyebrows and thick, sensuous lips. Hetty was immediately taken by the face. You could not call the man handsome, but there was something fascinating about him.

He removed his hat. 'Evening,' he said. Instead of moving on, he stopped, seeming curious, but then was unsure what to say.

'Everything all right?' he asked. 'Are you waiting for someone?'

'In a manner of speaking,' Hetty said coyly. She couldn't stop looking at him. She had never seen a man quite like him before.

The man stood still, gazing at her. In his eyes she thought she saw interest, a touch of humour – and desire. He turned away for a moment to look back along the street. There were a few other people about and he seemed to be locked in a struggle with himself. Still holding his hat, he stepped closer, looking apprehensive now.

'Are you working?' He spoke so quietly she could barely hear.

Her heart started thumping. He didn't look like her usual sort of customer.

'I am,' she murmured, lowering her eyes.

There was a silence, but he could not afford to stand there in uncertainty. It would be too obvious to everyone what transaction was taking place.

'Oh, Lord,' she heard him breathe. For a second he hesitated, then hurriedly came close to her and reached out his arm. 'Come on.'

He told her he worked for the engineering firm to which he had once been apprenticed. He rented a couple of rooms nearby and smuggled her upstairs. In her turn, Hetty told him she was eighteen, though this was two years older than the truth. There was something about him, a mixture of fraught desire and decency, that humbled her and she tried to speak nicely.

From the beginning, James had been in no doubt about what she was, where she had come from. At first she thought he was trying to save her soul while satisfying his own needs. But once he had let off steam the first time, he made her tea. He looked at her in a way no man ever had before – directly, into her eyes. When he asked her name, she said, 'Phyllis,' just like that, as if somehow she already knew she was to be someone else. It was a name she had once seen in a story book and she thought it sounded gracious. It sounded like the person she wanted to be.

'Tell me about your family,' he said, that first time she sat in his simple, bachelor's sitting room.

'They ain't no good,' she told him, lowering her head in shame. 'I ain't seen my mother or father for years now.'

'And this is how you live?' he asked, seeming surprised. Did he think she was out there for the fun of it?

Face thick with blushes, she nodded.

'A lovely girl like you,' he said sadly. He couldn't seem to stop looking at her. 'Shouldn't you like to be living a different life?'

Her gaze met his. Something lit in her then that had never gone out. She felt as if with him, she could be different.

'Yes,' she said longingly.

Fifty

All that week Rose kept the poem close to her heart, tucked between her dress and camisole. She read it over again until she no longer needed to look to know the exact words. The line, '*. . . time nor ties, nor distance make love less*', burned in her mind. *He loves me, he still loves me . . .* After the way he had looked at her, his anger and hurt, she had doubted whether even that could be true. But he had sent her this ardent message. He had not wanted their love to die.

She did not like to think about another line of the poem, '*friend of my former day . . .*' Those words made the message a final, regretful goodbye. It was too unbearable to believe that.

A plan began to form in her mind. It was the only way she could ease herself. She would go to Arthur that Sunday and say that she was prepared to face whatever it took for them to be together. She would leave Harry, taking Lily with her; they would run away, go anywhere, so that no one would know them. She would be his wife and care for him, he could get work somewhere . . .

The idea gave her a new lease of energy. She took the tram out to Moseley with Lily to see Mrs Lacey and came away promising to bring her a set of tea-table linen, each mat embroidered with cowslips, bluebells and hollyhocks.

'They'll be so pretty!' she told Mrs Lacey. 'I can see them already. I'll buy the finest cotton to work on.'

'I'm sure, Mrs Southgate,' Mrs Lacey assured her. 'No one has ever been disappointed with your work yet. If you could do even more I'd be happy!'

From the draper's she bought a length of fine white cotton and the coloured threads she needed and got to work. Summoning up all the patience she could, she gave Lily some scraps of cloth and showed her how to begin stitching – running stitch, then chain stitch – and Lily took to it very well.

'You'll be able to make lovely things when you're bigger,' Rose told her. Lily beamed at her approval.

She found patterns for the flowers and set to work. Even though she was in a state there was always a magic to the work that Mrs Mount had taught her, threading the colours in and out until these beautiful shapes were etched on the cloth. This was one thing she was good at. And she was burning with energy and ambition. She would make money to bring away with her. She was stitching her way to freedom, to love! Perhaps, once she was safely with Arthur, she could begin her own little business in some small town somewhere in the north where they could be safe and no one would know their background.

As much of the day as she could she spent sewing. Once it grew late enough for there to be any chance of Harry coming home, she packed it away, neatly rolled up in a box at the back of the cupboard in the front room. When she took Lily to Muriel's house for her piano lesson, she managed to be calm, chatty and polite. Because now, inside, she kept telling herself there was going to be an end to this, a way out. And she was happy.

Every second of Sunday morning hung heavily. It was sunny and Harry pottered in and out to the yard, the back door open, fixing his bike, fiddling with his fishing tackle. His permanent expression now was one of self-righteous aggression. *I am the man of the house*, his bearing said. *And I am hard done by. The rest of you can fall into line.*

'You not going to church then?' he asked, as Rose made no attempt to ready herself and Lily. There was an edge of sarcasm to his tone, as there was when he'd quip, 'Say one for me,' whenever she set off. The fact was that she really only went to church to get away from him and find some other company. Most of what went on there went right over her head, though she did like the chance to sit still and think her own thoughts.

'Not today,' she said. She was standing at the back door, squinting against the sun as Harry bent over his bike. There was a chasm between them, widening with every day, with every word they spoke and every gloomy silence. Once she would have cared, but now all she could feel was a cold indifference.

He turned back to the dangling chain. Rose watched him, arms folded, hearing the very faint crackle as she stroked the paper message tucked inside her dress and thinking how bodies that are not cared for start to give off waves of need and resentment.

'I'll start the dinner,' she said.

*

Seeing Harry cycle away after dinner gave Rose a moment of pure relief and joy. There was just Lily now, standing in her way. *Come on, Aggie!* she urged in her head.

The child came, subdued and thin in the face, and even in her moments of extreme tension and anxiety, Rose could feel for her. She knew Aggie's father had been a good man, and she remembered the desolation of those days following her own mother's death.

'How's your family?' she asked kindly. 'Are you getting along all right?'

Aggie, who was squatting down, helping Lily fasten her shoe, looked up at her.

'Mom says we're gonna have to move out,' she said. It was hard to tell from her general flatness whether she was upset by this.

'Oh, no!' Rose said. She felt so sorry for poor Jen Green. 'Is it the rent?'

Aggie nodded. 'We're going to the Mansions. It'll save us a few bob, she says.'

This grown-up information wrung Rose's heart.

'Well, at least it's not far, is it?' she said. 'We'll still see you . . .' She could have cut her tongue out. What was she saying? She was going away with Arthur, wasn't she? She might never see Lilac Street again! 'And I mean,' she added hurriedly, 'it's near your pal Babs, isn't it?'

Aggie nodded, straightening up, poor solemn little thing.

'Hold my hand, Lily,' she said. 'We'll go and get Silas and Ann.'

Rose stood at the door, half unable to believe that she was about to be alone at last and free to go . . . The gaggle of bare-legged children set off along the street and she watched them for a few seconds to make sure that they had truly gone. But as she was about to close the door, she saw a familiar figure turn in at the end of the street and walk determinedly towards her.

'Oh, no! Oh, heavens!' Rose whipped round and dashed inside the house, shutting the door. Muriel Wood – and she was obviously making straight for here. She hadn't said anything about visiting when they had seen her in the week. Rose stood in a complete fit of panic behind the door. Muriel surely had seen her – she could not pretend to be out.

Sure enough, moments later came a polite tapping at the door. Rose clenched her fists. Trying to look normal, she opened the door to see Muriel's homely face smiling at her.

'I knew I'd find you in,' she said. 'How lovely! We missed you at Communion this morning.'

It was an hour and a half before Muriel left, during which time Rose brewed and drank tea, trying to chat amiably with so kind a person. Muriel shared little snippets of news about fellow parishioners, some of whom Rose could barely remember.

But suddenly she got to her feet and said, 'Oh, my goodness, look at the time! We've had such a lovely talk I'd forgotten I was also on my way to see Mrs Woodward. What a chatterbox I am. But how lovely to see you, Rose.'

Rose beamed at her, almost delirious with relief. How long was it until Lily would be back? She had the best part of an hour, she calculated.

As soon as Muriel was out of sight, she set off,

walking with as much decorum as she could along Lilac Street. Once out on the Ladypool Road, she hurtled along as fast as possible. Another hour without seeing Arthur now seemed too much to bear.

When she reached the house, she was suddenly at a loss. Before, they had had an arrangement – he would have been waiting behind the door. But shortage of time and her own impatience overcame her and she knocked.

In a few moments there were sounds behind the door, the bolt slid back and Rose had her first sight of Mrs Terry, a tall, rather severe-looking middle-aged woman in spectacles. She looked like a school teacher, Rose thought.

'Yes?' she said suspiciously.

'I've come to see a Mr King,' Rose said. 'With a message from his sister.'

The lie sprang to her lips almost without her thinking.

'Oh.' Mrs Terry looked perturbed. 'Well, it's lucky for you I heard you knock because I'm rather hard of hearing. I'm afraid Mr King's not here.'

Rose tried to look neutral. 'Oh, dear. Will he be long, d'you think?'

'I don't know for sure. I assume he's just gone out for a little walk, to get a bit of sun on him as it's such a nice day. Not that he can see that, poor man.'

'I see,' Rose said. 'All right, then. Thank you.'

'Shall I tell him you called?'

Clearly she was going to anyway, so Rose agreed and said a pleasant goodbye. She walked along, feeling frantic. Where would Arthur go for a walk? If it was anyone with sight they would try to get to the nearest park, but that was not much help to him. She remembered him telling her that he liked the sounds and smells of the trains. It felt futile but she had to do something. She made her way across to St Paul's Road, to where the railway bridge crossed the road. There were children playing, spilling out of the avenues along the road.

The railway bridge cast a deep blue shadow. Emerging the other side into the sun, she saw a pair of legs and feet. Someone was leaning against the soot-grimed bricks, soaking in the sun. She would have known those feet in their brown shoes anywhere.

'Arthur?'

His head was back, face bathed in light, and he jerked forward, eager at the sound of her voice, but then she saw him remember and his face fell. He withdrew into himself and into silence.

'Arthur. Please. It's me.' She went to touch his arm but he shook her off.

'Don't! I know it's you. Don't you think I'd know your voice?'

She quailed at the sound of so much hostility in his tone. This was not the man she remembered. It was as if he had built a fortification round himself.

Where could she begin? 'You sent me that poem.'

'To say goodbye.' His face was so pained.

'It said you still love me.'

There was another silence. His face was working, trying to gain control.

'I could love you for ever,' he said acidly. 'But what difference does that make to anything? You're married, Rose. And that's that. You should never, *never* have let me get involved with you the way you did. Have you any idea how this feels, to be played around with like that? I thought I'd found –' He stopped, turning his face down, emotional and bitter.

Rose wrung her hands, longing to touch him but not

daring. As well as Arthur being so forbidding, there were people about. She moved closer, speaking in barely more than a whisper.

'I wasn't . . . I'm *not* playing. How can you say that? I've almost gone mad this week! Arthur, it's you I love . . .'

'That may be so,' he retorted. 'But that doesn't alter the rather inconvenient fact that you already have a husband, does it?'

'I don't love Harry – in fact, I loathe him!' she said passionately. 'It's torture living with him when it's you I want to be with. All I can think of is you – being with you, leaving him and—'

'Oh, Rose . . .' He was wretched now, past anger. 'For God's sake. Just stop doing this – to both of us. Can you imagine it – divorce? Do you know how vile it all is? How much it all costs? People like us don't get divorced! Then there's me – a blind, useless wreck.'

She tried to protest but he made a fierce gesture with his hand, his anger returning.

'Just leave me, woman. You've done me enough damage, letting me hope there might be something for me. I can't stand this. Just let me be alone again and get used to it without coming and disturbing me.' Almost weeping now, he said, 'Just go away – *please*.'

Rose stared helplessly at him. How could he be saying these things, after all her dreams of them being together again? She couldn't leave, not like this. Her own tears came then.

'Arthur,' she said between sobs. 'Don't talk like this. I love you – I'll do anything to be with you. We won't divorce – we'll just go where no one can find us. Just tell me . . .'

But he had pushed off from the wall and was walking

as fast as he could away from her towards the Moseley Road. As she went to follow, he swung round.

'No! Damn it – just leave me alone. Get away from me!'

And all she could do was watch him recede from her, along to the corner, turning right on to the main road. She moved back into the shadow of the bridge and put her hands over her face.

Fifty-One

The Greens moved a few days later, on a baking hot morning. Aggie and John were kept home from school to help and to keep May out of trouble. Jen had hired a handcart and they loaded it with all their chattels. Jen's elder brother Bill turned up to help, a big, stocky man with faded sandy-coloured hair and a freckled face.

Aggie and John helped lift things on and carry smaller things out – pots and pans, a stool, rugs and bedding – and they were piled around their humble sticks of furniture.

'It doesn't add up to much,' Jen said, eyeing the drab collection.

'Good job,' Freda commented. She could not do much but stand nursing her arm in its cast. 'There's not going to be a lot of room where we're off to.'

Neighbours milled around offering help and comments. 'You're not going to be far away, bab – come and see us,' and, 'Don't bother putting that on, I'll carry that down for you.'

Aggie, standing on the dusty cobbles holding May's hand, had a nice warm feeling with everyone chatting and wishing them well. While they were packing up, an ice-cream barrow came along the street and one of the neighbours treated her, John and May.

While she was standing relishing the cool oblong of ice-cream, sandwiched between two wafers, Aggie saw the door of number fifteen open and Mr Southgate stood in the doorway, sleeves rolled, thumbs tucked in his braces. He seemed as if his mind was on something else altogether to start with, a frown pulling at his brows. Then he took in what was going on along the street and stepped over to them.

'D'yer need a hand?' he asked. What with Nanna's bad arm and Mom expecting, they weren't up to much. 'I ain't got to go to work till a bit later.'

Soon he was chatting to Aggie's uncle Bill. Aggie watched Mr Southgate. Though he had looked surly and frowning when he first came out, like someone who had been dragged unwillingly from his bed, he gradually relaxed and Aggie saw him laugh, leaning back, his face lifting. She thought he didn't look so frightening after all, when he smiled. Then she thought about Mrs Southgate and the bruises on her face, and what Nanna had said about having the piano tuned, and she wondered. None of it made much sense to her.

'Right,' Bill said at last, when the cart was stacked so high that its load was in danger of swaying off. 'Let's get this first lot along then, eh?'

Just as they were about to move off the milkman's dray appeared, the horse's hooves loud along the street.

'Hang on a tick,' Jen said. 'I'll just see him before we go. Aggie – get the jug. Look – it's on top there!'

As she went to fetch the white enamel jug from the cart, Mr Southgate reached up for it and handed it down to her.

'Here you go,' he said gruffly. She caught a whiff of him, sweat and smoke. He gave her what was almost a smile and it lit up his dark eyes.

'Ta,' Aggie said shyly. She decided maybe he wasn't so bad after all. She glanced across the road wondering if Mrs Southgate would come and wish them well, but there was no sign of her. Aggie felt rather hurt by the way Mrs Southgate hardly ever asked her in now. She took Lily to Sunday school but she rarely went into the house. Somehow these days she'd got bored of spying too. She never seemed to find out anything nice.

She took the jug over to the milkman, a man with a jolly expression who reminded her, with a pang, of her father.

'Going to your new house today then, are you, bab? Going up in the world!'

Aggie heard her grandmother give a snort behind her. 'Oh, yes,' she said. 'Heaven on earth, that's where we're going.'

'Nowt wrong with the Mansions,' the milkman said chirpily, ladling milk into the jug from one of the churns on his cart. May was tickling the horse's nose and the blinkered horse kept jerking its head back which made May laugh. Aggie stroked its neck, enjoying the animal's hot smell. 'One of Brum's many fine palaces,' he chuckled. 'Long as you stove it reg'lar.'

'Huh,' Jen said, but he had brought a smile to her lips.

'Here you go.' He handed Aggie the well-filled jug. 'I've put in a bit extra for luck. See you tomorra.'

So Aggie trailed after the cart with the heavy jug of milk. As they set off, the men at each end of the cart, its wheels squeaking as they turned, a low cheer rang along the road and they were showered with good wishes which brought tears to Jen's eyes all over again.

'Doing a moonlight, Jen?' an aproned lady called from her doorstep.

'If I was going to do that I'd get a lot further away from you lot, I can tell you!' Jen quipped.

The woman laughed. 'Bet you would, bab! I'll be round for a cuppa once you're settled.'

And soon, on a tide of goodwill, they were washed along to the entry off which the two yards of the Mansions divided, which was as far as the cart could go.

'Should only take one more load,' Bill said, hoicking up his trousers, which kept shrinking down under pressure from his generous gut.

'Give us a shout,' Mr Southgate said, moving away. 'I might still be about later.'

'Ta very much!' Jen said. She looked at her mother. 'He seems cheerful for once.'

Dulcie Skinner was at the end of the entry, waving.

'You're good and early,' she said, hooking her arm through Jen's. 'All right, are yer?'

Aggie saw her mother smile and pat Dulcie's arm. 'I'm all right. Glad you're here.'

Aggie carried the jug along the dark entry. She often came down here to visit Babs, but now they were going to live in the next yard. In the heat she could already catch a strong whiff of refuse from the rubbish tips at the end of the yards.

'Stinks,' May remarked behind her.

'Sshhh,' Aggie said. 'Don't upset our mom.'

May made a mutinous noise, her lower lip sticking out.

'Shurrit, all right?'

Aggie wanted to take in the new place without May rattling down her ear. She stepped into the yard. 3/2 The Mansions was their new address. There were three houses each side of the yard facing each other, a gas lamp placed squarely halfway down. Further along was a tap, free-standing in the middle of the yard. It was dripping steadily, so that a mucky brown snake of water squiggled across the uneven bricks. The place was quiet enough to hear fat bluebottles buzzing round and some-one splashing water in the brew house at the end. This was next to their new home, at the end, on the left.

The houses all looked much the same, but outside some there were signs of efforts to cheer the place up. Inside number two you could make out red-and-white striped curtains, and the family at number four had pots on their sills outside full of red and white tobacco plants and geraniums, and hanging chained to a nail outside the door was a soldier's helmet, full of petunias of pink, white and mauve. Aggie thought they looked lovely.

'Look,' she pointed and saw May take in the colours with a pleased gleam in her eyes.

Number six, by the yard entrance, was Mary Crewe's, though there was no sign of her, and her sister, Eliza Jenks, was out at work. Theirs, down in the opposite corner, was a dingy, neglected-looking house, with filthy windows and all its paintwork cracked and split with only hints remaining of its original green.

'Here we are,' Nanna said, limping along the yard. 'It'll do us.'

Mom came along after her and Aggie heard her murmur something to herself. Her eyes were full of dismay.

Cautiously, they pushed the door of number three open. It seemed queer going into the old man's house. His possessions had been cleared out and it was bare and covered in dust and grime. The range looked as if it hadn't been blackleaded for years and there was a strong smell of mould. As they stepped inside, things scattered away from their feet, at lightning speed.

'Dear God,' Jen said. 'We're going to be eaten alive in here.'

The house needed the spring clean of a lifetime. And it was considerably smaller than their house in Lilac Street. For a start there was no attic. Downstairs there was one room only, with a little scullery at the back with a sink, but no running water. They had to fetch that from the tap in the yard. On the upper floor were two bedrooms. After the extra rooms upstairs and down that they had had before, it was a comedown, all right.

All the same, the children found it exciting to explore, their feet clattering on the bare boards. These were so rotten in some places that they'd splintered off and there were rough holes in the floor. They ran upstairs to investigate where they were going to sleep.

'Don't bang about so much!' Mom kept yelling up the stairs. 'You'll come through the ceiling, else!'

Aggie, John and May came back down. The fourth step was broken and Aggie helped May jump over it.

'Are we having the big room, then?' John asked, standing, as he did these days, with the air of the little man of the house.

'Don't keep on,' Jen snapped, peering into the range, which looked as if it hadn't been lit in living memory. 'How're we even going to get a cup of tea in this place?'

'It'll be all right,' Freda said. 'Just stoke it up.'

'I bet the chimney hasn't been swept in years,' Jen fretted. 'We could have a fire. Burn down the whole yard!'

'Well, we *could*,' Freda said dryly. 'Or we *could* try looking on the bright side.'

'I'll see to it,' Bill said, wheezing. He was also

perspiring heavily, his face nearly as pink as the flowers outside. 'I'd've thought it was hot enough already.'

'I need a cuppa,' Jen persisted. 'And how're we s'posed to cook, else?'

Once they had brought along the second, smaller, cartload of their things – this time without Harry Southgate's help – and had wrenched themselves away from number nine Lilac Street, the day suddenly felt like a holiday, especially when nearly all the other children were at school.

A pale, almost silent little boy appeared out of the flower house, number four. He was accompanied by two baby sisters who were too young to be at school and all of them stared apprehensively at the new arrivals. The little girls stood half hidden behind the boy, who positively cringed when John went over to him.

'What's your name?' John asked him, towering over him.

'Peter,' he muttered, his pasty face turned towards the ground. 'I've 'ad the mumps.'

'Are there any more of you – at school like?' John asked.

'A brother and a sister,' the boy mumbled, squinting defiantly. 'My brother's bigger 'un you.'

'So what?' John said, strolling away scornfully.

Jen had asked the men to carry the big bedstead up to the smaller room. Once it was put back together, it just fitted in. She and her mother were going to have to share. And the children would sleep, as they had in the attic before, all in together.

Aggie came upstairs that afternoon to find her mother and grandmother looking in through the door of their room, where there was scarcely space to move round the bed.

'I'm sorry, Mom,' Jen said. Her apology contained regret for all she knew of her mother's life, that they were back in a place just like where they started.

'Well.' Freda edged her way in and sank on to the mattress. 'That's life, bab – ups and downs, swings and roundabouts. All I want just now is to be able to lie down for a bit – just anywhere. And this looks like a perfectly good bed to me.'

She lay back, her face pale and pinched with pain, nursing her arm to her chest. 'O-o-oh, dear,' she muttered, closing her eyes.

'D'you want a cuppa tea?' Jen asked her wearily. However tired she was herself, and however much she had to report for duty at the fish shop that evening, she could see that her mother was all in. 'Come on down and leave her,' she whispered to Aggie.

They went down the twisting staircase. The room looked a little bit more cheerful with their few bits and pieces in it. Bill had got the range going and the room was stiflingly hot. They had brought the last of their coal with them. Aggie could hear John and the others, now back from school, running about in the yard, but it was hot out there as well and she could see Mom needed her help.

Jen sank down on a chair as they waited for the kettle to boil again.

'I need summat to eat – we all do,' she said. 'Get that loaf out, it's in the crock there.' As Aggie was doing as she was asked and trying to locate the bread knife, her mother said bitterly, 'I never thought it'd come to this. Not all this again – cowing bug-ridden place. I'll have to stove it tomorrow.'

Aggie found she didn't mind as much as she had thought she might. Babs was in the next yard and other things were not so far away. Everything felt strange and sad these days, and the aching absence of their father was always there, but at least in this house they were not expecting to see him, to hear his voice or his coughing from the bedroom upstairs. It put his death just a little bit further away. She was too young really to understand what it was like for her mother to have lost the man she loved and to have this step backwards, further into the poverty she had watched her own mother battle as a child.

'Never mind, Mom,' she said, sawing at the bread. 'It's not so bad. It'll be all right.'

As if seeing her daughter with new eyes, Jen looked over at her. 'You're a good kid,' she said.

And for the first time that day, at this rare gentleness, it was Aggie who had tears in her eyes.

Fifty-Two

Aggie's first night in the Mansions felt very strange. Dulcie came round and lent a hand and Babs too, once school was over. Gradually they got their things organized, the familiar crocks on the rickety shelves and on the table, the pots and pans and their bedding in the upstairs rooms, and even though it was drab and dirty, the place started to feel a little bit more like home.

Some of the neighbours came to say hello, including the mother of the timid Peter. The woman, Mrs Peters, was very new to the area. She had a scarf tied tightly over her hair even in the evening and she was thin and shrieky. They were to hear a lot of her shrieking in future, mostly at Stan, the oldest boy. When she talked about Stan, she implied that John had better watch out. As she left, Aggie wrinkled her nose.

Jen stared after the woman. 'Hm – I'm not so sure about her,' she said. 'And anyhow –' She deposited the wooden box which held their eating irons on the shelf with a clatter. 'What the hell's she playing at, calling her boy Peter when her surname's Peters? Daft if you ask me – not that anyone did.'

She sank down suddenly on to a chair. 'Oh! How am I going to keep going all evening?'

'I could do it instead,' Aggie offered.

Her mother smiled wearily. 'I wish you could, bab. But I can't send someone else along my first day, can I?

If we can keep the dinners going from here as well . . . Maybe,' she said, speaking really to herself, 'we might just get by for now.'

Aggie felt relief flow through her.

They waited, that night, for her to come back from Price's. Nanna, having had a rest, was there with them and her very presence made the place home. No one wanted to go up the strange stairs to bed, so they sat round and at half past nine they heard Jen's footsteps along the yard.

She came in looking tired but quite cheerful and accompanying her was the most delicious smell.

'Chips!' Silas cried, suddenly wide awake again. Aggie felt the saliva rush into her mouth.

Jen brought the warm, newspaper-wrapped bundle to the table. 'He slipped a bit of fish in an' all,' she said. 'Such a nice man, that Mr Price. Come on, kids – tuck in.'

'You're to have the fish,' her mother instructed. 'You need to keep your strength up.'

The smell of hot potatoes and vinegar was spreading round the room.

'No, there's enough for all of us,' Jen said. 'Tell you what – I'll have this end. Mom, you take some. And kids – you all have a bit each.'

They gathered close round the table, relishing the chips. Aggie noticed that John tore a piece off the fish to eat, then had second thoughts.

'Here, Mom – you're to have mine,' he said gruffly. 'You need it more.'

'Good lad,' Nanna said.

'Oh, John!' Aggie could hear the emotion in Mom's

voice. Mom could see John was determined so she took it graciously. 'Ta, love. When these two arrive,' she stroked her stomach, 'we'll tell 'em they owe you!'

Mr Price had been generous with the chips and Aggie enjoyed the blissful feeling of swallowing the hot tasty potatoes. Though the place was strange, the creaks and other noises different from the house they were used to, they slept all the better for having nice, full, warm stomachs.

From Aggie's point of view life went back almost to normal. They were still all grieving for their father, but Aggie and the others had to go to school and for the moment Nanna was at home to help with the dinners and Mom working every hour she could at the fried fish shop. The children were all trying to bring in any money they could manage still and John found some work after school in a little toy works the other side of the Stratford Road and was very proud of his few shillings he brought in every week.

There was more earning for Aggie as well. A few days after they had moved, as she walked back from school, pleased to see the old neighbours in Lilac Street, she found Mrs Southgate hovering near the entry into the Mansions.

'Aggie!' Rose Southgate called to her, her voice soft but urgent.

She was dressed in a summer frock in a lovely soft green and her pale golden hair was caught prettily up at the back. But when she got closer, Aggie saw that the woman's face was pinched with distress.

'Please, Aggie,' Mrs Southgate said, her voice only just steady. Aggie wondered with alarm if she was going to cry. 'I really need you to run an errand for me . . . Look, come along to my house. I don't want to talk about it in front of the whole street.'

She led Aggie inside, where Lily came running to greet her.

'Aggie!' she cried and threw her arms round Aggie's waist, which was cheering.

Mrs Southgate put on a forced, cheerful tone. 'I expect you're hungry? How would you like a piece of bread and jam?'

'Yes, please,' Aggie said instantly. Whatever else the woman wanted she wasn't going to throw up the chance to be fed. But she did feel wary of her nowadays.

'Come and sit down with Lily . . .' She took them into the kitchen and the two little girls sat at the table where Aggie saw there was already a plate of bread and raspberry jam waiting. Mrs Southgate sat tapping her fingers on the table as the little girls ate. She seemed quite unable to sit still. As soon as Aggie showed signs of having had enough, she jumped up.

'Now, Aggie dear – come into the front with me a minute, please.'

Closing the door of the front parlour, she took a deep breath.

'I need you to take another message to Mr King – to speak to him again. I need a reply straight away.'

Aggie frowned. 'Why don't *you* just go and see him?'

Rose Southgate forced a smile. 'Well, I have been rather busy, you see, and Mr King is at the works all day or out with customers. I can't keep going to and fro all that way with Lily . . . Anyway, the thing is, I'd like you to go now, as fast as you can and wait for Mr King, all right?'

Aggie nodded.

'And Aggie – this is our secret. No one else is to know. There's a shilling in it for you.'

Before Aggie could say anything she moved closer, bending down as if someone was eavesdropping on them. She smelled faintly of flowers.

'You *must* see him, d'you understand? Don't let his landlady put you off. Tell her it's an emergency – a family matter. When you *do* see Mr King, you must tell him you've something from me, Mrs Southgate.' She spoke very deliberately. 'You tell him Mrs Southgate is unable to come herself, but that she urgently needs to meet him. Say to him . . .' She looked away, desperately, over Aggie's head for a moment. 'Say –' Her eyes drifted down again. 'Oh, dear . . .' She crumpled for a moment. 'This is so very difficult. His being blind makes everything so . . . Look, ask him where he can meet me, will you? Just anywhere, but get an answer, Aggie, for God's sake. Now do go, please, dear, at once.'

'I've got to run a message for Mrs Southgate,' Aggie announced at home.

'Oh, have you now,' Jen said. 'And what's that exactly, then?'

Trying to dodge the question, Aggie added, 'She's giving me a shilling for it.'

'A *shilling*!' Jen shot her mother a significant look. 'Must be mighty urgent. Who to?'

Aggie squirmed. 'She said I wasn't to say.'

'Would it be anything to do with piano tuning?' Nanny Adams asked.

'No – not really,' Aggie said truthfully. She wasn't sure about the way Mom and Nanna kept looking at each other.

'Well, you'd better get on with it,' Jen dismissed her, muttering, 'A *shilling* – must have money to burn.' She didn't ask Aggie to take May with her. One of the new developments about moving was that May was thick as thieves with another little girl in the yard and Aggie didn't have her trailing after her every moment of the day.

Fortified by the bread and jam Aggie set off again. As she went back along Lilac Street and was just turning the corner into Turner Street, she almost collided slap bang into Mrs Taylor.

'Watch where you're going!' the woman exclaimed. As usual she was proceeding along with a bag on each arm like a ship in full sail and beside her was Dolly, who scowled at Aggie.

'Sorry,' Aggie said, running on and wandering why Dolly Taylor was always so snappy with everyone. Or at least she thought it was Dolly. But afterwards, she realized she seemed to have a mole on her cheek. Had it been Rachel? She was confused.

She was just rehearsing to herself what she had to say to Mr King when she almost ran into someone else. The someone didn't let her go, but grabbed hold of her shoulder. Aggie gasped and looked up to see a crone of a woman with a matted mop of yellowish grey hair and lips parted to show a few peg-like teeth.

'Who's that?' the woman demanded. 'D'you know who that is?' She nodded vigorously along the street. Phyllis Taylor was just disappearing round the corner.

'What d'you mean?' Aggie asked.

'That woman – one with the girl with 'er. You spoke to 'er. D'you know 'er?'

'A bit. She lives down the road.' Aggie tried to pull away but the woman dug her fingers in.

'You can go once you tell me what 'er name is. Is it Hetty summat?'

'No!' Aggie said. 'That's Mrs Taylor.'

The woman relaxed her hold, sinking back in a satisfied way. 'Taylor. First name?'

Aggie's mind went blank. She was always called Mrs Taylor but she was sure the name wasn't Hetty.

'Got a 'usband, 'as 'er?'

'N-no. I think he passed away.'

At last the woman released her. 'And she lives just along there, you say? I'm an old pal of 'ers, see.'

Aggie nodded doubtfully. Anyone who looked less as if they could be a friend of Mrs Taylor's she found hard to imagine.

'Number?'

But Aggie was backing away. 'I dunno . . .' She ran off down the street, rubbing her shoulder. She'd had enough of adults being funny with her already that day and felt she had said too much already.

The landlady in Oldfield Road peered over her spectacles disapprovingly at Aggie. Aggie looked down at the woman's well-polished brogues.

'Mr King is not home yet,' she said, eyeing Aggie's stained dress. The brown shoes Mrs Southgate gave her were now very worn and down at heel. 'And I really can't think what he'd want with you if he was.'

'All right, ta then,' Aggie said, backing away. She'd just have to wait.

She guessed that Mr King would be coming from the piano works, so she walked along in that direction. She wished for a moment that she could go into some of the gardens that she knew were behind the houses. It was such a hot, sleepy sort of afternoon. She imagined how it would be to go and lie down in the grass under an apple tree. Out here there was no green and though the sun was sinking down now, it was still oppressively warm.

Waiting on the corner, she picked at little growths of moss from between the sooty bricks and wondered if Mrs Southgate was in love with Mr King. How could that be though, since she was married to Mr Southgate? Mom and Nanna had been making comments about it but Aggie wasn't fully sure if that was really what they meant. And why did it always involve tuning the piano?

She became aware of a light tapping along the street and turned to see Mr King, feeling his way along with his stick. Aggie began to move slowly towards him. It seemed unfair, as she crept along, that she could see him when he could not see her. His black jacket was unbuttoned, as was the top of his shirt, and he was not wearing a tie.

Suddenly he was very close.

'Mr King?'

'Yes?' He spoke amiably. 'Who's that?'

'It's Aggie again. Mrs Southgate sent me with another message.'

His face tensed, an odd expression passing over it for a second.

'I see.' He swallowed. 'Well, Aggie, as you've come all this way again, you'd better deliver your message.'

Aggie did as she was bidden. Mr King listened carefully. Just for a moment he lowered his head as if to gather his thoughts.

'Tell Mrs Southgate that I shall call at her house on

Sunday afternoon. About three. If that's not convenient
... Well, if it's not then perhaps she'll send you back to
tell me.'

'Sunday, at three,' Aggie murmured.

'That's it, exactly.'

When Aggie gave Rose Southgate the message, it was
like watching the sun come up, the joy that spread over
her face. And Aggie came away with a shilling, gripped
tightly in her palm.

Fifty-Three

'So come on, out with it – what the hell d'you think you're playing at?'

Phyllis had barely got the door shut before she launched into Dolly, letting out the fury that she had been containing all the way home. She dumped her bags down on the table and glared at her youngest daughter, looking fit to explode.

'Nothing, Mom!' Dolly protested. 'It weren't me. I was just walking along minding my own business and he came up and—'

'And you let him sweet-talk you until you're prancing about with that grinning 'apeth like any other moll on the monkey-run!'

Phyllis had happened to be on the Stratford Road, picking up a few bits of shopping, and lo and behold, who should appear but Dolly and likely lad, arm in arm.

'It was nothing,' Dolly said mutinously. 'Just a bit of fun. I was only on my way home and he came up and started asking me my name and that, and we was—'

'Were,' Phyllis said. 'There's no need to talk common as well as acting it.'

'*Were*,' Dolly rolled her eyes. 'We *were* just canting, that's all. Why shouldn't I? There's no harm! You just want me locked up here, day in, day out. I feel like the Prisoner of Zenda!'

'Oh, yes – why shouldn't you?' Phyllis leaned across the table. 'Let's just think about this, Dolly.' Her voice was dripping with sarcasm. 'Why shouldn't you go about doing exactly as you please, eh? What's stopping you? Only the fact that you're more than six months gone with a bastard baby, or had you forgotten all about that for the moment?'

'God, I wish I could!' Dolly roared, stamping out of the kitchen and up the stairs.

'Don't blaspheme!' Phyllis shouted after her. Soon she heard Dolly's angry sobbing from upstairs and rolled her eyes furiously.

'Bloody stupid little bint,' she muttered, fishing a handful of carrots from her carrier. She was shaking with rage. 'No idea, that one. No sodding idea at all.'

She heard footsteps at the back. Susanna came in from work.

'D'you know what that flaming girl's done now –?' Seeing Susanna's worried frown Phyllis cut short her tirade. 'What's up with you?'

'It's just . . . It may just be nothing, but, you know Rachel said about that filthy old lady who she met?'

Phyllis felt her circulation start to pump much too fast. She stood very still, having to hold on to the back of the chair.

'Well – she's standing out there, staring at our house.'

The blood was banging in Phyllis's ears. She wanted to sink down on the chair, but Susanna was staring at her.

'Are you sure?' She forced a casual tone. 'Bit odd, that.'

'She *does* look odd.' Susanna moved through to the front. 'She looks horrible. I'll go and have a peek, see if she's still there.'

408

Phyllis followed Susanna's padded, solid figure to the front. She went to the window and peered out from behind the nets.

'She's going now – I can still just see her, look –'

Phyllis joined her at the window. Further along the street she could just see a scruffy, shuffling figure. Was that Ethel? It was impossible to be sure from here. Maybe it was all a mistake? She felt herself breathe more easily.

'Bit queer,' she said, releasing the curtain. 'Perhaps the old duck isn't right in the head.'

'She gives me the creeps,' Susanna said, shuddering. She pulled at the edge of the padded burden she was carrying. 'Ugh, it's so hot. I can't wait to get this lot off. That blasted baby can't come soon enough, is all I can say.'

It wasn't until the next day that there was a knock on the door. Phyllis heard it as she stood in the kitchen, rubbing fat into flour. She froze, drawing herself up straight. After a few seconds she began to breathe again and moved silently to the scullery to rinse her hands and take off the apron, uncovering her navy, belted dress made of stiff cotton. As she did so she heard it again, the sharp rapping. Phyllis did not have visitors in the normal run of things. She kept herself very private.

Thoughts rushed through her mind as she crept to the front door. As she raised her hand to open it the knock came again. She drew the door open.

The two women regarded each other, each trying to overcome the erosion of the years and find recognition. Those were Ethel's eyes all right, the narrow set of them, and their almost unnaturally pale blue. In every other respect the woman looked like a tramp, hair straggling out from under a greasy-looking square of cotton, grey, threadbare clothes and a black wool shawl, even in this warm weather. She was scrawny and her haggard face an unhealthy yellow colour.

To Phyllis's surprise, Ethel seemed abashed at the sight of her, almost cringing as, in a grating voice, she brought out the words, 'Well, Hett – tracked you down at last.'

Phyllis stood back. She must get Ethel out of sight. 'You'd better come in.'

She led Ethel into the parlour, walking over towards the window with its spotlessly clean net curtains and turning to face her. Ethel stood just inside the door. Phyllis had never been exactly sure of Ethel's age, but it had not been too far off her own. Now though, Ethel did not look like a woman in her early forties – she looked twenty years older. Phyllis saw her staring hungrily round the room at the two matching upholstered chairs facing the fireplace, the elegant clock on the mantelpiece, the little Chinese rug by the fire and her ornaments which she had collected over the years with James. *Take a good look*, Phyllis thought.

At first Ethel seemed surprised, cowed by the smart, respectable room. But soon a sly expression crept back over her features.

'See yer got some nice knick-knacks 'ere, Hett.'

Phyllis cringed at the use of the term. *Knick-knacks* – cheap and common, like baubles picked up at a fairground. She clenched her fists as Ethel shuffled in her broken-down shoes, which had long lost their laces, over to the mantel and put her face close to the framed wedding photograph of herself and James. She felt violent loathing rise in her that Ethel's breath was steaming up the glass, and had to resist such an over-whelming desire to grab this slovenly wreck of a woman and shove her out of the house, that she found she was shaking with the effort.

'What d'you want, Ethel?' She managed to sound calm.

'I was married once, yer know.' Ethel turned, her voice petulant. Phyllis could hear the old Ethel again, the child.

She didn't say anything.

'I had a son. 'E's gone off and left me now, all grown.'

'I said, what do you want?'

Ethel looked her in the eyes for the first time, her piercing, calculating stare. 'Bet none of these round 'ere know who you are really, Hett. Hetty Barker? I kept asking. No, no one knows who Hetty Barker is.' She took a step closer. 'But I know what kind of piece you are really, Hett, for all your finery. What you've been.'

'I was forced into it,' Phyllis retorted. For a horrified moment she felt tears rising in her. What chance had she ever stood, back then, of a better life? It was as if everything she had strived for since, all she had tried to be, a wife to James, bringing up her children the best way she could, now counted for nothing. She was still to be tarred as a fallen woman. Ethel didn't even know about Ma Hegarty's and what she had been forced into in Birmingham, but *she* knew – about that life that she had been running away from ever since.

She tried to steady herself. She must not get into a barney with Ethel! No – she must keep her dignity. She must do everything in her power to get rid of her before the old crone went blabbing around. Oh, yes, there were plenty round here would love to know all about her past and rub it in her face. Phyllis had no illusions that she was popular.

Ethel was even closer now. 'I thought you was my friend . . .'

'*Friend?*' Phyllis said, thrown into bewilderment. Everything between them had always been based on barter and threat, who could get what out of whom.

'Yes, friend. We was in it together – and that day you ran off, just ran to save your own miserable skin, the day she—'

'I thought the police would come. All that blood . . .' Phyllis shuddered. The memories kept forcing themselves at her. 'Why didn't you leave her? You didn't owe that trollop anything – everything she did was for herself. She used us, both of us for anything she could get . . .'

'She was *my mother*!' Ethel flared into her face.

Phyllis stepped back, in stunned horror. 'Your . . . ?' She tried wildly to recall Ada, any resemblance. But Ethel had had flame-red hair, those eyes – nothing like Ada's.

'Yes – my mother. No, I didn't favour Ada, not in looks. Must've taken after my father, whoever the hell he was. You never saw it, did you, never wondered why I stayed with 'er? You thought I was just after saving my own skin. But I'd've done anything for 'er – she was all I had. When I came out of the reformatory I was back there with 'er, we was working as a team, looking after the boys.'

Everything was rearranging itself in Phyllis's head. 'The babbies – Eddie and Alf . . . ?'

'My brothers – half-brothers, any road. They were as much my own as anyone.'

'But . . .' Phyllis began.

412

'Why didn't we tell yer? That what yer want to know – eh?' Ethel came up close, and Phyllis shrank from the stink of her rotten teeth. 'You think a whore like my mother has no pride? That she'd want a soul to know she was selling her own daughter?'

There was a moment when they stood, eyes fixed intensely on each other.

'The boys were done for, both of them. You know who did it? That quiet one used to come. The Quiet Gentleman.' Ethel looked down brokenly for a moment, and Phyllis almost pitied her. When she looked up, her harsh tone was back. 'She died, soon after if you want to know. Not from that – she was bad anyway, summat inside 'er. A growth. So –' Her tone toughened more, into sarcasm. 'I carried on the business. Married one of 'em, but 'e died – drink finished 'im, that and bad luck. My son – well, 'e might as well be dead too for all I see of 'im. No gratitude from that one.'

Phyllis held herself stiffly, feeling as if she was watching a snake that might pounce on her at any moment.

'You're not short of a bob, Hett, I can see that.'

Phyllis gave a harsh laugh. 'I'm a widow – and this isn't a palace, in case you can't tell.'

'All the same –' Ethel peered around. 'Look at you – a few things yer could pawn in 'ere.'

Phyllis's mind was racing. So it was clear, what she was after.

'You could spare me a bit, Hett, for old times' sake,' Ethel wheedled. 'I ain't had your luck. Never had none of that going, not me. If you help me out – you know, proper like, I'll keep away after that. You won't see me again. Never.'

'How much?'

Ethel looked taken aback for a moment, as if having

413

her request granted was more than she ever really expected. She struggled to fix on a figure. Screwing up her face, she pronounced brazenly, 'Fifty quid. Get me fifty.'

Phyllis kept her face a mask of calm, but her mind was racing ahead, planning, calculating.

'It's a lot of money,' she said at last.

'Worth it though, eh, Hett?'

Phyllis looked down at the floor for a moment, giving the impression of deep thought.

'Course, I don't have that sort of money around me,' she said, looking up into Ethel's face, which was now showing signs of a repulsive excitement. 'But I tell you what I'll do. I don't want to carry that sort of sum about, not round here. You hang on a couple of days and I'll send my son to you.'

Ethel's face darkened. 'How do I know I can trust him?'

'My Charles is a lay preacher,' Phyllis said haughtily. 'There's none more trustworthy than him, I can tell you. And he'll do what I say.'

She named the place and time. Ethel still looked doubtful.

'We're a Christian family, Ethel,' Phyllis said, ushering her firmly towards the front door. 'He'll be there – don't you worry. Just keep your head down till then. And keep away from here.'

Ethel turned on the step, her face eager, almost childlike. 'I won't forget this, Hett.'

'We go back a long way, us two,' Phyllis said.

She watched for a second as Ethel turned to go along the road, then quickly she disappeared back inside.

Fifty-Four

All Rose could think about was that Arthur was coming on Sunday afternoon.

The weather was warm and good for both house painting and fishing, so Harry was away from home a good deal of the time. Every spare moment while he was out, Rose worked on her embroidery for Mrs Lacey, intent on earning as much money as she possibly could. The set of flowered table places was already finished and looking fresh and pretty and she had begun on a tea cloth in a similar design.

Every hour felt like a mountain that had to be conquered. One of the hardest things was having Harry in the house and trying to behave as if everything was normal. Harry's behaviour towards her now was cocky, sneering, as if he had won a battle and was glorying in it. He had her just where he wanted her. All because, Rose thought contemptuously, he could put his *thing* in her whenever he wanted now, as if that was all that mattered. What a fool he was – like an animal!

She still wore the letter, with the poem from Arthur, tucked into her clothing. It was her greatest comfort, knowing it was there.

On the Sunday morning she sat through church, standing and sitting automatically for hymns and readings, smiling vaguely at the other parishioners and not taking in a thing. When the clock struck eleven, at the end of the service, she thought, *Four more hours*. And it seemed like the eternity that the Bible was forever mentioning. She already knew what it was to live in eternity, she thought.

By ten to three, she was alone at last, sitting in the front room, her chest tight, ears straining to take in any sound, above all that of a stick tapping on the pavement. The waiting seemed to go on and on. Then she heard it, unmistakably. In a second she was at the door, pulling it open. And there he was, coming towards her.

He stopped at her step, and because he couldn't see her waiting for him, half hidden by the door, she called softly, 'Arthur.'

His face held a combination of eagerness, fear and possibly resentment, she wasn't sure. She shared the fear, but all else she could feel was immense relief that he was here, and the tenderness of longing to be in his arms.

'Come in, quickly,' she said, reaching out her hand.

Behind the closed door, in the front room, they stood close together, but at a loss, each hearing the other's breathing. They could not embrace – nothing was resolved. Arthur hung his head as if he suddenly did not know why he was here.

'You came,' she said eventually.

He nodded. She could see now that he was regretting it, as if he had given in to something wrong.

'That child – Aggie. I had to tell her something. And then when I'd told her—'

'Arthur,' she interrupted. 'Please. *Please*. Let's leave here. Let's just go away together. I can't think of anything else. I love you, I want to be with you whatever it costs. I just can't bear this life . . .' She

416

gestured round the room, even though it was wasted on him.

'It's all very well,' he said despairingly. 'But how am I to work? I'm all right in the firm here, but—'

'You'll find work,' she said passionately. 'You can tune pianos just as well as anyone who can see. And I thought you said St Dunstan's would help, that they'd help wherever you were living? We could go north, to some town where no one knows us or any of our business and we can just be together, you, me and Lily.'

As she spoke, Rose found she was panting. Both of them were, they were so pent up with nerves.

'You don't seem to realize what you're saying,' Arthur said. 'Neither of us has much money—'

'I can work. I'll do anything, especially once Lily's at school. And I can sew. I've got some money saved and I'm working on more. Mrs Lacey says my work's some of the best – she'd still buy off me and I could find others . . .'

He seemed stunned by her determination.

'But the shame . . . Divorce . . . It's a terrible thing. I'd feel as if it was all my fault – you know, the Vile Seducer, like in the pictures. And my family . . .'

'Arthur.' She went up close to him now, laying her hands gently on his shoulders. 'Do you love me?'

He face was working, twisting with inner conflict. 'You know I do. Though God knows, I've tried not to.'

'Oh, my darling . . .' Her voice was full of tears. 'And I love you. I just can't stand life without you – with Harry. I don't care about shame. There are worse things. Loneliness is worse than shame and I've had so much of it.'

Arthur nodded. She could see that he was moving

417

towards her, that they would be together, and it was wonderful and terrifying. 'Loneliness.' He sighed. 'Yes. Oh, God, yes.'

Only then, they held each other. She could hardly believe even now that he was here, that she had her arms round him and could feel him warm and close to her.

'Here –' She guided his hand to her ribs, where the paper, softened by being pressed to her for so long, could just be felt under the cotton of her dress. 'I've kept it close to me all this time – your poem.'

Arthur smiled, moved. 'Not my composition, I'm afraid. But it seemed right.'

She moved her face towards him, her lips reaching for his. He kissed her with hungry need and for a moment they were lost in each other, but then Arthur drew back.

'Look – not now, here, like this. If we go on I'll want you so much I'll lose my head and we just can't do that. Especially not here, in this house. To tell you the truth, I've been so worried . . .'

'Why?'

He looked solemnly at her. 'When we were together before, we didn't – I mean, I was afraid there might be an outcome. That perhaps that was what you needed to tell me?'

'A baby?'

'That's the normal thing, isn't it?' He was teasing now, gently. 'But there isn't, I take it?'

'I don't know, for sure. But I don't think so. Arthur.' She couldn't tell him she had missed twice. Not now. 'Come and sit down. I'll make tea. Come to the back with me while the water boils. I can't bear not to be with you every minute.'

They drank tea in the kitchen, at first intoxicated by excitement. They had given in to their feelings for each other. They could not be denied, and Rose sat holding Arthur's hand, full of a sense of the miraculous. He was here. They would be together and at first it was like a haze around them. But then the cold realities began to reach then, like fog seeping into a warm room.

'Arthur – what are we going to do?'

He sat looking ahead of him for a few moments. 'I feel so shocked – at myself, at all of this. I can barely think. We need to take a while, to make plans. Nothing sudden, not at first.'

'But if we go,' she said. 'That'll have to be sudden.'

'Yes, I suppose so.'

'We'll have to just walk out one day with everything, and get on a train and never come back.'

'We'll need to arrange somewhere to go.'

'Yes, dear.' She could see that his lack of sight made everything more difficult, the world an even bigger obstacle than to her. 'I think for Lily's sake we must do our best.'

Arthur turned to her. 'You astonish me, Rose. Your voice is so soft and gentle. But you're made of steel. I never would have thought it, not at first.'

'Not always,' she said, thinking about it. 'Not most of the time. But with you, I know it's right. Even if it's wrong, so far as everyone else is concerned.'

Arthur put his arm round her. 'I believe you've got more guts than me.'

'No, I've never done anything! Not been a soldier and all those terrible things you've had to do. But just for once, I'm sure. And we mustn't wait too long, dear. We can meet at weekends and plan.'

'What about Mrs T?'

'She doesn't know who I am, does she? Why can't I just openly come in? I'll take my wedding ring off.'

'Oh, Mrs T'd be funny with you whoever you were.'

'Well, we can meet outside sometimes. The park or somewhere if it's difficult with her. And work out what we're going to do. And I can still send Aggie if necessary – so I'm not up and down to your house too much.'

Arthur shook his head. 'This is madness, Rose. Pure and simple.'

'*No* – it isn't!' She squeezed his hand tightly. A power seemed to flow through her. She could do anything, get past any obstacle so long as she knew that the two of them were in it together. Nothing else mattered. 'We're going to manage it, whatever anyone else might think or say – and they're not going to know, are they? Just you and me. Whatever it takes, we *must* be together – and soon!'

He turned to face her, reaching out a hand gently to stroke her cheek. 'God, I do love you, Rose. You're an amazing woman. Whatever else . . . However wrong this is . . . I feel as if I've just been given back my life.'

She leaned forward to rest her forehead on his shoulder, and for several moments they sat in silence, in the wonder of it.

Fifty-Five

Phyllis sat with her children round the table that night. She had roasted a bit of beef and the smell of the meat and crisp potatoes filled the house.

'You're not eating much, Mom,' Susanna remarked as Phyllis took two small potatoes and some cabbage along with a modest slice of beef.

'I don't seem to feel that hungry today,' she said. 'Must be the heat.' She was perspiring heavily, but she knew that it wasn't much to do with the muggy evening. She kept eyeing the clock. Its tick was ratcheting up the tension inside her though time itself seemed to be moving very slowly, as if arrested by the thickness of the evening air.

Attention was soon removed from her by Dolly, squeaking, 'Ooh! It's kicking me again!' She pressed a hand to her right side, beneath her ribcage. 'Oh, my word, I'm sure I can feel its foot sticking out the side!' Dolly never spoke of the baby as 'he' or 'she'. 'It feels really peculiar.'

'Well, what d'you expect?' Rachel retorted.

Charles looked very displeased to have the reality of the baby forced upon him.

'Dolly, quiet,' Phyllis cautioned her, feeling as if she was going to explode. She was so taut with nerves that the last thing she needed was Dolly's carry-on. She got

421

up from the table. 'Get this lot cleared up. I've got to go out.'

'Where're you going, Mom?' Susanna asked.

'Madge Lines's. I said I'd give the Cradle Roll to her. It won't take long.'

'Oh,' Susanna said, surprised. It was so unlike their mother to go out of an evening, except to a very occasional Bible study, for duty's sake.

'I'll just go up and get the papers.'

Upstairs, out of sight, Phyllis's movements became faster, more furtive, but with no hesitation. She had thought this through many times over. Now all she had to do was act.

In a cloth bag she had put some papers to look like the Cradle Roll, the church's list of babies and young children. She already had one or two other items in the bag and now she went to her drawer and drew out one of her little brown bottles of smelling salts and slipped it into the pocket of her dress. She looked in the glass over her chest of drawers to make sure her hair was tidy, then slipped a cardigan on, despite the heat. She cursed. Why did this have to happen in the summer? It was just coming up to ten to eight and still light outside. If it was November or December it would have been dark for hours, making her job much easier.

Her face looked back at her from the glass, its fleshy folds pulled into a grim expression.

'So,' she whispered, narrowing her eyes. 'Come on, Hett. Time to get moving.'

Going downstairs she could hear the clash of pots and pans and Rachel and Dolly squabbling over the washing-up. Normally she would have waded in but tonight she was not going to get involved.

'Shan't be long,' she called from the front. She was

about to open up, but changed her mind and went through to go out the back way. She could feel the family looking at her, but she ignored them and went out into the yard.

The air was full of the smells of smoke and cooking, of fried onions and boiled cabbage. She walked through the entry and the street was alive with children playing out, ropes swinging and boys running wildly back and forth. Phyllis eyed the street carefully to see if anyone who mattered was looking at her. That tattling bitch Dorrie Davis was nowhere in sight. She pulled herself upright, and made her stately way to the end of Lilac Street.

Half past eight was when she'd instructed Ethel to meet Charles. Once again she cursed the fact that there was no darkness to hide in, but if she'd suggested meeting much later it would likely have scared Ethel off.

'I don't want you near my house, you understand that, don't you, Ethel? Charles is a good lad. I'll send him with the money. After that you must leave us alone. It's a lot of money, Ethel – there won't be any more.'

Ethel, avid with expectation of this windfall, would have agreed to anything.

Ever since, Phyllis's mind had played with images of things she'd like to do to Ethel. If only she could have thought of a place where they could meet next to the cut. She pictured herself rolling Ethel's body over the canal side into the black water, the splash of her foul existence and the memories that went with it disappearing for ever! It was no good – Ethel might be greedy but she wasn't completely stupid. She would never have agreed to meet by the cut and in any case on a hot summer evening it would still be crawling with joeys and other boats. At the time, the first place that had come to mind was St Paul's churchyard. It seemed a good place for her religious-minded son to appear before Ethel.

Phyllis lengthened her stride. She did not want to draw attention to herself but she was determined that she would be there first. Sweat broke out under her arms and down her back. Turning into the end of St Paul's Road, the street stretched before her, seeming endlessly long. Suddenly she was filled with dread that there would still be something going on in the church: it was Sunday, after all. But surely by now, the evening thing they did – evensong, wasn't it – would be over?

By the time she passed under the railway bridge she was in a state of such nerves that when a train came roaring over it, she emerged shaking.

'Come on – for heaven's sake pull yourself together,' she admonished herself.

She walked on past the entrance to the churchyard to check how busy it was. In these crowded streets any secluded space was a lure for kissing couples. A man turned out of the gate as she came along but she could not see anyone else and it seemed to her that the church was quiet as well, though the porch door was open.

Reaching the end of the street, she turned round and made her way back as if she was out for an evening stroll. As the road was clear, she went in quickly through the gate, and ducked down to hide behind the wall and a bush growing at the edge of the graveyard. The light was fading, though it was nowhere near dark. The church clock said eight twenty-five.

Time seemed to crawl by and she could feel her heart thumping. There were footsteps in the distance and a young couple came along arm in arm and disappeared under the bridge. As soon as the next lot of footsteps approached under the bridge, she knew it was Ethel. Crouched low, she watched. The dark-clad, shuffling figure was in view now. Phyllis shrank even lower, shaking with nerves. She reached into her bag and withdrew something which she inserted into the left sleeve of her cardigan. Then she tucked the bag down at the edge of the bush. With her right hand she took the little bottle from her pocket.

As Ethel turned into the churchyard, Phyllis cowered behind the bush until she had moved past, then as fast as she could, slipped soundlessly across the grass as the woman shuffled towards the entrance.

'Where are yer, then?' she heard Ethel muttering resentfully, at the porch door. 'Anyone in there?'

Ethel didn't hear her at all. Phyllis, who was at least a head taller, shoved Ethel into the dark porch, and reaching round with her right arm, pushed the bottle of smelling salts close under her nose. Its vicious blast of ammonia made Ethel's head shoot back and she let out glugging sounds of distress. But Phyllis had her pinned from behind with both arms. Ethel struggled, whimpering at the pain of the vapours knifing up through her nostrils.

'Right, Ethel,' Phyllis said, her mouth next to Ethel's right ear. 'It's me, Hett, in case you're wondering. Thought you were coming here to get rich, didn't you? Only it doesn't happen like that – not if you tangle with me. I'm not falling for blackmail, having you round my family like a bad stink.' She jerked Ethel, who whimpered, obviously still suffering.

'What if I was to give you money, eh? You'd be back, sucking on us like a fat grub. I don't owe you, Ethel. I've lived my life and worked hard to better myself and you –' She gave a yank with her arms, pulling Ethel so that she whimpered. 'Are not going to wreck it.'

She reached inside her sleeve and drew out the size ten knitting needle, thin and sharp.

'See this? This is what's going to happen if you ever, *ever* come anywhere near me or my family again. I'll stick this thing in your ear and up into your rotten, filthy head. And when they drag you out of the cut, no one'll see the tiny hole in your ear – they'll think your heart gave out, an old lag like you. No one'll ask too many questions.'

Ethel squirmed, trying to protest. Phyllis gripped her harder with her right arm though she had removed the bottle from under Ethel's nose.

'Don't mistake me, Ethel.' Her voice was a growl now. 'You come near me or mine one more time and I *will* finish you. Without a thought. You're not getting any money – not now and not ever. If I see you in my neighbourhood ever again, I'll come for you. I swear it. You got that?'

Ethel nodded, a whining sound coming from her.

'You get right away from here,' Phyllis warned, beginning to release her. 'And don't you ever come back.'

Ethel turned and in the gloom looked into Phyllis's eyes. 'Never thought you'd be like this with an old pal, Hett,' she whined.

'I'm not Hett. Hett's dead. And you're not my pal. Never were.'

Ethel stared at her. Her eyes were still running and had gone red as had her nose. She looked truly pathetic. 'You're a bad woman, Hetty Barker. You may look all respectable, but . . . Saying things like that to me – in a church! You're evil, you are!'

426

'Well, that makes two of us, then,' Phyllis said, tucking the needle back into her sleeve. 'But don't you ever forget what I've said. Come near us again and –' She made a slashing motion across her throat.

Leaving Ethel in the porch, she went and retrieved her bag, put her bits and pieces into it and disappeared into the gloom under the railway bridge.

July 1925

Fifty-Six

Aggie soon felt at home in the Mansions. The family set to and cleaned up the house, bit by bit. All the children did what they could. It was as if with their dad passing away, everyone had grown up a little and they were pulling together to support Mom.

'Lucky I'm not further on,' Jen said soon after they arrived, eyeing her growing belly. It was the time in a pregnancy when she had most energy. 'Another few weeks and I'll be the size of a battleship.'

'I just wish I could get this off,' Freda said, looking gloomily at her plaster cast. She could move it more now but it was still always in the way. 'I could curse it, I really could. I can't get down to anything properly.'

'Oh, it'll be gone soon enough,' her daughter said. 'I should make the most of it.'

'I expect I can sort those curtains out,' Freda said.

Jen set about sweeping and washing the house out and burning sulphur candles to get rid of the roaches and silverfish and any lurking bedbugs. Although it was a school day when she did it, Jen kept Aggie home and shut up the house for the day to fumigate it. Aggie spent that warm day playing out with May and the other little children who were not at school. Another day she helped her mother polish the old range, which had been much neglected, and cleaned up the heavy Dutch oven, which had been left behind as well.

Now she was living so close to Babs, their friendship grew closer. Aggie barely thought about going to see Mrs Southgate any more. Instead of being relaxed and sweet the way she had been before, Mrs Southgate was now odd and intense in a way that made Aggie uneasy. Every so often she ran an errand for her and was glad of the money, but these days she was having much more fun with Babs and her brothers, who were a harum-scarum bunch, full of laughter and mischief. They had an orange box shackled on to some old pram wheels and liked to push each other in it, roaring up and down the yard until everyone shouted, 'Get out from under my feet!' and banished them to the pavement outside.

The two yards were almost identical and because Aggie had often been to Babs's house in one yard, she found the other quite easy to adjust to. Even Mary Crewe felt familiar as she came in and out, looming in the entry, muttering to herself. The girls walked to school together, and once home, they ran back and forth along the entry in and out of each other's yards. There were some people she didn't like much, like the Peters kids next door, but she kept out of their way as much as she could.

It already felt to Aggie as if they had been there for a long time.

One Saturday, in mid-July, something very sad happened. Aggie was playing at the bottom of their yard near the brew house with May, Babs and the others, when a kerfuffle broke out. Loud, distressed wailing noises were coming from Mary Crewe's house. The noises grew louder. Aggie and Babs stopped their game of fives. Everyone looked round.

'Where is it?' Mary was shouting hysterically. 'Give it back! Who's got 'er? Someone's stole 'er – give 'er back to me!'

Aggie felt her stomach turn over. She had never heard anything quite like it before. Mary's shouting made her sound like a big, shrieking child.

Babs made a face, pushing her bottom lip out and rolling her eyes. 'It's Mad Mary. Sounds like trouble.'

Aggie got to her feet. 'Come on –' She pulled on Babs's arm. 'Let's go round to yours.'

Babs shrugged. 'All right, then.'

They slipped round the entry into the other yard, but Mary Crewe's yells followed them, echoing round the yards, and there was no escaping her.

'Who's got it?' she was yelling to anyone who would listen. 'I know one of you's stolen 'er. Give 'er back, now!'

'Oh, my,' Dulcie Skinner said. She slipped round to find out what was going on and came back looking upset.

'It was her "babby",' Dulcie said. 'That bundle she carries about with her. Someone must've slipped in and took it.'

Aggie found herself hoping it hadn't been John or one of the Skinner boys. Whoever it was would be in for a hiding.

'So has she got it back then?' Babs asked.

'Yes – it was one of them Dawson boys,' Dulcie told her, shaking her head. 'Went in and took it for a joke – he thought it was funny. D'you know what was in there? A rag doll – a little scrappy thing. Poor soul.'

Aggie felt the sadness of this go into her.

They thought that was the end of it, but the next day, Mary Crewe disappeared. No one saw her go out of the yard, and her sister Eliza was beside herself, saying Mary must have got up in the night or early that morning but she hadn't heard a thing.

Soon everyone on the street was talking about it. Dulcie, who had known the sisters for years, tried to comfort Eliza.

'She'll've just gone on her wanderings, bab – she'll be back. Don't you worry.'

But by six o'clock that evening, people were out searching the streets for Mary. Dulcie called round at the Greens.

'Cooee?' Her head appeared round the door. Freda and Aggie were clearing up the tea. 'Jen not 'ere? Oh, course – she's down at Price's, I'd forgotten with all this going on.'

'Cuppa tea?' Freda asked. 'Kettle's boiled.'

'Ooh, no, I'd better not . . . Oh, go on, then. Joe's gone out searching with some of 'em. Poor Eliza, she's beside 'erself. I mean, Mary's always been a wanderer – but this is different.'

Freda brought the pot to the table and sat down creakily.

'That arm of yours feeling any better?'

'Not so bad,' Freda said, nursing it in her lap.

'Flaming nuisance that must be.'

'I remember Mary as a child,' Freda said, changing the subject. 'Her family lived up the road from us.'

'I remember Jen saying,' Dulcie nodded. 'Was she always a bit – you know?'

'No. Not the sharpest, ever, but she was all right. It was her mom dying young the way she did, then that husband of hers running off, and then the children . . . Everything piled on top of her, that was what did it.'

'Well, that's the queer thing,' Dulcie said, sipping her

tea. 'About what happened. I mean, the lad should never've done it but it were only a few minutes and he gave it back. He thought it was a joke but she scared the living daylights out of him. It was as if her whole world had fallen apart, just in a few minutes.'

'Poor soul,' Freda said. 'I hope she's not done summat hasty.'

Aggie and the others were already in bed that night when the news came. The neighbours had carried on searching and those still at home were in and out of each other's houses talking about it. Mary Crewe had been seen up and down the street as regular as clock-work for years. Everyone felt they knew her even though she spoke scarcely a civil word to anyone from one year to the next.

Aggie was lying beside May, who was already asleep. They had stayed up late to wait for Mom to come home, and they'd had a few chips each, but still there was no news that Mary Crewe had come home. Aggie's eyes were closed and she was drifting off, when she heard the knock downstairs. She raised her head and listened. It sounded like Dulcie.

May and Ann were both asleep and she slipped off the bed without disturbing them, but she found John getting up as well.

'Who is it?' he whispered.

'Mrs Skinner, I think.'

They crept halfway downstairs.

'It was at Moor Street,' Dulcie was saying in hushed tones. 'She managed to get right out along the track.'

'Oh, dear God,' Aggie heard her mother say. 'Ooh, I feel quite peculiar.'

'Come on, bab – you sit down,' Dulcie said. Aggie and John looked at each other in the gloom of the staircase.

'She's thrown herself under a train!' John whispered and Aggie was infuriated by the objective relish in his voice.

'I *know*,' she hissed. 'And it's horrible. How can you say it like that?'

She left his side enraged, and went back to bed. She found she was shaking, and it took her a long time to sleep. All night, her mind was full of it: Mary out by the dark tracks, and the sadness and the horror of it. All the next day she felt sick and exhausted.

Fifty-Seven

'I'm always chasing rainbows!' Rose sang out in her sweet voice as she worked.

She was scrubbing her way down the stairs, sleeves rolled up. As she reached the bottom and stood up, for a moment she was overcome, her head swam and she steadied herself against the wall, breathing deeply to push the feeling away.

'Why're you singing, Mom?' Lily asked. She looked genuinely puzzled.

Rose felt a blush spread over her cheeks. She hadn't realized Lily was watching her.

'Was I?' She wiped her arm across her forehead to move wisps of hair out of her eyes. 'Oh, I don't know. Must be because it's a nice day. Come on –' She held out her hand to distract Lily. 'I'm going to make a cup of tea and then how would you like to come and help me wash the windows?'

She had scarcely noticed the terrible events with Mary Crewe because she had spent the afternoon with Arthur, and on returning had stayed at home with Lily and closed into her own thoughts. When she heard eventually, on the Sunday, she could see what a tragic event this was, but nothing seemed to be able to dent her own happiness.

*

On Saturday, she had asked Muriel Wood if Lily could spend some time at her house because she had to visit her sick sister, and on Sunday Lily had gone to Sunday school with Aggie and the others. Rose felt pangs of guilt about her untruths to Muriel, but Muriel was so kind-hearted and would welcome Lily anyway. And above all, the force of her need to be with Arthur had overridden everything.

She persuaded Arthur to introduce her to Mrs Terry as his fiancée.

'She doesn't know anything about me, does she?' she reasoned, though Arthur, ever truthful, was very hesitant.

'I don't know,' he said. 'It seems devious. Supposing she finds out?'

'But how could she do that?' Rose said. 'Oh, please, Arthur – otherwise it's going to be so awkward, all this creeping about smuggling me into the house, or having to stay out all the time. That's not very honest either, is it?'

Arthur had to concede that this was true. So he announced to Mrs Terry that he was engaged and that Rose would be visiting him. Mrs Terry was surprisingly accommodating about it and Rose realized that crusty as she was, she had a soft spot for Arthur.

So they had spent two delicious afternoons being able to come and go as they pleased and planning a new life.

'Maybe we'd be best off in London,' Arthur said.

'I don't see why,' Rose said as they cuddled up on the bed, half clothed in the warmth. 'Can't you just advertise yourself as a piano tuner anywhere?'

'I suppose so.' He sounded doubtful.

'London's so big,' she said. 'It frightens me a bit.'

After a silence, Arthur said, 'It's my family that's really troubling me. How will my parents feel – and Connie and Ede? I feel so underhand taking off like this, not saying a word, after all they've done for me.'

Rose lay thinking about it. It was so long since she had had her own mother and father. She would have loved to know Arthur's mother and father, to get to know them and be accepted by them. But in their circumstances, how could this ever happen?

'I don't know –' she sighed, really burdened by this. 'I'm bringing you so much trouble, my dear. Could you ... perhaps write to them, later, when we are far away, and explain? Would they hold it against you for ever?'

'They're very old-fashioned,' Arthur said. 'They don't like to stand out, or have any scandal. But since the war – I suppose that's changed things. I know they'd rather I was alive and happy ...' He turned and kissed her. 'I can't imagine being happy without you, Rosie. It's just all rather a lot to think of at once. So ... Where would you like us to make our home?'

'What about going to Manchester or . . . I don't know, York? There must be plenty of pianos up there.'

Arthur laughed. 'Oh, I'm sure there are. You're an adventurous soul, aren't you?'

She rolled over to look at him and kissed his warm cheek. 'Only when I'm with you.'

Arthur pulled her close, laughing joyfully. 'Oh, Rose, my beautiful Rose. God, I love you. This is all terrible and not how it should be – not at all. But why doesn't it feel wrong?'

'It's *not* wrong,' she said fiercely. 'Not you and me. It's right –' She kissed him between the words each time. 'Right, right!'

The more they talked, the more they felt that going

north would be best. To Manchester or Leeds. And soon.

'I don't know what to think,' Arthur said. 'Losing my sight makes me much more timid. Do we just go, pack a case one day and take our chances, like vagabonds, or do we prepare ahead? What about Lily? She needs to go to school.'

'No – not yet,' Rose reminded him. 'She's only little.'

'I'd forgotten. Yes, I suppose she just needs to be where you are. But she'll miss her father.'

'You can be her father,' Rose said. She thought of the queasy feelings she'd been having from time to time. She kept ignoring it, telling herself she was a little bit ill, or that it was the heat. She knew in a part of her mind that she was expecting a baby and that, the way things had been, only Harry could be the father . . . But she just wouldn't let herself admit it. She couldn't worry Arthur with it. Not now, when he was so apprehensive about everything else.

All she wanted to think about was that soon, she and Arthur would walk away and never come back, and that that momentous day was coming very soon.

For now, though, with Harry, she had to carry on pretending.

One afternoon that week, he came home early, having finished a job. Rose was in the kitchen cooking. She had let Lily go and play out with the Green children and some of the others and she had been embroidering. Luckily she had just put her sewing away and started on a stew. All afternoon she had been in a dream, her mind fixed on Arthur, on their plans. She jumped when

440

Harry suddenly appeared at the back window, wheeling his bike.

Rose arranged her face into pleasant lines. She might as well try and be nice. What did it matter now?

'You're back early!'

'No sense hanging about. We'd finished.' He looked round. 'Where's the kid?'

'Out playing. I'll put the kettle on,' she said.

But Harry came up behind her and laid his hands over her breasts.

'Careful,' she said, trying to wriggle away. 'You'll dirty my dress – you've got paint on you, look!'

But he was insistent. 'It's dried. Won't do any harm.' He took hold of her again, his eyes already glazing with desire. 'Come up with me. While we're on our own.'

She could think of no reason to object and she wanted to do anything to avoid trouble. With his hands at her waist, Harry steered her up the stairs, stopping once or twice to nuzzle at the back of her neck. She could smell his sweat, the plaster dust, paint, white spirit on his clothes. Nausea twisted her insides at the smells and she had to swallow hard, but she went with him, quiet and docile. Harry was too caught up in his own desires to take any notice of what she was doing.

In the bedroom he pawed at her clothes.

'I'll do it,' she said, not wanting him to tear anything.

'No, let me,' he insisted. He seemed as excited by undressing her as anything. Usually she undressed in the dark with her back to him. He undid her buttons clumsily, pulled off her dress, her underclothes.

'Lie down,' he ordered.

He undressed only as much as was necessary and took her, hard and urgently, his eyes closed. Rose turned her head so as not to look at him, holding her mind apart. After her love with Arthur, who saw her far more with his blinded eyes than Harry ever did with his unharmed ones, it was horrible to be shamed like this. She felt dirty and small, his weight forcing her down, pressing on her lungs, his stale breath panting into her face. She made herself think about Arthur. Soon this would end. It would be over for ever.

Harry's need was soon satisfied and he rolled off her, on to his back, and yawned. Rose turned from him and sat up, reaching for her bloomers, longing to go and wash.

'Make us a cuppa tea, bab,' he said sleepily. 'I'll 'ave a kip, just for a minute.'

She dressed hastily and went downstairs. As she did so, Lily came running in with a scraped knee.

'Oh, dear, never mind,' Rose said, thanking heaven she hadn't fallen over even a few minutes earlier. She sorted Lily out while the water boiled, then gave herself a quick wash, before taking Harry up a cup of tea.

She expected to find him lying prone, but instead, he was sitting up in bed, covered by the sheet. His eyes were fixed unwaveringly on hers as she came through the door; this was startling and she stopped, unnerved by it.

'I thought you were going to have a sleep,' she said, forcing herself forward with the cup of tea.

'Nah.' Harry pushed himself into a more upright position. 'I wasn't sleepy in the end.' He added, 'Ta,' as she put the cup on the chair by the bed.

As her steps receded down the stairs, Harry reached under the sheet. He had leaned over the side of the bed earlier to look for the po to relieve himself. As he did so, he saw something on the floor under Rose's side of the bed. He unfolded it now: a well-worn sheet of paper with a poem written on it:

. . . time, nor ties, nor distance,
   makes love less. A

Harry folded it up again, and reaching down, slipped it under his side of the mattress. He straightened up again, his features pulled into an expression of grim triumph.

Fifty-Eight

'So they won't have her in the churchyard, will they?' Aggie heard her mother and Nanna talking. 'Not as she took 'er own life. Poor Eliza's in a terrible state.'

Mary Crewe's funeral had been delayed to allow for an inquest, but the coroner decreed that she had died at her own hand 'while of unsound mind'.

'And it means,' Jen reported back after much talk in the yard, 'that Mary wasn't in control of her own actions so she can have a funeral like anyone else.'

It was a humble affair. Eliza was as poor as a church mouse and some of the neighbours had a whip-round to help her out a bit. The street gave Mary the best send-off they could manage in the circumstances. Aggie and the others were at school when it all happened, but she was haunted by Mary Crewe. When she was going to sleep at night, she kept seeing herself lying on the railway track, like the ladies in the pictures, when they lay there trembling and the piano drummed louder and louder as the enormous engine bore down on them, billowing smoke. Sometimes she scared herself so much she sat up, trembling, hugging her knees in the darkness, and Ann would grumble sleepily, 'Stop it, Aggs, you're pulling all the covers off!'

That week a number of odd things happened. One day Aggie came home from school to find Mrs Southgate waiting for her.

444

'Oh, no,' she groaned to Babs. 'I bet she wants me for summat.'

She was beginning to feel resentful towards Mrs Southgate, although the bits of money came in handy of course and pleased Mom.

'Aggie,' Mrs Southgate greeted her as if she had just stumbled on her by accident. Her manner was exaggeratedly cheerful. 'What a good thing I've met you! Can you run an errand for me, dear – straight away?'

As Aggie trotted along Lilac Street, hurrying to get it over with, a voice called out to her, 'Aggie! Come over here a minute will you, bab?'

Mrs Best had a chair in the street outside her door, her husband in his wheelchair behind her in the doorway, and standing beside her was Mrs Davis.

Aggie went over to them. Dorrie Davis was staring at her and Aggie could tell she was eager for information of some sort. She always was.

'Aggie,' Mrs Best said gently, looking at her through her watery eyes. 'Where're you going?'

Aggie immediately knew that Mrs Southgate would not want her to tell these women anything. But it was tricky because she liked Mrs Best.

'On an errand.' She couldn't think what else to say.

'Who for?' Dorrie Davis asked immediately.

Aggie swallowed. 'Mrs Southgate.'

The two women looked at each other.

'Sends you on a lot of errands, does she?' Dorrie asked.

'Sometimes,' Aggie agreed.

Irene Best's face wore a gentle, concerned look, the sort of face people put on when they knew someone was about to receive some bad news.

'You will be careful, won't you, bab?' she said.

Aggie stared at her.

'She won't know what you mean,' Dorrie said.

'I just mean,' Mrs Best struggled on, 'well . . . Don't get too involved, that's all. You don't have to run errands for Mrs Southgate if you don't want to. Just keep your wits about you, won't you, Aggie?'

Aggie nodded, backing away. She hurried past the Mission Hall and on towards the Ladypool Road. She didn't know what Mrs Best was talking about, not exactly, but in another way she did. She knew that Mrs Southgate had secrets; that she, Aggie, was running errands for her that no one was supposed to know about. That there was something queer about it all and that Mrs Southgate had changed. But she didn't know what it was all about and she also didn't feel she could get out of it now even if she wanted to.

Mrs Terry answered the door in Oldfield Road.

'I've got a message for Mr King,' Aggie announced.

'I see,' Mrs Terry said. 'Well, he's only just this moment back. Mr King!' she called up the stairs. 'I'm afraid you'll need to come down again. That girl's here again with a message – probably from your fiancée.'

Arthur King came downstairs quite fluently, skimming his left hand down the wall. He looked very cheerful and different from when Aggie had last seen him.

She didn't want to ask Mom or Nanna, so she waited until school the next day.

'Miss Neal?' she asked her form teacher, just as they all poured out at break time. 'What's a fiancée?'

Miss Neal, an older lady with glasses, looked amused. 'A fiancée? Well, it's a French word, meaning a woman

446

who is promised to a man in marriage.' She turned to the blackboard and wrote *FIANCÉE*. 'It has two e's because it's feminine, in French. For a man it's spelt the same but with only one e.'

Aggie stared at the word. 'Is that the only thing it means?'

Miss Neal was wiping the board. 'Well, yes – so far as I know.'

Aggie ran outside into the playground, her mind full of confusion. Was Mrs Southgate playing some sort of game? Why was she calling herself a 'fiancée' when she was already married to Mr Southgate?

She ran over to where Babs and their friends were playing. The adult world seemed bewildering and frightening. She threw herself into a game of tag and decided she'd been a fool not to stick with playing with Babs in the first place – never mind *Agnes Green: Spy*. So far as she could see, spying didn't get you anywhere.

Rose felt that everything she did these days was secretive. She had started going shopping further away, to avoid gossips like Dorrie Davis. She liked to go later in the afternoon to get some air, after she had been sitting sewing.

As she shut the front door behind her and Lily, the realization struck her, forcefully: *By the end of the month, I'll be gone, and I'll never see this house again!* Taking Lily's hand, she thought tenderly, *And you'll be with me, my little darling. Just you, me and Arthur.* This filled her with a sense of bliss. By the end of July, they had decided, they would go and start their new life.

Once she had done her shopping people were starting

to come home from work. Just as she was approaching the end of Lilac Street, someone familiar was coming from the other direction. But she had to look again, to check. Yes, it *was* Susanna Taylor. Susanna saw her and waved, quickening her pace.

'Hello,' Rose said. 'Haven't seen you about in a while.'

'Hello – and hello, Lily, love,' Susanna said, smiling at the little girl. She was her usual rather reserved self but she did seem distracted. She looked very hot and flustered.

'Just back from work?' Rose asked as they turned into the street.

Susanna said that she was.

'How're you all keeping, then?' Rose asked questions quickly so that Susanna could not ask her any. She couldn't help noticing that Susanna was overdressed for the weather, in a rather thick navy cotton dress and a heavy cardigan buttoned over the top. Her cheeks were very round and pink. All of a sudden, Rose couldn't help noticing, Susanna seemed *portly*. Her body was quite substantial and her face had thickened up as well.

'Oh, we're all right,' Susanna assured her with determined cheeriness. 'You know, going along as usual.'

'Well, that's good. Have you got a date with David yet – for the wedding?' Rose asked in a friendly, teasing voice.

'Not yet. Next year, we hope.'

Susanna was the same, reserved young woman, Rose thought. Just . . . bigger. As they said their goodbyes, Rose watched her walk away. If she didn't know better, Rose realized, she'd have said Susanna was expecting. But that just wasn't possible! Not Susanna – such a dutiful, religious girl. No, it couldn't be. Rose narrowed her eyes, watching. Although Susanna seemed bulky at the front, she wasn't walking like someone carrying a child. Her gait was brisk and unencumbered.

'Well, she's getting a bit plump,' she said half to herself. 'Maybe it's because she's happy.'

Would she become plump and rounded once she was with Arthur?

Panic seized her again, as it kept doing. *Oh, God*, she thought, leading Lily into the house. *I'm the one who's expecting!* She couldn't carry on avoiding it. *I must be two months gone*, she calculated. *Harry mustn't notice. Nor Arthur – not yet.*

In her heart of hearts she was almost sure that the baby must be Harry's, but she didn't want to believe it. Her mind wrestled with the problem.

How can I possibly be sure? Maybe I got it wrong and it is Arthur's? Anyway, whatever happens, Arthur will be the father now. He'll love it, bring it up. It's his baby in my heart.

And there were the thoughts she could not admit aloud, even to herself. If the child turned out looking just like Harry – well, Arthur would never be able to see, would he?

Fifty-Nine

Phyllis stood just to one side of her front window, from where she could look out from behind the net curtain. She was perspiring in the humid day and she wiped a hand across her pink face.

Everyone in Lilac Street seemed to be going about their normal business. Phyllis saw Rose Southgate pass in front of her, in a pretty blue frock, with her little girl beside her. *A queer fish that one*, Phyllis thought. She watched Rose move out of sight with her shopping bag.

Even though it was getting on for a month now since she had had her encounter with Ethel Sharp, Phyllis was still on edge, was constantly looking out for her. She kept going to the window, many times each day, just to make sure that there was no one there, that Ethel wasn't standing across the street watching her house, taking revenge, spreading rumours. It had become an obsession. Her dreams were full of blood and violence.

We just need to get this baby over with, she thought. *That's taking it out of me. I can't rest easy until it's all settled. I hope to God Nancy keeps her word about it.* There were so many ifs and buts, far too many details to worry about.

She turned her back to the window and looked at her front room, her pride. Everything shone with care and elbow grease, the coal scuttle, the fire-tongs and clock, all her hard-won ornaments, her badges of ownership and respectability. Phyllis clenched her fists, thinking of Ethel. Nothing and *no one* was going to break into the castle of security she had built first with James and then on her own. It was all *hers*, her standing in the neighbourhood, her children, her things. No one was going to spoil it.

'Mom?' Dolly's sleepy voice broke into her thoughts. She appeared still in her nightdress, her long hair hanging down, looking like a little girl, except for the smooth, contradictory curve of her belly. She was big now, ripe. 'What're you doing in here? You're always looking out of the window. What's so interesting about out there?'

Dolly made as if to look herself, but Phyllis pulled her back.

'Don't you go showing yourself, Dolly,' she reprimanded her.

Dolly tutted. 'I feel like a prisoner.'

Stung, Phyllis snapped, 'Well, I should've thought staying in's a small price to pay!'

The baby was due in early August and last week Phyllis had instructed Dolly to give up her job and stay in the house until it was all over.

'That's when you'll really get to a size. You'd best stay out of sight.'

'Well, what about us?' Rachel had asked. 'Do we still have to wear all this blooming stuffing round us?'

'What you've got to do,' Phyllis emphasized, standing leaning over the table where they were sitting, 'is to put yourselves out and about even more. 'Specially you, Rachel.'

'Why?' Rachel said huffily. Dolly's sisters had had more than enough of the whole business.

'Because you're the one who looks the most like

Dolly. Lots of 'em say they can't tell you apart. So you go out in the morning – 'specially the weekend – wearing one frock and a hat. Later on you'll get changed – into something Dolly's been wearing – and go and put yourself about out there again. And put some chalk on that mole.'

Susanna looked shocked. 'Mom, that's – well, it's very *deceiving*.'

Phyllis's lips twisted with bitter amusement. 'You've just noticed, then? We've got to finish this, now we've started. It's just got to be done and you've all got to keep your traps shut.'

As usual they had agreed and obeyed her. It had all gone this far – what were they to do?

Now, with Dolly in front of her, complaining that she was hungry, Phyllis, for almost the first time, allowed herself to take in that within her daughter's belly there was a child growing. When she had had her own babies she had felt fulfilled and triumphant at her own capacity to give life and at the fierce love she felt for them. It had been the greatest time of her life, by far. She had felt like a queen. And James had taken great pride in her fertility, though they both agreed four was enough. But until now she had not allowed her mind to follow the reality of the situation, that inside Dolly was her grandchild. She felt a twist of almost overwhelming longing inside her. *But no!* They couldn't keep it here. Mustn't. She pushed her feelings away.

'Well, if you're hungry,' she said brusquely, 'go and have something to eat.'

'I've had enough,' Babs panted. She and Aggie were out in the street skipping, taking it in turns to run in and out and jump over the long rope. 'I'm all sticky and I need a drink of water.'

'Come on, then,' Aggie said. 'Ann – keep an eye on May, will you? I'll be back.'

It was stiflingly hot and the children, who had just broken up from school, were already in holiday mood. As Aggie and Babs ran into Aggie's yard they nearly ran full tilt into someone coming out of Eliza Jenks's house.

Aggie raised her eyes gradually, seeing first a pair of big, dusty boots, above which were faded black trousers topped by a magnificent belly, thrusting against a white-ish shirt. This was topped off with a faded black jerkin. His sleeves were rolled to display forearms bristling with curling grey hair and, on his left arm, a long colourful tattoo. At the top was a big, fleshy face and balding head with curly tufts of grey hair over each ear. Blue eyes looked at her very amiably, over the pinkest pair of cheeks Aggie thought she had ever seen. They were smooth and shiny as apple skins.

'Eh – canny on theya! You nearly 'ad me orva!' was what he said, in an accent so strange that Aggie took a few seconds to take in what he meant.

'Sorry,' she said, meaning it.

'Ah should think you are!' he chuckled. 'Well, noo I've met yee, yee can gissies a bit of advice. Should Ah come and live heor, in this canny good lady's house?'

Aggie and Babs looked at each other and giggled. He looked such a jolly, well-disposed person.

'Yes,' Babs said. 'You should. That's what I think.' And they both got the giggles again.

Eliza Jenks, Mary Crewe's sister, came out into the yard then, looking more cheerful than she had in a long time. Her grey eyes were full of amusement.

'Well, Mr Gates,' she said.

'That's me,' the man chuckled infectiously. 'Mr Gyets from Gyetshead. You'll think that's a jork, but it's not.'

'A jork,' Babs whispered to Aggie. 'I think 'e means a joke.'

'D'you want to take the room?' Eliza said. She had cleaned the place up spotless to make sure she could rent it to someone.

Mr Gates looked around the yard. 'Are the neighbours aal reet?'

Aggie and Babs nodded. 'I live over there,' Aggie pointed out importantly. 'That's my mother.'

Jen had just come out into the yard and caught sight of Aggie with the stranger. Curious, and a bit protective, she came over.

'Yee this one's mutha?'

Jen squinted at him, then nodded, starting to smile. You couldn't not smile at the sight of Mr Gates.

'You coming to rent off Miss Jenks?' she said.

'Aye – ahm thinking of deein tha.' He eyed Jen's swollen belly with sympathy, but didn't say anything. 'Seems aal reet heor. Ah've had a canny good welcome.'

As he was nodding his head, Jen understood that he was moving in, even though she could not make out much of what he was saying. She and Eliza Jenks both stood smiling.

'There's nothin' left fre me in Gateshead, so ah thought ahd myek a fresh start heor, see.' He grinned at their bemused faces. 'Yee divvent knaa what the hell ahm saying, dyer? It's leik a foreign cuntry doon heor!'

By this time Aggie saw that Nanna had come out and was listening in to the conversation, but she shook her head in bewilderment and went back inside again, though she was smiling.

Everyone wished Mr Gates welcome and when Aggie went in, Nanna said, 'I've had more luck making sense of a Frenchie than that. Is he moving in?'

'Looks like it,' Jen told her. 'I s'pose we'll get used to him. Any road, he looks a cheerful sort and goodness knows, we could do with a bit of that around here.'

Sixty

All the gossip that week was about Mr Gates. As the newest resident and being different, foreign almost, in everyone's eyes, all the tittle-tattle centred round him. Mrs Peters next door was very nosey and saved the others the effort of asking questions. By that Sunday morning she had most of the basic facts and was full of importance sharing them around.

Jen met Edna Peters outside at the tap at the beginning of what promised to be another stiflingly warm day. Jen wasn't overly fond of Edna, a small, sharp-faced little woman with faded blonde hair, but she was curious about what she'd found out.

'He must be a widower, I think,' Edna said, waiting with her bucket as Jen filled an enamel bowl of water. 'He's on his own and he's got some grown-up sons – one's away in the navy, that he did say. Not that you can make out much of what he's on about.'

'It's a big step, moving down here like that,' Jen said, grasping the heavy bowl, resting it on her belly. She nodded her head at the tap. 'I can't turn it off – you come and fill yours.'

'I s'pose it is,' Edna agreed as the water splashed into her bucket. 'I mean, he ain't young. Must be well on the wrong side of fifty. I just hope there's nothing – well, you know. Nothing he's got to hide, like.'

'By the sound of it,' Jen said, 'there's not so much

456

work up there as there is down here – and let's face it, there ain't that much here. I'll have to go – this is doing my back in.'

She waddled back to the house. Freda was downstairs now as well.

'I couldn't sleep, it's that warm,' she said, flexing her still-fragile arm. She had had the plaster removed and was trying to pretend that it was all completely better.

'I know,' Jen said, getting the kettle on. 'It's going to be sweltering in here today.'

'That one canting again?' Freda said, nodding out towards Mrs Peters, in the yard.

'Ar – as ever.'

'So what did she say, then?'

Aggie and Babs played out all morning and Mr Gates called a cheery greeting to them, but otherwise they didn't take very much notice. He went out for some time, causing speculation about whether he was a churchgoing man, but no one knew anything for sure.

By the time dinner was over and Aggie was getting the others ready for Sunday school, and so far as she knew, Mom and Nanna were both fast asleep. Jen was tired out from working every hour she could at the fried fish shop. But she didn't complain; she just went out and got on with it.

'Shurrup bossing,' Ann said grumpily as Aggie nagged her and the boys to get a move on. 'You ain't our mom!'

'Just shurrit yerself,' Aggie retorted. 'It's all right for you – I have to do everything round here.'

'Have we got to get Lily?' Silas asked, shoving his feet into Ann's cast-off pumps which were now his.

457

'Yes – so hurry up,' Aggie urged. 'Come on, May.'

It was oppressively hot, the sun right overhead and casting very little shadow. Babs was already on her way, a young brother in each hand. 'See you down there!' she called.

Mrs Southgate was waiting at the door with Lily. She seemed ready to go out, with her straw hat and cardigan on, and she closed the door behind her as she handed Lily over.

'There you go, dear. She's been ever so impatient, waiting for you.'

Aggie stared at Mrs Southgate and thought she was the one who looked impatient. Lily was quiet and if anything looked a bit sad. It seemed a long time since their cosy afternoons by the fire with the poems and Mata Hari.

Rose Southgate seemed disconcerted by Aggie's hard stare. 'Is there anything wrong, dear?' she asked.

All the things Mrs Southgate had said she would do and hadn't welled up in Aggie. The sewing was the thing she felt most bitter about. Her heart was hard with disappointment and she felt defiant.

'Are you going to pay me for taking Lily to Sunday school?' she dared ask. After all, she thought, Mom needed the money and how was it different from the other errands?

Mrs Southgate's face flushed with annoyance. 'Oh, no – I don't think so. I don't really think that's polite of you, Aggie. After all, you're going to the church yourself and it's not really what you'd call a *job*, is it? Have a nice time, Lily,' she said and walked off as fast as she could.

'Huh,' Aggie muttered, watching Mrs Southgate's

slender form speed away from her. 'Feels like a job to *me*. Oh, for goodness' sake, where's Silas gone now?'

There was a hiatus as Silas ran back in for his marble collection. He only had six marbles so far but they had to go everywhere with him.

Mrs Southgate set off in the opposite direction to them. Aggie thought she must be going to see Mr King. Again, she felt that sinking sense of betrayal. Why was Mrs Southgate going about telling people she was Mr King's fiancée? It didn't make any sense, but it added to the growing feeling that she couldn't trust Rose Southgate.

A figure came towards them on the shaded side of the street. Aggie was surprised to see that it was Mr Southgate, wheeling his bicycle with his fishing rods tied along the side of it. He was walking hurriedly, with an intense look, his eyes fixed on the far end of the street, where his wife had just disappeared.

'Dad!' Lily called to him. Aggie could see she was upset that he hadn't noticed. Both of her parents' minds were full of too many other things these days.

Harry's head turned. He looked shocked to see her there. 'See yer later,' he said carelessly, and hurried on.

Aggie turned to watch him. As she did so, she saw Mrs Best appear at her front door, her eyes following Harry as he moved up the road. Mr Southgate stopped at his house, leaning the bike against the wall for a moment. He carried the rods up the entry, and seconds later, reappeared without them, jumped on to the bike and rode off fast along the street.

Inside, Jen Green was having a lie-down, but was still wide awake. She had hoped for a nap, but felt restless and the babies inside her weren't quiet either. Limbs jostled about under her ribcage.

'Settle down, you little so-and-sos,' she whispered, shifting on to her left side to try and get comfy. It was no good on her back; she couldn't seem to breathe properly.

As usual her mind was going round and round, fretting about money and making ends meet. Mr Price was a kind man and she was truly grateful to him for giving her work, but her wages didn't amount to all that much. That and her mother's tiny widow's pension and the little bits the kids brought in were all they had to go on at the moment. Thank goodness they'd been able to move and save on the rent! And Mom was on about going back to work soon. She swore she'd be able to manage. Jen was worried to death about her, but she was that stubborn. And soon these babbies would arrive . . . What was she going to do then? She'd be unable to work, at least for a bit, and they'd all be crammed into this rotten little house like wasps in a bottle.

She felt tired to her very bones with the struggle of it all. So tired and so worried. She felt as if the flesh on her face was pulled tight with it all the time, the worry and tension. And she missed Tommy with a constant ache inside her. Not that he had been able to bring in much either, not for a good while. His health had finished him, however hard he'd tried. She smiled, sadly, picturing him, his laughing face, always ready for a joke. But the illness had eaten away at him, removing him from her. The thought that she'd never see him again would knife through her, suddenly, the pain fresh and raw every time.

There were so many widows about, all struggling. All those children without fathers. At least when they all got to an age when they could go to work, things would ease up. And her mother understood what it was like. Tears came to Jen's eyes. Both the men in her life, father and husband, had been taken from her so young. She had only been four when her father died. She had only a handful of memories of him. Mostly she remembered his boots, but she did recall a wide, smiling face and that he had been very big – or seemed so to her – a burly, comforting presence. She found herself aching for him as well, for strong, comforting arms to wrap themselves round her and ease her of all her worries.

461

Sixty-One

Rose walked back in the lazy Sunday afternoon warmth, brimful of happiness and expectation. She had spent a loving hour with Arthur in the privacy of his room.

'Let's go out, shall we?' she said afterwards. 'To the park? It's too nice a day to be inside.'

Arthur was cautious. 'Aren't you worried someone'll see us?' He was still lying on the bed and he half sat up and took her hand. 'We could just stay here, love.'

'I'm not worried round here,' she said. 'No one knows me. We could be any courting couple for all anyone else is concerned.'

'All right.' Arthur sat up. Rose sometimes had the feeling that he would always do whatever she asked of him. It was strange, to know that someone needed her so much.

As they walked towards Small Heath Park they could hear music drifting on the still air.

'There's a band today!' Rose said, excited. They were walking arm in arm and it felt so happy and free. She didn't know anyone else in Small Heath. How good it would be to be in Manchester where they could be completely sure that no one knew them or would find them!

They drifted across the green to the bandstand, where the Sally Army were playing cheerful marching tunes

462

which added a festive air. They strolled round at an easy pace in the Sunday afternoon atmosphere of pipe smoke and mown grass and ice-cream. People were lolling on the grass, chatting, smoking and just lazing in the luxurious heat.

'I feel so strange, don't you?' she said. As she turned to speak she longed, for a second, for Arthur to be able to move his head to her in response, to look deeply into her eyes.

'Yes,' Arthur agreed. 'It's hard to take in that this is real . . .'

'That after next week we shan't be here. That it's really *true*. I've never been anywhere except Birmingham. At least you know that other places really exist!'

'I hope I can get work.' He was forever fretting about this. 'I don't want to let you down, Rose.' He squeezed her arm. 'I feel I could be such a burden. As if I'm not – well, a full man.'

She moved her lips close to his ear. 'Oh, you're a full man all right, Arthur, my dear.' This brought a smile. Rose could see his need for reassurance. She squeezed his arm back. 'Look, you've got a bit saved up – you live like a monk – and so have I. We'll be all right, love. We'll find a place to lodge and get established. It may take a little time, but we can do it. We'll be together, working for each other.'

Rose looked across the park, scattered with knots of people. The band set off on another jaunty tune. She wanted to capture the memory of it. In another week they would be gone and they might never see this place again. However much she longed to leave, this was her home town, the only place she knew. The start of August meant the beginning of a new life. It meant Manchester, and Arthur and happiness. She had made her choice and she felt a thrill of power go through her. 'We can do anything, you and I, Arthur, when we're together. I know we can!'

He did turn to her then, as if hungrily seeking her face. Gently he held her upper arms and said, 'God, I love you, woman. Where would I be without you?'

It was always a dreadful wrench to leave him and go home, like waking from a dream and having to go back to her mundane reality.

'I hate to let you go, every time,' Arthur said.

'Soon I shan't have to leave you,' she said, kissing him goodbye, pressing her face close to his. They stood, their warm cheeks touching for a moment.

Once she had torn herself away from his loving presence, she strode home, needing to be back in time for Lily, and in case Harry should come back early, though that seemed unlikely. He might have cycled miles to fish on such a long, lovely day.

She walked along to the Mansions to collect Lily, thinking, as she hurried down the grim entry, how a few months ago she would never have thought of entrusting her daughter to a place like this.

Now that the sun was low in the sky the yard, which had been a baking rectangle of brick without the relief of grass, was in shade and many of the occupants had brought chairs outside and were sitting talking. Heads turned to look at Rose, neat and pretty in her blue frock. She saw Aggie's mother over by the tap with a pail – the redheads in the family were easy to spot – and there was a huge man with her who seemed to be offering to carry it for her. Rose never remembered seeing him before.

Goodness, Rose thought, Jen's getting ever so big now.

Freda Adams, the grandmother, was on a chair beside their door. 'Come for Lily, have you?' she called. 'They're in the next 'un.' She nodded her head towards the other yard.

'All right – thank you,' Rose called.

She found Lily with Aggie and Babs, all sitting in one corner, away from the boys who seemed to seethe around the yard getting in everyone's way.

Aggie looked up and Rose saw a closed, wary expression on her face, very different from the Aggie of a few months ago when she was so eager to please. Rose felt a pang of regret. She had always had a soft spot for Aggie, had liked to give her attention, but lately she had been so caught up in her own thoughts and feelings about Arthur. Love can be so selfish, she thought. She knew it, but could do nothing about it.

Lily saw her and stood up.

'Thank you, Aggie,' Rose said kindly. 'You are a good girl and I know Lily likes to come with you.'

Aggie still looked up with a reluctant smile. Babs, that strange, gawky little thing, was squinting up at her. In that moment, Rose felt overcome by shame, as if she had truly lost her own innocence.

'Here –' She reached in her pocket for the little rag in which she carried her change and found a twopenny piece. 'That's for you, Aggie.'

Aggie looked as if she was about to say something but then stopped herself. She reached out and took the money, saying, 'Ta,' and stowing it in her pocket.

Before Rose had even gone, with Lily, Aggie had turned away, and was talking to Babs.

*

Harry was late coming home. Rose cooked some fish for their tea, but there was no sign of him. By the time seven o'clock had passed, then eight, Rose was too hungry to wait. Once she had put Lily to bed, she ate and settled down to sew. When she heard him coming along the entry she quickly hid her sewing away and went to open the back door.

'You're late back,' she said, without resentment. 'Your tea's here if you want it.'

Harry was bent over, his back to her in the dusky light, detaching the rods from the side of his bike. He said nothing. Rose went and took the plate from the range where it had stayed warm. She moved the fish about a little with a fork so that it didn't look congealed and put it on the table.

Harry came in, heavily, and sat at the table. From his movements and the redness of his eyes she could see he had been drinking.

'I don't want that –' He pushed the plate away with a look of disgust.

'Oh,' she said. There was something bunched up about him, as if he was coiled, waiting to spring, and her insides tightened.

'D'you want a bit of bread instead? Cup of tea?'

'Nah.'

She sat down, nervously, opposite him, wondering what was on his mind.

'Nothing then?' she asked, and she could hear the way her voice had gone higher.

Harry looked back at her with a bleary ferocity, his bloodshot eyes struggling to focus.

'What I want to know –' he said, slurring his words. There was a long pause. Rose's heart began to thud, the way he was looking at her. 'Is who the hell "A" is.'

Rose could not get her breath for a moment. She worked on arranging her face, blank at first, then in an expression of casual puzzlement.

'"A"? What d'you mean?'

Harry slid two fingers into the inside pocket of his jerkin. To her horror she saw a familiar piece of paper drawn out and held up before her. Arthur's poem! Surely she had hidden it in her drawer upstairs, with her stockings and undergarments? Hadn't she? Otherwise she had had it on her at all times: how had he got hold of it?

'What's that?' she said lightly.

Harry's stubby fingers struggled to unfold it. The paper was limp and well worn from being tucked close to her skin, and from her having looked at it over and over again. It was almost as familiar as her own hand as he held it out to her.

'A *poem*.' His voice held both venom and disgust. 'From "*A*".'

Rose affected a glance at it as inspiration came to her. 'Oh,' she laughed. '*That*. Where on earth did you find that? God – I've had that for years. It was my mother's. Alice, her name, remember? She gave it me before she died. It was her favourite poem. I think my father had taught it her somewhere along the line when they were courting. His family tried to stop them marrying...' She was making this up, fast, as she went along. 'And in the end they did marry. But while they had to be apart he'd given her that and she wrote it out and kept it.'

Harry stared at her for a moment, then his face took on an ugly sneer.

'Your mother's?' The words were spoken with such contempt that they were like a slap.

He pushed the chair back and came for her, round

467

the table, pushing his hand round her throat. His big body loomed over her, his breath hot and pungent on her face.

'What kind of fool d'you take me for?' His hand tightened. Rose sat completely still, terrified. Any tighter and she would not be able to breathe.

Harry stood looking down at her. She could tell his mind was full of something but he was too drunk to find words for it. For those moments they were locked together, her eyes staring back at him.

He swayed, then pushed her away with a roar of disgust. She felt the chair tilt back and had to scramble forward to save herself. Fear filled her to the back of her throat at what he might do now. But he turned away, his feet clumping heavily up the stairs to bed. She did not follow until she was sure he was asleep.

Sixty-Two

'I'm going to go mad,' Dolly moaned, lolloping from side to side on the bed, trying to get comfortable. 'It's sweltering. I can't stand it!'

She knew the others weren't asleep. The three girls lay staring into the hot, humid night. Their beds felt damp under them and there wasn't a hint of movement in the air. The open window gave no relief. Dolly knew her sisters resented her, but she longed for some company and reassurance.

'Oh, shut up,' Rachel said unsympathetically. 'Just go to sleep.' She sat up and lifted her long hair up and off her neck, trying to cool herself.

'Don't you think I would if I could?' Dolly complained, tears rising in her. 'You don't know what it's like . . .'

'No, and I don't want to either,' Rachel retorted.

Dolly began to cry then. She had kept her feelings in for so long but now they spilled out. She felt so mixed up about everything, full of powerful, conflicting emotions. The bigger the baby had grown, the worse it had become. She could feel it in her now, twitching and squirming. Alive; real.

Susanna turned on to her side and Dolly could feel her quietly looking at her in the gloom.

'It'll soon be over,' she said, more gently than Rachel. 'Two or three weeks and . . .'

'We can forget all about it and stop walking about padded up like a lot of clowns,' Rachel said grumpily. 'And I can stop flaming well pretending to be you, Dolly!'

Mom had sent Rachel out on all sorts of errands that week. 'You want to put yourself about – make people think all three of you are going about your business as usual . . .'

'Mom says you've got to do it bit by bit,' Dolly said. 'You can't just take it all off. People'll notice.'

'Oh, sod that,' Rachel retorted. 'Once the babby's out of the way, what does it matter what anyone thinks?'

'Oh, it'll matter to Mom,' Susanna predicted gloomily.

Rachel's words made Dolly break out in sobs. 'Don't talk like that!' she said, her voice suddenly small and vulnerable. 'It's moving – I can feel it, all the time now. I think it's a boy.'

There was a moment of shocked silence from her sisters. For months, all of them had barred their minds from thinking of the baby as a real child, a person and part of the family.

'Oh, Dolly,' Susanna said, and Dolly could hear that she was emotional. 'A little boy? Why d'you think that?'

'I dunno. It just feels like it.' Dolly felt very old compared with her sisters these days, even though she was the baby.

Rachel had sat up again and now she spoke more kindly. 'What's it feel like, Dolly? All of it, I mean? Now it's big.'

'It feels heavy, and tight at the front,' Dolly said through her tears. 'Like a drum sometimes. And it keeps going all tight. It hurts . . . It's like being taken over by . . . I mean, it's *someone* in there. It's hard to believe, but it is. And it's got to come out. How'm I going to manage? I'm so scared. Mom says I've got to go next week – to this Nancy person. I don't know her, and then I've got to leave him with her, and I don't know . . .' She really broke down now. 'I don't know if I want to any more! I don't know what to do!'

As Dolly lay sobbing, she felt her sisters move over to her, their weight beside her on the mattress.

'Come on – sit up,' Rachel said, and even she sounded choked up. They had been through so much of all this together – but it was only Dolly who could do the real part, the last, terrifying act of birthing the child.

Dolly sat up, feeling the baby lurch inside her. Her sisters' arms came round her and they sat huddled together, speaking in whispers, smelling each other, sweat and Lifebuoy and a hint of Susanna's perfume.

'Mom'll be there,' Susanna told her. 'And they'll help you. They've all had babbies – they'll know what to do.'

'Mom'll give you your marching orders,' Rachel said. 'And us. Hey –' She nudged Dolly. 'You'll be all right. You're a strong 'un, you.'

Dolly let herself cry as they held her, her body trembling. 'I'm so scared,' she sobbed. 'And . . . Oh, this is making my belly clench up – feel!' She took her sisters' hands and laid them on her swollen front.

'Crikey,' Rachel said, in awed tones.

'Like a drum,' Susanna said. 'Oh – I felt it! I felt him kicking!' They had never done this before, allowed themselves to know.

'Sometimes I feel as if he's ruined my life,' Dolly said. 'And then other times I feel him moving and I

471

think, he's a little baby, a person who'll grow up and get big, and . . . He's *mine*.' She wept again. 'Oh, I don't know what to feel. Sometimes it feels as if my head's going to fall off, my mind's spinning so much. What if I have him and I don't want to be parted from him?'

'What – you mean keep him? Bring him back here?' Rachel said, stunned. 'God, Dolly – Mom'd *never* let you do that. Not after all this . . . What'd people say? You know what she's like.'

'And you're so young,' Susanna pointed out gently. 'And no father. It's no good, is it?'

Dolly lowered her head. She cuddled closer to Susanna, warmed by her sisters' closeness. 'No,' she said, in a small voice. 'I s'pose it isn't.' Then she burst out again. 'But he's my little babby!'

By then, all three of them had tears running down their faces.

Rose woke very early the next morning, filled with terror. When Harry had confronted her with Arthur's poem last night, he had been half knocked out with drink and barely able to keep awake. But what would he say now?

She lay looking at him. The light was already bright outside and though it was early, she could feel the heat building up. Harry lay on his side facing her, his features relaxed in sleep, his chest a cave of coarse black hair. She tried to summon up tenderness for him, even the smallest amount, to make herself feel guilty and sorry. But her neck was still sore after last night; and after his silent contempt, the painful, aggressive way he had forced himself on her in bed over these weeks, his thuggish way of dominating her, she felt nothing now except contempt in return. She had to leave him, had to be with Arthur, whatever it cost.

She knew there was only so long she could deceive him now. How had she let that poem get into his hands? How could she have dropped it? Round and round spun her mind. Had she got away with it?

She slipped out of bed, full of tension about what would happen when he woke. She must try to make everything seem normal, not make him suspect anything else.

She went about her morning tasks, boiling water, making breakfast, with a grim deliberation, waiting. As soon as either Harry or Lily came downstairs, her act would begin that everything was normal. *In ten days, I'll be away from you*, she said to him in her head. It was thrilling, terrifying. But what if he knew more than he was saying? What if he came down and confronted her? But how could he possibly know? He had been fishing all afternoon, miles away . . . This was the whirl of her thoughts.

When she did hear him coming down, her heart thudded madly, all her body on alert. She turned her back and studied the task of making tea and he came in and sat with a loud sigh at the table. When she turned, with the tea, he was rasping his hands down his stubbly face.

'Needs to stand a minute,' she said, putting the pot down.

Harry nodded. He seemed subdued: the effects of the drink.

Rose cut bread and put it in front of him, then poured the tea, eyeing him for any reaction as if he were a dangerous bull. But he said nothing. He seemed low in himself and sunk in his own thoughts.

Life in the Mansions had become more interesting with the arrival of Mr Gates, so much so that Aggie and Babs chose to play in their yard now more than in Babs's. One thing about Mr Gates was that he either did not notice, or chose not to notice, when people were disagreeable.

'Even Mrs Peters is quite nice when he's about,' Aggie told Babs. 'Most of the time she has that face on her, you know. But I saw her smile at him this morning.'

Babs looked impressed. 'Well, there's not many can make that happen.'

'And everyone's always trying to get him to speak so they can try and make out what he's saying.' Aggie did some impressions of Wally Gates's broad Geordie. 'I think I know what he's saying now, mostly.'

'I think he's nice,' Babs said.

The weather had brought everyone outside. That evening, it was so hot in the house by the time Jen had cooked tea that they ate as fast as they could and went out again. She hurried off to work, saying she didn't know if she'd be able to stand it in Mr Price's in this heat.

'God, it's close,' Freda said, perched on a chair by the door. Most of the other neighbours were out too, waiting for the evening to cool, for any breath of fresh air.

The smell from the lavatories and the dustbins was very strong and spoiled the atmosphere. The whole city was baking, the dirt cooked to dust, the air gritty with it and flies seething round everything. They all longed for rain to ease the suffocating atmosphere.

'Your arm all right now, is it?' one of the neighbours asked Freda.

'Ooh, not so bad,' Freda Adams said, though she winced as she moved her fingers.

'Given you a rest though, hasn't it?' one of the neighbours, a Mrs Roberts said with an air of reproach. Everyone knew that Freda was going back to work, and it seemed wrong at her age. But, as she would have retorted, what else was she supposed to do – sit on her backside and watch her family go under?

The burly figure of Mr Gates appeared from the entry and everyone looked his way.

'Quite a gent, that one, I gather,' Mrs Roberts said, leaning close to Freda.

'Seems decent enough,' Freda replied. 'When you can make out a single flaming word he says.'

Mrs Roberts chuckled.

Mr Gates stood looking at the kids dotted round the yard and spoke to Aggie, Babs and the few other older ones.

'Any of ye fancy a game of cards?' He held up a pack in his large hand.

Aggie and Babs looked at each other. 'All right!' Babs called out.

Mr Gates brought out a rickety folding table of Eliza Jenks's and they all gathered round. He sat on a chair, legs apart to grip the table with his knees.

'D'you know hoo te play whist, or shall Ah larn yee?'

His thick, work-worn fingers dealt the cards skilfully and then he looked up at them. Turning to Aggie, his big eyes looked into hers and she felt a thrill of something: the feeling of being paid attention to. And she liked the smell of his beery breath – it reminded her of Dad.

'D'you want to stort, pet? I'll explain as we go.'

Sixty-Three

'You're nothing but a whore, are you?'

Rose thought at first that his voice was the continuation of her dream, the next morning. But as her waking brain made sense of the words she lay rigid with fear. The voice was light, almost teasing, but laced with a terrifying venom.

'No one'd think it looking at you, lying there. Pretty little bitch, spreading your legs. You're a filthy little whore. You're no one's wife, you're just a tart . . .'

Harry's charming monologue went on and on. Rose kept her eyes shut but could feel her eyelids trembling. Surely it must be obvious to him that she could hear him?

He blew softly on her ear. To her it felt like a dagger plunging into her. His hot chest was pressed up against her back as he leaned over her. He seemed massive, as if she was propped against a hillside.

'I should've married an ugly woman, not a pretty little whore like you, Rosie,' he said. 'A whore and a cock teaser . . .'

The filthy words kept pouring out of his mouth. Soon Lily would wake, Rose thought. Would she come into the room to hear this horrible gush of language washing all over her mother? She could tell that the longer he went on the more he was working himself up and she couldn't lie here with her eyes closed for ever.

As if she had only just woken she stirred and tried to roll on to her back, but of course he was blocking the bed. Rose opened her eyes, pretending puzzlement, and she jumped, which she didn't have to pretend to do, even though she knew he was there.

'Oh, Harry!' She drew back a little. 'What on earth're you doing?'

She went to sit up but he pressed her down.

'Don't make out you're so surprised to see me,' he snarled. 'I know you heard what I said. Now you listen to me . . .' He pressed down on her so that she could not move. It was hard to breathe. 'You think I'm a fool, don't you?'

'No!' But this seemed to aggravate him further.

'Don't pretend with me, you lying tart! All your flannel about, "Oh, Harry dear, it was my mother's." A love poem from your mother? That you was wearing in your clothes? You must think I was born yesterday.'

Rose lay very still.

'Now you listen to me. I know you're a whore and an unfaithful bitch. I know there's another bloke. And I intend to make sure that 'e never comes near my wife again – whatever it takes . . .'

'No!' she cried, horrified. She couldn't hide or deny any longer. Struggling, she tried to get up, but Harry slapped his hand across her face. He punched her hard in the ribs. Pain ripped across her side and the air left her lungs with a moan.

'So – the truth at last out of your lying mouth! D'you know –' He crouched over her and once again fastened his hands round her neck. Rose gasped, feeling her eyes bulging as he tightened his grip for a moment. 'I could kill you, easy. Just like that.' He squeezed again. 'If I wanted.'

He got up, abruptly, as if disgusted all of a sudden.

'You're not my wife any more,' he said. 'You ain't been the woman I married in a long while. You're just a slag.'

And he left the room. She lay panting, holding back the sobs as his feet pounded down the stairs. All she could think was that she had to get away from him, go to Arthur, had to – now!

Jen could not bear her bed any more, the shifting back and forth trying to get comfortable. She never slept well in the last months when she was carrying a child, and the heat made this worse than ever she could remember.

'It's like treacle,' she muttered, getting slowly up out of bed. It made it impossible to do anything fast. She decided she'd get up and have a wash to cool down before everyone else was on the move.

The yard was still in shade and it was a little more bearable outside, though the air already had the intense, charged feel of the beginning of another scorching hot day. The Peters boy was out there, ambling about in a purposeless way. He seemed a bit simple, Jen thought. She stood in the doorway for a moment, leaning against the frame, breathing in the morning air, metallic and smoky even at this time. She thought sadly for a moment of Mary Crewe.

Footsteps came down the stairs and she cursed, having hoped for a time of peace. It was Aggie.

'You're up early,' Jen said. It wasn't even seven o'clock yet.

All Aggie had on was her long vest, which came down nearly to her knees. 'It's too hot,' she said. 'I couldn't sleep.'

''Ere – as you're up – go and fetch us a pail of water. I want a wash.'

Aggie went out barefoot, tiptoeing across the blue bricks, the mud of wet days long dried to a crust. She stood watching the bright thread of water pour into the bucket, letting it fill until it was teetering at the top ready to spill. As she picked it up water sloshed out all over her feet, deliciously cool.

'Heor,' a voice said, that could only belong to one person, 'let me tyek tha' – it's too heavy for a little 'un.'

She stood back to let Mr Gates pick up the bucket and transport it easily, splashing across the yard. She saw Mom watching, looking a bit embarrassed that this big man had involved himself.

'Oh, she can manage,' Jen told him. 'But ta very much, any road, it's nice of you.'

Mr Gates inclined his head.

'Oh, it's ne trouble.'

Jen nodded amiably. She felt very aware of how big she was out at the front, of her swollen neck and ankles. She felt very heavy and ungainly.

'Well, ta,' was all she could think to say again.

Mr Gates smiled, his pink face crinkling, and was about to move away, but he added humbly, 'Ah must gan an get mesel some work. Can yee tell me some likely places? A've worked in big firms in the northeast, and Ah'd turn me hand to owt, like.'

Jen looked at him, trying to guess his age. In his fifties, she thought, and strong. Work was hard to find for anyone, but there was something about him that inspired confidence.

'Oh, there's plenty of firms round here,' she told him. 'All you need to do is go about and look. You may not be lucky at first – it won't be easy, but keep trying. Tell you what, though, when my mother comes down we'll have a think of where might suit you best.'

Mr Gates backed away, thanking her and touching a non-existent cap. Jen found she was smiling as she poured water into a bowl and began on her wash. Smiling felt unfamiliar, stretching her cheeks in a pleasing way that she had almost forgotten.

By the time Rose had dressed and got herself downstairs, taking tiny, shallow breaths because she was in such pain, the fight seemed to have gone out of Harry. He was in the backyard. Rose hurried to the front parlour and fetched something from a drawer. It was still early. There'd be enough time if she hurried. It was too late to worry about hiding. She had to do the one and only thing she could do now. For a second she hesitated. Should she take Lily? Was it safe to leave her with Harry? But he'd never shown any sign of hurting Lily before. He took little notice of her. If she was quick, he would barely notice she had been gone . . .

Painfully, she crept out of the front door and hurried to the Mansions. Turning in to the entry she met a burly, middle-aged man coming out who stood back with a kind air to let her pass.

'Thank you,' she breathed.

'All reet, lass,' he said. Rose was too caught up in her own troubles to notice much more. She turned in to the yard and hurried to number three.

It was Aggie who answered her tap on the door. She saw the shock on the little girl's face at the sight of her.

'Mom can't come out – she's having a wash,' Aggie said.

'No – it's you I need, dear,' Rose said. Even speaking

hurt. 'I need you to run an errand for me – now, quickly, before it's too late!'

Her desperation communicated itself. Rose did not realize quite how bad she looked. The bruising had not yet come out on her face but there were cuts and her left eyebrow was already swelling.

Aggie looked uncertain.

'Look –' Rose held out a half-crown. 'This is for you – here, take it. But go now, please. Go to Mr King in Oldfield Road. Don't go away until they open the door. Say you've come from me – tell Mr King he mustn't go out. D'you understand, Aggie? He mustn't go to work, or anywhere. Tell him it's an emergency – he must wait at home for me.'

'Who're you talking to, Aggie?' Jen Green's voice came from the back.

Aggie looked round, then back, in confusion.

'Tell her,' Rose urged. 'Tell her you've got a quick errand to run.'

'Mrs Southgate's give me half a crown to run an errand for her,' she said, hoping the money would smooth things.

'Blimey,' Jen's voice came through. 'She must've won the pools.'

'Go on,' Rose said frantically. She looked so deranged that Aggie felt scared. 'Now, Aggie – and run, please!'

Harry left for work, without a word to her, with a slam of the back door. The second he had gone, Rose began to make her final preparations to leave. Bit by bit, she had already taken a large number of her possessions to Arthur's. She did not have the suitcase she had stored in his room, planning to bring it home and pack it at the right time. Instead, she made three bundles of her and Lily's remaining possessions.

'We're going on a little journey,' she told Lily urgently, upstairs. Her nerves were at screaming pitch, yet at the same time it was as if she had slipped into a dream. Nothing seemed quite real. Was she really doing this, gathering her underclothes and Lily's toys? All she could think of was getting away. Harry knew about Arthur, and she didn't know what he might do, he was in such a dark rage. That look on his face when he had his hands around her throat . . . She had to get to Arthur, safe in Oldfield Road. Harry didn't know where Arthur lived, of that she was certain. How could he possibly? If she could just get away this morning, everything would be all right. And soon they'd be on their way, out of his reach for ever.

Rose put the bundles down in the front and looked around. She had all she needed, her few possessions, her savings. They were going. It was too late to wonder what anyone else made of it. In any case, she was not carrying a suitcase.

She made Lily put her coat on to save carrying it and did the same herself. Lily already looked hot and fed up.

'Come on then, dear,' she said, handing her a bundle. 'You can carry this little one with your dolly in and I'll take the others.'

'Where're we going?' Lily said grumpily.

'Just for a little walk,' Rose insisted, her nerves frayed to pieces. 'Come *on*, Lily!'

With a last glance round, she let the two of them out, scarcely noticing the pain she was in now from the injuries he had inflicted on her. Trying to walk normally was the hardest part. All the time Rose's back was prickling with the expectation that Harry was hiding somewhere, that he had not gone to work at all, and was behind them. If they got to the corner and looked back and he was there, she would go somewhere else, anywhere, catch a bus into town, make sure they lost him.

After what seemed an eternity, they reached the corner and she looked back. There was no sign of him.

'Oh, God,' she breathed, hand on her chest. She pulled her daughter round the corner. 'Oh, thank God – come on, Lily, walk quickly now!'

Sixty-Four

Phyllis wandered round the Rag Market. The bag she carried over her arm was already weighed down with groceries – mutton and vegetables. She looked round from under the wide brim of her navy straw boater with its cluster of white flowers pinned at one side. She knew she looked splendid in it. That was what James used to say: 'You're a splendid woman, Phyllis.'

All the time she was aware that she was on guard in case any familiar faces suddenly surfaced in the crowd. Still, always, she was on the lookout for Ethel. Ethel had kept away from her – her threats had been genuine and she realized that Ethel had understood that. But she might be out there somewhere and might appear suddenly, like an evil spirit, threatening everything that Phyllis held dear.

And it wasn't just Ethel. Today she had no wish to meet anyone she knew, no faces from Lilac Street. She'd had bits and pieces left over from the layettes she'd put together when her own babies were born. Sentimentally, she'd held on to them. But there were still a few things needed for Dolly's baby. Nancy could not be expected to provide for the brat. But the last thing Phyllis wanted was for anyone to see what she was buying. She picked up a white, soft blanket on one stall and stowed it away. Some napkins on another.

Looking round again, she sauntered away, towards

the tram stop, trying to look like the last woman in the world who would be carrying baby clothes in her bag.

As she turned in to Lilac Street, its features, so often obscured in fog and rain, were lit up by the intense sunlight, its blemishes full on display. The slates on the roofs were uneven as a mouthful of bad teeth, grimed with soot and rashes of lichen. Every pore of the brickwork had absorbed the filth. Most of the houses had scrubbed steps and swept pavements in front, even if that meant refuse being swept briskly into the gutter. The fight with dirt was constant, but today the street reminded Phyllis of an unwashed maiden caught blushing in her underclothes in this bright, exposing light.

The sight dragged her down. At least the inside of her home was its own little world, full of her things, the fruit of her hopes. She had longed for so much more and had James lived, she would have had it. They would have moved to a better neighbourhood, kippers and curtains, the lot. Things would have been very different. But, she told herself, considering where she'd started out, she was lucky to have all that she'd got and she revelled in it.

She called a smiling greeting to Irene Best: 'Very warm again, isn't it?' *Poor cow*, she thought, as she always did. If there was one thing worse than a dead husband it was one that might just as well be.

It was a relief to push the front door open and go into the shade. Phyllis was perspiring heavily and longing for a drink and a sit-down. She closed the door behind her. The house felt blessedly cool in comparison with the street.

'Mom?' Dolly appeared from the back of the house.

486

She was wearing her white shift and her hair hung loose. For a moment Dolly looked to Phyllis as she had when she was eight or nine and the huge belly on her seemed a cruel mockery.

'Get me a drink of water, Dolly,' Phyllis said. 'I need a sit-down.'

They went through to the back and Dolly poured the water and gave it to her. Phyllis drank gratefully, kicked off her shoes and tipped her head back against the wall, closing her eyes.

'Mom,' Dolly said again, timidly. 'I've had something come away – sort of pink and . . .'

Phyllis's eyes snapped open. 'What – a gush of it – as if you've wet yourself?'

'No,' Dolly said, sitting down. Her cheeks were flushed. 'It was just a little bit. I just feel a bit funny, that's all, as if I can't sit still.'

'Well,' Phyllis said exhaustedly. She longed for a doze. 'We'll have to keep an eye on you. But it's too early yet.'

Phyllis closed her eyes again. She would not let herself think about this, about the grandchild curled in Dolly's belly just feet from her. If Dolly had been married, if everything was regular and right . . . There was nothing she liked more than a baby coming. It had been the finest thing of her life. But not like this – a little bastard whelped when its mother was barely more than a child. No – she couldn't afford to let her heart get involved. There was too much at stake.

Dolly saw her turn her face away and, not receiving anything more in the way of reassurance, got up and moved away. She went up to their room and lay on her bed, trying to get comfortable. As the day wore on the sky clouded over. The air was so still, so heavy with threat and moisture, that she felt as if her head might explode. She dozed for a while, and woke to find a warm, melting sensation moving across the lower part of her body.

Sixty-Five

'This is terrible.' Arthur sat on the bed, his sightless eyes staring ahead of him in anguish. 'It should never have come to this!'

Rose, full of a terrible, agitated energy, was transferring her belongings to the suitcase they had prepared.

'Mo-o-om,' Lily said, from where she was standing, bewildered and forgotten just inside the door.

'*Shush*, Lily,' Rose snapped. 'You're just going to have to be quiet and wait today. Arthur and I have got a lot to do.'

Lily's face crumpled into tears.

'No!' Rose rushed to her and put her arms around her. 'You must be quiet. No noise, Lily! Look, we'll find one of your books – here's *Ameliaranne* – you sit and look at that quietly.'

Lily quietened, appeased for the moment. Rose was full of a sense of steeliness. Arthur seemed to be in shock, first from Aggie's appearance earlier with the frantic message, then Rose and Lily's arrival. He had not been able to see Mrs Terry's pursed lips but could guess at what she must be thinking when she saw Lily. Arthur was a law-abiding, usually pliant man, not used to confrontation. He appeased Mrs Terry, telling her that they would soon be gone, that he would pay her extra. But Rose could feel that she was the one who was going to have to be strong, upon whose shoulders everything rested.

'My love –' She sat beside him and took his hand. 'I know things aren't as we wanted. It *is* terrible, I know.'

'There shouldn't be all this . . . Trouble for . . . For *him*. Your husband. And sneaking about, disgrace. It feels all wrong.' For a moment she was filled with a dreadful foreboding. Was he going to stay with her, to see this through now? Had he the backbone?

'I know,' she said gently. 'It's very bad – for everyone, and I'm frightened, Arthur. But in the end it'd be the same, wouldn't it? We'd have to leave here, make the break, We want to be together . . .' She squeezed his hand. 'Don't we?'

Arthur nodded wretchedly. 'More than anything, love.'

'So it just means we have to do everything a bit sooner than we planned, that's all.'

Arthur took a couple of deep breaths, gathering himself. 'Rose – love – I'm *sorry*. To be so weak. It's all been so sudden. And I'm so slow – everything takes me such an age. I need to gather my things, go into work – I can't just disappear . . .'

'You *can*, Arthur.' She spoke very intensely. 'And you'll have to. We have to go straight away –' She saw that he could hear the iron resolve in her voice. 'I'll help pack today. We'll go first thing in the morning.'

Arthur turned. 'You're right. But you said he doesn't know anything – about here, this house?'

'He *doesn't* know, I'm sure. He can't know. But we can't take any chances. Suppose he finds out somehow? He's crazy – he's really frightened me. You haven't seen how he's been – what he's done to me. But if we go soon – in a few hours, get on a train and get away from here, everything will be all right. He won't have any idea where we are then.'

They sat for a moment, embracing, still trying to absorb the enormity of what was happening.

'Come on then.' Arthur released her gently. 'We must make a start.'

By the late afternoon the sky had darkened; there was a slight breeze, and a hushed sense of expectation seemed to fall over everything in the dusk-like atmosphere.

When Dulcie Skinner hurried along to Dorrie Davis's little shop for a few bits and pieces that afternoon, she went in saying, 'Ooh – I'd best get back home quick, or I'm going to get a soaking!'

But Dorrie had her mind on other subjects than the weather. She could hardly contain herself, leaning over the counter, her sharp-nosed face taut with a gossip's excitement.

'I don't know if you've heard. Most likely not up at your end.' She stood back and crossed her arms, full of the power of withheld information.

'Well, I don't know if I have or not if you're not going to say what,' Dulcie retorted. She thought Dorrie Davis was a spiteful troublemaker and pointedly glanced towards the door, as if she had better things to do. But all the same, now she wanted to know what it was she may or may not know already.

'It's that Mrs Southgate,' Dorrie said disdainfully. 'That blonde bit from number fifteen.'

'Yes, I know who she is,' Dulcie said impatiently.

'Well, Irene saw her and the girl take off this morning, with everything bundled up by the look of them.

And so far,' Dorrie unfolded her arms and leaned triumphantly on the counter, 'she hasn't come back!'

'Well, that doesn't mean . . .' Dulcie began. She'd always found something a bit odd and mysterious about Rose Southgate. As if she was always in a dream, her mind somewhere else and the real Rose was round the corner somewhere out of sight.

'Oh, Irene's seen plenty – comings and goings. And she's had that kid of Jen Green's running errands for her. There's a man in the picture, you can be sure. And the husband – goes in and out looking dark as a thunderclap,' Dorrie said, nodding at the pregnant sky.

This seemed slim evidence of anything to Dulcie. 'Well – she could've taken the child on a visit somewhere . . .'

'She could've,' Dorrie said. 'But there's more to it than that, I'll bet you any money. I've seen her sort before. One of them quiet, scheming types, that one. We'll see, won't we?'

'I daresay we will,' Dulcie said, tired of the woman already; it never took long. 'I'll have a packet of Bisto and one of Swan Vesta, ta, Mrs Davis. Oh, and Joe's ciggies.'

There came the first distant grumbles of thunder.

'Here we go,' Freda Adams said, hastily pulling washing from their line in the yard. Other women rushed out to join her, all looking up at the thick belly of sky.

''Bout time,' Mrs Peters whined. 'I feel as though my head's fit to burst.'

Aggie, Babs and the other children all skipped about like excited calves.

'Look at the colour of that!' Aggie said. The sky was

a deep mauve-grey, waiting to break over them. At first a few big drops spattered on to the dust, then more and more. Everyone shrieked and held their hands out and their faces up to the rain.

'Come in!' Jen yelled over the noise of the rain. 'You're going to get soaked!'

But no one took any notice. After the sultry heat over the past week it was glorious to hear the loudness of the drops and to let the cool water run over them. In the end Jen joined them, laughing as her clothes soaked through and her hair straggled into rat's tails. Even Freda turned her face up to it and Eliza Jenks came outside, a smile lighting up her strained features.

The Green and Skinner children did barefoot rain dances in the puddles. Aggie felt the water seep right through her clothes. The rain made her feel better than she had in weeks, full of a happy, bubbling excitement. Soon the yard was awash with water and they jumped in pools of it, screaming with excitement.

'Join hands!' Babs yelled, and a ring of them twirled round, laughing and shrieking.

Susanna and Rachel were on the way home from work when the storm broke. Rachel saw Susanna ahead of her, dashing along with her head down, and called out to her.

'Wait for me!' She ran and caught up.

Both of them were already saturated, their loose bits of dark hair clinging to their cheeks. The street appeared to be bouncing, so many large drops of water were falling on to the already wet ground, and the street was full of the sound of it. For a moment they looked at each other in dismay.

Susanna was leaning forward. 'I'm worried about getting this flaming bag of tricks wet,' she said, bent protectively over the sawdust stuffing tucked beneath her frock.

'It'll all go into lumps,' Rachel said, pressing it with her hand. Hurrying along in the pelting rain they exchanged glances, water running down into their eyes. 'It's like walking about with a vat of porridge strapped to your belly!'

Susanna, suddenly overcome by the absurdity of the entire situation, and all they had gone through in the past six months, creased up, doubled over with laughter. She had to stop and lean against a wall, weak with it, and Rachel joined her, both of them soaked to the skin and soon hysterical. Susanna tried to say something, making several attempts which were drowned out by rain and laughter.

'When . . .' she began, several times, then managed, 'when I'm at work I think to myself, *What would they say if they could see . . .*' And she was off again. The ritual of getting dressed in the morning in their house at the moment was strange indeed. Rachel was helpless with laughter as well.

Among the other people hurrying along to get under cover, a large figure loomed towards them from out of the torrent of rain and a voice said, 'Well, there, lasses, it's canny good someone's finding summat te laugh aboot!'

He went on past, smiling, and the girls sobered down a bit, staring after him.

'Who was that?' Susanna asked.

Rachel shrugged. 'Dunno. He looks jolly though. Come on – we'd best get home.'

*

494

Phyllis rolled her eyes at the state of them when they got into the house.

'Go and get that lot off,' she ordered. 'And wake Dolly up – she's been asleep for an age.'

The two girls dripped off upstairs, still giggling. Their laughter stopped abruptly as soon as they went into their room. Dolly was on her hands and knees on the bed gasping in pain.

'Dolly! What's – you're not . . . Are you sick?' Susanna cried and both of them went to her.

'I think it's coming,' Dolly groaned, her face contorted with pain. 'It's been going on and on.'

'Mom!' Rachel yelled at the top of the stairs but at the same time there was a huge crack of thunder which drowned her out and she ran downstairs again.

'Mom – quick! Dolly's having the babby!'

For a moment she saw utter panic on her mother's face. 'She can't be,' Phyllis said wildly. 'It's not due till . . . We'll have to get her on the train . . .'

'No, Mom – it's too late for that!' Rachel insisted. 'She couldn't even get downstairs, she's that far gone.'

She saw her mother rally, her features tightening into a determined expression.

'Right,' she said. 'I'll get some pans on. Get the papers from by the fire – put them under her on the bed. Tell her I'm coming.'

With trembling legs Rachel ran back upstairs, her hair still dripping.

'What did she say?' Susanna said, getting out of her wet things and trying to comfort Dolly at the same time.

'She's coming,' Rachel said. She looked with awe at her younger sister, who for the moment did not seem to be in pain and had lapsed down on to her left side on the bed, her eyed closed. 'It'll be all right, Dolly,' she said, not having the first idea whether it would or not. 'Look – I've got to put this paper under you.'

They prepared the bed around her as the rain tippled down outside, a great wash of sound, splashing off roofs and gutters, seeming to seal them into their own little world in the house, away from everyone else. They heard Phyllis's feet on the stairs and Dolly began to moan as another wave of pain rose up in her.

Phyllis looked gravely down at her daughter writhing on the bed. The other two could see her thinking, calculating.

'You can stop making that noise, for a start,' she told Dolly. 'There's no call for that.' Then she added, rather less harshly, 'At least with all that going on out there, no one's going to hear you.' She looked round. 'All the same – keep the window shut. And here – you can pull on this.' She had a long strip of a ragged sheet with her and tied it to the end of the bed.

'Shouldn't we fetch Mrs Sissons?' Susanna said, looking rather faint.

'No!' Phyllis said emphatically. 'We don't need anyone else. I know what to do.'

'Have you ever done it before?' Susanna said.

'Not . . . exactly,' Phyllis admitted. 'But I've had my own. We'll manage.'

They heard a sound from downstairs, the back door closing.

'That'll be Charles,' Phyllis said. She nodded at Rachel. 'Go and tell him to stay down there and keep the range going. He won't want any part of this.'

'I'm not sure I do either,' Rachel muttered, on her way downstairs. She was frightened at what was to come. She spoke to her brother, who'd come in soaked to the skin as well.

'She's having the baby *now*?' he said, bewildered. 'Oh, dear God.' More endearingly, he added, 'Is Dolly all right?'

'I don't know – I think so,' Rachel said. 'Just keep the water boiling, will you?'

She usually found her brother's stiff stuffiness aggravating, but now she was in sympathy with him. She made a pot of tea and spent as much time as she could down there, hanging up the wet clothes and trying to stay out of the way of the disturbing events unfolding upstairs.

Sixty-Six

By early evening the rain abated, leaving the gutters streaming and yards puddled with water. Aggie and the rest of the family were finishing off their tea when they heard someone come sploshing across to their door.

'Jen – it's me!'

'Come in, Dulce!' Jen called.

Dulcie pushed the door open, laughing. 'My feet're soaked, just coming round here!'

'Leave the door open,' Nanna said. 'It's nice now.' There was a cool, fresh feel to the air. She edged her chair close to the door.

'There's a drop of tea left if you want, Dulce,' Jen said.

'No, ta, I'm not staying,' Dulcie said, leaning up against the door frame with an air of someone who knows something.

'Sure?' Freda Adams said.

'Yeah – you're all right. You carry on . . . Oh, go on, I'll sit down for a minute then . . .'

'That's it, John – give her your chair,' Jen said. 'And clear off, you kids. Except you, Aggie – you can clear up.'

For once Aggie didn't feel resentful at this, as her younger brothers and sisters rushed off outside. She liked it when Dulcie came round. It felt reassuring, like old times. And she could see that Dulcie had something to impart, and she didn't want to miss out on it. She stood in the scullery, slowly scraping off bits of mutton gristle and piling the dishes up to wash.

Mom was complaining about her swollen ankles and how they'd got even worse in the heat.

'I can't think whether I want it all over with now or whether I don't,' she said, hands resting on her swollen belly. 'Either way it's a blooming ordeal.'

Dulcie made a wry face. 'That's for sure. You sure there's two in there?'

Aggie saw her mother nod. 'Well, if there ain't, it must be an octopus.'

'I went into Dorrie's – just before the rain come down,' Dulcie said, rolling her eyes as most people did when they spoke of Dorrie Davis.

'Oh, ar – and what did that one have to say for herself?' Freda said.

'Well – course I dain't take any notice,' Dulcie said. 'But –' She lowered her voice. 'Irene reckons that Rose Southgate woman's done a bunk – with another man!'

Jen raised her eyebrows, shifting in her chair to get comfortable.

'What makes her think that?'

'She saw her and the girl setting off carrying bundles – and they ain't come back.'

Jen frowned. 'Aggie? Did Mrs Southgate say anything to you about her going away?'

Aggie shrugged. 'No.'

'Oh, it's just Dorrie putting her spoke in,' Freda said. 'You know what that one's like. She'll find trouble anywhere for the sake of it.'

'I tell you what,' Jen called, impishly, towards the scullery. 'You go over there, Aggie, and knock for her – see if she's come back.'

Aggie emerged, frowning. She didn't want to do as she was asked. 'What'm I s'posed to say to her?'

Jen and Dulcie were both grinning now. 'This is daft, Jen,' Dulcie said.

'I know – but it won't do any harm. Say to her – does she want you to take Lily to Sunday school this week . . . Summat like that.'

'Oh, Mom!' Aggie protested. She knew Mrs Southgate would want her to take Lily – she always did.

'Oh, go *on*, Aggie – run along. It won't take a minute.'

Reluctantly, Aggie went outside, barefoot, not wanting to spoil her shoes. The entry was almost completely flooded and she had to hold on to the slimy wall and climb along at the very sides. Then she ran along to number fifteen, hopping over puddles. There were lots of children out playing now, barefoot, splashing.

Heart thumping, she knocked. *Please don't let Mrs Southgate be back*, she prayed. It was such a long time before anyone answered that she was turning away, relieved. Then she heard the door open. It was Mr Southgate. Aggie's heart thumped harder.

'Yeah?' He looked sullen, but that was normal.

'I came to ask Mrs Southgate—'

'She ain't in,' he interrupted brusquely, and shut the door.

'He said she weren't in,' she told the expectant faces in the house.

'Is that all – dain't 'e say anything else?' her mother wanted to know.

'No,' Aggie said. She eyed the door. 'Can I go out now?'

The women were giving each other significant looks.

'It's most likely just Dorrie being silly,' Freda said, getting creakily to her feet. 'Go on, Aggie – off you go.'

It was Susanna and Phyllis who stayed with Dolly. Rachel ran up and down fetching and carrying anything that was needed. She and Charles stayed out of the way, Charles trying to lose himself in a book and Rachel asking him questions to try and get him to talk to her to distract both of them from the sounds from the upper floor. All the time there came the movement of feet back and forth, of Mom's and Susanna's voices and an occasional muffled cry from Dolly. She was remarkably self-controlled.

'D'you think anyone can hear her?' Rachel asked Charles. Now the rain had stopped it seemed so quiet.

Charles listened, then said, 'No – I don't think so. Let's hope not.'

Rachel got out some mending and tried to concentrate on that. The rain had made the atmosphere cooler and less stifling. But all the time she was full of nerves and a certain horror about all that her sister was experiencing.

'Good God,' she said to Charles after a sudden, anguished cry came through the floorboards. 'When will it be over?'

Charles looked round at her, his pale face also tense, and Rachel realized that he was suffering with Dolly as well but did not know how to say so. He'd always had a soft spot for his baby sister, despite all her ragging of him.

'It's a natural thing,' he said, trying to sound knowledgeable.

'Or the curse of Eve,' Rachel retorted. She felt angry suddenly, though she wasn't sure why.

Charles stared ahead of him. 'There must be a reason why God made it happen this way.'

'If you say so.' Rachel got up to put some more water in the kettle. All she could think of doing was making cups of tea. 'I still can't really believe she's having a baby – a child, a *person* . . .'

Charles, suddenly vulnerable and uncertain, said, 'D'you know what Mom's planning to do?'

Rachel turned to look at him. 'Get rid of it. Take it to this sister of hers out of the way.'

She was surprised by the conflict she saw on her brother's face.

'It seems all wrong, doesn't it?' he said. Then as if he had given too much of himself away he looked back down at his book.

Rose slipped out of the house in Oldfield Road and fetched some fish and chips for herself and Lily, while Arthur ate the meal cooked for him by Mrs Terry, as usual, even though he said he was going to find it hard to eat anything at all. Mrs Terry was furious with him. He couldn't bring himself to lie to her and say that Rose was a widow.

'I thought you were a gentleman, Mr King,' she said disgustedly. 'I began to think of you almost like a son.'

When he had paid her an extra month's rent, she was a little appeased, but added, 'I don't want to know anything about your life, or that woman who's got her claws into you. I just want you gone.'

'We shall be,' he assured her. 'First thing tomorrow.

And I'm so very sorry for your trouble, Mrs Terry. You've been very good to me while I've been here.'

They had spent the afternoon hastily sorting out their things. Their plan was to walk to Brighton Road station very early next morning, to catch the first stopping train into Birmingham, then another on to Manchester. Much of their talk had had to be about practical things, which items were essential for their new life and which not. How much could they carry and what would they need first?

By the time the evening came, they were both exhausted by the strain of it all.

'Come on, Lily,' Rose instructed her daughter. 'I'm going to make you up a nice little bed on the floor.'

Rose had lit two candles and stuck them on the dressing table, their light doubling in the mirror. They made the room very cosy.

But Lily was tired and fed up. 'When're we going home?' she said miserably as Rose tucked her up, with a blanket for a mattress. There was a little space on the floor at the end of the bed where she would not have the light in her eyes while they were still up. 'I don't like it here.'

Rose knelt and cuddled her, feeling again that her whole being was involved in holding together the two people she loved and who loved and needed her.

'Very soon, sweetheart,' she told her, kissing her soft cheek and stroking her head. 'The sooner you go to sleep, the sooner things will be better. We're going on a little journey tomorrow, and then we'll be home.'

And soon, feeling safe in spite of it all, because her mother was there, Lily was fast asleep.

Sixty-Seven

Rose and Arthur lay curled together in his narrow bed, he with his back to the wall, his arm round her and his hand resting on the gentle round of her stomach. For a moment she was nervous about this, but she soon knew that he would not guess. There was nothing showing of the child. Not yet.

They had decided on an early night – 'Such an early start tomorrow,' Rose said. And there was little else that they could do now, even though it was barely nine o'clock, except quietly undress in the candlelit room. Very sweetly and quietly, they made love together, wincing as the springs squeaked, determined not to disturb Lily. But she was exhausted and very deeply asleep. They lay in the warm night, with no covers over them for a time, their bodies sated, cooling down together.

Rose twisted round on to her back so that her face was nearer his.

'My darling,' she whispered, filled with tenderness, and reached her hand up to stroke his cheek. She felt, rather than saw, him smile. 'Do you feel you're in a dream, as if all this might just fade away?'

'I certainly feel strange,' he admitted. 'And worried – but so happy, my darling.' Thinking about it for a moment, he added, 'It's this strange feeling of not knowing what's going to happen, even the next day. I remember feeling it in the war sometimes. You'd be on the move, travelling to a new place and not knowing where or what it was going to be like. So you have a constant feeling of life being a sort of blank in front of you – when in normal life you usually know where you'll be the next day and what you'll be doing.'

'Manchester,' she said, wonderingly. That was the whole feeling that night – one of wonder. That they were here at last, cleaving together as if they were husband and wife. They had done it! They had escaped! His beautiful face was here beside hers and they had made this gigantic step to be together. And tomorrow, first thing, they would go from here, walk away, and begin their new life.

'D'you think we'll stay in Manchester for ever?' she said.

Arthur gave a low laugh. 'I told you – I can't even visualize tomorrow, never mind for ever!'

'We might never come to Birmingham again.'

Arthur squeezed her tightly for a second. 'Should you mind?'

'I don't know – I was born here. I've never been anywhere else.' She moved even closer to him, her arm across his warm chest. 'I don't think where we go matters much,' she said. 'It's being together, you and me – and Lily. If I went somewhere, however nice, and you weren't there, then it would be miserable. I'm sure Manchester will be the best place on earth – because you'll be there with me.'

'Oh Rose.' Arthur looked moved. 'My dear love – you are so extraordinary. You're prepared to risk everything – and not only that, to take me on. I'm a wreck – I'm not up to much.'

'Arthur,' she said seriously. She took his face in her

hands. 'Please – don't keep saying that. I know your being blind makes things difficult in a way – for you especially. But it's not the main thing. I love you *so much*. Why d'you think I'm here?' She kissed and kissed his face. 'Because with you I'm alive. That's what it is – loving you and knowing that you love me . . . All this time with Harry, I felt only half alive, and even the half-alive part he was crushing, as if he stopped me breathing. But you . . .'

Arthur made a joyful sound and held her close. 'You amazing woman! You're just . . . you're light for me, that's what you are.'

They kissed and held each other, still with the same sense of miracle. Then Arthur said, 'Let's go over it all again. I had hoped to buy tickets in advance. It's a shame I haven't managed that.'

'Never mind. Let's get up very, very early. Get away before Mrs T is awake and get the first train. We shan't meet anyone at that time. We can go to Brighton Road – then get our tickets to Manchester and . . .' She drew in a deep breath. 'Off we go – free! Oh, it does feel strange.'

'I'll write to my mother and father,' Arthur said soberly. 'They'll take it hard at first – but I think in the end they'll understand. And they can come and visit – and we don't need to stay away from here for ever, Rose. We just need to get ourselves sorted out.'

'But how?' Rose said. 'Harry won't divorce me – I'm sure of it,' She looked soberly at Arthur. 'I'd barely thought as far ahead as us getting married. How can we?'

Arthur pushed himself up on one arm, his optimism dented. 'It may take some time, of course. We must . . . All I want is for you to be my wife . . . But if we can't . . .'

'Your wife,' she said, overcome again by a sense of wonder. 'Mrs Arthur King!'

'Will you marry me?' he asked, with sudden touching seriousness. 'Rose – will you?'

Laughing in the face of all the obstacles in front of them, she pulled him down into her arms again. 'Of course I will, you silly. I'd marry you tomorrow, if I could!'

A few streets away, in the Taylor household, Charles had been dozing. Rachel felt she could not have slept if someone paid her to do it, she was so on edge. It was nearly half past nine, but it felt as if the night had gone on already for several days. She felt a bit guilty that she was hiding down here, but told herself that she'd only be in the way and Susanna was older and a much calmer person. Rachel had been up and down, taking cups of tea and fresh candles, but as soon as she could she came down again, away from the sight of Dolly's writhing, sweating agony.

Charles suddenly jerked awake at a cry from upstairs. He looked confused. 'What was that?'

Another sound came, somewhere between a wail and a grunt. They heard Phyllis's voice, low and urgent. There were more goings-on, and then a noise which electrified both of them: the outraged, grating cry of a tiny baby.

'Oh, dear Lord,' Charles said.

'It's here!' Tears rushed into Rachel's eyes. For a second she felt as if she could have sat and wept for ages, but she tore upstairs.

Her mother and sister were both bent over the bed, Phyllis in the middle of cutting the cord. Dolly was panting, half laughing, half crying, her eyes stretched wide with amazement.

'Oh!' she exclaimed in amazement. 'It's real – it's a baby! Look, a baby!'

Susanna was cradling the little fellow wrapped in a piece of towelling, tears streaming down her face. 'It's a little boy,' she kept saying. 'Oh, a boy – hello, little one!' she addressed him emotionally.

Rachel bent over to see his bloody, wrinkled, indignant face roaring out of the towelling. Phyllis tied off the cord.

'Give him here,' Dolly said hungrily.

'No!' Phyllis's voice was like a whiplash. 'No holding him – not more than you need. You don't want to get fond of him – he's not staying.'

All three of them were silenced. They all stared at her, still as statues. Only now did they really take in the enormity of what this meant; the giving up of a baby. Dolly's face was pale with shock.

'But Mom . . .' Rachel said. Here was a flesh-and-blood child, a person, a *relative* – and he was to be sent away . . .

'No buts. She can feed him – for the moment. Keep him quiet. But that's all. He's not staying, and that's that. First thing, I'll be taking him to Coventry.'

Rose and Arthur, despite their keyed-up excitement, fell gradually into a doze, warm and intimate, wrapped around each other, her gold hair like a curtain on the pillow beside his curls. After a time she stirred. In such a narrow bed it was hard to move without disturbing each other. She extricated her arm from under Arthur's and tried to turn over. He half woke, muttering.

'Sorry,' she whispered. 'I'd best get out and blow out the candles.'

Someone was knocking on the front door. It was the hard aggression of the knock which alerted her. Whoever would knock on Mrs Terry's door at this time? It must be gone ten. Her heart began to thud, blood pounding in her ears. The knock came again and after a moment she heard Mrs Terry moving about downstairs.

'I wonder who that is,' Rose murmured. She had a terrible feeling of dread. But no – it was impossible to take in. Not Harry coming here. He didn't know where she was. Harry belonged to another life, another world now. Whoever it was had begun hammering again and even louder, but then Mrs Terry must have opened the door and it stopped abruptly. Rose gave a half gasp, half scream. His voice. She heard him, so familiar that she could tell, without hearing any clear words, that it was him.

'What – what's the matter?' Arthur said, as she jerked to sit up beside him. But then she was paralysed. There was nowhere to go. She could hear him on the stairs, hear that already it was too late.

'Where are they? Tell me where they are, woman – now!'

'It's him,' Rose squeaked. She could hear all his rage, his pounding feet. She started to get out of bed.

Arthur was half sitting up as well when the door flung open and Rose saw Harry, his eyes, his body, so familiar, but his face was twisted with rage and there was something dark in his hands and it was pointing at them in the candlelight, it was straight and black and somewhere Mrs Terry was crying out something and Harry was screaming at the top of his voice, 'Bitch! You bitch! There you are, you whore and you, you thieving bastard, there you are, I've got you – *got you*!' And it was so fast there was a huge blast, a bang exploding round them in waves, and Arthur sagged beside her and she begged, 'No!' but a second later another blast and the last stunned light in her eyes and then blackness and she knew nothing more.

September 1925

Sixty-Eight

'Aggie!'

Lily broke free from Muriel Wood's hand and came running along the pavement. She flung her arms round Aggie's waist and clung to her so tightly that Aggie could hardly breathe.

'Hello, Lily!' she said, laughing. 'Hey – loose me a bit – you're hurting!'

Lily obeyed but seized Aggie's hand instead, her thin, strained little face looking up imploringly at her.

'You're coming with us, aren't you, Aggie?'

'Hello, dear,' Muriel Wood said, reaching them. 'Are you ready?' She looked tired and sad, and she spoke very gently.

Aggie nodded. She had agreed that sometimes, as well as Sunday school, she would go to church with Mrs Wood and Oliver and Lily, who was now living with them.

'It's such a good thing for Lily,' Mrs Wood had told Jen Green when she called round to ask if it was all right for Aggie to go. 'She so needs to see familiar faces around her after all that's happened.'

'Poor little mite,' Jen said. 'Of course Aggie can come, if you think it helps.'

Mrs Wood had looked at Jen Green, now hugely pregnant, her face and ankles swollen.

'My dear,' she said. 'You have such an awful lot on

your plate. If there's any help I can give you, don't hesitate to ask.'

Rather awkwardly, Jen thanked her, warmed by the woman's unaffected kindness.

Aggie walked along with Muriel Wood, Oliver and Lily, who clung tightly to her hand. The little girl had lost so much weight after the shock she had experienced, that she looked waif-like, almost transparent. Everyone was concerned for her. Aggie loosed her hand and put her arm round Lily's bony shoulders.

Lily looked up at her. 'Will you be my sister, Aggie?' she asked.

'I'll try,' Aggie said solemnly.

Looking up at Muriel Wood, she saw that the woman was wiping tears from her eyes.

'Is Mrs Southgate getting better?' Aggie asked.

Muriel Wood tried to regain a cheerful demeanour. 'I think she is,' she said. 'But it's going to take a very long time.'

In the days after the shooting, there was no other subject of conversation in the street. The shock was total. Huddles of people stood casting glances at number fifteen Lilac Street, which now stood empty. Harry Southgate had fled from the scene as soon as he had finished firing the gun. He had not seen Lily, on her little bed on the floor, had not been thinking of her, so caught up was he in his own rage and agony. He had not tried to run away; he had simply gone home again. The police had no difficulty in finding him.

Poor, terrified Mrs Terry had found Lily cowering at the end of the bed, only inches from all the blood and the apparently lifeless faces of her mother and Arthur

514

King. Arthur had died almost instantly. Rose, though bleeding grievously, was found to be still alive.

It had taken some enquiries to establish that Lily could go to Mrs Wood's house, somewhere gentle and familiar, and Muriel Wood, good woman that she was, had not hesitated to say that she would care for her for as long as necessary.

'That poor child,' were the words on everyone's lips. 'However will she recover from a thing like that? That father of hers will swing for this.'

'I knew there was summat about that man,' Irene Best kept saying. 'He was a brooding sort of a person. I tried to warn that young Aggie not to have anything to do with him . . .'

There were endless discussions about Rose Southgate. Dorrie Davis tried to persuade everyone that she'd seen it all coming.

'Well, that's a load of old rope if ever I heard it,' Freda Adams commented. 'What does Dorrie think she is – some kind of fortune teller with a crystal ball?'

In the yards at the Mansions, all squabbles were forgotten. Everyone huddled together, fonder, involved with each other, life put in perspective for the time being by the horrific events so close by.

And one morning, Muriel Wood walked quietly up the entry into the Mansions, in search of Freda Adams.

'I've been to the hospital,' she told her. 'Rose – Mrs Southgate – asked for you. She wondered if you'd be kind enough to go and see her.'

'Me?' Freda said, startled.

'She said, of everyone in the neighbourhood, you were so very kind to her.'

*

The one person who was completely bemused by the whole episode to begin with was Mr Gates. Seeing Freda Adams and Jen sitting outside that Saturday afternoon, Dulcie Skinner with them and the children all around, he came over, hesitantly.

'So – Ah hear there's been bad news, like?' He stood looking awkward, his burly shape towering over them. Aggie saw her mother squint up into his pink face.

'Get yourself a chair, Mr Gates,' Jen said. 'We'll tell you about it – what we know, anyway.'

He carried a chair out and joined them. Aggie, who was playing jackstones with Babs and Ann nearby, heard her mom and nanna telling him about Rose Southgate and how her husband had turned a gun on her and her lover in his jealous fury.

'He dain't stand a chance, poor man,' Jen said. 'Shot through the heart – and in any case he was blind. Not a hope of getting out of the way. But by all accounts she was on the move when he shot at her. He got her here –' She indicated the left side of her pelvis.

Mr Gates's face was a picture of horrified astonishment. 'He shot his own wifie?'

'It's worse than that . . .' Freda lowered her voice. 'I've been to the hospital to see her this afternoon, Mr Gates. She's in a bad way. They don't know if she'll walk again – or not proper, like. It's made a right mess, smashed the bone. But . . .' Freda wiped her hand over her face as if to dispel her emotion at the thought of Rose's white, despairing face in the hospital, the way the young woman had clung to her hand. 'There was a child as well – she was carrying a babby, but . . .' She shook her head, running out of words. It was one of the very few times in her life that Aggie saw her grandmother close to weeping.

Jen's eyes were full of tears too, as she listened. 'Whatever she did, she dain't deserve all this,' she said.

Freda drew in a deep breath and went on. 'She looked terrible, lying there – white as the sheet. Her voice was thin somehow. She said to me, "I've lost everything, Mrs Adams. I don't want to go on living, not after this." So I said, "No you haven't, bab, you've still got Lily, and you're going to have to soldier on and build a life for her." Well, she was full of how she had nowhere to go and how she'd have to move away, where no one knew her, be surrounded by strangers. So I said, "Why do that? Why not come and live nearby? Everyone knows you, they know what happened and they know Lily. There'll be those'll cant for a bit, but they'll get over it, we'll all rally round. Why not stay where you've got friends?" Well – that gave her summat to think about. And d'you know . . .' Her tears were close to the surface again. 'She turned her head and kissed my hand . . .'

'She always did like you,' Jen said.

'Oh, her heart's in the right place, from what I've seen of her. Quite a kindly soul really,' Nanna said. She cleared her throat, her tears banished. 'A dark one all right, though. Pleasant enough, but you'd never know what she was thinking. And all that time she must've been carrying on with him.'

Aggie half listened. She was constantly trying to shut thoughts of Mrs Southgate out of her mind, not to allow herself to picture what had happened in that night-time room, the two of them caught together in bed. And now of Mrs Southgate lying shattered and weeping in hospital. It made her feel too frightened and upset. And Mr King – that nice Mr King! They had been on the point of running off together, the landlady had said.

Nothing had been quite how she thought. Aggie remembered Irene Best saying, 'Be careful, Aggie . . .' It made her feel fear and distrust of other adults, of what they might be after. All she wanted at the moment was her own home, Mom and Nanna, the yard, her family and Babs's mom and dad. People she had known for years, who she was sure of.

'It was a German gun, they say,' Dulcie was saying. 'A Luger. I mean, why did he have one of them?'

'He must have brought it home – he was in the army in the war, wasn't he?' Jen said, shifting on her chair to get comfortable. 'Got it from somewhere over there, brought it back? Fancy.'

'D'you think he'd kept it all this time?' Dulcie said. 'I wonder if *she* knew he had it?'

'A Luger,' Mr Gates said thoughtfully. 'That's a pistol. He must've tyaken it off a German soldier. Hoo else would the feller've had it?'

'Ooh,' Jen shuddered. 'It gives you the creeps to think about it.'

Aggie had gone cold the first time she heard about the gun.

'Told you, dain't I?' was all John said. 'I told you I saw it.' But he looked stunned and upset as well.

Aggie and John discussed endlessly whether there was anything they might have done. Aggie told Babs about it, who was riveted by this information. But they didn't tell the grown-ups. Not then and not ever. The thought that the gun had been up there in that tool bag, just waiting all this time, chilled them all and burdened them with guilt.

'What if you'd told?' Babs said gravely.

'But we dain't, did we?' Aggie felt bursting suddenly

with frustration, with anger. 'And you wouldn't have done neither.'

They hadn't known what Harry Southgate would do. How could anyone know or expect a thing like that? Why was life so horrible? It let your dad die, it allowed a man to turn a gun on his wife. All feelings were heightened then, this terrible event making everyone see things differently. All those messages she had carried to Mr King from Mrs Southgate! Didn't that somehow make it her fault as well? Sometimes Aggie felt like weeping and never stopping. But all she said, in a bitter voice, was, 'Don't talk daft.'

That afternoon they sat, playing half-heartedly, reassured by the rumble of the adults' voices. Aggie liked it that Mr Gates was out there, his big, comforting presence.

After a time, Jen got up. 'I'd best get ready,' she said. 'Got to get to work.'

Mr Gates looked up at her. 'Should ye be ganning out working, tha' far on?'

Jen smiled. 'Who else is going to do it? I've no husband. My Tommy died not long back.'

His face creased with concern. 'But what aboot when the bairn comes?'

'Bairn?' Jen flexed her back. 'Bairns, yer mean.'

'No!' Mr Gates sat back, a look of wonder on his face. 'Twins, like?'

'That's about it,' Jen said. She grinned suddenly. She felt a bit like a wonder of the world, carrying two babies.

'But how're ye gonna manage? Earn a wage?'

'I'll be back – next week,' Nanna said. Aggie saw Nanna take her right wrist in her left hand, as if to check on its progress. 'They're taking me back, for my sins.'

Mr Gates looked even more astonished by this. 'A woman of your age!'

'Oh – there's a bit of life in me yet, ta,' Nanna said spryly. 'We get by, any way we can.'

Jen walked heavily across to the house. Aggie saw Mr Gates's eyes follow her. He looked kind and concerned, but he didn't say anything more.

On a sudden impulse, Aggie got up and ran to her mother. She felt more grown up suddenly. 'D'you want some help, Mom?'

'Well,' Jen joked. 'You could go to work for me if yer like.'

'I'll go!' Aggie said. 'I will, if you want.'

Jen looked at her, seeing the need in her daughter's eyes. With a smile she ran a hand roughly over Aggie's head. 'It's all right, bab. I can manage for now. Your turn'll come soon enough.'

Sixty-Nine

Phyllis Taylor was saying goodbye to her old neighbours.

On a mellow Sunday in mid-September, after church, the Taylors progressed grandly along Lilac Street. Phyllis took her leave of the people she had known, at arm's length at least, though she had never taken people into her confidence.

Her children accompanied her, politely saying goodbye. The family were moving on. Now that all four of them were out at work, Phyllis informed everyone, they were moving out to a better class of house with more space. When quizzed as to where exactly, Phyllis was vague on the subject. Out west, she told them, towards Smethwick.

She even went so far as to grace the yards of the Mansions with her presence, to speak to the Greens.

'We just wanted to say goodbye,' Phyllis said, restricting her gaze from looking round too carefully at the yard and its houses, as if for fear of what she might see. The place reminded her far too much of Spon End, of so many things best forgotten. She carried herself mightily. She wanted everyone to know she was moving up and out.

'Well, best of luck to you,' Jen said. She didn't like the woman much, but as she was on her way out they would all be pleasant. 'I hope you have some nice neighbours where you're going.'

'Oh, I expect we will,' Phyllis said, as if, in the area she was moving to, you could expect nothing less.

The four young people murmured their goodbyes and the family trooped out of the yard again.

Jen watched from the doorway for a moment.

'Funny –' She frowned. 'Those Taylor girls seem smaller than I remembered. They seem to have *shrunk*.' She turned to her mother. 'I could've sworn they were big strapping wenches – and that youngest one looked as if she was expecting, earlier on.'

Freda looked up at her. 'Don't look like it,' she said indifferently.

Jen dismissed it, shaking her head. 'Must've been seeing things. Ah, well – that's them gone, anyway. Another lot moving on. I wonder who'll move in there instead?'

Before dawn, on the Saturday after Dolly's baby was born, Phyllis got everyone up, except Charles who was to stay behind, and marched them all along to Brighton Road railway station. Charles, if anyone asked, was to say that the women had gone to visit his mother's sister, which fortunately for Charles's fastidious mind, also had the benefit of being true.

Dolly, young and healthy, was recovering well physically from the birth. Emotionally she was in a bad state, confused, mutinous, one minute wanting the baby taken away and never to have to see him, the next passionately opposed to being parted from him at all. Susanna and Rachel were also upset, and scandalized by the granite hardness of their mother's resolve that the little boy, however lovely and however much their flesh and blood, had to go. She was not having any bastard babies in the family and that was that.

Phyllis did everything she could to close her own mind to the child, forcing herself to think of him as an object that had to be disposed of. She was the one who carried the little newborn at first, well wrapped up and hidden under a shawl she draped over her shoulders.

The journey, from the walk through the deserted streets at dawn to the train ride out to Coventry, the bus ride to the farm, was all lived through in a state of sullen, welling emotions.

Dolly sat pressed close to the window on the rumbling old bus, her baby clasped in her arms. He had been quiet while they were on the train, and she had insisted on her mother handing him over. Phyllis could hardly make a fight about it in front of the other two passengers. As they travelled, Dolly's gaze scarcely left his little face, her eyes drinking in the way his lips and eyelids twitched as he slept. However much Mom would have liked to keep him away from her, she was the one who had to feed him. And in those two days, she had already begun to know him and to feel as if she had known him all her life.

On the bus, he began to stir and started yowling lustily. Dolly felt her mother prodding her shoulder from the seat behind.

'You'll have to feed him – keep him quiet,' she hissed.

Dolly said nothing in reply, but she was raging inside. *I know!* she wanted to shriek. *Of course I know he needs feeding – he's my babby. I know what to do better than you. Stop bossing me!*

She fed him very discreetly under the shawl. Pain shot through her as he latched on, so sharp that she almost cried out. Her breasts, new to the whole experience, were sore and leaking so that everything about it was distressing. And all she could think was, *He's mine. He's mine and she's making me give him up. I hate her . . .* She felt so torn with emotion that she cried nearly all the way and Susanna who was next to her was soon in tears too. They arrived at the farm in a hot, fraught, tearful condition.

When the bus stopped, somewhere out in the country, their mother suddenly said, 'This is it, I think. Quick – off, all of you!'

They only had to walk a quarter of a mile along the road and they had arrived at the farm, where they were to stay one night, to settle the baby in with Lizzie and the family.

At the gates, round which was a sea of mud, Dolly saw Susanna and Rachel exchange despondent glances. Dolly shot them both a despairing look and clung even more tightly to the baby. But what else could they do but follow?

Phyllis led them, picking her way across the mired farmyard, full of dread and misgivings. The house, of faded bricks, did not look too bad, but the place was a dirty, functional farm. None of her children had been in the country before. Panic seized Phyllis for a moment. Nancy's letter had been welcoming, but what did she really know of her sister's life? It was years since she had seen her. What was she bringing them all to?

The yard was coated in cow's muck and bits of straw, and hens were strutting about, squawking away from them in panic. Their arrival set the dogs off. Three creatures, one black and white, the others of muddy, mongrel colours, came tearing out barking hysterically.

Dolly let out a shriek. 'Get them away!' she cried, terrified. Rachel and Susanna clung together.

'Oi – get back! Go on – all of you!' A young woman rushed out of the house with a child clasped on her left hip and a poker in her right hand which she was swishing at the dogs, who retreated with whimpering, defeated noises. The young woman was curvaceous, with hanks of long, mousey hair taken up in a loose bun and dreamy, but friendly-looking grey eyes. The little girl on her hip had the same eyes and a cap of brown hair. She seemed worried by the sight of so many strangers and buried her face in her mother's shoulder.

'Are you my auntie Het?' the woman said.

'I am,' Phyllis admitted, sensing the puzzlement of her daughters on hearing this name. 'Only I've gone by the name Phyllis for years now. I like it better.'

'Het!' Another voice rang from the house and Nancy came hurrying over. She was a less heavily built woman than Phyllis, with faded hair and dressed in a workaday brown frock with an apron over the top. She had aged a good deal since Phyllis last saw her. 'So you've got here all right – oh, and look at you all!' Her lined, good-natured face took in all her nieces. 'What a lovely-looking lot of daughters, Het! This is my girl Lizzie and her little 'un, our Susan.' The young woman smiled. She was staring at them all with great curiosity. 'Now you must be . . . ?'

'Susanna,' Susanna said.

Nancy went along them all and when she got to Dolly she said, 'Oh, now here's the babby – let's have a look. Oh, isn't he lovely! He looks nice and healthy!'

Dolly's eyes filled again and she looked away.

'Come on inside – I s'pect you need a cup of tea,' Nancy said.

Phyllis suddenly felt a deep sense of comfort. Her sister had always been more of a mom to her all those years back, and in that moment she felt the reassurance of that all over again.

As soon as she walked into the farmhouse she could see that Nancy had made a good life. There was no great wealth. Farming, as Nancy told her, was always a struggle. But there was an atmosphere of chaotic cosiness, a sense of home in the big, busy kitchen. The table was still dusted with flour, there were big blackened pots and kettles steaming gently on the range and Nancy's choice of colours for curtains and crocheted rugs on the chairs was bright and cheerful.

She bustled about making tea, telling them to sit, that her husband Wilf and the three lads would be back later, as well as Lizzie's husband, who worked on the farm. Nancy seemed harassed but happy. She told them how lucky she was to have so many sons – it meant the burden of the farm was shared, enough hands to go round.

'This was Wilf's family's farm,' she told them. 'He inherited it off his father – there've been Pearsons here for years and years.'

The girls sat quiet, overwhelmed by the whole experience. Lizzie had sat down and begun feeding her little girl. Phyllis tried not to look, either at her or Dolly. She wrestled to keep her own feelings tightly shut down. All those emotions and sensations of having a child, a baby at your breast, that had filled her so vividly with life when she had her own, were waiting to rush at her. She must not let herself soften. How was

Dolly supposed to make a life with an illegitimate child? Her reputation would be ruined before she even started.

'Look Het—' Nancy began.

'Phyllis,' she said firmly, seeing her older girls' ears prick up at the name. Dolly was too lost in her own misery to notice that she had heard the name Hetty before.

'Phyllis. I'll have to get used to that. You can tell me all about everything later. I can see you're in a fix, though God knows, he is your own flesh and blood. But I daresay you've got your reasons. Now look, I've been thinking – I'll tell people he's my sister's child, a younger sister who's too sick to care for him. Not that we see all that many people out here, except for the lads on the farm.' She turned to Dolly. 'And you can come and see him when you like. You know where we are.'

Phyllis was touched by the thought Nancy had put into everything. Unspoken between them was the sense that Nancy felt she owed Phyllis protection from things long past. She knew they needed to talk, in private, to know each other again. But not now, with her girls there. They did not need to know her, Phyllis thought, not her childhood and how it had been. She could explain Ethel away as an old neighbour, not right in the head. She'd think of something. They didn't even need to know the half of it. All that could stay in the past.

Dolly, looking down at the little boy in her arms, had begun to cry quietly again. It felt as if everything was decided and that she had no say in anything. Being in this strange place, added to the shock of the baby and her sore, bleeding body, made it all feel overwhelming.

'Don't you worry, wench,' her new auntie told her

kindly. 'He'll be well looked after. I know you'll see us right, Het, with enough to take care of him. After all, he is yours to care for really. But Lizzie here's still feeding Susan so she can take him over and see he gets his milk.'

Dolly couldn't help openly crying now.

'Oh, you poor young wench,' Nancy said. 'Don't want to part with him, eh? But your mother's right, Dolly – you're only a child yourself . . .'

'I'm nearly seventeen!' Dolly protested, looking up into Nancy's face, the kindliness of which made her cry all the more.

'My – you look younger,' Nancy exclaimed. 'Now look, Dolly, does your little lad have a name?'

Dolly shook her head wretchedly. They had held off naming him, none of them wanting to feel that he was Him, a real Someone they then had to part with. She saw that her sisters were both tearful too.

Lizzie brought a stool over and sat beside Dolly. 'You feed him for today,' she suggested carefully. 'Then tomorrow he can come to me.'

Dolly nodded, her face wan. But she couldn't help being drawn in by Lizzie's earthy kindness. All the girls were happy to find that they had these new relatives.

'We can't let him go on without a name,' Lizzie said. 'What about christening him, for a start? What're you going to call him, Dolly?'

'I don't know,' Dolly said mutinously.

'Well, you should name him,' Lizzie insisted. 'You had him – it's yours to do.'

'But he's not mine, is he?' Dolly burst out. She stood up, still holding the baby clutched close to her, her face creasing with distress. 'I never thought I wanted him. I never wanted a babby! I didn't know what it'd be like and . . . I never knew what I'd feel about it.' She spoke to Lizzie. 'Mom says we can't keep him and that's that. But –' She was crying heartbrokenly now. 'I don't want to give him up. I don't know as I want to keep 'im either . . . I just don't know.' She burst into sobs.

It was Rachel who got up and put her arms round Dolly, but Dolly pushed her away and went over to her mother.

'Look, Mom –' She held him out to her pleadingly. '*You* hold him.'

Phyllis found herself presented with the little boy, wrapped in a blanket and sleeping peacefully despite the storm around his head.

'There he is,' Dolly pleaded. 'Look at him – properly for once. You can't just pretend he's not there, that he's just a parcel or something!'

Phyllis felt the warmth of the small, milky-smelling body in her arms. The very posture of holding a child brought back so many memories. She felt a faint memory of tingling in her breasts. For the first time she allowed herself to look, really look at him. He was very much like Charles had been as an infant, the same colouring and expression of bafflement. The powerful feelings she had tried to push away started to rise in her.

'I'm going to call him after our dad,' Dolly said. 'James. That's his name. And his second name can be George, after the King. There.'

'James is a nice name,' Nancy said.

Phyllis felt a deep ache in her for the man she had lost. James – her James. How he would have loved seeing this little boy! What would he have done? She found herself thinking. 'Be kind,' that was James's motto. 'Better to be kind than to be right.' She could hear his voice in her mind and her eyes filled. Her chest was suddenly bursting with emotion. His kindness had always softened her. She could feel her girls all watching her and she struggled to gain control. It was a moment before she could look up.

'It is,' she said. 'That's a very good name.'

The house Phyllis had chosen was a roomy villa in Erdington, not Smethwick as she had told her neighbours. When she walked in through the front door, into a vestibule instead of walking straight into the front room, Phyllis felt like weeping with relief and pleasure. It was all she had ever dreamed of.

As the four children explored the rest of the house and they waited for the van to arrive which she had rented to carry their things, she stood in the front parlour, the sun pouring in through the as yet uncurtained windows. She would buy some new, quality nets for those. She had an inner tremor of pleasure. How lovely all her things would look in here, arranged round the elegant little marble mantelpiece.

She heard the footsteps on the boards upstairs, her children's voices. Susanna would be married and gone in the new year, she knew. But she wouldn't be too far away. And for now, they were all here together. By evening they would have arranged many of the things in their places. They would sit together and eat a meal. Soon they would branch out. Charles would travel back to their old church on a Sunday for a time, as he had responsibilities there. But the rest of life was a fresh start: a blank sheet. No one knew them. Once little James was weaned, a few months down the line, he would be joining them. He was to be the child of Phyllis's youngest sister, who had died tragically in childbirth. He would be hers to look after while Dolly went out to work. Phyllis's fleshy face spread into a smile. Nothing like a child to give you a sense of the future, of fruition and purpose.

Phyllis looked out into the street. Strangers moved back and forth. Blessed strangers who knew nothing. And her family still knew very little about her – only a few sketchy details. The past was dead; everything was about now and the days to come. She took a deep breath of contentment, and smiling, went to call her children.

Seventy

'Hey – they're coming!' Silas came tearing along the entry as if his shorts were on fire.

'Mom's back!' the cry went up, and the welcoming committee – the Greens and most of the people from the Mansions – came out to see Jen return from the hospital.

One of the twins had been lying across the base of the womb and the doctor thought they would have to birth them by Caesarean section, but the babies made some last minute rearrangements and managed a natural, though arduous, birth. Jen stayed in the hospital, recovering. Everyone was very excited. She'd had a boy and a girl.

'Are they gingers or brownies?' Aggie asked when they heard the news.

'The boy's ginger and the girl's another little May,' Nanna said.

May looked up at her, big-eyed.

'You're a big sister now,' Nanna told her. 'You're not the babby any more – you've got someone else to love now, bab. How's that?'

Nanna was fully in charge again. She'd gone back to the factory, even though her wrist still gave her some 'gip' as she called it. But even with their mother missing, the Green children knew they were in safe hands.

And there was even more help on offer. Some surprises were being prepared for Jen. Since Mom had been away, Mr Gates had been making himself busy. He was fixing the door which had been off its hinges for ages and nailing down floorboards, replacing one or two of them. He had put up a few shelves and mended the chairs which had loose legs, which was most of them. He was, as Nanna said, 'very handy'. And he seemed to have a soft spot for all of them.

'Heaven help ye,' Mr Gates said, red-faced as he worked at fixing the door hinge. 'Ye lot are gonna have yer hands stowed when they get back.'

Freda Adams and the children had grown used to the sound of hammering. They'd also grown accustomed to Mr Gates. Aggie, John and Ann got into the habit of waiting for him outside the Eagle, the way they used to with Dad, until he came out. He would laugh, seeing them there, and say, 'Howay then, ye little monkeys – we better get ourselves home!' And they would skip along the short distance back to the Mansions behind his large, lumbering figure. He had a habit of laying his beefy hand on their heads, and Aggie loved the warm feel of it when he did.

Jen arrived home by ambulance, and there were cheers as she got out, carrying the baby boy. A nurse followed with the little girl in her arms. Dulcie ran and put her arm round Jen's shoulders.

'Let's have a look at him. Ooh, he's so like you, Jen! They're not a bad size, are they, considering?'

As Aggie followed her mother into the yard, she felt a thrill of relief and pleasure. It had felt so strange with Mom away and she looked thinner in the face now, but she was well, and smiling at the sight of them all. Soon everyone was gathering round, cooing over the babies and admiring them.

'Let her get into her house!' Dulcie protested after a time. The nurse, smiling, handed Dulcie the baby girl, wished Jen well and departed.

Inside, they all took turns to hold the new arrivals. Other children from the yard, Babs among them, came and wanted to look as well. The little girl was dark haired and as Nanna had said, very like May.

'I thought we'd call her Lilian,' Jen said. 'And him –' Fondly, she looked down at the little boy. 'I know he's nothing like Tommy in looks, but he's got to be called after his dad.' She filled up for a moment, but quickly wiped her eyes. Aggie felt a terrible pang. How Dad would have smiled and joked over these two. How proud he would have been!

'They're the last, that's for sure,' Jen went on. 'So one've them had better be called after their father.'

'They look very good, Jen, for twins,' Nanna said and Aggie saw the tears of joy and pride in her eyes.

'Oh,' Jen said,' they're a couple of guzzlers. I'm at it morning, noon and night.'

Nanna had made tea and they'd all talked non-stop about the babies for some time before Jen said, 'Hey – where the heck did those shelves come from?'

Aggie watched her grandmother's face take on an amused, knowing look. 'Ah – well, wouldn't you like to know? And that's not the only thing. See the door ain't hanging off any more? And you'll find there's no more holes in the attic floor – or any other floor, for that matter. I think it's safe to say that you've found an admirer.'

Jen stared at her, an obvious blush seeping right up her cheeks. 'What d'you mean? Who?'

'Who?' Nanna teased. 'Now don't pretend you haven't noticed. The man's been here working like a dynamo for you all week.'

Ann couldn't hold back and called out, 'Mr Gates! He did all of it.'

Aggie was standing just inside the door, with the sun on her back. She could feel a grin spreading across her cheeks watching her mother's face. She felt a bit funny about the way Mr Gates had taken so obvious a shine to her mother and was always helpful and protective towards her. *He's not our dad*, Aggie told herself defiantly. *He never will be.* But Mr Gates was someone they were quickly getting used to. You couldn't help yourself liking him: he was so reassuring and kindly. And he put a smile on Mom's face.

Aggie slipped outside and sat down on the ground, drawing her knees up, her back against the warm bricks. The air was balmy and tinged with the smells of smoke and cooking. Some of the little children were playing out in the yard but they took no notice of her. She looked up at the clear late-afternoon sky, lit by a mellow sun, hearing the chink of teacups from in the house, and all their voices, Mom and Dulcie, Nanna, her brothers and sisters and Babs. There were so many thoughts she didn't want to dwell on, that could take over her mind if she let them in. She tried not to think too much about sad, terrible times: about Dad, and Mary Crewe and what had happened to Mrs Southgate. Although Nanna said Mrs Southgate was getting better, so maybe things would be all right. Those afternoons she had spent in Mrs Southgate's house already seemed a long way off, like another life in which she had wanted different things.

She heard Babs, her best friend, giggling and the others joining in. Nanna was better. Mom was safely home with the babbies. The sky was blue and, for now, what she could hear from inside was laughter.

My Daughter, My Mother
ANNIE MURRAY

Two daughters. Two mothers.
The secrets of two lifetimes.

In 1984 two young mothers meet at a toddler group in Birmingham. As their friendship grows, they share with each other the difficulties and secrets in their lives:

Joanne, a sweet, shy girl, is increasingly afraid of her husband. The lively, promising man she married has become hostile and violent and she is too ashamed to tell anyone. When her mother, Margaret, is suddenly rushed into hospital, the bewildered family find that there are things about their mother of which they had no idea. Margaret was evacuated from Birmingham as a child and has spent years avoiding the pain of her childhood – but finds that you can't run from the past forever.

Sooky, kind and good-natured, has already been through one disastrous marriage and is back at home living with her parents. But being 'disgraced' is not easy. Her mother, Meena, refuses to speak to Sooky. At first her silence seems like a punishment, but Sooky gradually realizes it contains emotions which are far more complicated and that her mother may need her help. Meena has spent twenty years trying to fit in with life in Birmingham, and to deal with the conflicts within her between east and west, old ways and new.

This is the story of two young women discovering the heartbreak of their mothers' lives, and of how mothers create daughters – and learn from them.

ISBN: 978-0-330-53520-5

FOR MORE ON

ANNIE MURRAY

sign up to receive our

SAGA NEWSLETTER

Packed with **features, competitions, authors'
and readers' letters** and **news of exclusive events,**
it's a must-read for every Annie Murray fan!

Simply fill in your details below and tick to confirm that you would
like to receive saga-related news and promotions and return to us at
Pan Macmillan, Saga Newsletter, 20 New Wharf Road, London, N1 9RR.

NAME _____

ADDRESS _____

_____

_____ POSTCODE _____

EMAIL _____

☐ *I would like to receive saga-related news and promotions (please tick)*

*You can unsubscribe at any time in writing or through our website where you can also see
our privacy policy which explains how we will store and use your data.*

Bello:
hidden talent rediscovered

Bello is a digital only imprint of Pan Macmillan,
established to breathe new life into previously
published, classic books.

At Bello we believe in the timeless power of
the imagination, of good story, narrative
and entertainment and we want to use digital
technology to ensure that many more readers
can enjoy these books into the future.

Our available books include:
Margaret Pemberton's *The Londoners* trilogy;
Brenda Jagger's *Barforth Family* saga; and,
Janet Tanner's *Hillsbridge Trilogy*.

For more information,
and to sign-up for regular updates visit:

www.panmacmillan.com/bellonews

B E L L ◎